THE RESURRECTION

REAPER TRILOGY BOOK 3

STEVEN DUNNE

Huge thanks to the ever-obliging Ed James for his help and guidance.

Massive thank you for the book title suggestion by Sue Blood.

Cover by Emmy Ellis at Studioenp

BOOKS BY THE SAME AUTHOR:

The Reaper (Reaper - Part 1)
The Disciple (Reaper - Part 2)
Deity
The Unquiet Grave
A Killing Moon
Death Do Us Part
Blood Summer

Full details
www.stevendunne.co.uk

Copyright © 2021 Steven Dunne

All rights reserved.

All characters in this novel are fictitious and any resemblance to real persons, living or dead, is coincidental.

Cover design by Emmy Ellis at Studioenp

1

November 23rd 2008 - Holland Park, West London

Professor Victor Sorenson drained his malt whisky and set the heavy glass down. He put aside the thin volume of the A-Z of Derby and stood from behind his antique Italianate desk, strolling across to the circular porthole window at the other side of his study. Pulling back the catch on the top half of the window, he allowed the clamour of evening traffic on Holland Park Avenue to invade his home. The cold breeze freshened both Sorenson and the coal embers glowering in the grated fireplace.

'It's going to be a long, cold winter,' he said, gazing down from the third storey of his home across to the small residents' park beyond. It was dark and deserted, the trees nearly bare, the decay of mulching leaves permeating the air. 'For those that survive past Christmas.'

He turned from the window and picked up a CD case from the desk, flipped out the disc of Gustav Mahler's Ninth Symphony then padded across to the music centre in a corner of the room. He slipped Mahler's final work into the machine and an expression hinting at future pleasures, creased around Sorenson's black eyes. The Ninth - a work finished with Mahler's dying breath.

He flicked at the stereo's remote to choose the correct track - the adagio - and Mahler's weeping violins flowed from the speakers. Sorenson closed his eyes, the better to allow the beauty of Mahler's symphony to flow over him like pure oxygen.

'Envy the family that departs its miserable existence with such a feat of grandeur waving them off to eternal rest.'

Sorenson returned to his desk, pulling a sheaf of papers towards him and reread the report from his most trusted disciple. It had been a long wait but now it was time for the Reaper to strike again.

'It will be good to see you after all these years, Damen.'

He unlocked a drawer of his desk and pulled out a pre-paid, disposable mobile phone from amongst a set of twelve. It had a white sticker with the number one, written in Sorenson's elegant hand. He turned it on and thumbed re-dial to engage the only number stored in the phone.

'Good work,' said Sorenson. 'You've found some deserving families and I've given it a lot of thought. I think we'll go with the Wallis family. I'm sure the hard-pressed residents of Derby will be thrilled to see them go. The teenage son, Jason, is perfect for our needs.' A pause. 'Of course, the daughter too. What earthly use is she to anyone? Before Christmas would be ideal. I'll set a firmer date when I know Brook's duty roster.'

He listened for a moment.

'No, forget about Derby for now. You have bigger fish to fry. I'll sort out the logistics with Charlie Rowlands.' A pause. 'I know he's a bit doddery but he'll be fine. He doesn't have a lot to do. I've already purchased an apartment as a base of operations. It's quiet and central and it's been stocked with everything we'll need for our visit. This will be my final contribution and I intend to take the reins personally.'

2

11th December 2010 - St Mary's Wharf, Derby Division Police Headquarters

Jason Donovan Wallis strutted through the smoked glass doors accompanied by his solicitor, Mr Dorrell. As soon as they were clear of the building, Jason sparked a fresh tab, pulling long and hard on its toxic comfort before crunching across the frosted ground towards the throng of journalists. His solicitor's car was beyond, engine running but, seeing photographers, Jason rolled to a halt to soak up the attention, beaming at the cameras.

'What did I say?' muttered Dorrell, under his breath. 'Get that grin off your face. And lose the cigarette.'

Crestfallen, Jason dropped the cigarette to the ground and lowered his head in an attempt at humility.

'Have you been charged, Jason?' shouted a journalist.

'Jason has *not* been charged and we are appalled that Derby Constabulary should even consider such a course after my client's ordeal,' said Dorrell, placing a paternal hand on Jason's shoulder. 'A few short weeks ago, six people were horrifically slaughtered at the Ingham family home, just yards from the house where Jason's own family were murdered two years ago.

'It's clear to me that a notorious serial killer is targeting this poor boy and, while we must give thanks that he survived both attacks, it should be obvious to all that Jason is as much a victim of the Reaper as those who perished. Jason was, and remains, profoundly traumatised by the murders of his friends and family.

'For the police to take the decision to arrest my client on a completely erroneous assault charge, is nothing short of an outrage. This is clearly an attempt by Derby CID to deflect attention from their own shortcomings and they are grievously mistaken if they think we are going to let them get away with it. Their treatment of my client is unforgivable and we will be pursuing an action for damages against them.'

'Are you seeking financial compensation?' called another journalist.

'Nothing can compensate this boy for the horror of losing his loved ones,' said Dorrell. 'That said, if a financial penalty means that other traumatised victims of violent crime are spared malicious prosecution then it would be remiss of me not to explore such a course of action.'

A middle-aged journalist thrust a recorder towards them. 'Mr Dorrell. Brian Burton, Derby Telegraph. Do you know if Detective Inspector Brook was behind the decision to arrest Jason?'

'I can't speak to that, Brian...' began Dorrell.

'Brook's always had it in for me ever since my family were cut open,' sneered Jason, before a squeeze on his arm brought a halt.

'Brian, I'm aware your newspaper has been rightly critical of Derby CID and the poor quality of the investigations run by Detective Inspector Brook into *both* Reaper killings in the city. But my only purpose today is seeking justice for my client. Jason has been cleared of the assault on Ravinder Singh and he leaves custody without a stain on his character.'

'Jason was the sole survivor of both Reaper killings,' shouted a reporter at the back. 'What do you say to people who think that's suspicious?'

'Here, what you saying?' protested Jason.

'That's a monstrous insinuation,' said Dorrell, patting Jason's shoulder again. 'My client was unconscious at *both* crime scenes and incapable of defending himself. Investigating detectives made it very clear that my client had no hand in either attack...'

'He does have a long record of juvenile offending,' said Burton.

'After the horrific murder of his parents and sister two years ago, I believe Jason suffered post-traumatic stress disorder and, in my opinion, has never recovered,' said Dorrell. 'And, yes, under the yoke of that psychological damage, a few petty offences were committed. But any reasonable person could see those acts were a cry for help from a distressed young man. What my client needed was treatment *not* incarceration in a Young Offenders Institution.'

'White Oaks has been described as a holiday camp by former inmates,' suggested Burton.

'Whatever the nature of the confinement, Brian, my client was denied the kind of care that might have made a difference to his decision-making. His association with the three young criminals who died on the Drayfin Estate just weeks ago might have been avoided if proper steps had been taken to treat this boy's psychological condition.'

Jason took a sly peek at the crowd, hunting in vain for Brook's face for a chance to gloat.

'You can't deny Jason was present when Ravinder Singh was assaulted,' said Burton.

'We have never sought to deny it, Brian,' replied Dorrell. 'We admit Jason was there but he was an innocent bystander and the assault was committed by his three friends. Images gathered from Jason's mobile phone prove conclusively that he wasn't involved.'

'How is filming his friends committing an assault not involvement?' demanded Burton.

Jason bristled but Dorrell gripped his arm. 'Brian, the only other living witness to the assault was the victim and his statement absolved Jason of active participation. Paul Gretton, Stephen Ingham and Benjamin Anderson attacked Ravinder and the fact that all three died at the hands of the Reaper, a few hours later, doesn't alter that. We have no further comment at this time and my client wants to go home and be left alone to grieve. Thank you.'

Dorrell guided Jason through the crowd towards his waiting car and, once inside, the vehicle crawled past the animated press pack to the exit.

∽

FROM A THIRD-FLOOR WINDOW, Detective Sergeants John Noble and Jane Gadd watched the journalists disperse.

'The shit rises again,' said Noble.

'As Brook predicted,' replied Gadd. 'What does the little fucker have to do before we can put him away?'

'Now, Jane,' said Noble, winking. 'Bad language is a symptom of a mind not under control.'

'We're allowed to vent with the boss off the premises. Are you going to tell him about Jason?'

'I'll text him.'

'So, he should know in about a week.'

Noble laughed. 'Harsh. He's improving. Turns on his phone every other day, at least.'

'You've spoken to him?'

Noble hesitated. 'Briefly.'

'What did he say about your meeting with the Chief Super?' said Gadd. No reply. 'You haven't told him, have you?'

'Not until I know what it's about,' said Noble.

'You know what it's about. The Reaper enquiry is going nowhere without an SIO.'

'It already has one.'

'Brook's suspended and the investigation is drifting.'

'Thanks,' said Noble.

'You know what I mean,' said Gadd.

'No, I don't. Besides, he's not suspended...'

'As good as. You've got to speak to him, John. He's being replaced and he has the right to know.'

'And if he's being replaced by a clock-watcher like DI Ford, what do I say?'

'You tell him he's being replaced by DI Ford,' said Gadd. 'Simple.'

'I'll cross that bridge when I come to it.'

'By which time he'll have found out from the Derby Telegraph.'

'He doesn't read the local rags.'

'But he *will* find out and it should come from you,' said Gadd. 'And you never know, maybe it won't be Ford.'

'If it happens, it's Ford,' said Noble. 'Who else could it be?'

'What about Hudson and Grant coming back up from Brighton?' said Gadd. 'They've got the background and they were good.' Noble shot her a glance. 'Not as good as the boss obviously but they were professional and the squad liked them.'

Noble shook his head. 'It's not them. I asked a mate in Sussex. DCI Hudson's close to retirement and he's staying put. It's a Derby case now. It'll be Ford.'

'So, you accept we need a new SIO.'

'No,' said Noble. 'But with an officer-involved fatal shooting, it's obvious the boss will be in limbo for a while.'

'Especially if he's not co-operating with the board.'

'Why wouldn't he be co-operating?'

'Per-lease,' scoffed Gadd. 'When has he ever volunteered information to Brass? Charlton hates him for that and, if he gets a chance to replace him, he will. I only hope it stops there.'

'What does that mean?' said Noble.

'There are six fresh vics on the slab, John, and Charlton needs a result. He doesn't need his SIO dropping off the grid at the height of a murder investigation then turning up in the middle of the night, carrying a gunshot victim into hospital. If the shooting board think it looks dodgy and Brook isn't co-operating, he could be finished.'

'You're exaggerating.'

'Am I?' said Gadd. 'Two ex-FBI agents shoot at each other and one of them dies. Brook was there.'

'It was a domestic. McQuarry drew first and Mike Drexler was forced to shoot back.'

'But why were they armed and why was the boss there?' demanded Gadd.

Noble shrugged. 'It was just bad luck. Brook barely knew them.'

Gadd narrowed her eyes. 'You know something, don't you?'

'Only what you know,' said Noble. 'Drexler moved into the cottage next to Brook and his name came up in conversation. But I'd never heard of Edie McQuarry until the night she died and I don't think the boss had either. That's it.'

'Did you speak to the FBI?'

'Only to confirm the basics,' said Noble. 'McQuarry and Drexler were partners at the FBI. In 1995, they solved a big case then both left the Bureau suddenly.'

'So, they have history.'

'Like I said. It's a domestic.'

'Fifteen years later?' said Gadd. 'That's some quarrel.'

'Americans,' shrugged Noble. 'Why argue things through when you can settle it with guns?'

'You're sure the boss never mentioned McQuarry.'

'Not to me.'

'And he'd never met her before the shooting.'

'He says not and I've no reason to disbelieve him,' said Noble. 'What's your point?'

'My point?' said Gadd. 'Forget suspension or dismissal, John. If the shooting board goes bad, DI Brook could be looking at charges. Three people in a field, in the middle of the night. With guns. McQuarry dead and Drexler seriously wounded.'

'Bad blood which turned into a firefight,' argued Noble. 'These things happen.'

'No, they don't,' insisted Gadd. 'And if a regular scumbag fed us that bullshit, we'd be on the floor laughing.'

'What do you want me to say? I wasn't there.'

'But Brook was and you've spoken to him.'

'He told me two shots were fired and McQuarry was killed instantly. But before she was hit, she returned fire and Drexler was wounded. End of story.'

'John, there were three of them,' said Gadd. 'They recovered *three* guns, all unlicensed and untraceable.'

A smile turned Noble's lips. 'You make it sound so suspicious.'

'That's because it is and if Brook was a punter, we'd be all over him. Three guns, John. Do the math.'

'Are you American?' asked Noble.

'Don't change the subject.'

'The third weapon was disabled, Jane. The board know that. Plus, Brook's prints aren't on any of the guns and GSR tests prove he didn't fire a weapon...'

'Ever heard of gloves?'

'Look, he's a DI. We have to give him the benefit and so will the enquiry.'

'I'm not taking Charlton's side but you must see how it looks.'

'Doesn't matter. He's been in Charlton's bad books before and always come out on top.'

'That won't help if the Chief Super wants him gone.'

Noble glanced at his watch and gathered up a pile of papers from his desk. 'Do you trust him, Jane?'

Gadd hesitated. 'Of course.'

'Then he'll be fine.'

Gadd stared beyond Noble to the car park. 'Oh, Christ!'

'What is it?'

'You were right. It's not Ford.'

3

Noble waited while Chief Superintendent Mark Charlton examined the reports in front of him. Beside Charlton sat Detective Inspector Robert Greatorix, riffling his own stack of papers. If it wasn't clear after Noble watched him lumbering across the car park, it was clear now - Greatorix, newly restored to health after a lengthy absence, was taking over the Reaper Inquiry and this briefing was for his benefit.

Noble ran a discreet eye over the difference in his appearance. Before his intestinal problems, Greatorix was notorious for his girth, his excessive perspiration and subsequent body odours, a consequence of his penchant for wearing the same sweat-stained clothes for weeks at a time.

But now the flab was largely gone. Slimmed down, Greatorix had a healthier sheen to his skin and was infinitely better dressed. He now wore a clean white shirt under a simple woollen jacket and seemed at ease with himself, his hair greyer and less abundant than Noble remembered but the sickly jaundiced tint that had once discoloured his sagging jowls had gone.

Greatorix glanced up to catch Noble looking. 'With you in a sec, John.'

'Sir.'

Eventually Charlton looked across at Noble. 'I've called this meeting to inform you that DI Greatorix will be taking over as SIO for the Ingham enquiry. He will also assume command of all

Reaper-related casework in the city, including the murder of the Wallis family two years ago.

'I realise that Brook and DCI Hudson concluded the Ingham murders were the work of a copycat. Nevertheless, the connection to the Wallis murders stands and, as that enquiry was under DI Brook's purview, DI Greatorix will take command.' Charlton beamed at Noble before turning to Greatorix. 'Robert?'

Greatorix nodded at Noble. 'John, I've been through the murder book for the Ingham killings because this case offers the best chance of progress with the trail relatively fresh. What's the status regarding current suspects?'

'We don't have any,' said Noble.

'That's what I thought,' sighed Greatorix. 'John, we need to shake things up, get this investigation out of the doldrums where DI Brook steered it. I notice John Ottoman and his wife, Denise, haven't figured in your thoughts since the husband's release. I must say, from afar, they look a good fit to me.'

'I...we thought the same,' said Noble.

'Which is it?' said Charlton.

'DCI Hudson, DS Grant and I were very keen on the Ottomans at one point, sir,' said Noble.

'And Brook?'

'He was never convinced.'

'Well, I'm with you on this one, John. I see a wealth of solid evidence against the Ottomans.' Greatorix began to count on his pudgy fingers. 'John Ottoman admitted carrying out a campaign of harassment against Jason Wallis because of the lad's previous assault on his wife. He admitted following Wallis and his friends to the Ingham house on the night of the killings. He also admitted entering the crime scene where Jason's three friends were found dead. Forensics also found Ottoman's partial on Jason's mobile phone. We know he was there. He had opportunity, he had motive.'

'Sir, I...'

'Then, at sparrow's fart the next day, Ottoman and his wife threw a few suitcases into a car and high-tailed it off to France. A search of their home revealed blood-stained clothing, the blood later matched to three of the victims, as well as a bicycle, used by Ottoman to flee the scene, smeared with identical blood samples.' Greatorix gazed at Noble. 'Were Ottoman and his wife eliminated from enquiries on Brook's say-so?'

The Resurrection

'DI Brook wasn't SIO,' answered Noble. 'DCI Hudson had the final call and he agreed with DI Brook's analysis.'

'Then explain it to me,' said Greatorix.

'You're right about the bloodstains on the bike and Ottoman's clothing which matched blood from the three dead boys in the Ingham yard. But they only found samples on the bottom of his trouser legs, which confirmed Ottoman's account of walking around the crime scene checking for signs of life. Not a single bloodstain suggested Ottoman could be an assailant who severed three carotid arteries with a scalpel. If Ottoman had been the killer, his clothing would have been covered in blood spatter.'

'And the print on the phone?'

'Having checked for signs of life, Ottoman used Jason's mobile to call the emergency services, at which point he realised he might be implicated and panicked. He left on the bicycle, transferring blood smears from his trousers onto the frame.'

Greatorix produced the blurred image of a middle-aged woman looking down from an upstairs window of the house opposite the crime scene. 'What about this image of a woman clocking the Ingham house from a vacant property, a few days before the killings?'

'Ottoman knew nothing about it and insisted it wasn't his wife. And the property wasn't vacant, it was unoccupied and the owner, Mrs North, in Australia.'

'But you'll admit, this picture shows a woman of similar age to Denise Ottoman,' continued Greatorix.

'Yet, a local postman who saw the woman at Mrs North's house failed to identify Denise Ottoman,' countered Noble.

'In fact, this postman saw the female driver of a car that picked up Mrs North from the property and took her to the airport two weeks before the murders, long before this image was taken,' said Charlton.

'Exactly,' agreed Greatorix, brandishing the blurred photograph again. 'This could easily be Denise Ottoman inside Mrs North's house, whereas the driver may simply be a random cabbie or chauffeur for hire.'

'A driver we've mysteriously been unable to trace,' said Noble. 'Sir, we covered this ground. If you'd met Denise Ottoman in the two years since being attacked by Jason Wallis, you'd know, not only was she incapable of this level of violence, she was psychologically unfit to leave her home. To suggest she could break into a property and prep the murder of six people, four of them healthy young men, is...unbelievable.'

'She was capable enough when the pair escaped to France.'

'If packing a car in her driveway points to someone being a killer, we're going to have a lot of work on, sir,' said Noble. 'Besides, Denise Ottoman died of a heart attack the night we arrested her husband...'

'Stress caused by guilt,' suggested Greatorix.

'Then what would the stress of participating in multiple violent murders have done to her?' Noble looked to Charlton. 'Sir, you were there. We discounted their involvement after the interview with John Ottoman. DCI Hudson and DI Brook agreed. You heard Ottoman and you went along.' Charlton didn't answer. 'Watch the film, Inspector. Ottoman doesn't present as a stone-cold killer. They were teachers and what Ottoman saw at the Ingham house was way beyond his experience and he left the crime scene in a state of shock.'

'Opinion not fact,' said Greatorix.

'Experience,' countered Noble. 'And not just mine.'

'You can't deny the Ottomans had motive and opportunity,' argued Charlton.

'No, I can't,' said Noble. 'But that's the problem. If Jason Wallis was their target, why was he the only survivor? Why kill his friends yet leave Jason alive? It doesn't make sense. So, with the forensics supporting Ottoman's statement, we *all* took the decision to treat him as a witness, not a suspect.'

'Maybe he was saving Jason until last and got spooked before he could finish him,' countered Greatorix.

'Spooked having already killed six people?' scoffed Noble. 'Six! Chelsea Ingham, her partner Ryan Harper and Chelsea's nine-year-old son were all killed *inside* the house and there wasn't a shred of forensics to place Ottoman in the building. No blood transfer, no fibres, no foot or fingerprints.' He directed his gaze at Charlton. 'You saw his reaction when we told him there were more bodies in the house. He was genuinely astonished because he'd only seen the bodies in the yard.'

'And he admitted finding those,' said Charlton, nodding.

'And calling it in when he could have left undetected,' added Noble.

'And why do that if he killed them?' agreed Charlton, glancing at Greatorix who shrugged his reply.

The Resurrection

'What about Jason himself?' said Greatorix. 'He survived *both* Reaper attacks without a scratch.'

'Of course, we looked at Jason,' said Noble. 'Long and hard. He's a nasty little shit and, if the facts had supported his guilt, we'd have happily put him away for the rest of his life. But Jason was incapacitated at *both* crime scenes, drugged and unconscious. We tried to punch a hole in the tests but we couldn't. Physically, Jason couldn't have killed his family two years ago or committed the Ingham killings last month. He's in the clear.'

Greatorix and Charlton stared at Noble.

'Well, this has been helpful, Sergeant,' said Charlton, dismissing Noble with a flick of the eyes. 'Your experience is going to be very useful to DI Greatorix going forward and I anticipate a positive result.' Noble stayed in his seat. 'Something to say, Sergeant?'

Noble hesitated. 'I don't know if it's appropriate to mention it but I have been looking at another line of enquiry, sir. I haven't been able to confer with DI Brook...'

'Is this about the shooting?' barked Charlton.

'Indirectly.'

'Speak.'

'The dead woman, Edie McQuarry, was also middle-aged and it crossed my mind that maybe she was the face at the window in Mrs North's house.'

'Any evidence for that?'

'Not a scrap but, at one point, early in the investigation, DI Brook floated the possibility that Mike Drexler might have been involved in the Ingham murders.'

'He's the ex-FBI agent who rented the cottage next door to Brook,' Charlton explained to Greatorix.

'The one Brook dragged into the QMC with a bullet in him?' said Greatorix. 'I didn't see anything in the murder book.'

'That's because he wasn't interviewed,' said Noble. 'It was a hunch which DI Brook later discounted.'

'Based on what?' asked Charlton.

'Based on seeing Drexler in the crowd at the Ingham crime scene; based on the timing of his arrival in Derbyshire and his history in law enforcement.'

'But nothing concrete,' said Greatorix.

'No,' confirmed Noble. 'But DI Brook gave me a beer bottle Drexler had handled and asked me to compare his fingerprints against the partial on Jason's mobile phone. This was before we matched the print to Ottoman. He also asked me to run it through the American database, IAFIS, and confirm with the FBI.'

'Confirm what?'

'That Drexler was who he said he was, which it obviously did.'

'You think a pair of former FBI agents killed the Ingham family?' enquired Greatorix.

'It's just a theory, sir.'

'Why?'

'I've no idea.'

'Where would Brook get a beer bottle with Drexler's prints?' said Greatorix.

'A social occasion,' said Noble. 'I think DI Brook and Mike Drexler became friendly.'

'Friendly, how?'

'They were neighbours with a shared history in chasing serial killers - understandable they'd get together and talk. Drexler became an author after retiring from the Bureau and wrote a book about a case in California he and McQuarry worked - *The Ghost Road Killers.*' Charlton picked up a pencil and made a note.

'Still not seeing a connection to the Ingham case,' said Greatorix.

'Maybe Drexler came to Derbyshire to write a book,' offered Charlton.

'That's what DI Brook concluded,' said Noble. 'It even crossed his mind that Drexler might have been writing a book about the Reaper so he had a drink with him, hoping to find out.'

'Do you think this friendship could explain Brook's reluctance to come up with a convincing explanation for the shooting?' said Charlton.

'I didn't say that, sir.'

'Brook didn't even raise the alarm,' said Greatorix. 'He waited for the hospital to report it.'

'He was probably in shock,' said Noble.

'A hard-nosed detective like Brook?' said Greatorix.

'I'm a hard-nosed detective,' said Noble. 'But I've never seen someone shot dead in front of me. Have you?'

'Get to the point, Sergeant,' said Charlton. 'This is your theory. Were Drexler and McQuarry in the country when the Inghams were attacked?'

'They both were.'

'And two years ago, when the Wallis family were killed?'

'Neither were in Britain,' said Noble. 'But then they wouldn't need to be if the Ingham murders were copycat killings of the Wallis murders.'

Greatorix shook his head. 'If two ex-FBI agents carried out the Ingham murders, the scene would've been a lot more organised yet, according to the files, you were tripping over evidence.'

'Perhaps Ottoman blundering onto the scene disrupted carefully laid plans,' said Noble. 'The three vics in the house *were* executed with maximum efficiency, the three boys in the yard too. But when Ottoman stumbled onto the scene, things began to unravel.'

'It's a bit thin,' said Charlton.

'I know,' said Noble. 'But all the evidence pointed to a pair of killers, one a middle-aged woman.'

'Which brings us back to the Ottomans,' said Greatorix.

'It's not them,' said Noble, echoing the phrase Brook had used many times during the Ingham investigation.

'You've no motive for Drexler and McQuarry?' asked Charlton.

'No,' admitted Noble.

'Or why they might turn on each other afterwards?'

'No.'

'Did Brook ever mention McQuarry before the shooting?' continued Charlton.

'No.'

'So, you don't know if Brook had ever met her before that night.'

'He told me he'd never met her or even heard her name,' answered Noble.

'And you believed him?'

Noble remembered all the things Brook had kept from him about his past dealings with the Reaper. All the details he'd had to squeeze from him like blood from a stone. 'Of course.'

'What's your take on the shooting?' said Charlton.

'It looks like a domestic to me, sir,' said Noble. 'DI Brook was just in the wrong place at the wrong time.'

'According to Brook,' said Greatorix. 'McQuarry is dead and the only other witness is in a coma, so his *version* of events is uncorroborated.'

'That doesn't make him a liar,' said Noble, beginning to wish he'd gotten out when given the chance.

'It might when Drexler wakes up,' countered Greatorix.

'Sir, DI Brook's account matches the known facts,' said Noble. 'The GSR test confirms he didn't fire a weapon...'

'He could have worn gloves.'

'True,' replied Noble. 'But then if DI Brook hadn't rushed him to the QMC, Mike Drexler would be dead. If he had something to hide, he could've left Drexler to die, driven away and nobody would have known he was ever there.'

'Let's hope the panel can get to the bottom of it,' said Charlton. 'Anything else on this theory of yours?'

'Just background. McQuarry and Drexler were FBI partners from 1992. They had a decent record together and a good rapport, according to reports. Drexler even saved McQuarry's life when she was attacked by a drunk with a knife. She was badly cut on the hand and had to take a couple of months to recuperate. They both left the Bureau in 1995, shortly after solving one of California's most notorious serial killings.'

'The Ghost Road Killers?' said Charlton.

'Yes, sir,' said Noble. 'Over twenty recorded victims and some remains not found to this day.'

'And fifteen years later they exchange deadly fire in a field, near East Midlands airport,' said Charlton, rubbing his chin. 'Maybe I should read this book.'

'It's well written,' said Noble.

'Tell me,' said Charlton, looking at his watch. 'Broad brush.'

'The Ghost Road Killers were three members of the same family - Caleb Ashwell, his brother, Jacob and son Billy,' said Noble. 'Drexler tells us that upfront so it's not a spoiler. The Ashwells owned a dilapidated service station on a remote stretch of road in Northern California, where they gave away drugged coffee to selected tourists. After the driver lost consciousness, they'd hijack the occupants and tow their vehicle back to the station. They usually picked young families with children, killed the father and any male children. The mothers and daughters... well, you can imagine.'

'I can,' said Charlton. 'And the Ashwells?'

'All three were murdered in 1995,' said Noble. 'Caleb and Billy at the service station and brother Jacob in a Nevada motel room some weeks later. Nobody knows who did it but when police found Caleb and Billy, they searched the area and found the vehicles of all the missing families and some of the bodies. Drexler and

McQuarry came to the conclusion that someone had worked out what they were doing and executed them.'

'A vigilante,' said Charlton. 'Who?'

'They never identified a suspect,' said Noble.

'Sounds like most of Brook's cases,' quipped Greatorix. Charlton frowned at him.

'There was one other interesting detail. One of the murdered families was originally from Ashbourne. Name of Bailey. Mum and dad...two teenage daughters, Nicole and Sally.'

'Two daughters,' said Charlton, staring into the distance. 'And you think that could be why Drexler was in the Peak District. Writing another book.'

'It's a possibility,' said Noble.

'Interesting. Pity you couldn't rustle up a connection to the Ingham Inquiry.' Something in Noble's silence, piqued Charlton's interest. 'Sergeant?'

'Before they were killed, Billy and Jacob Ashwell were drugged using a combination of morphine and hyoscine. The common name for hyoscine in the UK is scopolamine and the combination of those two drugs was once called Twilight Sleep.'

'Twilight Sleep?' said Greatorix, eyes narrowing.

'The two drugs were used in combination to pacify the Wallis family and two members of the Ingham household, before they were killed,' said Noble.

'And not just the two Reaper killings, John,' said Charlton. 'DI Brook's ex-wife's second husband was murdered in Brighton a few weeks before the Inghams were attacked.' He waved an arm, to conjure up the name.

'Tony Harvey-Ellis,' said Noble.

'Right,' said Charlton. 'He was sedated using the same combination of drugs before being drowned in the English Channel.'

Greatorix nodded. 'Is that why Hudson and Grant were in Derby?'

'Brook was a suspect,' said Charlton, nodding.

'You're kidding?' said Greatorix, his face lighting up.

'Only briefly,' added Charlton, when Noble prepared an objection. 'John, he assaulted Harvey-Ellis two years ago. It was a legitimate line of enquiry.'

'Was Brook charged?' said Greatorix, a mocking smile playing around his lips.

'No, he was cleared immediately,' replied Noble.

'But Brook did turn up at the Ingham crime scene shortly after Ottoman had left and before the first patrol car arrived,' said Charlton.

'Really?' said Greatorix, eyes widening.

'He was lured there by an email supposedly written by a Reaper suspect in the first London killings,' said Noble.

'Victor Sorenson,' said Charlton.

'Sorenson?' exclaimed Greatorix. 'The guy who killed himself two years ago after Brook turned up at his house?'

'The same,' said Charlton.

'So, Brook was a suspect in the Ingham killings,' said Greatorix, a broad grin cracking his features. 'This gets better and better.'

'It was a set-up,' insisted Noble. 'He was cleared in about five seconds.'

'That's true,' conceded Charlton. 'But because DI Brook was temporarily tainted, I seconded DCI Hudson to take charge of the Ingham enquiry.'

'And here we are again with Brook back in the doghouse,' laughed Greatorix.

'Inspector,' said Charlton.

'Sorry, sir.' Greatorix eyed Noble, sorrow the furthest thought in his mind. 'Well this is interesting ancient history, Johnny, but I don't see how far it gets us. The Wallis and Ingham killings were three houses apart and obviously connected. But this Brighton drowning...'

'Edie McQuarry spent time in Brighton,' announced Noble.

'Around the time Harvey-Ellis was drowned?' said Charlton.

'I can't place her there on the day but credit card receipts say she spent at least a month there before his death.'

'And Drexler?'

'I have a request in with the Sussex force. Nothing yet.'

'Interesting,' said Charlton. 'Bear it in mind but, for now, I want you and Inspector Greatorix to bear down with renewed impetus on the Ingham and Wallis family murders. So, if there's nothing else...'

Noble considered whether to mention Victor Sorenson's whereabouts at the time of the Ghost Road killings in 1995 and opened his mouth to speak. 'No, sir.'

4

Jason Wallis shifted his position on the groundsheet and looked towards the cat. Pulling a plastic bag from his pocket, he removed pieces of cooked chicken and wafted them around to let the tortoiseshell cat pick up the scent. It powered across the shadows to the darkness of the overgrown laurel tree to nuzzle against the delicate white meat between Jason's fingers. Jason held onto the chicken to heighten the cat's desire before gently easing the meat towards its mouth.

'You're a cutie, innit,' he whispered, stroking the feeding animal. 'Yes, you are.' He offered another piece of meat and the cat butted Jason's hand to make him lower it to the ground. After the cat ate the meat, it began to purr and Jason stroked its neck. 'It's a shame about your owner giving me all that shit. She needs to show respeck, innit. Yes, she does.' Jason pulled out the final piece of chicken and laid it on the ground. The cat ate it quickly then looked longingly at Jason for more. 'Guess what?' Jason picked up the animal, continuing to stroke its neck. 'The next time she clocks you, I reckon she's gonna learn that.'

∽

DETECTIVE INSPECTOR DAMEN BROOK shrugged off the blanket and glanced at his watch by the light of the moon. He inhaled the hit of blue-brown smoke from his cigarette and ground out the butt in the soil of the herb planter beside his garden bench. As he exhaled the poison, he tipped away his cold tea, wishing it had been a relaxing glass of whisky and water.

Brook hadn't touched alcohol since the night Edie McQuarry had held a gun to his head in a remote field near the airport, the night he'd gazed into the abyss and accepted Death as a friend, come to claim him. Only Mike Drexler's intervention had saved him and tomorrow night he would raise a glass to his saviour.

But tonight, he had important work to do. Things had died down since the shooting but there were loose ends to tie up from that fraught night.

Brook flashed an instinctive look over the wall to the cottage next door, half-expecting Drexler to be in his garden, throwing wood onto his pot-bellied stove or preparing a barbecue. But the place was in darkness, while Mike fought for his life in the Queen's Medical Centre in Nottingham.

Only the Police tape draped across the tiny drive and the seal on the side door gave a hint that Rose Cottage had played a role in such drama. Both the police search of Drexler's rented cottage and Brook's unofficial search that had preceded it, had yielded nothing to concern or incriminate him. Most of Drexler's papers were notes for his latest book and it was doubtful anyone in the local force would make the connection between the Bailey family, murdered in California fifteen years ago, and the violence triggered by McQuarry and Drexler's broken relationship.

In the end, only Mike's spent train ticket had left the premises in Brook's pocket, to be burned in the log burner later that morning - no sense leaving evidence of Drexler's visit to Brighton a couple of weeks before the murder of Tony Harvey-Ellis.

Back in his kitchen, Brook gathered up the padded envelope from the table, left for him at the Midland Hotel reception desk by Laura Grant the morning after the shooting, before her own hasty journey back to Brighton.

He opened it to reassure himself of its contents - keys to McQuarry's Audi, keys for the Reaper apartment and a plastic card with a magnetic strip for accessing the car park beneath the building. Edie McQuarry's personal effects had also been in the envelope but had joined the train ticket in the log burner the previous month. Laura's long letter to him sat folded, and still unread, in the same envelope.

On the front of the envelope, after extensive research on the PNC database, Brook had written a deserving local villain's

The Resurrection

address then memorised the route to the address from the Reaper flat. Brook wouldn't have risked using the Satnav in McQuarry's rented Audi, even if the GPS had been working. But, according to Grant, McQuarry had disabled the system before leaving Brighton and Nottingham detectives looking into her death had been unable to locate her car.

Finally, Brook retrieved his black suit, still in protective wrap, and gathered his car keys. Hearing a gentle snoring, he looked up the stairs to see Bobbi, a black cat from the village, stretched languidly near the top step, dead to the world.

'How did you get in, you little monkey?' Brook trotted up to retrieve the languid ball of warm fur and the cat keened round his hands. 'You can't sleep in here.' Bobbi yawned disdainfully and, unimpressed by Brook's strictures, wriggled free and skittered down the stairs and out into the night.

A second later, Brook lay the black suit carefully on the back seat of his ten-year old BMW. Throwing the padded envelope on the passenger seat, he jumped in and drove through deserted Hartington streets to pick up the road to Ashbourne and on towards Derby.

∾

JASON WALLIS COULDN'T KEEP the grin from his face. This was gonna be sick. It was all he could do not to laugh out loud, except sound carried a long way at night and he didn't want to give away his hiding place. Still, residents in Borrowash weren't as twitchy as those on the Drayfin Estate. When he'd been staking out the Ottoman bitch's house, the merest rustle had somebody flicking on a light or pulling back a curtain, to see if someone was torching a dustbin or boosting a motor.

Feeling the cold seeping into his bones, Jason cast around the groundsheet for his plastic bottle filled with vodka and Baileys, filched from his aunt's drinks cupboard on a night she'd forgotten to replace the padlock. He put the bottle to his mouth and took a long draught of the chocolate-coloured brew then flicked at his mobile. Eleven o'clock. His birthday was an hour away and now he was bored. The disrespectful bitch had better show soon.

At that moment, the beam from a car's headlights swept through the undergrowth. Seconds later, a car drew to the kerb outside the house. Jason rolled up his groundsheet using the engine noise as cover and, when it was silenced, he crouched in mute readiness.

The car door slammed and a scrape of high heels approached the house along the garden path. From beneath the darkened tree, he could just make out a figure walking towards the front door until a sensor picked up the movement and a bright light flooded the doorway, illuminating the woman clearly.

A howl tore through the night and she appeared to stagger and fall onto her haunches. Jason's grin widened and he felt a semi start to tighten his crotch. He heard her sobbing and saw her pick up the dead cat and gather it into her arms like a baby, cuddling its cold, stiff body, its unsupported head, rolling against her cheek.

Jason slipped away regretfully. He would have preferred to drink in more of the woman's suffering, would have liked to step out in front of her and point out the obvious consequences of her disrespect but, having just been released from custody, he resisted.

As he walked the hundred yards down Station Road to his aunt's house he began to bask in his achievement. He missed the Drayfin Estate, right enough, but here, in the sprawling village of Borrowash, to the east of Derby, he was Mr Big, head and shoulders above the rest of the chicken shit kids running around the streets for whom making too much noise was the limit of their ambition. And now the adults were starting to get a taste of his power too.

'Fuck with me lady, you get fucked up double,' he said, turning on music from his phone to stave off boredom on the two-minute journey home.

～

FORTY MINUTES after leaving the deathly hush of the Peak District, Brook was driving through the dark streets of Derby towards the railway station. Two hundred yards before the station a large, brick building loomed up out of the darkness - Magnet House, a two-floor converted warehouse, divided into four apartments. Brook turned onto its short driveway and pulled up in front of a pair of imposing iron gates. He rummaged in the padded envelope and produced the entry card and waved the magnetic strip at a sensor on a post next to the driver's window. The gates swung back noiselessly and Brook drove down, underneath the building, to the residents' car park.

He silenced the BMW but turned off the lights only after identifying the location of Edie McQuarry's sleek black Audi, nestled in the farthest corner, driven there by Laura Grant after she'd parted company with him at the hospital.

Brook removed the Audi keys from the envelope and thumbed the fob in the direction of the vehicle. When the sidelights winked and the cabin light came on, he pulled on a pair of black leather gloves to match his black jeans and sweater then padded over to the car. Unable to see through the tinted window, he took a deep breath to combat the smell and opened the rear door. Laura had done as asked and covered the back seat with a couple of blankets to cover the large bloodstain caused by Drexler's gunshot wound.

He closed the rear door and opened the driver's door, ignoring the sickly-sweet stench that puckered his nose. To dissipate the reek of decay, he lowered all the electric windows then returned to his BMW to retrieve the apartment keys and his black suit, before trotting up the two flights of stairs to the top-floor flat.

Brook unlocked the door and pushed it open. No lights were on but still he cocked an ear for signs of occupation. This was the Reaper's lair, purchased three years ago by the late Victor Sorenson as a base for his network's murderous activities in Derby and discovered by Brook on the night of the shoot-out.

Sorenson, a wealthy industrialist, was the Reaper - a serial killer Brook had hunted for nearly twenty years. He'd purchased the apartment under a false name to serve as a base of operations for the slaughter of two dysfunctional families on the Drayfin Estate, two years apart.

After Sorenson's suicide at the turn of the year in 2009, the apartment had been used by ex-FBI Agent Edie McQuarry and DS Laura Grant of Brighton CID to plan and execute a second Reaper killing in Derby, a few houses from the first atrocity. Six people had been murdered, including a nine-year old boy and his mother.

Investigating the murders, Brook had uncovered the existence of a network of former and current law enforcement officers - the Disciples - recruited and indoctrinated by Sorenson to be a cadre of skilled vigilantes, programmed to execute anti-social families on hard-pressed estates. Brook had resisted all inducements to join. Only God and Victor Sorenson knew how many had not.

Satisfied the flat was unoccupied, Brook flicked at the light switch. Nothing happened. The light fuse was blown. In the radiance of moonlight streaming in through curtain-free windows,

Brook stepped across the threshold, laying his black suit over a chair. McQuarry might be dead and Grant safely back in Brighton but, when the network became aware of the fatal shooting of one of their number, other Disciples were liable to investigate and Brook's raised heart rate acknowledged the prospect.

Closing the door, he made his way to the small bedroom and flicked on the bedside lamp - the sockets were still working - and the room filled with soft light. He threw the padded envelope on the bed.

Back in the main room, Brook picked his way around the various artefacts stored there. There were cases of Nuit St Georges - expensive wine left behind at both crime scenes to suggest a celebration; flasks of a narcotic mixture - Twilight Sleep - and sealed packets of hypodermic syringes to deliver it, subduing victims before their execution. A camcorder's tripod stood in the corner, the camcorder missing after being used to film events at the Ingham house. The mountain bike used by Laura Grant to get back to the flat after the murders, stood against the wall. Everything appeared to have lain untouched since Brook's previous visit, the month before.

He took a moment to gaze in wonder and dismay at the room's contents. All the evidence he'd ever needed to convict the Reaper and confirm the existence of the Disciples was here. In the freezer, there were packets of barbecue meat, identical to those offered up as a prize to the Ingham family, a ruse to locate the family in one place, prior to their slaughter. In a kitchen cupboard, he'd found a box of Swann Morton Post Mortem scalpels, the brand used to cut the family's throats.

With time to search, Brook completed a brisk but thorough inventory and found more evidence of the Reaper's occupation. Under the sink, he discovered a bin bag full of protective suits and masks worn by Scene of Crime Officers, suits that McQuarry and Grant had worn to slay the Ingham household. Indeed, McQuarry had worn a second, clean suit and mask to walk away unchallenged from the crime scene, even winking at him from behind her mask as she strolled, unchallenged, to freedom from the empty house in which she'd been hiding.

'Unbelievable,' mumbled Brook. All those years hunting a single artefact to identify and convict the Reaper and here, in this apartment, he could scarcely move for incriminating exhibits.

That he was unable to use *any* of them, without compromising Laura Grant, failed to excite Brook's sense of irony.

After a final look around, he picked up the light-bodied mountain bike, checked the tyres were inflated and manoeuvred it to the top of the stairs, locking the apartment behind him.

Back in the underground car park, Brook set down the bike next to the Audi and opened the boot. The sickening scent of old blood was more manageable now and flattening the rear seats dowsed the smell further. He manoeuvred the mountain bike into the back of the car then retrieved a jerry can and a half-bottle of Polish vodka from the boot of his BMW and placed them in the back of the Audi. After locking his car, he jumped into the Audi, started the engine and drove slowly back to the main road.

∽

TEN MINUTES later Brook turned off the Audi's lights and rolled onto an empty driveway, coming to a halt and killing the powerful engine immediately. Heavy cloud and broken streetlights contributed to the gloom but Brook took nothing for granted, sitting perfectly still, gloved hand poised to restart the engine and drive away should the house's occupant came out to challenge him.

After two minutes, the windows remained dark. Marek Grabowski, the thirty-eight-year-old Polish resident, was either asleep or out, which didn't settle Brook's nerves.

During Grabowski's two-year stint as a plumber in Derby, he'd become a persistent thorn in the side of local law enforcement. Firmly of the opinion that he could drink himself to a standstill and climb behind the wheel of his, or anybody else's car, Grabowski had become Derby's most wanted car thief and drunk driver but had yet to be arrested and brought to book. That was about to change.

Stepping out of the car, Brook removed the jerry can, the bottle of vodka and the mountain bike from the boot, the latter carried to lean against an unkempt hedge facing the dark street. He removed the Audi's number plates then poured the contents of the jerry can liberally over the inside of the car. He then removed the fuel tank cap and pushed a petrol-soaked rag into the opening.

Finally, he placed the empty jerry can and the half-filled bottle of vodka on the step by the front door. Even the most obtuse investigating officer, couldn't fail to join the dots. With a match, he lit the petrol-soaked rag and tossed the flame into the cabin. Flames erupted immediately.

Glancing to the upper storey of the house, Brook was frozen by the sight of a heavy-set man in a white vest, staring groggily down at the flames on his driveway. When he retreated from the window, Brook sprinted to mount the bike and, with the number plates across his handle bars, peddled hastily away to a safe distance.

A hundred yards away, he turned to watch the blazing Audi, as the barefooted Grabowski - in vest and underpants - appeared and stood, shouting in his direction. After a loud crack in the windscreen, the man took cover and Brook peddled furiously away. Turning the corner, he heard a loud explosion.

A couple of streets away, Brook spied a blue recycling bin for metals and plastic, ready for the morning collection. He slid in the number plates and pushed them to the bottom, before cycling back towards Derby City Centre.

5

Having carried the bike upstairs to the Reaper flat, Brook made his way to the small bedroom and booted up the computer. While he waited for it to load, he plucked one of the bottles of Nuits St George from its box and opened it, pouring a generous glass of the red wine. From the padded envelope he pulled out three sheets of paper and sat down to read Laura's thoughts about the night of the shooting.

Damen

Computer p/word is DISCIPLES301137

I've just returned from the hospital and left the Audi under Magnet House as you requested. I'm now sitting in my hotel room shaking like a leaf, as you can probably see from the handwriting. Regardless, I must say thank you for what you've done for me. I'll never forget it. Ever. I feel I've woken from a deep sleep and can see properly for the first time. What a fool I've been.

You were right about what happened in California. I was waiting to die in that cabin until Victor Sorenson rescued me from Caleb and Billy. At 15 years old, I guess it was inevitable I would fall under his influence. I'm not trying to justify the lives I've taken on the professor's behalf, some of them kids. I won't even attempt it. I can only say that, if I have a future, I'm going to be the best person I can be to make some small amends for the crimes I've committed.

Of course, all this assumes the Disciples don't come after me. It was always an article of faith with Sorenson that anybody who'd served in law enforcement was untouchable, no matter how much they interfered with his work. You were living proof of that. McQuarry ignored that philosophy and rightly paid the highest price. Hopefully, if there's anyone still in charge of the network, they'll see what she did, remember the professor's code and leave us both in peace - well, hardly that but you know what I mean.

And, nobody got closer to Sorenson than you, Damen, not even Mike. The professor would turn in his grave if he thought ANYONE in his organisation could ever contemplate killing you. But he's dead now so better take care. I know I'll be looking over my shoulder for years to come and perhaps that's only fitting.

Last night, Ed was unrecognisable as the woman who took me under her wing and befriended me. After the murder of my family, she helped me a lot and I thought she was my friend. I see now she was insane and what we did at the Ingham house sickens me.

Brook broke off when the computer prompted him for a password and typed in DISCIPLES301137. He wondered how many Disciples there were. Maybe he'd find his answer tonight. He turned back to the letter while the program loaded.

I enclose all the keys you'll need, as well as Ed's passport and driving license. I couldn't face taking her luggage into the flat so I stopped on the way back and threw it in the river. You'll find the car in the darkest corner of the lot, the back seat covered with blankets to hide Mike's blood. God, there was so much of it. I hope he pulls through.

It's barely five in the morning and I'm sitting here ready to go back to Brighton and the only thing to decide is whether to face Hudson at breakfast and drive back with him or leave a note and take the early train. I've had to face up to so much in such a short time that I'm not sure I can look him in the eye without bursting into tears and confessing everything.

I still can't quite believe I'm free of this. You saved me, Damen. No-one has shown such faith in me since Uncle Vic. (Sorry, it's hard not to think of him without affection).

I want you to know, it's not too late to change your mind. You cracked the Reaper case; you deserve the credit. Please know you can turn me in any time if you need to. I deserve it and I won't fight it. I know you won't do it and I also know what covering for me will cost you. People will say the Reaper has beaten you again and your critics will have even more ammunition so please keep this letter as insurance.

If things go wrong, if you get caught disposing of the car or covering up for me in any way, this is your get-out-of-jail card. I mean it, Damen. Six people died at the Ingham house and I'm prepared to pay for that. Even the murder of my parents and sister can't excuse what I did.

You guessed most of what happened after Sorenson found me in the cabin. I was in a terrible state, physical and mental. I'd suffered a trauma that no teenage girl should have to endure and I was near catatonic. I remember on the way to Sorenson's house in Tahoe, I collapsed into a deep sleep, a coma almost, and I was out for days. Maybe it was relief, or the knowledge that I no longer had to fight for survival every second of every minute, or that I would no longer have to hear my sister's screams. My God, the nightmares, Damen.

When I woke, I was in paradise. I could hear water and see the sun. I'd been bathed and attached to a drip by a nurse Sorenson hired to make sure I made a full recovery. But all I really needed was time - time to come to terms with what had happened and to wonder where my future lay. You were right, of course. Sorenson had already made plans. I was to live with him until I was ready to work for the cause. From that moment, my life as Nicole Bailey was over. A week later, I became Laura Grant - passport and all. Fifteen years ago. Half my life.

I don't know if Mike laid it out for you but I was there when Ed killed Jacob Ashwell at the Golden Nugget Motel. The professor had Ed take me under her wing though obviously she couldn't visit Tahoe too often as she was still an active FBI agent, especially as Mike Drexler had taken to sitting in his car, watching the house.

Once they'd located Caleb's brother, they offered me the chance to be useful. Of course, I jumped at the opportunity to avenge my sister and my parents and no-one can blame me for that! I'd do it again tomorrow.

Mike was supposed to pull the trigger. The professor was certain he was Disciple material. He was on a downward spiral after the death of his own sister and estrangement from his father, the one he mentioned last night. He seemed the perfect recruit. Ed, who'd been on board for about three years, had flagged him up. Once they located Mike's abusive father, they thought they had the perfect bait. The best laid plans, eh?

I do know Drexler and Uncle Vic talked in the Tahoe house one night when Mike was working the Ghost Road case solo after Ed had returned to Sacramento. Subjected to the professor's persuasive powers, it seemed Mike had been convinced to join the Disciples. Uncle Vic even gave him a gun, the M9, to prove his worth when the chance came. And, Jacob Ashwell was the ideal first kill.

You'll know from Mike's book that Ashwell was working as a night manager at the Golden Nugget, about thirty miles away. Once Ed had found Mike's father in San Francisco, we were all set.

The Resurrection

First, the professor drove out to the Golden Nugget to scout around, making sure Mike followed him, of course. He booked all the motel rooms for one night the following week, when Ashwell would be on duty. That way, no innocent bystanders could get hurt or see something they shouldn't. And, of course, Mike took the bait. He got in touch with Ed and "persuaded" her to drive back to Tahoe for the showdown.

When the time came, I lay down on the back seat of the professor's car for the drive out to the motel; nice and slow so Mike and Ed could follow. We had everything we needed - a pair of hypodermics filled with the Twilight Sleep mixture, a small cassette player for music and a billycan full of petrol in the trunk to burn down the cabin when we were done.

When we arrived, the professor went to see Ashwell to let slip that he'd brought a drugged girl to the motel and didn't want to be disturbed while he partied - the ideal bait for that perverted piece of shit. Once inside the cabin, we set the trap. I stripped to bra and knickers and got into bed. I'd been practising with the hypodermic all week but I was still nervous. When the professor left the cabin, I knew I'd have to face Ashwell alone until Ed and Mike came through the door to 'save' me.

I could smell Ashwell when he came in, even from under the bedclothes - stale sweat and beer - and I wasn't sure I could go through with it, especially when I heard him pulling his pants down. But I kept thinking about what Sally went through and knew I couldn't let her down.

When Ashwell pulled the sheet away from me, I could almost hear him licking his lips. Dirty bastard. We thought he might recognise me but, even so, I still had time to stab the needle into his neck and I pushed the plunger down for all I was worth then started screaming so Ed and Mike could do their thing. The drugs worked perfectly and, within seconds, Ashwell was a dribbling wreck on the floor.

While I got dressed, Ed went through Ashwell's clothes, looking for ID so Mike would know they'd found Ashwell. After that, it was time for Mike to step up and rid the world of this cockroach.

But for some reason, he couldn't do it. Why, we were never sure. Worse, he wasn't going to let Ed put Ashwell down either. Fortunately, the professor had considered every possibility and we had a second hypodermic in case Mike didn't deliver. To be sure we had control, Mike also had a faulty gun - the same one he had last night, in fact. What goes around...

I didn't enjoy jamming the needle into Mike's neck but it had to be done. And while he was incapacitated, Ed put Jacob Ashwell out of our misery while I packed the car. We torched the cabin and took Mike back to the professor's house and left him there. The house had been mothballed and the professor was already on his way to the airport but it didn't matter. Ed had used Mike's back-up gun to blow out Ashwell's brains - Mike's gun, Mike's prints all over it - he was powerless to speak out in the aftermath.

You know the rest. Mike left the bureau shortly afterwards and Ed left to help the professor with his work. From that day to this, Ed and I worked as a team.

Brook broke off to look at the monitor. An online countdown was in progress and there were 353 days to go until it was complete. He pulled a calendar from the wall and, counting forward, worked out that 353 days would take the date to November $30^{th,}$ 2011.

The password on Laura's letter - DISCIPLES301137 - the thirtieth day of the eleventh month, nineteen thirty-seven. What had happened on that day? The answer arrived before Brook had finished forming the question - Victor Sorenson's birthday. In 353 days, the Professor would've been seventy-four years of age and Brook suspected the Disciples were planning further killings to mark his birthday. Reaper Armageddon, McQuarry had called it - RAG, for short.

Brook stared at the monitor. From Sorenson's pattern of recruitment, he knew most of the Disciples would have a connection to law enforcement, bringing a level of expertise as well as better access to deserving cases; dysfunctional families in which parents had toxified the lives of their children by rejecting honest work and self-improvement; families that embraced anti-social behaviour, dragging down whole streets and neighbourhoods, taking pleasure from misery caused to others.

And Brook knew from personal experience that the notion of eradicating these habitual criminals was unusually seductive for police officers, operating at the sharp end of their unlawful endeavours. Brook had no doubt Sorenson would have attracted plenty of willing recruits over the decades: disillusioned FBI agents like McQuarry and Drexler as well as British coppers like Brook's old mentor and boss, DCI Charlie Rowlands.

Rowlands had fallen under Sorenson's spell, the appeal to his vengeful instincts shaped by personal tragedy. Charlie's daughter, Elizabeth, had died from a heroin overdose and, unleashing the rage of a grieving father was a simple matter of identifying the dealer responsible for her supply. A simple matter, that is, for someone with Sorenson's resources.

> Time to go, Damen. I can't face Hudson. I'll leave him a note. I'm going to miss your steadiness. I know you have to dispose of the car and secure the flat but then I hope you can forget the Reaper and live your life. Forget the Disciples too. They can't be stopped and, if you don't interfere with their work, they shouldn't come after you.
>
> But, if you feel you must go on with this, a word of explanation. The password at the top of the page gets you through to The Disciples' encrypted website. That's as far as I've ever been and I can't get you further. Once there you'll see a number. It's a countdown to the next Reaper killings but there's something special happening, something big that Ed would only hint at and it will make the whole world sit up and take notice. Having carried out my first blood kill, I would've found out details in a few days but now I feel better not knowing.
> Christ, I want to sleep for a week. Last night seems like a million years ago. I'll hold a good thought for Mike and, if you see him, thank him for me. I won't forget what you've done for me and hope one day we can see each other again.

LG/NB x

Brook returned the letter to the envelope and gazed at the computer, cursor flashing, awaiting further codes. As he didn't have them, he closed the computer down and sat on the bare mattress, sipping wine and mulling over struggles with the Reaper that had defined his life and career. He'd lost his wife, alienated his daughter and very nearly surrendered his sanity. Now he had nothing left to lose but his life. And that made him dangerous.

∼

BROOK SWALLOWED AND, for a second, managed to keep his head still as he stared towards Sorenson's corpse. His mind and vision cleared and he found some control over his speech had returned.

'I'm not like you. I made a mistake.'

You are me Damen. You're ready. I came to Derby for you. Charlie did his best but you were always the one.

Sorenson's words rattled around Brook's head but he couldn't decipher their meaning. He closed his eyes. A sudden jolt roused him. He was on a stretcher in Sorenson's study. People were gathered around, carrying him.

Victor Sorenson was seated at his desk, his bald head turned to the window, his scalp and neck deathly white, like day-old snow. His wrists had been severed and the desktop was awash with blood.

Brook stared at the clenched fist, splashed with red, a necklace with little silver hearts stretched taut around marble-white knuckles. Then, welcome oblivion engulfed him and all was black.

It was over. Sorenson was dead. Brook was alive. He'd won.

Brook sat bolt upright, his mouth dry, eyes darting around to work out where he was. He located the lamp and turned it on, bathing the bedroom in soft light. Though still dark, it was the morning and he was in the Reaper flat.

He slid from the mattress fully-dressed, padded into the kitchen to wash and wipe his glass and drank from a tap to purge the sticky residue of red wine. Slipping on his shoes at the window, the city of Derby stretched out before him, dark and lifeless. He turned off the lamp, locked the flat and hurried downstairs to his car.

6

December 12th 2010 - Queens Medical Centre

An hour later, Brook sat bleary-eyed in a padded chair next to Mike Drexler's bed in his room at the QMC, eyes glued to his motionless friend, fighting for his life amongst the beeping hardware. The prognosis was good. All Drexler needed was time for his body to start the healing process, time for his brain to tell itself to wake.

Having slept fitfully at the Reaper flat, the rhythmic noise of the machines began to lullaby Brook and his bloodshot eyes closed. He dreamed of driving through dark countryside. He dreamed of being on his knees in a cold, dank field, McQuarry pointing a gun at him, Laura pleading for his life, breath steaming in the winter air. He dreamed of McQuarry's expression, turning to ice when Drexler raised his gun. He dreamed of the bullets speeding to their targets and the bodies of Drexler and McQuarry falling to earth.

Brook shook himself awake and stared at Drexler's slackened features. Somewhere in that shell of flesh and bone, somewhere unreachable, Mike was fighting his battle.

A nurse arrived and lifted a wrist from Drexler's inert form and began to take a pulse, smiling at Brook then staring intently at the upside-down watch attached to her uniform.

Brook found the ritual incongruous amongst so much technology. 'How is he?'

'Hanging in there,' said the nurse.

'Thank you for your efforts.' Brook stood to leave but paused, fumbling for a pen. 'Nurse. Can you do me a huge favour?'

∼

ON THE WAY back to his car, Brook took the time to locate any obvious security cameras, particularly around the ambulance bay, across which he and Laura Grant had carried Mike Drexler's body.

That night he'd parked the car away from the bright lights around the emergency doors to limit the ability of cameras to focus on occupants of the car. Cameras may have recorded Laura Grant helping Brook carry Drexler to A&E but identifying her would be difficult and placing her in the Audi with Drexler all but impossible, unless there was film of her jumping out of the car.

Brook drove his BMW to the car park's exit barrier and pushed in his ticket. But, instead of turning west towards Derby, he drove through the dark morning into Nottingham City Centre and into the underground car park beneath the Victoria Centre. At this hour, the city was only just stirring but even before seven there was light traffic on the roads and the wide pavements were sprinkled with low-paid wage slaves, eyes to the floor, cocooned by headphones, lumbering resentfully to their work.

Brook parked and returned to the ground floor and pushed open the heavy door onto the street. He emerged onto the pavement as the first drops of rain were spotting the concrete so he pulled up his collar against the cold and hurried to the steamy warmth of a nearby cafe.

Sitting down with a mug of tea to await his bacon sandwich, he pulled out a pair of mobile phones from his jacket and turned on both with a heavy depression of the thumb. He checked his regular phone for messages. There was only one from DS John Noble - the only colleague entrusted with the number.

You were right. Jason Wallis in the clear on the assault. Not enough evidence.

'Surprise, surprise.' Brook texted the same in reply though it was far from that. Ravi, the Asian boy Jason Wallis had filmed being assaulted by his soon-to-be-dead friends, was the only witness to the attack and his testimony was always likely to come under pressure. So, while Jason's fellow assailants had paid the ultimate price for their crimes, Wallis had walked away clean.

Noble replied. *Had meeting with Charlton. Bad news. DI Greatorix back on active. Taking over Ingham + Wallis enquiries. Sorry.* ☹

Brook stared at the message for thirty seconds before his face broke into a wide grin which turned to laughter. When it stopped, the smile remained and he bit cheerfully into his bacon sandwich. 'Laura, you're in the clear. Greatorix couldn't catch a snail with asthma.'

He picked up the other phone, a pre-paid mobile sent to him by Laura Grant, the week after her return to Brighton. He keyed in a text to the single contact number.

MD on the mend. Car sorted. All well. D.

He ate his sandwich, drained his tea then switched off both phones and walked the few hundred yards to the police station on North Church Street for his eight o'clock meeting with DI Connor Campbell.

Campbell hadn't yet arrived and Brook was shown to an interview room to wait. A projector hummed overhead and Brook wondered what film they had to show him - almost certainly the Audi hurtling around the hospital grounds. It was unlikely, but not impossible, they had a clear view of Laura, tending to the wounded Drexler in the backseat. And any film of a third person in the car would directly contradict his statement that he'd driven Drexler to the hospital alone.

He stood to walk round the room and noticed the red light on a camera and smiled into the lens and, in the same instant, the door opened. DI Campbell walked in, tall with mid-length brown hair and a fading tan, wearing a smart grey suit. He was about the same age as Noble - early thirties.

Behind him walked a female officer he hadn't seen before, younger than Campbell, with grey eyes and short brown hair, also wearing a suit. She clutched a folder under her arm and her eyes locked onto Brook before she'd stepped across the threshold. Both officers carried hot drinks and Campbell set down a mug of tea on the table and pushed it towards Brook.

'Tea with milk, no sugar, right?' enquired Campbell.

'You remembered,' said Brook, sarcastically.

'Basic Nottingham manners.'

'Do those manners not extend to punctuality?' said Brook, taking a sip.

'You have somewhere to be?' said Campbell.

Brook decided against mentioning the funeral. 'I have commitments.'

'Then let's press on, Inspector,' said the female detective, offering her hand to shake. 'I'm DS Kelly Tyson. Where's your Fed rep?'

Brook pulled up a chair. 'I'm fine without.'

'Seriously?' said Tyson, with a glance at Campbell. 'I don't think that's wise.'

'Noted,' said Brook.

'We could rustle up a duty solicitor...'

'I've nothing to hide,' said Brook.

'Everyone has something to hide,' said Campbell. 'We have a body in the mortuary and, if our findings go against you, your career is on the line. You do realise that, right?' Brook said nothing. 'Your funeral.' Campbell activated the recorder and made introductions for the record. 'DS Tyson is here representing Leicestershire CID and, for the record, DI Brook has once again waived his right...'

'Leicestershire?' said Brook.

'We have jurisdiction,' said Tyson.

'Turns out the field where the victim's body was found is actually in Leicestershire,' said Campbell. 'Near...' He glanced at Tyson.

'Isley cum Langley,' she obliged. 'It's on the county border. So, as Nottingham picked up the original enquiry and did the initial legwork, we've opted for a joint approach.'

'Meaning I have to go over everything again,' sighed Brook. 'Then let's start with my objection to characterising the deceased as the victim. Mike Drexler is the victim here and he's fighting for his life, shot by the deceased in the act of saving *my* life.'

'Objection noted,' said Campbell. 'But the status of participants won't be officially determined until the enquiry is concluded and the board delivers its verdict.'

'And when Mr Drexler regains consciousness, as appears likely, he may have a different story to tell,' said Tyson.

'Story?' said Brook.

'Figure of speech,' said Tyson, smiling.

'What if Mike can't remember and this nonsense drags on for months?' said Brook.

'We'll cross that bridge when we come to it,' said Campbell. He nodded at Tyson.

'Inspector, we'd like to know a little more about the three guns recovered from the scene...'

'I know nothing about the guns,' said Brook. 'I'd never seen them before that night and I didn't touch any of them, let alone fire one, as the GSR test confirmed...'

'You could have been wearing gloves,' said Tyson.

'I wasn't,' said Brook. 'Besides, only two shots were fired. That's a proven fact. Another fact. Tests confirm gunshot residue on Mike's hands and the deceased. I didn't fire a weapon.'

'Three people, three guns,' said Tyson. 'Even if you didn't fire a weapon, you could have been holding.'

'The third gun belonged to McQuarry and it was faulty,' said Brook. 'Thinking Mike was unarmed she gave it to him and ordered him to shoot me.'

'Why would she do that, if she knew it was faulty?'

'I can't be sure but my guess is she wanted to find out if Mike would do what she asked,' said Brook. 'By giving him a dud weapon, he'd effectively be unarmed until she knew he'd comply.'

'But he didn't?'

'No, he turned the gun on her and tried to disarm her.'

'Thinking the gun worked.' Brook's answer was a smile. 'Lucky for you Mike had another weapon.'

'Wasn't it,' said Brook.

'Did *you* know Drexler was armed?'

'No, of course not,' said Brook.

'Or why?' asked Tyson. Brook shook his head.

'Cautious about encountering his former FBI partner, perhaps?'

'You'll have to ask him.'

'But, it's fair to conclude that he and McQuarry had...issues.'

'It would seem so,' said Brook. Before they could follow up, he added, 'But, beyond their relationship in the FBI, I don't know what those issues were.'

'No hints? No pithy comments exchanged that might shed some light?'

'None.'

'Who fired the first shot?' said Campbell.

'Mike, by a whisker,' said Brook.

'Which could point to him as the aggressor,' said Tyson.

'No. McQuarry was about to shoot me so her attention was diverted. When Mike drew his gun, he had a split-second advantage that saved my life.'

Tyson dropped her eyes to the file on the table and pulled out a large photograph and pushed it across the table for Brook's scrutiny. 'Former FBI Special Agent, Edie McQuarry, 53 years old at time of death. Is that the person you say was trying to kill you?'

'It is.'

'And the person shot and killed by Michael Drexler on the night of November 10th?'

'Yes.'

'Have you anything you want to add to your previous statements?' said Campbell.

'No.'

'Something you may have remembered pertaining to the relationship between Drexler and the deceased,' said Tyson.

'I didn't know anything in the first place,' said Brook. 'They were on first name terms and had clearly known each other for some time but that's all I know.'

'Sorry we're covering old ground, Inspector. Being new to the enquiry, I hope you'll understand why I'm asking these questions.' Tyson stared at Brook and when he failed to object, returned her gaze to the file. 'Let's talk about *your* relationship with Mike Drexler. How long have you known him?'

'Mike rented the cottage next to mine in Hartington and moved in towards the end of October, I think. You'll have to check the exact date with the landlord, Tom Hutcheson.'

'So, you'd never met him until then,' said Tyson.

'No.'

'But you got to know him.'

'Well enough to call him Mike,' said Brook. 'That's about it.'

'For someone you barely know, you've been to visit him a lot in hospital,' said Campbell. 'Every other day, according to my constables.'

'Mike saved my life and I want to thank him to his face,' said Brook.

'Those visits stop now,' said Campbell. 'It's likely Mr Drexler will make a full recovery so he'll be under 24-hour supervision

The Resurrection

from now on. You can sit outside but there'll be no unsupervised access.'

'Understood,' said Brook.

'Did you and he socialise?' said Tyson.

'He invited me round to his cottage for a drink and a meal when he first arrived.'

'And you went?'

'Why wouldn't I?' said Brook. Campbell raised an admonishing eyebrow. 'Yes.'

'What did Mike tell you about himself?' said Campbell.

'He said he was retired from the FBI and worked cases in California out of the Sacramento office. When he retired, he wrote a book called The Ghost Road Killers, about one of his biggest cases.'

'A case he and McQuarry worked in 1995,' said Tyson, checking a note. Brook didn't contradict. 'The year both left the bureau.'

'So, I gather.'

'You think something happened between them on that case?' said Campbell.

'It seems suggestive,' agreed Brook. 'You'll have to ask Mike.'

'Did Drexler talk about the case?'

'Only in very broad terms about how he agonised over it. Families were slaughtered. Children were raped and killed. It was a bad one.'

'And Edie McQuarry?'

'I didn't know her and Mike never mentioned her.'

'So, you'd never heard of her before the shooting?' said Tyson.

'I never heard him speak of her but I knew McQuarry was Mike's ex-partner because he gave me a copy of his book. But, until the night of the shooting, she was just a name. Everything I know about her derived from reading the book.'

'I've read it,' said Tyson. 'Interesting case.'

'Yes,' said Brook.

'So, when the shooting stopped did you know the deceased was Edie McQuarry?'

'When I heard the American accent and Mike calling her Ed, I put two and two together.' The two detectives across the table waited. 'Yes, I knew.'

'Do you know why Mike was in Derbyshire?' said Tyson.

'He told me he was researching another book.'

'What about?'

'One of the families killed by The Ghost Road Killers was English, originally from Ashbourne.'

'The Bailey family,' said Tyson, peering at her notes. 'George, wife Tania, daughters Nicole and Sally. Tortured, raped and murdered by Caleb, Jacob and Billy Ashwell in California. Nicole Bailey's body was never found. Why would he write a book about them?'

'Mike was appalled by the publishing industry's appetite for books about serial killers and what drives them, every aspect of their psyches devoured by a public, hungry for sickening details. He thought it was important to remind people that even the most glamourized killers leave behind shattered lives and he owed it to the victims to tell their story.'

'Sounds like you talked to him a lot,' said Tyson.

'Enough.'

'What's he like?'

'Affable. Confident. We never ran out of things to talk about.'

'And did he seem...' Tyson paused, looking for the right word. '...pre-occupied?'

'You mean, worried that his ex-partner was planning to kill him?' said Brook. 'No. He was self-possessed, thoughtful and well-balanced, considering the things he'd had to deal with.'

'Did you envy him that balance?' asked Tyson.

Brook stared, unmoved. 'My breakdown was nearly twenty years ago.' There was a moment's silence that Brook decided to fill. 'No, I didn't envy him. In our business, control is everything but it's only ever a performance. Scratch the surface of any experienced detective and you'll see a different picture, as you should know.'

'Still waters running deep,' said Campbell, a wry smile on his lips.

'Something like that.'

Tyson's smile was apologetic. 'Sorry. We had to ask.'

'Glad I could answer without foaming at the mouth,' said Brook.

'You deserve a biscuit.'

'I've already eaten,' said Brook, taking a gulp of tea. The opening skirmishes were ending, the easy questions, lobbed up for him to hit out of the park. They had something else. Brook could feel it.

'Was the Reaper ever mentioned in your conversations?' asked Campbell.

'What do you think?' said Brook.

'You're the Reaper detective,' said Tyson. 'Famous the world over. Books have been written about the killings. For a writer like Mike Drexler...' She left the rest unsaid.

Brook shrugged. 'I was investigating the Ingham murders when we talked so, yes, Mike was interested in all the speculation. And yes, he mentioned the Reaper.'

'Only natural he'd ask,' nodded Campbell. 'What did you tell him?'

'Nothing he couldn't have read in the papers,' said Brook. 'Six people were dead, murdered in cold blood. I wasn't about to compromise the investigation with a few off-the-cuff remarks and Mike wasn't dumb enough to expect any.'

'What about before the murders?' said Tyson.

'Before?'

'Drexler's arrival in Derbyshire pre-dated the Ingham killings by a few days,' said Campbell. 'Did he mention the Reaper murders *before* the Inghams were killed?'

Brook went through the motions of thinking about it before deciding he had nothing to gain by lying. 'Yes.'

'So, he knew who you were,' said Tyson.

'Famous the world over,' said Brook. 'Your words.'

'How did he find out?' said Tyson.

'I had T-shirts made and gave him one,' said Brook. Tyson and Campbell stared coldly at him. 'The landlord mentioned it to him.'

'And, while you were investigating the Ingham killings, did you ever consider him a suspect?' said Campbell.

Brook stared. 'Who told you that?'

'Did you?'

Brook considered his answer. 'Briefly.'

'Long enough to ask a subordinate to check Drexler's fingerprints with the FBI.'

'Yes,' said Brook.

'Why?'

'Given Mike's past, I thought it a bit of a coincidence he should show up just before the Ingham family were attacked.'

'You suspected Drexler because he was in the FBI?' said Tyson.

Brook hesitated. 'When I was at the Ingham crime scene, I saw Mike in the crowd.'

'Where?'

'On the other side of the tape with the rest of the punters,' said Brook.

'When was this?'

'The night after the murders.'

'There's nothing in the files to that effect,' said Campbell.

'It was dark and I only saw him for a split-second,' said Brook. 'I couldn't be sure. I was with DS Noble, DS Grant and DCI Hudson and none of them saw him. Later, I mentioned it to DS Noble and we decided it wasn't worth committing to the record.'

'But you had Noble run his prints just the same.'

'I thought it best to be sure.'

'And Drexler consented to having his fingerprints taken?'

Brook looked away. 'Not exactly.'

'We're listening,' prompted Tyson.

'The next time I saw Mike, we had a beer in his garden. Without his permission, I secured a beer bottle he'd been drinking from and asked DS Noble, to check the prints against the print found at the Ingham crime scene.'

'And?'

'There was no match,' said Brook. 'When the FBI confirmed Mike was who he said he was, I didn't think any more about it.' Tyson nodded though she didn't appear to be finished with this line of questioning and Brook knew what was coming.

'Would it surprise you to learn that Mike Drexler arrived in Britain a full month before he moved into the cottage next to you?'

Brook tried not to overdo his shock. 'Yes, it would.'

'He didn't mention it?' said Campbell.

'If I didn't know then clearly, he didn't mention it,' said Brook.

'Or where he'd been before he turned up in Hartington?'

'Asked and answered,' said Brook, mustering a little impatience.

Campbell smiled his apology. 'My bad.'

'Your bad what?'

'My bad back,' said Campbell, faking a grimace.

Brook frowned at Campbell. If they'd found out Mike had been to Brighton to look for McQuarry, that would be the next topic of conversation.

'And McQuarry?' said Tyson.

'What about her?'

'Any idea when she arrived in Britain?'

'Not a clue,' said Brook. 'Have you?'

'That's not information we can give out.'

'I'll live,' said Brook. 'Thanks to Mike.'

Tyson turned a page in the file. 'When you visited Mike's cottage, did you have any inkling that he was armed or kept guns there?'

'Is that a serious question?' said Brook.

'A routine one,' remarked Tyson. 'For the record.'

'If I had, I would have acted on it. Obviously.'

'Is that a no?' said Tyson.

'That's a no.'

'Did you ask Mike about guns?' said Campbell. 'From a law enforcement point of view.'

'Did you check my file?' said Brook.

'We did,' said Tyson. 'In all your years of service, you've never fired a weapon and never visited a firing range.'

'Well, then,' said Brook.

'And privately?'

'I have never fired a gun,' said Brook. 'Ever. I've seen the damage they can do.'

'So, you don't know one of the guns recovered from the scene was an M9,' said Campbell. He pulled out a glossy photograph of the gun and pushed it towards Brook. 'It's an American military gun which suggests it was smuggled in by McQuarry or Drexler.'

Brook turned his gaze onto the gun, remembered staring down its barrel in the Reaper flat, the gun in Drexler's hand - before McQuarry put her own weapon to Drexler's head and took it from him. 'Fascinating,' he said. 'What of it?'

'The M9 was also the gun you claimed McQuarry gave to Mike Drexler,' said Tyson. 'The one she ordered him to kill you with.'

'If you say so.'

'But it didn't work,' said Campbell.

'No,' confirmed Brook.

'So McQuarry knew the gun wouldn't work before she gave it to him?' said Tyson.

'Asked and answered,' replied Brook.

'So, she wasn't expecting him to shoot you,' said Campbell. 'A test, you said.'

'That was my take on it,' said Brook.

'So, Drexler didn't, at any time, attempt to turn the gun on you,' concluded Campbell.

'No,' said Brook. 'I suspect McQuarry expected him to turn the gun on her.'

'Because of some dispute in their past, about which you know absolutely nothing,' said Campbell. Brook's only answer was a tight smile.

'And when he did turn the gun on her, she pointed out to him the M9 was faulty,' said Tyson.

'Yes.'

'And then she prepared to shoot you herself?'

'That was her intention,' replied Brook, remembering the feeling of complete helplessness, coupled with the strange taste of defeat in his mouth as he waited, on his knees, to be executed.

'But Drexler was carrying a second weapon in an ankle holster.'

'Yes.'

'And it was with this second weapon that he shot and killed McQuarry?'

'As she fired at him, yes,' said Brook.

'A spectacular fall out for two former FBI agents who were partners.'

'No argument here,' said Brook.

'And you have no idea how the guns got into the country?'

'None,' said Brook.

'Not your area of expertise?' said Campbell.

'No,' said Brook. 'But then, I don't work in the gun crime capital of the East Midlands.'

Campbell pursed his lips. 'I don't appreciate Nottingham being characterised in that way.'

Brook smiled. 'The stats don't do character profiles.'

'Nor do they tell the whole story.'

'Story?' said Brook. Campbell glared at him.

'More tea?' said Tyson.

'No,' said Brook. 'Will this take much longer?'

'It'll take as long as it takes,' said Tyson. 'Because the guns...'

'Where the guns came from is irrelevant,' said Brook. 'When Mike regains consciousness, hopefully he'll be able to tell you but that won't change the sequence of events. A Detective Inspector, with almost thirty years' service under his belt, witnessed a fatal shoot-out where the person who initiated it, met her demise. It was a good shooting, as the Americans say.'

'The problem is that's not how it looks to senior ranks, Inspec-

The Resurrection

tor,' said Campbell. 'Brass see *three* guns at a crime scene at which *three* people were present. You must realise the implications and how that could look.'

'I can't help how it looks to you, DS Tyson or senior ranks,' said Brook. 'But, unlike any of you, I was actually there and *saw* how it looked and continue to do so several times a day.'

'Must be tough reliving it like that,' said Tyson.

'I hope you never have to find out,' said Brook.

'We're just doing our job, you understand,' said Tyson.

'Of course,' replied Brook. 'But I've already answered these questions more than once.'

Tyson smiled. 'Blame me, Inspector. I'm new here.'

'Too new to read the transcripts?' asked Brook.

'Perhaps we should take a break there,' said Tyson, her smile becoming a little more mechanical.

7

Jason woke to the sound of knocking on his bedroom door.

'Happy birthday.' His aunt's muffled voice. 'Are you decent?'

Jason sat up, irritated, an empty Diamond White cider bottle falling to the floor. 'What do you want, woman?'

The door opened and his aunt walked in holding the hand of Jason's three-year-old sister, Bianca.

'Oi, I didn't say you could come in, did I?'

'This is *my* house and don't you forget it,' she growled. She carried an Asda bag and Jason fancied he could make out wrapping paper.

'What's that?' he demanded sourly.

'What do you think? Happy birthday.' Bianca gurgled happily at him.

'Presents?' Jason sat up further, smiled at his little sister and scratched idly at a nipple on his lean frame.

His aunt stepped over Jason's discarded clothing, empty cans and bottles and full ashtrays to the window. 'It smells like a brewery in here.' She hauled the curtains apart and opened the window. Jason shielded his eyes. 'Get some clothes on and come downstairs.'

'Give me some peace, woman, it's my birthday.'

'It's your birthday every day, at the moment. Me and Bianca are going shopping in ten minutes so, if you want your presents, get dressed and get downstairs.'

Two minutes later, Jason walked unsteadily into the bright kitchen in tracksuit bottoms and baggy T-shirt. He went straight to the fridge and pulled out a carton of orange drink and drained half a litre in one go. While he drank, he ran his eye over the packages waiting for him on the table, while his aunt was forcing the wriggling Bianca into her coat.

'Aren't you going to open them?' she asked.

Jason pulled a face. 'Can't see owt that looks like an iPad.' He went to unwrap the larger parcel. It was a copy of *In Search of The Reaper* by Derby Telegraph journalist, Brian Burton.

'A book,' wailed Jason. 'For fuck's sake.'

'Mind yer language round the lass, you ungrateful little shit. You're in it so I thought you might like to read it.'

Jason gave her a pitying look. 'My name's in a lot of stuff, woman. Where've you been the last two years? I'm a celebrity.'

'Shame you're not in the jungle.'

'Ha, ha,' sneered Jason, heading back to the stairs.

'Don't you want your main present?'

Jason sighed like he'd been asked to climb Everest. 'If it's as shitty...'

'You're welcome,' she said, nodding at the small gift-wrapped box on the table.

Wearily, Jason pulled off the paper and lid and dropped them on the floor. Inside was a key. He frowned and turned it round in his hand. When he saw the fob, his face lit up with excitement. 'A Kawasaki?' he gasped. 'Where?'

His aunt nodded at the back garden through the kitchen window. 'There's a helmet on the saddle and I've already put the L plates on for you.'

'I don't need plates, woman. I been on dirt bikes plenty.' Jason's face distorted in momentary contempt but he couldn't suppress his joy. Unlocking the back door, he almost pulled it off its hinges.

'What do you say?'

'Cheers aunty, you're the best,' he threw over his shoulder and raced out to start his brand-new Kawasaki KLX 125. A minute later he was revving it up then ran back into the house to get properly kitted out so he could ride over to Drayfin Community and have it large in front of the school gates, impress the jailbait.

∽

BROOK SIPPED on his fresh mug of tea and stared sullenly at the floor, exhausted from lack of sleep but determined not to let fatigue lead to carelessness. Campbell and Tyson were simply doing what detectives did the world over - wearing down the suspect. Then, when the suspect was sufficiently lulled by the boredom of it all, detectives would produce something that might catch them in a lie.

Campbell and Tyson re-entered the interview room for the next session and restarted the recorder.

'I'd like you to take us back to before the shooting,' said Tyson. 'Tell us about the sequence of events that led you to be in a car with Edie McQuarry.'

'We were in Derby, outside the Railway Station,' said Brook. 'McQuarry pulled a gun and forced us into her car. From there, we drove out to the field.'

'The same Audi you used to drive the wounded Mike Drexler to the hospital.'

'Correct.'

'Who drove to the field?' asked Tyson.

Brook took a discreet breath. Lying on the record wasn't his favourite thing. 'Mike.'

'Where were you in the vehicle?'

'In the back with McQuarry holding a gun on me.'

'And what were you doing in Derby?'

'I'd arranged to pick Mike up at the station.'

'What time?'

'Late,' said Brook. 'Gone eleven.'

'Where did you drive from to pick him up?'

'I was working late at St Mary's Wharf?'

'Do you often give a lift at that hour to someone you barely know?'

'No,' conceded Brook. 'But I owed him a few favours. And I often drive home at that time of night when there's no traffic. It's calming.'

'What kind of favours?' asked Campbell.

'He fed me a few times and gave me a copy of his book.'

'Did he ring to ask you to come fetch him?' asked Tyson.

'No, it was pre-arranged.'

'Verbally?'

'Yes.'

'So, there wouldn't be a record of any call or text then?'

'Obviously not.' Campbell and Tyson waited. 'No.'
'And where had he been?'
'He didn't say and I wasn't interested enough to ask.'
'Here's the thing,' said Campbell. 'Since your first interview we haven't found a single image of Mr Drexler on the station cameras. He wasn't on any of the platforms and none of the staff on duty that night recognised his picture.'
'Did I say he was taking a train?' said Brook.
'You said...'
'I said I was picking him up *outside* the station.'
'Outside?'
'It's a local landmark, easy to find.'

Campbell looked across at Tyson who flicked through several pages from her file. She glanced apologetically at Campbell. 'You're right. There's no mention of a train in your previous statement. Our bad.'
'Your bad what?'
'Our bad mistake,' replied Tyson, without missing a beat. 'So, you were picking him up at the station. Who arrived first?'
'I did.'
'Where did you wait for him?'
'I parked my car on the station forecourt. The station cameras should confirm the time. Then I wandered around, smoking a cigarette.'
'The CCTV shows you parking your car. Then you rummaged around in your boot and walked out of shot. What were you removing from the boot?'
'My cigarettes,' said Brook. 'I keep them in the boot. Helps stop me smoking in the car.'
'And then?'
'I think I crossed the road and just walked up and down to stretch my legs.'
'Be precise.'
Brook's expression suggested concentration. 'It was cold, so I walked up and down Midland Place, by the Waterfall pub. There might be film.'
'It's too far away from the station cameras.'
'What about the pub?'
'Not unless you were inside or at the front door,' said Tyson. Brook shrugged.
'When did Drexler appear?' said Campbell.

'A couple of minutes later,' said Brook.

'From where?' asked Tyson.

'The junction of Wellington Street and Midland Place,' answered Brook.

'Sticking to camera-free backstreets,' said Campbell. 'Why am I not surprised?'

'Go on,' said Tyson.

'I called out and Mike acknowledged but he was hesitant, nervous. Then, I noticed a woman walking behind him. When she stepped closer, I saw the gun.'

'One woman against two burly men,' said Campbell.

'Guns are great for an inferiority complex,' said Brook.

'Which gun?'

'No idea.'

'But if Drexler was armed at this point, how did she get the drop on him?'

'You'll have to ask Mike, I wasn't there.'

'What happened then?'

'McQuarry told me to walk in front of them or she'd shoot Mike. That's when I heard her accent.'

'Which direction did she tell you to walk?'

'Midland Place then right onto Calvert Street...'

'More backstreets,' sneered Campbell.

'With a gun, wouldn't you?' said Brook. Campbell waved a hand as though no longer interested. 'A minute later we were at her car...'

'Where was that parked?'

'Behind the Brunswick pub. We got in and McQuarry told Mike to drive.'

'Drexler was driving?' said Tyson, glancing down as though checking a detail.

'Right.' For a split second, Brook was back in the Audi, driving through deserted Derby streets, Laura Grant behind the wheel, dividing her gaze between the road ahead and the driver's mirror. He recalled the haunted look in her eyes, remembered staring helplessly back at her, her expression changing from anxiety to fear with each passing mile, as McQuarry's intentions became clear.

'And you sat in the passenger seat.'

Brook frowned. 'No, I was in the back with McQuarry, as I said.'

'Did McQuarry say anything, give any reason for abducting you?'

'All she did was direct Mike to the airport.'

'So, she knew the way.'

'So, it would seem.'

'She hadn't programmed the Satnav?'

'No.'

'Any conversation along the way?' said Tyson.

'Not much,' said Brook. 'Mike kept telling her to put the gun away and let me out, that I wasn't involved.'

'Involved in what?'

'Whatever it was McQuarry wanted to settle.'

'But she refused.'

'Yes.'

'She considered you a witness.'

'I guess so.'

'So, she was already planning to kill Mike and you were collateral damage,' said Campbell.

'It looks that way,' said Brook.

'How long was the drive out to Isley cum Langley?' said Tyson.

'Twenty minutes, though it felt much longer.'

'And when you got to the field?'

Brook paused. 'When we arrived it was pitch black, except for the headlights. McQuarry told Mike to pull over and ordered us both out of the car. She told us to stand in front of the headlights and I was ordered to kneel.'

'Then what?'

'There was a brief conversation between them about the old days in California,' said Brook.

'Details?'

'Drexler's father got a mention. He'd died and McQuarry passed on her condolences. Mike said something about making things right.'

'Anything else?' asked Campbell.

'I can't remember.'

'Course you can't,' said Campbell. 'A trained officer like you.'

'It's hard to follow chitchat with a gun pointed at your head,' replied Brook.

Campbell shook his head. 'Go on.'

'Then she gave Mike the M9 and ordered him to shoot me. Instead, he turned the gun on her and confirmed her suspicions.'

'What was her reaction?'

'She laughed and told him the gun wouldn't work.'

'What did Mike do?'

'He aimed the gun in the air and pulled the trigger but it failed to fire.'

'What was the exact sequence of events after Mike realised the gun wouldn't fire,' said Tyson.

'Mike dropped the faulty gun then McQuarry lifted her gun to shoot me but Mike pulled out another gun from his coat...'

'From his coat?' said Campbell. 'Not from his ankle holster?'

'No, it was in his pocket, I think,' said Brook. 'He must have transferred the gun while he was driving.'

'When did you figure that out?' said Tyson.

'A couple of days later, when I was going over events in my head.'

'But if he drew the gun from his coat, how did you know Drexler was wearing an ankle holster?' said Campbell.

'When Mike was wounded, I carried him to the car,' said Brook. 'His trouser leg rode up and I saw the holster.'

Campbell nodded. 'So, McQuarry hadn't searched him.'

'Not in my presence,' said Brook. 'But, if she did, she missed the ankle holster.'

'Pretty sloppy for an FBI agent,' observed Campbell.

'Ex-FBI,' said Brook.

'And after the shots were fired?'

'Mike was wounded and fell. McQuarry was dead.'

'And through all this you just stayed meekly on your knees,' said Tyson.

'I asked for a last cigarette,' replied Brook. 'I didn't get one.'

'And there were no last words before she fired. No hint about motive.'

'None.'

'Did you carry Drexler to the car on your own?' said Tyson.

There it was. They had something.

'I didn't have much choice,' said Brook. 'I was alone. Mike was dying.'

'You're sure there wasn't a fourth person present?' said Tyson.

She'd delivered the question innocently enough but both she and Campbell seemed to ease closer to catch Brook's answer. He wondered what they had. Footprints in the field? Laura on the QMC's cameras?

'Of course, I'm sure,' said Brook.

The two investigating officers paused for reflection. 'And before your dash to the hospital, you just left the guns where they were, in the field.'

'A man was dying. There wasn't time to secure the scene. I drove as fast as I could to the QMC and carried Mike into A&E.'

Campbell flicked at a remote control to turn on the projector, pressed a couple of buttons and the screen came to life. 'This is a still from footage taken by one of the QMC's security cameras.'

The photograph was an image of the hospital access road, Brook clearly visible through the open driver's window behind the wheel of the shiny black Audi. There was an indistinct blur on the back seat and Brook was relieved.

'Can you see the back seat?' asked Campbell, pointing. 'See here. That looks like it could be two people in the back - one sitting up and the other, presumably Mike Drexler, lying wounded.'

'The windows are tinted,' scoffed Brook. 'Those are just shadows. I can't see anything clearly. Is that the best shot you've got?'

'Would we be showing you the worst?' said Campbell.

'Perhaps you could clean it up a little,' said Brook.

'We have. You don't see the outline of two people?'

'No,' said Brook. 'But then I was actually there so I know Mike was alone in the back. Maybe his knees were up. That's just a shadow. The grounds were dark, remember.'

Campbell and Tyson stared and Brook was uncomfortable. He was lying to them and coppers, especially detectives, hated being deceived. They expected it - everybody lied - so detectives bent over backwards to expose the lie, any lie, be it a phoney alibi, a misleading statement or a small discrepancy in detail. Catch a suspect in a lie and they would break like a dry twig.

Campbell pressed another button to start a piece of film and Brook watched the powerful Audi pull up to the brightly lit emergency entrance at A&E. A second later, the car reversed away from the doors and around the corner, out of shot into darkness. Brook was surprised he'd been that obvious.

'That's you outside A&E,' observed Campbell. 'Why did you move the car?'

'The signs.'

'Signs?' said Campbell.

'Ambulances needing constant access.'

'But Drexler was seriously wounded.'

'I'm a copper. I can't disregard something like that. It only took a few seconds more.'

Campbell darted a glance at Tyson, who restarted the film. Brook readied himself, knowing - no matter how it sounded - he had to beat them to the punch. 'When I pulled around the corner, I dragged Mike out. He was heavy but there was a young lad nearby, having a smoke.' Tyson and Campbell stared at Brook then at each other. 'He helped me carry Mike from the car into A&E.'

'Young lad?' demanded Tyson.

Brook turned to the screen as he and the baseball-capped Laura Grant rounded the corner, carrying the crumpled frame of Mike Drexler. 'There,' said Brook, pointing at the indistinct image of Grant straining to hold up Drexler's legs, her short hair, slim build and cap hiding her gender.

'You didn't mention a young man in your previous statement,' snarled Campbell.

'Until I saw this film, I'd completely forgotten. Is it important?'

Campbell glared at Brook. 'Of course, it's bloody important. Who is it?'

Brook shook his head. 'Jim or Jack or something. I don't remember. He helped me get Mike inside and onto a trolley then I lost track of him.'

'You lost track of him,' repeated Campbell.

'Once Mike was on a trolley, he went on his way,' said Brook. 'Be great if you could find him. I'd love to thank him.' The three officers were silent for a moment and Brook's heart rate began to climb. If they had film of Laura getting out of the car, this was the time to confront him with it.

'Wouldn't we all?' said Tyson. 'Did it occur to you that this lad may have been the one who stole the Audi after you took Mike into the hospital?'

'No, it didn't,' conceded Brook. 'But then I wasn't overly concerned about security.'

'Which is why you left the keys in the ignition,' said Tyson.

'A man's life was at stake,' said Brook, shrugging. 'And it wasn't my car. Has it turned up?' Campbell shook his head. 'Odd,' said Brook. 'Doesn't a high-end car like that have GPS?'

'Usually,' said Campbell.

'It seems it was disabled shortly after McQuarry rented it in Brighton,' said Tyson.

'Covering her movements,' nodded Brook. 'Very suspicious, don't you think?'

'We can't be certain McQuarry disabled it deliberately,' said Tyson.

Brook smiled. 'Can't you?'

Campbell stood to signal the end of the interview. 'Thank you for your time, Inspector. For your sake, I hope Mike makes a speedy recovery and confirms your *story*,' he said, shuffling papers.

'I'm counting on it,' said Brook. 'My boss wants me back on cases.'

'Not the impression Chief Superintendent Charlton gave me,' said Campbell.

'That's just his manner,' said Brook. 'He's my biggest fan.'

Campbell formally ended the interview and turned off the recorder before walking Brook to the door. 'I hope you were careful, Brook.'

'Careful?'

'If there's *anything* to find, we'll find it. That's a promise.' Campbell walked away, fumbling for his cigarettes.

'Good meeting you again, Connor,' called Brook to his retreating back.

Tyson shadowed Brook to the entrance and held out her hand to shake his. 'Your reputation precedes you, Inspector. You don't go out of your way to be liked.'

'I used to, but it only made me more unpopular.'

Tyson's laugh was genuine and she appraised him coolly with grey eyes. 'I wish I'd had the chance to meet you two years ago.'

Brook's eyes narrowed and he shrugged his confusion. 'Two years ago?'

'I served a year on secondment in London on your old patch.' When Brook showed no sign of understanding, she added, 'Hammersmith.'

'I know where my old patch is.'

She laughed again. 'Sorry.'

'You did a year at Hammersmith?'

'Yes, I was there when the Reaper killed the Wallis family in Derby. And when you returned to London to follow up a lead.'

'Have we met?'

'No,' said Tyson. 'Though, having reviewed the Reaper case, I feel like I know you.'

Brook stared at her for longer than seemed polite. 'Reviewed the Reaper case?'

'That's right.' She smiled as though he'd know what she was talking about. 'This was *before* the Wallis family were killed, obviously. I was just learning the ropes so I was lucky to get a chance to work alongside DCI Fulbright.'

Brook stared some more. 'Richard Fulbright?'

'The same.'

'Richard Fulbright reviewed the Reaper case?'

'Just the London killings obviously,' said Tyson. 'Wait, you didn't know?'

'No, I didn't.'

'DCI Fulbright should have given you a heads up, professional courtesy and all that.'

'I would've remembered.'

'Then I'm sorry,' said Tyson. 'I assumed you knew. The usual protocol...'

'Did Fulbright instigate the case review?'

'No, Chief Superintendent Kerr did. Did you know him?'

'Only by name,' said Brook. 'Why would Kerr activate a review on an eighteen-year-old cold case?'

'I've no idea though DCI Fulbright said Kerr went to visit your old guvnor, DCI Rowlands, in hospital.'

'Kerr spoke to Charlie Rowlands?'

'A few weeks before he died, yes. I don't know what they talked about but, afterwards, Kerr was keen to have DCI Fulbright dig around in the files.'

'And you were involved,' said Brook.

'That's right.'

'We're talking about the Reaper killings in Harlesden and Brixton.'

Tyson was puzzled by Brook's inability to process information. 'Yes, of course.'

'Go on.'

'That's it,' said Tyson. 'DCI Fulbright took the reins and DS Ross and I helped out. It was great experience. Really fascinating cases and I envied you. And yet, I didn't. The stuff you'd seen. Young children...' She shook her head in sympathy. 'DCI Fulbright was SIO at Victor Sorenson's home, the night you were poisoned. He said you could've died.' Tyson stared at Brook's pallor. 'Are you okay?'

The blood had drained from Brook's face and he was having trouble croaking out his words. 'You were there that night?'

'No. But, DCI Fulbright said Sorenson got his doses wrong or you would've been dead meat. You had a lucky escape.'

Images of that night cascaded into Brook's mind. A night he'd never forget. A night he'd been prepared to die to know everything, yet lived to tell the tale - or rather, not tell it. Instead, Sorenson had died in his place, arteries in his wrists severed by his own hand. And, because of Sorenson's false confession to the murder of Laura Maples - ironically the one killing Sorenson hadn't committed - Brook had risen from the ashes, his ruined career resurrected.

Brook managed to work his speech centre. 'I don't know about that.'

'Well, I do,' insisted Tyson. 'I saw the tape. Sorenson thought he'd killed you. Bizarre timing, no? We start investigating an eighteen-year-old cold case and a couple of weeks later, the Reaper strikes in Derby. Stopped our review dead in its tracks.

'After the Wallis family were slaughtered, there didn't seem much point sniffing around ancient files when you had a fresh crime scene to investigate.' She laughed nervously. 'Listen to me, explaining the Reaper case to the world's foremost expert.' She smiled wistfully. 'Poor DCI Fulbright.'

'What about him?'

'He died. Last year. Didn't you know?'

'No, I didn't,' replied Brook, genuinely shocked.

'Car crash. Visiting his brother in the States. It was a shock. A big loss to policing.'

'No doubt.' Brook was keen to be away but Tyson had one more stiletto to slip between his ribs.

'You know, after reviewing the case, even for the short time I worked on it, I'd have stuck all the money in the world on Victor Sorenson being the Reaper.'

8

November 25th 2008 – Hammersmith Police Station, West London

Detective Chief Inspector Richard Fulbright fed coins into the drinks machine, yawning as he waited for his coffee. The cold dark mornings drained him but, as a senior detective in the Met, the long hours were inevitable. At least most of the armed robbers from the King Street raid were in custody so, apart from a few court dates, his diary was clear and he'd be able to kick back a little.

When the vending machine finished dribbling its bitter foam into a plastic cup, he took a warming sip, gazing absently across the open plan office. At this early hour, it was empty except for DS Jimmy Robinson taking a statement from a frail old man who had clearly been the victim of a crime.

Fulbright had seen that dazed expression on a victim's face many times - the shock of normal life being ripped away never to return and the realisation that a civilised existence depended on the whim of strangers. As Fulbright knew only too well, for the elderly, this shock could prove fatal.

He strolled across to Robinson's desk, the old man motionless on the stiff chair, staring into space, hands clenching and unclenching. His mouth moved briefly when a reply could be coaxed but communication was an effort.

'Morning, Jimmy,' said Fulbright. He nodded at the oblivious old man. 'What have we here?'

DS Robinson stood and ushered Fulbright away from his desk. 'Nothing you'd want to worry about guv. Home invasion. Some slag conned his way into Mr and Mrs Treadwell's home and cleaned out the cash and a few tasty baubles. Mr Treadwell was out and came home to find his wife in cardiac arrest.'

'She okay?'

Robinson shook his head. 'Gone. But zero chance of pushing it beyond manslaughter even if we nab him.'

'Description?'

'Before she croaked, she said the perp was her age, mid-sixties. Next door neighbour saw him leaving and confirms. White, about sixty to sixty-five, medium build and height. Cropped grey hair, glasses. Must have come over trustworthy or she wouldn't have let him in.'

Robinson went back to his desk and continued to interview Treadwell but Fulbright failed to move away, standing in the background, sipping his coffee. A second later, he beckoned Robinson back to him.

'I'm not busy if you need help with some of the footslogging.'

'Guv?'

'Whoever did this is no stranger to the life. I've been in this manor for thirty years and know all the local grifters. I could go through the database and any old mug books you can rustle up from the bat cave. Get you a list of possibles for the Video-fit at least. Might save some man hours.' He shrugged. 'Up to you though.'

'That'd be a big help, guv,' said Robinson, impressed. 'Thanks.'

∼

CHIEF SUPERINTENDENT KELVIN KERR put down his mobile phone, made a quick note on a pad and circled it several times. The rumour was true. His source at Division had confirmed. Charlie Rowlands, a legend of London policing, was dying and, as a former colleague and commanding officer, it was his duty to pay him a visit and pass on the Force's respects.

Kerr glared at his notepad. *Hammersmith Hospital*. He didn't like hospitals. People died there and Kerr wasn't overly fond of decay and death. In his position, he'd seen too much of it, had shaken the hands of too many grieving widows and ruffled the hair of too many disbelieving orphans.

I'm sorry for your loss.
Your husband was a credit to the uniform.
Your father lives with Jesus now.

The finest DCI he'd ever worked with would soon be no more. Lung cancer - both barrels. Not a surprise the way Charlie smoked. At least, he'd reached a decent age. What was he? Seventy? Kerr made a note to look it up.

He sighed. There was no putting it off. No matter his hatred of hospitals, Kerr knew his duty, knew the expectation that came with rank. He'd have to go and speak to Charlie one last time and pay his respects.

He ambled to the window, rubbing the ache in his pelvis, catching sight of his reflection in the glass, not liking what he saw. Fifty-six years old and turning to fat. His flabby chin and sagging jowls made him seem ten years older. What had happened to the body of the Glasgow Middleweight Amateur Boxing Champion? Maybe it was time to retire and get out of London. Get back to a simpler life in Scotland and enjoy the rest of his days on a fat pension. He'd always fancied a house in the Borders, away from the sprawl of the South. Away from all this...death.

The thought returned him to Charlie. He'd go see his old colleague and get it over. It was the least he could do for an old friend. He depressed a button on his intercom. 'Margaret. Cancel my one o'clock.'

∽

THE RECEPTIONIST LOOKED Kerr up and down. 'Are you a relative?'

'Chief Superintendent Kelvin Kerr,' answered Kerr, employing the tone that opened most doors. 'DCI Rowlands is an ex-colleague and a friend.' He pulled off his hat and stuck it under his arm, its job done.

'Policeman, is he?' She looked back at her computer screen. 'He never said.'

'He's retired.'

'He's in D52. Take the lift at the end of the corridor though he may still be resting after the chemo...'

But Kerr had already turned on his heel to seek his destination.

The Resurrection

~

FULBRIGHT CRACKED open the next book of ancient mugshots and flicked through, staring intently at each picture in turn. The phone on his desk rang.

'DCI Fulbright.' His expression soured. 'Andrew! How did you get this number? I don't care. Text or e-mail if you need to speak to me. Alright. What's up? Problem with our mother? No. How would you know? I'm busy. No, I haven't got time to meet you.' A pause. 'Okay, where?'

Fulbright slammed the phone back onto its cradle then quickly picked it up and pressed a button. 'I want a block on all calls from Andrew Fulbright, please. Make any excuse you like but he is not to be put through under any circumstance, is that clear?' A pause. 'My brother always says it's urgent. Same instruction.'

~

FROM THE HARD CHAIR, Kerr watched his old friend and colleague, Charlie Rowlands, as he slept. His eyes lingered on Charlie's bald head with its yellowing, slackened skin and sunken eyes. Where once Charlie Rowlands had seemed so tall and intimidating, there now seemed to be nothing but a random collection of sharp bones poking through an overstretched bag of translucent skin.

Kerr popped an Extra Strong Mint in his mouth and stood to leave - this had been a mistake. There was nothing to be done or said, even supposing Charlie was in a condition to hear it. He felt foolish, watching his dying friend's fitful slumber. He hadn't even brought flowers or, better yet, a bottle of Charlie's favourite Navy rum.

At the door, Kerr was halted by the low rumble of Charlie's voice from beneath the sheets.

'You're the Reaper!'

Kerr turned. 'What's that, Charlie?'

'You're the Reaper,' Charlie repeated, eyes closed, the words rasping through the tar, thin legs squirming between the sheets as though trying to run. 'Brooky was right.'

'What about the Reaper?' said Kerr, returning to the bedside.

'I won't do it, professor,' mumbled Charlie. 'I won't.'

'Won't do what, Charlie?'

'No more killing. I won't do it.'

'Who's the professor, Charlie?'

But Rowlands had drifted off again and was soon snoring gently. Kerr was transfixed for a moment. Absently, he opened the bedside cabinet, not sure what he was looking for. It was bare apart from a half-bottle of Navy Rum, with just a tot left in the bottom. After closing the cabinet, he stood, lightly touched Charlie's papyrus hand and left.

∼

FULBRIGHT STIRRED ANGRILY at his second coffee and glared at the restaurant's entrance. As usual his brother was late, even for a meeting he himself had deemed urgent. He looked at his watch. It was nearing four o'clock and Wimbledon's Cafe Rouge was easing down after the lunchtime rush.

'Hello, Richard. You look well.'

Fulbright looked up to see his younger brother, Andrew, flashing his million-dollar smile, courtesy of his newly whitened crowns. His tanned face and bleached blond hair were guaranteed to draw the female eye and a pair of thirtysomething ladies-who'd-lunched did a onceover of his slim frame.

'Andrew.' Fulbright declined to stand.

Andrew sat and beckoned over a waiter. 'Andy. When will you learn, bro?'

'Andrew is the name our parents gave you.'

Andrew shook his head, amused. 'Whatever you say, bro. Refill?' Fulbright shook his head and Andrew checked his chunky diver's watch, raising eyebrows in feigned surprise. 'Booze o'clock. Think I'll have a glass of vino. Not often I get to see my only brother. Are you sure you won't join me?'

'I'm on duty.'

'Of course, you are.' The waiter arrived with a menu but Andrew waved him away. 'Just bring me a glass of your most expensive red wine.' The waiter turned away. 'Wait!' Andrew called after him. 'Make it a bottle. And make sure I get the bill.'

'Celebrating, little brother?' asked Fulbright, when the waiter had gone.

'I'm only two years younger than you so I'd appreciate it if you wouldn't keep calling me that,' hissed Andrew, his good humour dissipating for a second. 'And yes, I'm celebrating.' His smile returned. 'You should be congratulating me. I've been offered a job in the States.'

Fulbright refused to show the surprise and delight his brother's announcement demanded. This was a road he'd been down many times. 'Seriously? Doing what?'

Andrew's expression betrayed an injury. 'I have skills, bro. Maybe not skills you'd appreciate but skills nonetheless.'

'Such as?'

'I'm good with people. I entertain them.'

'Really?'

'Yes, really! I'm amusing and charming. Good company. When I want to be.' The waiter arrived with a bottle of wine and poured a large glass. Andrew took an appreciative slug.

'And there's the rub,' muttered Fulbright.

'Sorry?'

'Do you want some grub?' said Fulbright.

'No, this is fine.' Andrew took another pull on the wine.

'These skills,' said Fulbright. 'There are people willing to pay you for them?'

'There are,' said Andrew, a broad grin creasing his mouth. 'I was head hunted.'

Fulbright laughed. 'You mean a friend worked his way up to a position of influence and you tapped him up for a job.'

'Your cynicism wounds me, bro,' said Andrew.

'Where?'

'Los Angeles.'

'The high temple of artifice. You'll blend in perfectly.'

'That's not nice.'

'But accurate. What are you going to do there, Andrew?'

'I'm going to be a consultant to a sales division.'

'A salesman - you?'

'No, Richard, a consultant. They want me to use my immaculate English accent and winning ways to charm potential customers, show them a good time, grease the wheels a little.'

'Like a con artist, you mean.'

'No, like the kind of person who helps get business done. Jesus, bro, it's the way money gets made in the real world.'

Fulbright smiled finally. 'The real world? When have you ever lived there? Most people in the *real world* don't receive a cheque for three grand every month.'

Andrew's features hardened. 'I haven't received a cheque like that for two years as well you know. Not since you assumed full power of attorney over mum's estate.'

'Just as well or there wouldn't be anything left to keep her going.'

Andrew took another sip of wine. 'There's a million quid tied up in mum's bank accounts and you're willing to let it drain away to keep her hooked up to those machines in that...place.'

'It's a hospital.'

'It's a fucking mausoleum,' said Andrew, angrily. The two lunching ladies glanced across so he tempered his indignation. 'You talk about the real world but I'm the only one at this table who can accept that she'll never recover...'

'You don't know that.'

'She's a fucking vegetable, bro, and the sooner you switch off those machines the sooner we can all get on with our lives.'

Fulbright tensed in his chair but decided against delivering the punch his brother deserved. It wouldn't look good in the Police Gazette. Instead he stared down at the floor coming to a decision. 'You know what? You're right. We should be celebrating.' He called the waiter for another wine glass and poured a half measure when it arrived.

'To your new career, Andy.' He raised the glass for the toast and took a modest sip without looking at his brother. 'I really hope it works out for you this time.'

Andrew smiled, though suspicion remained. 'Thanks, bro.' His demeanour changed and he ran his finger around the rim of his glass. 'Now all I have to do is scrape together the air fare and buy a few clothes...' He let the rest of the sentence hang, looking expectantly at his brother.

'How much?'

Andrew shrugged. 'Six grand should cover it.'

Fulbright hesitated then took out a large grey chequebook and wrote out a cheque which he tore off and held out to Andrew. When Andrew moved to take it, Fulbright yanked it away. 'I'll be ringing the hospital tomorrow evening. This cheque will be cancelled if I find out you haven't been to see mum and practised some of those people skills on her.'

Andrew prepared to object then thought better of it. 'Fine.' He went to pocket the cheque, glancing briefly at the amount. 'This is only three grand.'

'Try club class. I hear it's perfectly adequate.' Fulbright put down his wine and threw three twenty-pound notes onto the table then paced towards the door. 'Goodbye, *Andy*.'

~

'WHAT ARE HIS CHANCES, DOCTOR?' asked Kerr, in the corridor.
'Zero. He has inoperable tumours on both lungs.'
'Chemo?'
'We've been trying to slow the growth but he's asked us to stop if it's only going to give him a few more months of pain. Today was his last round of therapy. He'll be going home the day after tomorrow.'
'So, he knows it's hopeless.'
'Oh, yes. And he seems at ease with it.'
Kerr nodded. 'How long?'
'Six months. Probably less.'
'Thank you, doctor.' Kerr replaced his hat and walked towards the lifts. An old man, late sixties, medium height and with greying, red hair appeared before Kerr, carrying a half bottle of Navy Rum in his withered hand. As they crossed paths, the old man glanced in his direction and Kerr stared into the blackest eyes he'd ever seen.

The old man passed serenely by and Kerr turned to watch the conservatively dressed figure walk towards the door of Charlie's room. The man seemed to hesitate for a second as his head turned imperceptibly back towards Kerr, before he continued past Charlie's room to the end of the corridor and out of sight.

Kerr strode back to the Reception Desk. 'The old man with the rum - did you get his name?'
'Which old man?' asked the receptionist.
'The old man carrying a bottle of rum - he was visiting someone. He walked right past me, coming from this direction.'
The woman looked back at Kerr and shook her head. 'I didn't see anyone.'

9

November 26th 2008 - Hammersmith Police Station

Chief Superintendent Kerr sat in his office thumbing through papers from a dog-eared folder marked "REAPER - HARLESDEN 1990". He'd read both digital and paper reports and transcripts pertaining to the investigation, some produced by DCI Charlie Rowlands though the majority seemed to be the work of Detective Sergeant Damen Brook.

Brook was the *Reaper* detective, a stellar profiler who was on his way to the very top when he was called out to investigate the first recorded crimes of a serial killer who slaughtered two families in their London homes - the first in Harlesden in 1990, the second in Brixton a year later. He was never caught.

After the Brixton killings, Brook had suffered a nervous breakdown followed by a long period of rehabilitation, finally returning to light duties before transferring out of the Met, a broken man by all accounts. Kerr seemed to recall Brook had headed north but couldn't remember where. He made a mental note to find out.

Reading through the murder books painted a grisly portrait and the Scene of Crime photographs confirmed it. In 1990, the family of small-time lowlife and petty criminal, Sammy Elphick, had been murdered in their grubby flat above a laundry in Harlesden. Both parents had been bound and their throats cut. Their young son had been strangled then hung from the cord of a ceiling rose. Two of his fingers had been removed post mortem, the severed digits placed in the breast pocket of the dead boy's pyjamas. The reason for this gruesome ritual had never been established.

Kerr glanced unconsciously at the grinning face of his own grandson beaming at him from a picture frame on his desk then stood to rub his back, strolled over to his open window and closed it, extinguishing the background hum of rush hour traffic crawling along the busy Hammersmith bottlenecks.

Having given up smoking a year ago, Kerr popped an Extra Strong Mint into his mouth then flipped open a second folder marked "REAPER - BRIXTON 1991" and pulled out various papers, photographs and reports to compare with the digital record. That case hadn't been investigated by Hammersmith CID but Rowlands and Brook had done a reconnoitre of the crime scene as a courtesy to Brixton Division.

For reasons unknown, Rowlands hadn't pushed for a joint task force, despite identifying the Brixton killings as the work of the Reaper. It was almost as though Rowlands and Brook wanted nothing more to do with it and, after examining the crime scene, they'd effectively washed their hands of it. If he could summon up the nerve to go back and speak to Charlie, Kerr made a mental note to ask why.

He sat back to remember the first Reaper killing. It seemed like only yesterday he'd been outside Elphick's Harlesden flat in the early hours of a winter's morning, watching the three bodies being carried down the rain-slicked, metal stairwell connecting their hovel to the outside world.

'Eighteen years?'

He flicked again through the Brixton photographs. If anything, they were worse than Harlesden. A young girl - Tamara Wrigley - tiny and undernourished had been tied to a chair before having her throat cut. Both chair and victim had ended up on their side in the death struggle.

Kerr stared at the image of the two blood-soaked corpses of the parents, tied together on the cheap plastic sofa. He didn't have a problem with their fate, especially the man, Floyd Wrigley, who hadn't distinguished himself in his thirty-four years on the planet and no-one mourned his departure from it. Floyd was a nasty piece of work with a jacket full of previous, much of it violent. It was even rumoured he'd pimped out his young daughter to local nonces, in exchange for drug money, though never proven.

'Good riddance!' Kerr smiled. That was Charlie's phrase whenever some lowlife overdosed or said the wrong thing to a punter in the pub and got a knife in the guts for his troubles.

From both files, Kerr compared pictures of the writing covering a wall at either crime scene. In Harlesden, that word was SALVATION, in Brixton it was SAVED. The ink was the blood of the victims. Kerr pondered its meaning but got no further than the usual "religious nutcase" theory that had been mooted in the file.

The last thing he read was a memo from DS Brook that had been photocopied and added to the BRIXTON file.

LEEDS KILLINGS IN 1993, NOT part of Reaper series, in my opinion. MO inconsistent with Harlesden and Brixton, notably choice of weapon. The Reaper prefers subtlety and sharp blades for a quiet kill. Choice of victims also wrong. They may share petty criminal background with other Reaper victims but are not a family unit like the Elphicks and Wrigleys. Although Leeds victim Roddy Telfer's girlfriend was heavily pregnant, there is only one generation present. The Reaper requires children be involved so that lessons can be learned.

'LESSONS CAN BE LEARNED,' mumbled Kerr, wondering what Brook had meant by that. He shuffled the papers back into their respective folders and put them to one side then picked up the final folder marked "REAPER - LEEDS 1993". In it were copies of the main murder book documents sent down from Yorkshire.

The file was thin but its contents seemed to back up Brook's opinion. Telfer's head was blown off with a shotgun and his girlfriend strangled. Only the daubing of SAVED on the wall pointed to The Reaper.

'Nineteen-ninety to ninety-three,' said Kerr, closing the file. 'Three murders in three years, then nothing.'

He flicked through the Harlesden file again and located the report he'd folded at the corner. It was a routine account by DS Brook of a visit to a Victor Sorenson, a wealthy industrialist who manufactured chemicals worldwide. Goods, presumed stolen by Sammy Elphick, had been recovered at the Harlesden crime scene and one of the artefacts, a video recorder, had been listed as missing by Sorenson after reporting a burglary at his West London home.

'Professor Victor Sorenson,' Kerr mumbled, after skimming Sorenson's potted biography. Kerr turned to his laptop and keyed the name into Google, then selected *Images*. To his immediate satisfaction, he was rewarded with a picture of the old man he'd seen at the hospital carrying the bottle of Navy rum, a gift for Charlie Rowlands. The same dusty red hair, the same inky black eyes.

'Hello, Professor.'

～

DCI FULBRIGHT SAT in the Chief Superintendent's office sipping bitter coffee, staring at Kelvin Kerr's stiff uniformed back. The chief seemed to be weighing up what to say so Fulbright let his eye wander over Kerr's desk to the pile of folders that sat on his planner. He sat up and half turned his head to look at the label on the top folder and Kerr turned back to his desk.

'Do you recall the Reaper murders, Richard? Course you do. Harlesden. You were there too, remember? We both were.'

'Sammy Elphick and family,' said Fulbright. 'Bitterly cold night, as I remember. Why the trip down Memory Lane? It must be all of...'

'Eighteen years,' said Kerr.

Fulbright grunted in disbelief. 'Seems like yesterday.'

'Doesn't everything? And the following year Brixton. Then Leeds, two years later, though there was some doubt about chalking it up to the Reaper from one of the Harlesden case officers.'

Fulbright smiled. 'Damen Brook.'

'You remember him?' said Kerr.

'Oh, yes,' said Fulbright.

'I can't place him. What was he like?'

'Hard to forget his arrogance and the way he unravelled after Brixton. It was quite a fall from grace. He was a whisker away from the funny farm before transferring out, marriage and career in tatters.'

'Transferred where?'

'They shuffled him up to the frozen north. Derbyshire somewhere. Made him a DI to sweeten the deal. What's all this about?'

'DCI Charlie Rowlands was SIO on the Reaper investigation. Brook was his DS.' Fulbright looked expectantly at Kerr. 'Charlie's got cancer. He's in Hammersmith Hospital and not expected to live more than six months.'

'I see.'

'You didn't know?'

'We weren't close and I haven't spoken to him since he retired. Has he had a brainwave about the case?'

Kerr ruminated for a moment, not wanting to give too much away. 'Not exactly.'

'Then I don't understand. The Reaper case is colder than Siberia. He stopped killing fifteen years ago and is either rotting in prison, out of the country or dead.'

'I want you to revisit the files,' said Kerr. 'Set up a small team and give it the full treatment for a week or so. Examine every angle, see if anything was missed.'

'Sir?'

'You're not busy, are you?' asked Kerr, in a tone that suggested the answer would be irrelevant.

'I'm trying to put a face to a conman involved in a home invasion.'

'Sounds like small potatoes.'

'Not to the couple who let him into their home,' said Fulbright. 'The wife had a heart attack and died.'

'Sorry to hear that. Still, it's manslaughter at best and beneath your talents.' Fulbright's expression turned to ice and Kerr held up his hands. 'I'm sorry. I know something similar happened to your parents...'

'Someone pretending to be from the council, blagged his way past my mother and into the house. When my father tried to show him the door, he was pushed to the ground and hit his head, causing a haemorrhage and subsequent brain damage. He died three days later without ever recovering consciousness. My mother blamed herself and suffered a stroke. She's been in a coma ever since.'

'Terrible,' said Kerr, eyes lowered. 'I see it's still raw but all the more reason to hand it off.'

'I don't own it,' said Fulbright. 'It belongs to DS Robinson.'

'Progress?'

'A description. White male. Mid-sixties.'

Kerr nodded. 'Robinson's a capable officer. Let him wade through the mugshots. That's what lower ranks are for.'

'And eighteen-year-old cold cases are what retired detectives are for. I can suggest some names if you...'

'No!' Kerr's reply was brusque. He nodded at the Reaper files. 'I want *you* to take a gander. The Cold Case Unit weren't in Harlesden and they didn't know Charlie.'

Fulbright pondered the relevance of the last remark. Was Kerr looking to clean dirty laundry? A last favour for a dying friend.

'What exactly is it you want me to do?'

Kerr pushed the files towards Fulbright. 'I want you to check everything that could have been done, was done, by Charlie and DS Brook both. If there's anything they overlooked or any lead that wasn't ticked off, I want it followed up. Understood?'

Fulbright sighed and glanced down at the tatty manila folders. 'Is the network down?'

'For a case this cold, the original files are always useful. There are more titbits. Little whispers that don't get onto the mainframe.' Kerr managed a watery smile. 'Just have a look, will you? A week should do it.'

'Without new evidence, I'll be done in two days,' said Fulbright, gathering the files.

'Actually, there was something,' said Kerr, avoiding eye contact. 'From Charlie.'

Fulbright looked up. 'You've spoken to him?'

Kerr turned back to the window. 'I went to see him, yes.'

'Sir, a dying man's memory...'

'I didn't ask for a medical opinion,' snapped Kerr. 'You'll find a report in the Harlesden file about a Professor Victor Sorenson, a wealthy industrialist. He reported a burglary in 1990. Stolen goods belonging to Sorenson were recovered in Sammy Elphick's Harlesden flat.'

Fulbright's eyes narrowed. 'What of it?'

Kerr turned. 'Is it possible Elphick burgled Sorenson's house in Kensington? Because, if so, it's also possible that Sorenson took revenge.'

'By killing Elphick and his family?'

'People have been murdered for less,' said Kerr. 'And there may be details we don't know. Elphick may have swiped something he shouldn't.'

'Presumably Charlie or Brook looked into it and dismissed it.'

'I don't want assumptions, I want hard facts,' said Kerr. 'It feels wrong. Elphick was small time and Kensington and Holland Park were never on his radar, from what I read. So, I want you to look closely at this Sorenson and get back to me.' Kerr opened his arms wide to signal the end of the meeting. 'One more thing.' Fulbright turned from the door. 'Charlie's on his last legs and I don't want him bothered.'

∼

Fulbright spied DS Frank Ross, a bullet-headed gym nut, flirting with DC Kelly Tyson next to the water cooler. Despite the cold, Ross was jacketless so Tyson could admire his well-developed torso, straining against his tight, short-sleeved shirt. Ross was close to minimum height and tended to overcompensate with an aggressive manner which, though often crude, Fulbright sometimes found useful.

His ability to get under the skin of certain criminals bore regular fruit in interviews. Not that Ross was subtle or probing - Fulbright always took the lead - but often a suspect would crack under the pressure of Ross's disdain and brag about what they'd done to impress him, hoping to gain grudging respect. Rapists were his speciality - many times a suspect had confessed in front of Ross in an ill-advised attempt to confirm his manhood.

However, there were villains Ross could never be allowed near. Suspected child abusers, for example. Ross had once assaulted a paedophile during an interview after the suspect suggested Ross was suppressing urges similar to his own - urges that Ross wouldn't understand and which would frighten and disgust him. And, in men like Ross, fear produced violence.

Ross understood rape and could imagine why men less fortunate than himself might need to force themselves on victims. He could even secretly condone it in certain circumstances. But children? That was sick.

'Frank!' called Fulbright. 'My office. You too, Kelly.'

DC Kelly Tyson was taller than Ross with long brown hair and grey eyes. She wore tight khaki trousers and a green cotton shirt. Her demeanour towards Ross was as polite as required by a junior officer required to respect rank but Fulbright was aware Ross had made several unwelcome attempts at courtship.

The Resurrection

Fulbright dropped the Reaper files onto a desk, already strewn with hard copies of mug shot folders.

'Whatever you're working on drop it. We've got a cold case to review. Have you heard of the Reaper, Kelly?'

'The serial killer?'

'The same,' said Fulbright. 'Frank?'

'Sure. Donkey's years ago.'

'Eighteen, since his first kill,' said Fulbright. 'The Reaper was the killer of three families in their homes between 1990 and 1993 - two in London and one in Leeds. The London murders were highly ritualistic and brutal. The parents had their throats cut and the children weren't spared either. The first strike was in Harlesden in 1990, a family called Elphick. Father Sammy had form for burglary, fencing and other small-time blags. His wife and son died with him.

'A year later, the Wrigley family were killed in Brixton. Parents and one daughter - their throats were cut. There was a third killing in Leeds, two years later but we concentrate on the London end because we can physically follow-up with witnesses.

'The files from the crypt are there. Cross check against the database in case something crucial wasn't uploaded. Unlikely but the Chief wants a big push on this so spend the rest of the day reading everything you can. Kelly, you take Harlesden. Frank, Brixton. We meet in my office tomorrow morning at seven for first impressions.'

'Earlies, guv?' said Ross, with a look of pain.

'You heard me. I want this done thoroughly but I don't want to take all week over it. I want thoughts on the crimes *and* the original investigation. What may have been overlooked, what lines of inquiry were properly investigated, what weren't. Also, any ideas about why the Reaper was never heard from again after Leeds, beside the usual death or prison angle.' He beamed at Tyson. 'Kelly, you bring fresh eyes so I'm expecting originality. See you in the morning.'

Tyson jumped up, an excited look on her face, and gathered the heavy Harlesden files and left the office. Ross remained seated.

'The Reaper, guv? Seriously?'

'Have you ever known me to be less than?'

'But it's ancient history. Is this coming from Brass?'

'Directly,' said Fulbright. 'I have my orders, Frank. Now you have yours.'

'Isn't Kelly a bit green for this? I mean, why aren't the dinosaur squad picking up?'

'Because it's been dumped in my lap, Frank,' said Fulbright. 'This is direct from the Chief Super. He's got a bee in his bonnet about Charlie Rowlands and he wants the investigation reviewed.'

'Any idea why?'

'Charlie's dying,' said Fulbright. 'Maybe the Chief is hoping to give him a decent send-off. There's not going to be one but we have to go through the motions and cover our arses.' Fulbright walked over to a kettle and flicked it on. 'And think how much Kelly can learn from working closely with you on this, Frank.'

Ross smiled. 'Fair point.'

10

November 29^{th,} 2008, West London

Sorenson stared at the calendar on the desk then at the document in his hand. 'I've acquired the information about Derby CID, Charlie,' he said into the mobile. 'Brook will definitely pick up the case.'

'When?' said Rowlands.

Sorenson could hear Rowlands struggling for breath. 'Before Christmas. Then you'll see your friend. Rest assured.'

'You can't guarantee that,' said Rowlands.

'Brook will get the message, loud and clear. He'll be back to London before the year is out and, when he does, he'll want to see you.'

'I may not live that long.'

'Nonsense. You're as strong as an ox. And when we get back from Derby, you'll have time to recover.'

'I'm not coming, professor. I'm too ill.'

'You're coming, Charlie, and that's final. I've been preparing this too long to change personnel now.' He waited for a comeback from Rowlands but heard only wheezing. 'By the way, what did Chief Superintendent Kerr say to you the other day?'

'Kerr? What do you mean?'

'He came to see you in hospital. I saw him outside your door.'

'*You were there?*'

'I came to visit but Kerr was hanging around in the corridor so I left. What did he want?'

'*I don't know what you're talking about.*'

Sorenson paused. 'Are you lying to me, Charlie?'

'*Why would I? I've been completely out of it with the chemo. If he came to see me, I must have been asleep because I didn't see him and he didn't speak to me.*'

~

EARLY NEXT MORNING, Fulbright was sipping black coffee, clicking absently through the PNC database. The ancient files of photographs were off his desk and back in storage. Instead, he clicked his mouse every three seconds, sifting through mugshots of London's elderly criminals.

The database needed updating. His search field for local offenders, between sixty and seventy-five years of age with a jacket for theft and deception, had thrown up some old villains he knew for a fact were dead. He clicked again and loaded a picture which gave Fulbright pause and he rubbed his tired eyes to stare hard at a face with familiar features.

'Vincent Muir,' he mumbled, making notes, before turning off the monitor as Ross and Tyson approached through the outer office, clutching cups of coffee. They mumbled a greeting and sat, Tyson pulling a notepad from under her arm. Ross carried nothing.

'Morning.' The pair looked back at Fulbright as if to say something contradictory before thinking better of it.

'Frank?'

'Guv, I've been over the files with a fine-tooth comb,' he said. 'I don't know why the Chief thinks this is a runner. There's nothing new to go on unless there's something he's not telling us. Seems straightforward. You get some wound-up, religious fanatic keen on washing the streets with the blood of sinners and you look for the trigger. It could be anything. Wife not putting out, football team takes a caning, knife and fork the wrong way round at dinner. Who knows with these freaks? So, he seeks out a pair of scumbag families and slaughters the lot, then boasts about saving their souls by writing it in their blood on the walls. End of story. Who cares?

'After the third one in '93, my guess is he can't live with what he's done and tops himself. Either that or he signs up for missionary work in the jungle so he can make amends for being a twisted little fuck.'

There was silence while Fulbright steepled his hands over his mouth to absorb Ross's analysis. 'Interesting.'

'Thanks, guv,' beamed Ross.

'Kelly?'

Tyson shuffled her notes and took a deep breath. 'Guv, serial killers are overwhelmingly male and almost always strike against their own ethnic and social group first. The first victims, the Elphick family, are white and so is the Reaper...'

'The Brixton family were black,' said Ross.

'That muddies the waters,' agreed Tyson, in her soft Leicestershire burr. 'But the first family in the series were white and first principles apply. Most serial killers are white males so the Brixton killings are an aberration, especially as the third family in Leeds were also white. My opinion, obviously.' Fulbright nodded encouragement.

'But the Reaper is different because he strikes outside his social group and goes out of his way to let us know. The attacks are premeditated, well organised and without frenzy. This man is cold blooded and calculating. He uses precision cutting tools for a swift and efficient kill because Mr and Mrs Elphick's throats were each severed by one stroke of either a scalpel or a Stanley knife.'

'So, he doesn't kill in anger,' said Fulbright.

'The Reaper has no emotional connection to his victims at all. There's no show of jealousy, vengeance or any signs of sexual deviancy driving him, except in one instance. The wounds inflicted on Floyd Wrigley in Brixton are savage and suggest a personal grudge, though that's at odds with the rest of the scene which matches the detached MO of the Harlesden attack. But, because of his wounds, I think Floyd Wrigley might even be the key to this whole series but don't ask me how. Yet.'

'Interesting. Any other observations?'

'Before he kills them, I think he spends significant time with the family...'

'Pulling one off?' cracked Ross.

'No,' said Tyson. 'These murders are not psychosexual and I don't think the actual killing arouses the Reaper, either during the act or subsequent to it. But he is putting on a show, especially for the parents, that's why mum and dad are immobilised on a sofa at both crime scenes so he can show them something.'

'What?' said Ross.

'This is speculation,' said Tyson, apologetically. 'But I think he wants them to watch their children die.'

'Sick fuck,' snarled Ross.

'Yes,' said Tyson. 'But also, no. Killing kids is indefensible, agreed, but he never physically tortures his victims. But he does want the parents to see what he's doing and I think he wants something back from them at the moment he kills their children.'

'What?'

Tyson sighed. 'I think he wants them to feel something. Shame? Fear? Anger? Despair? I don't know. But the Elphick parents cried. That's on record.'

'They were scared,' said Ross.

'Of course,' said Tyson. 'But it's more than just fear. The Reaper wants them to feel that they've caused this in some way and make them feel ashamed.'

'Of what?'

Tyson shrugged. 'The way they lived, the way they brought up their kid. The Reaper is punishing them, I think. So, by making them witness their child's death, he's sending them a message. Us too.'

'But the Elphick boy was dead before the Reaper strung him up,' said Fulbright.

'True, but the parents didn't die until they'd seen his corpse and watched the Reaper remove his fingers to demonstrate he was dead and that they were next. Having done that, he kills them quickly and leaves. No taunting, no hesitation cuts. Nothing.'

'Interesting.'

'It's more than that,' said Tyson. 'It's incredible. The care that's been taken in and around the crime scene borders on the fanatical. No witnesses to entry or exit. No fingerprints or usable fibres in the kill zone. Significantly, no DNA either.'

'DNA testing was still in its infancy back then,' said Fulbright. 'If the perp didn't leave semen or blood, there was little chance of detecting a sample until the technology developed.'

'But that's my point,' said Tyson. 'If perps weren't worried about DNA, why weren't there any samples of hair, saliva or skin? Why bother to be such a neat freak? Across two crime scenes there should've been something usable. But there's nothing. No trace on any artefacts in evidence and, despite advances in testing, periodic re-exams have drawn a blank. That's unbelievable and, once you rule out a fluke, it suggests incredible foresight.'

'Meaning?' said Fulbright.

'I think the perp knew about the upcoming importance of DNA. Why else be so cautious?'

'So, the Reaper was a copper?' asked Ross.

'It's possible,' said Tyson. 'But I'd be more inclined to think he was involved with the science.'

'A SOCO?' suggested Ross.

'*Or* he was, maybe still is, a member of the scientific community. Which would also explain his intelligence and high-level organisational skills. This guy's analytical, guv.'

'So, why is he targeting pondlife like the Elphicks?' said Fulbright. 'If he's a scientist, the vics are way outside his social group.'

'I can't explain motive, except to say the Reaper isn't your *usual* serial killer.'

Fulbright nodded. 'Anything else?'

Tyson looked down at her notes. 'There was one odd thing in the Harlesden file - a suggestion that Sammy Elphick, may have burgled a house in Kensington belonging to a rich businessman called Professor Victor Sorenson. Stolen goods - a high-end VCR - from a break-in at Sorenson's home were found in Sammy's flat. Interestingly, this Sorenson is an industrial chemist.'

'A scientist?' said Fulbright. 'Did you dig any deeper?'

'I checked Sammy's jacket but every blag we ever nicked him for was local to Harlesden or surrounding boroughs. He never strayed as far as Kensington and he would've stuck out like a sore thumb.'

'And Sorenson?'

'Squeaky clean,' said Tyson.

'But he was interviewed.'

'He was but DS Brook's reports on Sorenson are pretty flimsy,' said Tyson. 'It's like he interviewed him just to tick it off.'

'Anything else taken in this burglary found at Sammy's?'

'No, which is odd in itself. Sorenson's a multimillionaire and this would be an expensively-furnished home containing more valuable *and* more portable things to steal.'

'Maybe Sammy already fenced those,' suggested Ross.

'I cross-checked the burglary report. The VCR was the only thing Sorenson reported.'

'What does that tell you?' said Fulbright.

'That maybe there was no burglary,' said Tyson. 'That maybe this Sorenson faked the theft for some reason.'

'Why?' said Fulbright.

'Sorenson had a twin brother, Stefan. The year before, 1989, Stefan was beaten to death in his own home. Theory was it was a burglary gone wrong and the killer was never found.' She looked at Fulbright and Ross in turn. 'It doesn't take a huge leap to wonder if Sorenson, with his resources, set about looking for that burglar...'

'And if it turned out to be Sammy Elphick...' said Fulbright.

'Then Sorenson takes a very personal and savage revenge and slaughters Elphick and his entire family.'

'Okay,' said Fulbright. 'But there are a couple of flaws in your argument.'

'I know,' conceded Tyson.

'Flaws?' said Ross.

'If the Elphick killings are personal, there's no viable motive for subsequent killings,' said Tyson.

'So, why kill the Brixton family the year after?' nodded Ross.

'Or the Telfers in Leeds.'

'Maybe he got a taste for it,' said Ross.

'Anything's possible,' said Tyson. 'But it's a bit of a reach considering he seemed to lose the taste entirely after '93, by which time Sorenson's living abroad.'

'Where?'

'He has property in California,' said Tyson. 'A penthouse apartment in Los Angeles and a house in Lake Tahoe. In 1992 he moved out there though he kept the Kensington house for his sister-in-law, Sonja, and her kids to live in. Obviously, with extensive business interests on both sides of the Atlantic, he pays the odd visit.'

'Might explain why the killing stopped in England,' said Ross.

'Was Sorenson here when the Telfer family died in Leeds?'

'For a couple of months either side!' said Tyson. 'Though that proves precisely nothing, obviously.'

'Good work, Kelly,' said Fulbright. 'Not sure the Chief will spring for a flight to California for an interview though.'

'Actually, that's not a problem,' replied Tyson. 'I checked. Sorenson is back in London and living at his Kensington house.'

Fulbright smiled. 'Is he now? Think we should pay him a visit?'

'Rude not to,' said Tyson, grinning.

'You said a couple of flaws, guv,' said Ross.

'Kelly?' said Fulbright.

'Given all the careful planning and execution that went into Harlesden, it makes no sense for Sorenson to wipe out the Elphick family, leave no trace of ever being there but then leave behind his VCR for DS Brook and DCI Rowlands, to find. That's just nuts. It's the only direct link between Sorenson and the murder. What's it even doing there?'

'I see what you mean.'

'There's something else, guv,' said Tyson. 'Though it's a bit delicate.'

'You're amongst friends, Kelly,' said Fulbright. 'Speak freely.'

'I'm new at this but in 1990 Brook and DCI Rowlands were very experienced detectives,' said Tyson. 'They must have arrived at a similar conclusion and yet they didn't make nearly enough of the lead on Sorenson. You knew them, guv. How could they miss this?'

'From what I remember, Brook made all the running,' said Fulbright. 'Charlie Rowlands took a back seat after losing his daughter to drugs. To be honest, Brook carried him. He was a good detective, brilliant even. Maybe he gave it a go but gave up for lack of evidence.'

'It should still be reflected in the files,' said Tyson.

'I do remember there was talk about Brook stalking a suspect,' said Fulbright. 'Was that in the file?'

'Not that I saw,' said Tyson. 'I'm sorry if Brook was a friend...'

'I only knew Brook through Rowlands,' said Fulbright. 'Charlie thought the sun shone out of his backside but everyone else thought he was an arrogant prick and I had no cause to disagree.'

∼

FULBRIGHT SAT in the canteen staring down at the report, his coffee cold and untouched. The details of Detective Sergeant Damen Brook's nervous breakdown from his personnel file were highly confidential and only available to senior officers charged with assessing an officer's fitness for duty.

Fulbright had read it three times, pondering its relevance. And Tyson was right. There was nothing in the murder book to indicate Brook's suspicions about Sorenson. In fact, no suspects were ever unearthed, despite a year-long investigation into the Elphick killings. And yet, here in black and white, were the police psychiatrist's own comments about DI Brook's 'period of obsessive stalking.'

The Reaper had been a big deal in the papers and on TV and Brook had worked the year-long investigation exclusively, apart from a short break in the summer to follow up on a Jane Doe in Ravenscourt Park. And the questions to which Kerr would want answers, glared out at Fulbright from the yellowing pages of the report. Who was Brook stalking and why was there no mention of a suspect in the murder book? Had Charlie Rowlands filleted the file to cover up Brook's incompetence or, worse, his misdirection? Or was the absence of detail less sinister; a result of Brook's mental deterioration?

One thing was clear. The year after the Elphick murders, Floyd Wrigley and his brood had been slaughtered and Brook's disintegration as a police officer began to accelerate.

'Penny for them,' smiled Kerr, sitting down opposite Fulbright with a cup of tea and a biscuit.

'I wouldn't want to overcharge you,' said Fulbright, closing the file.

'How's it going?'

'Early days, sir. We're looking at a few angles.'

'Don't wash my balls with claptrap. How is it going?'

Fulbright hesitated. 'I'm concerned.'

'Tell me.'

'This Sorenson you mentioned. His whole connection to Harlesden is a bit off. Even my raw DC, Kelly Tyson, spotted that.'

'What did she say?'

'She thinks there's a good case for this Sorenson burglary being a fake. Elphick wouldn't have gone out of his comfort zone for just a VCR, having taken the trouble to break into a rich man's home so far off his turf.'

'Why would Sorenson fake a burglary?' Fulbright raised an eyebrow so Kerr came to his own conclusion. 'So, he can take the VCR to Harlesden to fence and kill Elphick and his family.'

'A ticket into the flat,' nodded Fulbright.

'Sounds workable,' said Kerr.

'But what's the motive?' said Fulbright. 'Sorenson's wealthy and successful. People like Elphick don't cross his path.'

'Unless they break into his house,' said Kerr.

'Then we're back where we started. If the burglary was real it provides some kind of motive but then how does a personal grudge become a series? And if Sorenson killed the Elphick family, for whatever reason, why leave the VCR in the flat? If he removes it, there's not a single thing to connect Sorenson to the murders and he's in the clear. In fact, why report a burglary at his home if it didn't happen?'

Kerr pondered. 'Maybe he was taunting the police, knowing there was no proof.'

'Then we'd know about it in the reports.'

'True,' conceded Kerr.

'I did work up another angle.' Kerr encouraged Fulbright with a nod. 'Just throwing it out there but what if Sammy's death was more mundane. Say he did break into Sorenson's home but with a partner. We only recovered a VCR from the Harlesden crime scene but there were likely more valuable things in Sorenson's house.'

'And Elphick and this partner had a falling out splitting the proceeds.'

'It's not very sexy and it doesn't explain a series,' conceded Fulbright. 'But we're looking at Elphick's KA's to see what pops up.'

'You think a known associate killed Sammy and his family over an argument about the spoils? Seems extreme.'

'Criminals are stupid, sir.'

'Which is why they get caught,' said Kerr. 'And why go to the trouble of staging the crime scene like that?'

'That, I don't know,' said Fulbright.

Kerr rubbed his chin. 'I don't like it. But find me an accomplice and a list of other stolen goods from Sorenson's home and we'll look again.' He drained his cup, standing to leave, then hesitated. 'Will you pay this Sorenson a visit?'

'We're considering it if we can come up with something more solid.'

'Any idea where the old man lives?'

'The same house - Queensdale Road, Kensington.'

'Talk to him and get a feel for him,' said Kerr. 'See what you can shake out. And keep me informed.'

Fulbright stared at the Chief Superintendent's retreating uniform. 'What do you know that you're not telling me?'

11

December 1st, 2008 - London

Victor Sorenson read the news cutting from the Derby Telegraph for a third time, pleased with his choice. Jason Wallis was perfect for the Reaper's attentions and his lawbreaking the ideal lure for Damen Brook. The threatened rape of a local teacher was the tip of a very large iceberg of offending for that vicious young man. He and his grubby family had been beyond the reach of the law for too long.

He smiled, anticipating future pleasures. When the Wallis family went under the knife, people would be reminded of the Reaper's message.

'It's time, my friend. It will be good to see you again after all these years. And this time you won't slip through the net.'

∾

DCI FULBRIGHT WALKED to the counter and nodded to the woman on duty. 'I'm here to see Charlie Rowlands.'

'Heavens, Charlie is popular all of a sudden,' she said. 'He's in Room D52.' The receptionist jotted down his name, drawing Fulbright's eye to the notepad. When she swivelled round to tap his details into the computer, Fulbright leaned over and flipped the pad round to scan the list of visitors.

All entries except his own had been crossed through to remind her that she'd entered the names in the database. Above his own name, signed in half an hour before, Fulbright saw *DCI Joshua Hudson*.

He flipped the notepad back. Josh Hudson up from Brighton? Rowlands and Hudson had been close until Hudson's move from Hammersmith out to Bromley, then further out to Brighton, in search of a quiet life.

'I was supposed to meet another colleague,' said Fulbright. 'DCI Hudson. Have I missed him?'

'Already in with him,' beamed the receptionist.

'Thank you,' replied Fulbright. Charlie was receiving plenty of visitors, yet Kerr's strict instruction had been to keep away. Odd. If Kerr wanted him to conduct a thorough case review, why discourage a visit to verify a few facts? Rowlands wouldn't be around much longer and none of Charlie's friends and ex-colleagues seemed to be leaving him in peace.

～

THE LIFT DOORS opened and DCI Joshua Hudson stood in front of Fulbright, a look of recognition, if not warmth, spreading across his face. 'Richard. Good to see you.' He held out a hand.

Fulbright stepped from the capsule and shook Hudson's hand. 'Joshua.' He nodded his head into the distance without knowing where Charlie's room was. 'How's the old man?'

Hudson shook his head. 'Mentally okay but physically struggling.'

'Hardly surprising,' replied Fulbright.

'No,' agreed Hudson. 'But I was here a couple of days ago, and he was in great form.'

'I'm sure chemo can do that to you,' said Fulbright.

'Good days and bad,' agreed Hudson. 'And, after Elizabeth, maybe he's more reconciled than he might have been.'

'Elizabeth?'

'His daughter,' replied Hudson. 'Heroin overdose at Edinburgh University nearly twenty years ago.'

'Of course,' said Fulbright.

'Charlie wasn't the same man after.' He shook his head in

sympathy then returned his gaze to Fulbright. 'You worked with Charlie?'

'I joined his CID team when I was just starting out,' answered Fulbright, his features severe. 'I wasn't with him long.'

'He touched many lives.' Hudson drew out a packet of cigarettes. 'These bloody things.' He offered the pack to Fulbright.

'I don't smoke or drink much.'

'That's right,' said Hudson. 'Unusual, in our game.'

'So, I've been told,' said Fulbright. 'Though yours was the politest version.'

Hudson laughed. 'I can imagine.'

Fulbright looked beyond Hudson. 'I'd love to stay and chat but...'

Hudson put an arm across his path. 'He was sleeping when I left. Leave him for now.'

Fulbright studied Hudson. Why was everyone trying to stop him seeing Charlie? 'Whatever you say.'

∼

A HALF HOUR LATER, Fulbright finished his aimless walk around Hammersmith Broadway and returned to Rowlands' hospital room.

'Charlie,' called Fulbright, stepping inside and closing the door. Rowlands seemed shrunken, diminished, the bed too large for his wasted body.

'Who's that?' said a grizzled voice from the bed. Ex-DCI Charlie Rowlands was sitting up, reading a newspaper and peered over his half-moon glasses. 'Let me see you.'

Fulbright walked to the bed and sat on a chair.

'Tricky Dicky Fulbright?' chuckled Rowlands, folding the paper. 'The fuck do you want? Come to gloat, Constable?'

'I've been a DCI for five years,' said Fulbright, looking around. The only colour in the room was provided by a bowl of untouched fruit and Charlie's jaundiced hue.

'Have you now?' said Rowlands.

'Like you didn't know.'

'Got a cigarette for your old guvnor?' enquired Rowlands. 'Course not. Too up yourself for such filthy habits, as I recall.'

'I bet you wish you hadn't started either,' said Fulbright, with more sourness than he intended.

The Resurrection

Rowlands rasped out a laugh which nearly cut him in two and he took a few moments to recover with the help of some water, held out to him by Fulbright.

'Cheeky fucker,' said Rowlands, gasping. He handed back the glass. Fulbright could smell spirits when he put the glass to his nose and noticed a suggestion of colour in the liquid. 'What are you doing here?'

'Paying my last respects to a valued colleague,' said Fulbright, pulling open a small side cupboard to reveal the half-full bottle of Lamb's Navy Rum.

Rowlands laughed again but with more comfort and control. 'Come to dance on my grave more like. Can't say I blame you. I didn't cut you much slack, did I?'

'Not much. But then I didn't expect any.'

'Just as well. You were a useless twat. Buggered if I can remember how you blagged your way into CID.'

'And all the way to Detective Chief Inspector,' said Fulbright.

'Incredible!' said Rowlands, shaking his head. 'Still credit where it's due. To get this far with so little talent...'

'If only I'd been the great Damen Brook,' replied Fulbright.

Rowlands' brief levity dissolved. 'Don't say his name. You're not fit to clean his boots.' It was Fulbright's turn to laugh. 'Who let you in here? I told Josh Hudson I didn't want visitors.'

'Don't blame Joshua. He did warn me off so I waited for him to leave. I'm only here because Chief Superintendent Kerr asked me to take another run at the Reaper killings for you.'

Rowlands' expression hardened. 'You what?'

'You heard me. The Reaper.'

'That Scottish cunt never could leave well alone.'

'No argument here,' said Fulbright. 'Can't see the point of going over ancient ground myself but if the Chief tells me you've had fresh thoughts about the case then who am I to argue?'

'What fresh thoughts? I haven't seen the charmless bastard and I wouldn't be talking to him about the Reaper case, if I had.'

'That's odd.' Fulbright pretended to think it through. 'He seemed to think you still harbour suspicions about Victor Sorenson.'

'Sorenson?' Charlie's red-rimmed eyes dropped briefly. 'What about him?'

'Something about a fake burglary that Wonder Boy investigated. Kerr seemed to think there was more to it than met the eye.'

Charlie's face flushed with what little blood was left in him and he seemed suddenly winded, his head slumping as though weighed down.

'If there's anything you want to get off your chest, Charlie, now's the time.'

'How about two cricket ball-sized tumours?'

'Such self-effacing courage,' mocked Fulbright. 'I'm welling up.'

'Well, fuck off and do it somewhere else, you sarcastic cunt. If you want to waste your time, check the files. It's all there.'

'Oh, but it isn't,' retorted Fulbright. 'I looked at the files and they've been sanitised - virtually every mention of Victor Sorenson has been removed. Now who would do that, do you suppose?' No reply from Rowlands. 'My money's on Brook but you're a close second, Charlie.'

'Don't call me Charlie, you jumped up fucker. Equals we ain't.'

Fulbright smiled without mirth. 'That's right. Play your little games, dead man. But you're hiding something and when I find out what it is, *I'll* decide whether what you and Brook are hiding can stay that way.'

Rowlands stared beyond Fulbright. 'I wouldn't worry about the Reaper, laddie. It was all a long time ago and if I had anything to confess it would be to a priest.'

'That bad, eh?'

'You wouldn't understand, even if I told you. You'd need a soul.'

'The suspect was surly and uncooperative,' said Fulbright.

Rowlands grunted in amusement. 'I haven't long left so I want to put at least one thing right before I head for the flames. You're different from what I remember. You're still a cunt but you've got a bit more nous about you. I didn't give you much of a chance after Damen got sick. That was because of what was happening to him and I want to apologise for that, at least. You're entitled to think ill of me and I don't expect forgiveness. But I'm sorry just the same.'

Fulbright studied him. 'I'll accept your apology when you tell me what there is to know about Sorenson.'

Rowlands turned his attention back to his newspaper. 'Goodbye, Richard. It's been good catching up. Don't come back.'

Fulbright stood. 'Until the funeral, then. I'll bring my dancing shoes.'

'And I'll polish the coffin lid so you break your fucking neck.'

The Resurrection

~

WHEN FULBRIGHT HAD GONE, Charlie Rowlands pulled open the drawer of the bedside cabinet and turned on one of two mobile phones.

'It's me. We have to call it off.'

'Call what off?' replied Sorenson.

'Our trip to Derby.'

'We can't. It's all arranged.'

'I've just had a visitor who's doing a case review into Harlesden and Brixton. He mentioned your name.'

'Who?'

'DCI Richard Fulbright.'

'Fulbright? Do you know him?'

'From way back. He's been given the Reaper files to look over and seems to be taking it seriously.'

'Is he any good?'

'He's no Damen Brook but he's dogged.'

'Did he say who put him up to it?'

Rowlands hesitated. 'Chief Superintendent Kerr.'

'The same Kerr who was outside your room the other day. What have you said, Charlie? Have you been indiscreet?'

'He may have visited but I haven't spoken to Kerr and that's the truth,' said Rowlands. 'Why won't you believe me?'

'Because I understand the urge to confess your sins before meeting your maker. Start your time in eternity with a clean slate. Is that how it was?'

'I haven't seen him and if I had I wouldn't be talking about my old cases. I've got a lot more to lose than you.'

Sorenson scoffed. *'In your condition, it would never come to trial.'*

'Trial?' said Rowlands. 'You think I give a shit about prison? I have a reputation...'

There was a dry laugh from the other end of the line. *'The greater the corruption, the greater the desire to appear principled.'*

'Fuck you.'

'Vanity, Charlie. Don't let it poison your mind.'

'Expect a visit. That's all I'm saying.'

'You worry too much.'

'And we're calling it off.'

'Our trip goes ahead as planned or I'll make sure your reputation is ruined forever. You're getting soft in your old age.'

'Soft? Do you think after what I've done, I give two shits about taking out some lowlife family in Derby?'

'That's the spirit, Charlie. Leave Fulbright to me. And remember, I'm in the same boat as you when it comes to life expectancy so don't play that card again. I'll deal with Fulbright if it comes to that.'

'Deal with him how? I don't like the bastard but I didn't sign on for killing coppers.'

'If we're careful, it won't come to that, Charlie. Now get some rest. We've got a lot to do.'

12

December 3rd, 2008 - Hammersmith

DCI Fulbright looked across his desk at Ross and Tyson. 'I've divided up Sammy Elphick's known associates still living.' Fulbright handed a sheet of paper to both. 'The five in the left-hand column are either still in prison or no longer in London. It doesn't mean they're out of the frame for a historical but, with just the three of us looking at an eighteen-year-old case, it means we have to take decisions about who we can reasonably cover. So, treat the ones on the left as duds unless something compelling presents.'

'And the three names on the right?' said Ross. 'Gus David. George Canning. Vincent Muir.'

'All three have a connection with Elphick, have extensive CVs for petty theft and house breaking and all three are still in West London, according to our best information.'

'They worked blags with Elphick?' said Tyson.

'Or shared his cell, courtesy of Her Majesty,' said Fulbright. 'Kelly, you take Canning. Frank take Gus David and I'll look at Muir. Last knowns are on the back of the sheet.'

FULBRIGHT STRADDLED the urine-coloured puddle and pressed a gloved thumb against the button for the lift. He was surprised to hear a lurching noise somewhere deep within the crumbling grey building, although whatever machinery was spluttering into life sounded in need of a serious overhaul.

The damp concrete steps snaked their way through all seven storeys of Block C of the King Edward Estate and Vinny Muir was six flights up. Despite that, he decided not to risk the lift and picked his way around puddles, packets of scorched aluminium foil floating on the surface.

Minutes later, he took a moment to recover his breath on the sixth-floor walkway before rapping on the glass panel of a door. A filthy lace curtain shrouded the interior from inspection but he fancied he heard a radio playing somewhere inside. He turned to study the view to the other two arms of the U-shaped estate and beyond, to Hammersmith's metropolitan sprawl.

'Premium Bonds Officer, Mr Muir,' shouted Fulbright. 'Are you in there, sir?'

Fulbright pulled out the form he'd mocked up with the National Savings and Investments logo at the top with various slogans and some random numbers and letters.

'Mr Muir,' Fulbright shouted through the letterbox. 'We need to confirm your numbers before we can proceed with the financial award.'

A dead-eyed, overweight woman holding a young baby pulled the door back, a glazed expression on her face. The baby wore only a grubby white vest, stained by the river of spittle that hung from its chin and the woman, a shapeless and brightly coloured robe.

'Is Vincent Muir at home, miss?' said Fulbright.

The woman's mouth hung open as she tried to process Fulbright's question. She could've been in her mid-thirties but her face looked much older, her cheeks sagging and dull. Her brown hair was lank and matted and she had a sore looking bald patch on her crown.

'Have we won some money?' slurred the woman. At first Fulbright thought she might be drunk but then the wind caught the woman's voluminous sleeve and pulled it up to her elbow revealing a series of needle marks.

'If Mr Muir's bond numbers correspond.'

The Resurrection

The woman thrust out a tobacco-stained hand for the forms. 'I'm his daughter. You can give it to me.'

'It doesn't work like that...' At that moment the crash of loud music drowned him out and the baby began to cry and reach for the ground.

'Liam!' screamed Muir's daughter. 'Turn that fucking thing off. And you can shut up you little bastard,' she added, almost dropping the squirming child onto the concrete. As she bent over an enormous breast fell out of her robe and she righted herself making no attempt to cover up. 'See anything you like?' she asked, with a lascivious grin.

'No,' replied Fulbright.

Her grin hardened and she turned to scream back into the flat again. 'I said turn that off, you knob. I'm trying...'

The music stopped and a young man emerged from the back of the flat, his slim muscled torso naked and his trousers slung low. With a sinking feeling, Fulbright recognised Liam's face.

'What the fuck does he want?' said Liam.

'Premium bonds,' slurred the woman, pulling her robe tight. 'We might have won summink.'

'Are you trippin', yer dozy mare? He's a fucking copper. I seen him darn the nick.'

'You what?' screamed the woman, wheeling round to Fulbright, face deformed by hate. 'You lying cunt.'

Fulbright shrugged. 'Guilty as charged.'

'We could sue,' added Liam.

'Right,' said Fulbright. 'Where's your old man?'

'Deception, innit?' continued Liam. 'Now fuck off, old timer, before you get shanked.' Liam pulled the woman inside and slammed the door.

Fulbright stood for a second, listening to the parent being told off by the child above the din of the wailing baby. He walked back towards the stairwell pulling his collar up against the harsh winds.

'Are you coming to sort out that Muir lot, officer?' Fulbright turned towards the voice coming from behind a barely opened door, two units along.

Fulbright approached and the door widened slightly. 'You know the family?'

'Terrible people,' said the white-haired old woman in a soft Irish brogue, opening the door a little wider. 'Evil and godless, they are.'

'So, I see.'

The frail old lady looked him up and down with her milky white eyes, her head tilted up and back to allow the good part of her vision to focus. 'My, you're a fine-looking young man, no word of a lie.' She squinted harder at his hand. 'And no wedding band to claim you. Now why would a handsome fella like yourself not be married?'

'Long hours and not much of a social life.'

'Hard worker. A fine catch then.' She smiled, extending a gnarled purpled hand. 'Ursula O'Hare. Mrs.'

'Richard.' Fulbright took off a glove and shook her hand. She held onto it with surprising vigour.

'You have a good grip. My Patrick had strong hands before he passed. Not at the end, of course...' her lips pursed momentarily but stoicism reasserted itself quickly. 'I'm from Donegal, originally. We came over in '75. Or was it '74? Not a good time, after Guildford and all...'

'And the Muirs?' said Fulbright.

'Terrible people. No respect for others or themselves. We've given up complaining to the Trust. Noise all night, every night. Music, screaming, fighting, banging on doors. And if they need something there's not a flat on the landing that hasn't been broken into for them to help themselves to whatever they want.' She nodded towards a pane of her glass door, replaced by chipboard. Fulbright didn't need to ask.

'My own fault. I'm such an eejit. Left my purse on the hall table in full view.' She dabbed at an eye. 'It was just a few pennies. But I do miss the pictures I had in there. Carried them everywhere I did. Even asked for them back but that little bastard Liam laughed in my face. Excuse my French.'

'We should see about getting that window fixed for you.'

'No use fretting over trifles. Just tell me you've come to take them away.' For the first-time Mrs O'Hare had a pleading look in her mother-of-pearl eye.

He smiled weakly back at her, his regretful demeanour revealing the answer. 'I'm actually looking for Vincent Muir.'

'Vinny?' The old lady managed a smile. 'Poor fella. He moved out. His own daughter and grandchildren, but he couldn't stand to live there. Nice man - not as good looking as yourself, mind.' She winked at him. 'He's on parole with yourselves. Said he couldn't take the risk living there, not with all that lawlessness and such.

The Resurrection

He moved across the landing over onto Block B.' She indicated the building opposite. 'The red door there, though he won't be in now. He washes up at the Greece-e-Spoon on the high street over lunchtime.'

'What's the cafe called?' asked Fulbright.

Mrs O'Hare chuckled. 'It's called the Greece-e-Spoon. Some Greek fella owns it.'

'Thanks.' Fulbright prepared to leave. 'Must be hard for you up here on the sixth floor with a dodgy lift.'

'Ah sure, it's fine. I don't go out any more. Don't dare, not even during the day. I've got cataracts, see. I'm on the list for an operation but who knows when that'll be. My son brings me groceries every few days. Never misses a visit - a good boy, he is. But he has to sneak the shopping round, mind, or they'll have it.' She nodded her head back towards the Muir residence. 'Before seven in the morning usually, while they're still out for the count. And he picks up my pension for me but I let him hang on to it to buy my food. No point keeping money in the place - asking for trouble. Have you time for a cuppa, Inspector? I've got a nice packet of custard creams with your name on them.'

Fulbright was touched. 'Thank you, Ursula, but I've got to work. I'm grateful for the information.'

'Don't mention it. It's a pleasure talking to nice people like yourself, so well-mannered and nicely turned out. And if you ever need a bit of an old chat...' She smiled at Fulbright as he walked away.

~

VINNY MUIR PULLED off the rubber gloves with difficulty and gingerly dried his aching hands with a grubby towel. Winter exacerbated his rheumatism and putting his hands in water for hours at a time, even in Marigolds, was not good for them. He attempted a fist but the pain was too great and his hand wouldn't close so he hooked a thumb in the strap of his sopping wet apron and pulled it over his head to drop in the laundry basket. He then massaged his hands with a little of the cheap hand cream Theo had seen fit to provide kitchen staff.

With the crisp tenner, secure in his back pocket, he picked his way over the slippery floor to the curtain that separated the kitchen from the customers. He was starving and looking forward to his staff lunch. Shepherd's Pie and gravy today - his favourite. It would sustain him until his free lunch tomorrow with maybe a cream cracker for supper if he couldn't hold out.

When he pulled the curtain aside, Muir stood frozen for a split second before stepping back from the welcoming warmth and light of the steamy cafe as quickly as his aging reflexes and aching hips would allow.

Copper! Corner table, nursing a cup of tea, pushing fifty, soberly dressed, neat haircut and - the giveaway - polished Doc Marten shoes.

Muir glued an eye to the crack in the curtain and stared, trying to place him. He didn't recognise him but hadn't seen him in the cafe before either. Not during his lunchtime stint at any rate. His breathing slowed. He hadn't missed a parole appointment so maybe it was just a coincidence. Or maybe it wasn't even a copper.

'You're being paranoid,' he muttered, running a gnarled hand through the stubble of his greying-red hair, feeling the hunger gnaw at his belly. Through a crack, he could see Theo plating up the only decent hot meal he'd have for a day and was sorely tempted just to step out into the cafe and eat his food.

A second later he pulled on his donkey jacket and slipped out of the back door into the alley behind the cafe, then marched as fast as his joints would allow towards the high street.

~

'IT WOULD BE a shame to let that shepherd's pie go to waste, Vinny.'

Muir stopped in his tracks, briefly reviewing his options before deciding that a burned-out old blagger, on parole with no skills and no prospects, didn't have any.

Turning, Muir managed a smile, gracious in defeat. 'Wouldn't it just,' he replied, his heart sinking at the expression of supreme confidence on the face of the man from the café. A feeling he'd experienced often during his felonious career washed through him. It was that special brand of helplessness a convicted criminal experienced when the giant maw of the justice system had him in its grip and was preparing to grind up his bones. And even though Muir was sure all his debts to society had been paid, that familiar dread pulled on his gut. 'I know you?'

'DCI Fulbright,' said the copper, flashing a warrant card and indicating the way back to the café with an outstretched arm.

'A DCI?' Muir passed Fulbright and headed for the condensed warmth of the cafe. *Christ, what am I in for?*

A minute later Muir pawed energetically at the first forkful of shepherd's pie, thrusting it clumsily into his mouth, unable to savour it. This was nothing new. Like most ex-cons at mealtimes, he ate quickly and kept a beady eye out for bigger beasts looking to steal his food. Old habits. With a copper at the table, his anxiety only deepened.

Fulbright watched him eat, saying nothing. When Muir could stand it no longer, he clattered the fork onto the oval plate. 'I'm not going back inside,' he muttered, through teeth spotted with minced beef. Fulbright smiled and an eyebrow lifted. 'And no, that's not an admission. I ain't done nothin' to go back inside for. I served my time and if I have to starve or freeze to death on the streets, I'll take it. I'm never looking at another whitewashed wall or pissing in a swill bucket as long as I live.'

'Fine words, Vinny.'

'I mean it.'

'They always do.'

'I'm done thieving, Inspector.' Muir lifted his gnarled old hands in the air like a surgeon about to be gowned. 'Even if I had the hands for it.'

Fulbright's grin faded. 'Detective. Chief. Inspector.'

However low Muir's heart had sunk before, it fell further. 'What do you want?'

Fulbright nodded at Muir's hands, still raw from the washing up. 'No prison ink?'

Muir looked down at his hands as though just noticing. 'My hands were my living and I wasn't gonna let some pill-popping con stick dirty needles in them?'

'Smart man.'

'Yeah, ain't I the dog's bollocks,' said Muir, arthritically picking up his fork to spear sullenly at the slab of mashed potato and beef. 'Now, what do you want?'

The DCI put a hand in a pocket and pulled out an old mugshot of Sammy Elphick and turned it towards Muir. The ex-con looked at the picture and back at Fulbright several times.

'Who's that?' he finally asked through a mouthful of food.

'His name is Sammy Elphick.'

'If you say so.'

'You shared a cell with him in the Scrubs in 1988.'

'I've had a lot of cellmates.' Muir lay down his fork and pushed his empty plate away. 'Don't know how I'm supposed to remember one from twenty years ago.'

Fulbright tapped the picture. 'Take a longer look.'

Muir stared hard at the photograph then shrugged. 'It could be anybody.'

'It's Sammy Elphick.'

'The name don't do nothing for me neither,' replied Muir. 'I'm being straight. Then again there's not a lot of use for names in the nick. Did he have a trade name?'

'Not to my knowledge. Sammy was a burglar, same as you. Worked out of Harlesden.'

'Harlesden,' muttered Muir, unimpressed. 'Ain't a thing worth stealing round there?'

'Sammy lived there. Minet Avenue, above the launderette. Eighteen years ago, he's *alleged* to have burgled a house in Kensington.'

Muir narrowed his eyes. 'Nineteen-ninety? What is this shit?' For the first time, Muir noticed Fulbright hesitate and it cheered him.

'We think he had a partner with him.'

'Me?' Muir lifted his mug of tea to his mouth with both hands and drained it. When he set it down, he fixed his black eyes onto Fulbright, a smile playing around his mouth. 'Is this a joke?'

'I look like I'm joking?'

'You're investigating an *alleged* eighteen-year-old burglary and you tell me it's not a joke.'

Fulbright broke eye contact. 'We're re-investigating it.'

'A burglary?' Muir smiled. His expression tightened suddenly. 'Someone died, right? Why else would you be having another look?' Fulbright's silence confirmed it and Muir's expression turned to a mix of fear and anger. 'Well, you're not pinning it on me. I never attacked no-one on a blag, or anywhere else, let alone snuffed anyone...'

'We know you didn't,' said Fulbright, holding up a hand to pacify. 'But we're not totally convinced that the householder was being truthful about it. That's why I'm asking you.'

'Because you think it was me and Sammy?'

'Was it?' Muir looked at Fulbright in disbelief. 'You can tell me, Vinny. Tell me what I want to know and you get a free pass.'

'How wet behind the ears do you think I am that I'd believe a crock like that without my brief to hear it?'

'Because we're more interested in who you robbed and what was taken.'

Muir eyed him suspiciously. 'Well, it wasn't me.'

'You mean you can't remember.'

'No, I remember just fine. It wasn't me. I've never pulled a job in Kensington. Too much money means too many alarms. Plus, it's hard enough to stay out of stir without having some partner knowing your business. I always blagged alone and, if he was any good, I reckon this Sammy Elphick did too.'

Fulbright grinned. 'You knew him then.'

'No. But I remember a few Harlesden-based blaggers and, if Sammy was one of them, he was a lone wolf like me. They all were. I don't recognise that picture and I ain't never done no blag with no partner and that the God's honest. But if you think we pulled jobs together on his say-so, get him and his brief in a room with me and mine and I'll swear on a stack of bibles that he's lying.'

Fulbright stared. 'We can't. He died, along with his wife and kid, murdered by a serial killer called the Reaper.'

Muir was sombre. '*That* was Sammy. Tough break. I'll be sure to say a Hail Mary the next time I'm on a church roof.'

'You think this is funny?' snarled Fulbright. 'You think I can't bust you back to stir any time I like?'

Muir held up his hands in apology. 'I just want to be left in peace. This is nothin' to do with me. You're barking up the wrong tree.'

Fulbright smiled in that unsettling way coppers had. 'Fair enough.' He made no attempt to leave. 'Glad you're finally going straight.'

'Pretty hot on fake concern, aren't you?'

'My speciality,' said Fulbright.

Muir struggled to his feet, patting his jacket theatrically. 'Been great catching up...'

'Sit down.'

Muir hesitated but didn't bother going through his options again. 'Got a cigarette?' he asked, sitting. 'I used to roll my own before mi' hands...'

'I don't smoke,' said Fulbright.

Muir gawped in disbelief. 'A copper what don't smoke? Never

heard of such a thing. You got to have some kind of vice in our game, whatever side of the fence you work. What is it? Skirt? Booze?'

'I met your family,' said Fulbright.

Muir lowered his eyes. 'They told you I was here? I'm surprised they could even speak.'

'They didn't tell me anything.'

'Mrs O'Hare,' concluded Muir, nodding. 'Nice old bird. And having to live within screaming distance of my lot. Ain't right.'

'Hardly your fault,' said Fulbright.

Muir's response was a bitter smile. 'No? The number of times I've said *it weren't me* to coppers. And my teachers before that. Well, there ain't no getting me off the hook for the state of my lass and those kids. I'm sixty-nine years old. I been inside for thirty-five of those years - more than half my life. I failed my daughter and I failed my grandkids. That makes it my fault.'

'That why you moved away?'

'I didn't move away. I could've gone to Bristol and got well shot. I only moved to a different block so I can keep an eye out. I wish I could help them lads, Liam and Jordan, but you can't tell them a thing cos they already know everything. They're a nightmare and they're heading down a worse path than me. Drugs, aggro and blagging are the least of it. Mark my words, they're gonna kill someone someday.'

'That bad?'

'You don't know the half of it. Things have changed, gradual like, and I don't know how or when but things are different. At least in my day, criminals used to know they were criminals. Now, most of these kids on the estate think they're God, think they can do whatever they want and if anyone calls them out on it, it's...' he cast around for the right word, '...disrespectful. Can you believe that? They think they've got the right to kick the living shit out of people and just the fact they want to, makes it okay. I mean, when did all that start?'

Fulbright shrugged. 'How long have you got?'

'Worse thing is I can't even give money, even if I had it to give. It'd just go in Debbie's arm or up Jordan's nose. And there's nothing I can say to make them stop because I lost that right. I've lived like that, every minute spent thinking about getting money to get ahead and never a thought for the pain I was causing my parents or the aggro I was dishing out to innocent people.

The Resurrection

'It's not so bad doin' some rich bastard with insurance but it's not like that anymore. Liam and Jordan won't do over some swell's pad, they wouldn't know how, don't have the skills. They'd have to break the door down to get in. No discipline, see. So, it's the single mums and the helpless old dears like Mrs O'Hare, who get the shit stick. They're the ones getting done over and worse, if they so much as look at my grandsons wrong. I might be to blame but they never learned that off me.'

'Mrs O'Hare said she liked you.'

'She wouldn't if she'd met me when I was Liam's age.'

Fulbright pushed back his chair. 'I may need to speak to you again.'

Muir shrugged. 'You know where I am.'

Fulbright turned to leave but hesitated, fumbled in a pocket and put a ten-pound note on the table. 'Get yourself some cigarettes.'

Muir looked at the ten-pound note on the Formica table and laughed. 'Get on with shortening my life, you mean.'

Fulbright smiled and pointed a leather finger at him. 'Straight and narrow,' he said and walked away as Muir clawed the money towards him.

'Chief Inspector?' Fulbright turned at Muir's voice. 'Thanks for the note.'

13

December 12th 2010 - Derby

Brook drove back to Derby in a daze, trying to piece together what he'd learned from Tyson. DCI Richard Fulbright, the officer who'd given Brook a hard time after Sorenson's suicide, had re-opened the investigation into the London Reaper killings just a couple of weeks before the Wallis family were slaughtered in Derby. Then, the following year, Fulbright had met his own untimely demise in a car crash in America.

He'd known Fulbright as far back as the Harlesden killings in 1990. While Brook and Charlie Rowlands were looking for clues amongst the blood-spattered remains of the Elphick family, Fulbright was a uniform on crowd control, stretching police tape across the roads.

Later he'd made the move to CID and even worked as a DC with Charlie after Brook's breakdown. Rowlands hadn't been impressed and had given Fulbright a hard time. Brass, however, had taken a different view and Fulbright's career had prospered all the way to Detective Chief Inspector and, despite his differences with the man, Brook was saddened by his banal and senseless death.

The Resurrection

~

BACK IN DERBY BY MID-MORNING, Brook parked his BMW in the station car park rather than Magnet House's underground parking bays, wary of residents starting to become suspicious and perhaps jotting down his license plate.

Five minutes later, Brook closed the apartment door behind him and changed into his black suit. He knotted his black tie loosely then donned his coat and a baseball cap and left the building.

Arriving shortly before the service at St Anne's, Brook parked away from the church for a quick getaway. Discarding his baseball cap onto the back seat, he ambled the few hundred yards to the church through a stiff wind and light rain. Turning the corner, he was surprised to see the size of the crowd - a couple of hundred - huddled under umbrellas, waiting for the coffin to arrive.

Brook assumed most of the adults would be Denise Ottoman's former teaching colleagues and the teenagers, her ex-pupils come to pay their last respects. Some youngsters had worn black though few were soberly dressed. Like all social occasions - even a funeral - it was a chance to impress peers.

A TV crew was filming and interviewing the great and the good of Derby and Brook was glad to be anonymous in the large crowd. The media presence was only to be expected after the Ottomans' dramatic flight to France after the Ingham family killings. Their equally dramatic capture and subsequent exoneration - thanks, largely, to Brook - had also been front-page news.

Looking around the sea of faces, Brook spotted Noble and a few other officers standing apart with Chief Superintendent Charlton. Amongst them was DI Robert Greatorix, fully recovered from his intestinal problems and weighing-in several stones lighter than Brook's memory of him. Greatorix had improved his wardrobe but, next to him, Charlton was even more resplendent in camel coat, black suit, scarf and leather gloves, waiting to be interviewed by the TV crew.

As Brook made his way towards Noble, a couple of photographers spotted him and headed in his direction. His heart sank when he noticed Brian Burton, crime correspondent for the Derby Telegraph, trailing in their wake.

'Inspector Brook,' shouted Burton, alerting others to Brook's presence. 'Any comment on the death of Denise Ottoman?'

The cameras flashed and Brook resisted the urge to put an arm across his face, as though he had something to hide. Charlton had been very specific about giving off-the-cuff interviews and unrehearsed sound bites to reporters so Brook needed no encouragement to keep silent. Indeed, there was still a chance that John Ottoman blamed Derby CID for the stress that preceded his wife's heart attack and any unguarded comments were to be avoided, in case of subsequent legal action.

Brook brushed past the throng of reporters, keeping his mouth closed and eyes trained on his destination but he was slowed by a photographer kneeling in front of him for a picture.

'Inspector Brook,' persisted Burton, shouting after him. 'Do you feel any responsibility for her death?' The question slowed Brook but he kept moving towards Noble and Burton gave up the pursuit.

Brook nodded at assembled colleagues Detective Sergeants Rob Morton and Jane Gadd and Detective Constables Cooper and Bull, all members of the Ingham investigation team. They were huddled in a group, some pulling heavily on cigarettes. Brook spotted DCI Hudson, standing with Greatorix, and gestured a greeting.

'Hello, stranger,' said Noble, lighting a cigarette.

'John.'

'How did it go in Nottingham this morning?'

'Fine. Can I have one of those? Left mine in the car.'

'Fine?' Noble snaked a look at Brook and shook out a cigarette before lighting it for him.

'What can I say? The Chief wants my blood this time.'

'You're fighting it though,' said Noble.

'As much as I can be bothered,' said Brook, inhaling smoke.

'So, I'm stuck with Greatorix,' said Noble.

'He's a fine detective, John.'

'We're at a funeral. Please don't make me laugh.' Brook faked an innocent expression so Noble changed the subject. 'How's Mike Drexler doing?'

'Fine,' said Brook.

'Why not just say *no comment* and have done with it.'

'He's unconscious but stable and they're confident he'll pull through.'

'Some good news then,' said Noble. 'Let's hope he can confirm your story.' Brook looked sharply at him. 'Statement.'

'You can't hurry a gunshot wound, John.'

'No. Any idea why ex-FBI partners were shooting at each other?'

'Not a clue.'

Noble nodded, a thin smile playing around his lips. 'I suppose working closely with someone, there could be a million irritations that can turn into murderous rage.' Brook didn't take the bait. 'Maybe the answers are in Drexler's book,' continued Noble. 'I read it. It's very good. About a case in California in the mid-nineties. California. Where Victor Sorenson had a home.' Brook could feel Noble's gaze on him but kept his eyes front. 'Here's a fun fact,' persisted Noble. 'California is over four hundred thousand square kilometres in size.'

'When does the fun arrive?' said Brook, stone-faced.

'Fun fact number two,' continued Noble, undaunted. 'Sorenson's house on Lake Tahoe is no more than twenty-five miles from the scene of the Ghost Road murders? In a state of that size. How big a coincidence is that? And yet there's not a single mention of Sorenson in Mike's book.'

'Should there be?'

'There should if Drexler and McQuarry interviewed him in 1995.'

Brook looked at Noble and then away. 'And did they?'

'I don't know but Sorenson bought gas and coffee at Caleb Ashwell's service station the same night Ashwell and his son died. There's film of him talking to Ashwell at the station plus a record of a check on his license plate.'

'Is that true?' said Brook.

'I've surprised you? Didn't Mike tell you?'

Brook paused before replying. 'I knew Sorenson had a house in California, John. But will you take my word that I had no idea he'd been interviewed in connection with events in Mike's book?'

Noble stared at Brook's profile. 'If you give it, I'll accept it.' Brook nodded. 'So, what do you think?'

'I don't know,' said Brook. 'I'll have to think about it.'

'In other words, stop asking.'

'It's interesting,' conceded Brook. 'Something to ask Mike when he regains consciousness.'

'We could ask him together,' said Noble. 'Wouldn't that be fun?'

'Joyful,' retorted Brook.

'Speaking of fun, fact number three - George Bailey, father of the last family murdered by the Ashwells, worked for Victor Sorenson's company in California. Another coincidence?' Brook maintained his silence. 'Throw in the fact that this was the last case Drexler and McQuarry ever worked together and you start to see a pattern.'

'I'm all ears,' said Brook.

'I think, whatever Sorenson was trying to hide from a federal investigation, he'd have a much better chance of covering it up if he got his hooks into one of the investigating agents, don't you?'

'Any thoughts on which one?'

'Drexler wrote a book about the case without mentioning Sorenson which seems significant. On the other hand, he killed his ex-partner to save your life so, take your pick.'

'Do you have evidence for any of this?'

'I'm still at the wild speculation stage. That's why it's just between the two of us.'

Brook nodded. 'Good to see your mind is as sharp as ever.'

The hearse drew up outside the church and various cars pulled to a halt behind it. An ashen-faced John Ottoman stepped out of the lead car and five other men in black suits joined him at the rear of the hearse to receive the coffin and carry it into the church.

'What about your mind?' said Noble.

'What about it?'

'How are you getting on with the shooting? Psychologically, I mean.'

'Fine,' said Brook.

'What does the shrink say?'

'We're still at the bedwetting stage,' replied Brook. Noble laughed, then lowered his eyes when a red-eyed mourner turned to the source of levity.

DCI Hudson detached himself from Greatorix and made his way over. When Charlton turned to see where he was going, he caught Brook's eye and nodded coldly before turning away to converse with Greatorix.

Hudson held out his hand which Brook shook firmly. 'Damen.'

'You've come a long way, Joshua,' said Brook. 'No DS Grant?'

'She couldn't make it,' replied Hudson. 'Work.'

'So, no more joint Task Force,' said Brook.

'Afraid not,' said Hudson.

'What *will* we do without you?' said Brook.

'We?' grinned Hudson. 'I thought you were still up shit creek, paddling with your hands.'

'For a while yet.'

'They're taking their sweet time clearing you for duty, aren't they?'

'Somebody died,' said Brook. 'I'll know soon enough.'

'You might sound like you care a bit more,' chipped in Noble.

'What doesn't kill you...' said Hudson.

'You met the new head boy?' said Brook.

'I did,' replied Hudson. 'This Greatorix...I assume he's not as big a wanker as he seems.'

'Assume away,' said Brook.

'Jesus,' muttered Hudson. 'If we couldn't close it out with a fresh trail, laughing boy has no chance. Did you tell him the Ingham killer was a copycat?'

'I brought him up to speed,' muttered Noble. 'For what it was worth.'

'Has he formed any opinions?' said Hudson.

'He's been through the paperwork, seen everything we've seen,' said Noble. 'He was pushing the Ottomans for it.'

'Superficially, they're a good fit,' said Hudson, shrugging. 'Lucky, he has you to set him straight.'

'Lucky for who?' said Noble.

Hudson grinned. 'Come on, John. How much damage can he do to anything other than Charlton's arsehole? If he were up there any further, they'd be Siamese twins.'

'Thanks for that image,' said Brook, grimacing. Noble's amusement was all the greater for Brook's distaste.

Hudson lit a cigarette. 'Ridiculous to hand the enquiry to a DI who's been in bed for a year.'

'Charlton's not a copper,' said Brook. 'He's a politician.'

'The problem with modern policing in a nutshell,' said Hudson. 'Be careful, Damen. Charlton will have your...'

'Chief Superintendent,' called Brook, heading off further comment from Hudson. 'A sad day, sir.' Greatorix stood behind Charlton, an expression of suppressed animosity aimed at Brook.

'How did your interview go this morning?' said Charlton, brusquely.

'Extremely well, sir,' replied Brook.

'Really?' said Charlton. 'So, the polar opposite to your previous Q&A...'

'They're going in,' said Hudson.

Charlton held his tongue and they walked with the crowd towards the church doors. Much to Brook, Noble and Hudson's relief, Charlton peeled off to have a word with a local councillor so the three CID officers ploughed on alone.

As they were about to pass through the church doors, Brook became aware of a rise in noise levels. He followed the shocked expressions and turning heads, past the photographers and TV crew who were sprinting full pelt away from the church.

'What the actual fuck is he doing here?' said a teenage mourner.

Jason Donovan Wallis dismounted from his motorcycle. He wore a shiny black tracksuit top, zipped down to the waist and matching trousers, sporting an embossed gold dragon down one leg. White basketball shoes adorned his feet and scuffed along the ground as he walked. Carrying his helmet, he strutted towards the church, a large grin covering his face when photographers and the TV crew rushed towards him. He slowed to let them gather.

'Jason, what are you doing here?' shouted one reporter.

'Disrespectful little scumbag,' muttered Hudson. 'Has he no shame?'

'Not a single ounce,' said Brook.

'I'm here to pay me respeck to me teacher, Mrs Ottoman,' announced Jason, in his best ghetto accent. 'Despite what she done to me with her lyin', right?'

'Any comment on the charges brought against you?' asked a TV reporter.

'I'm a free man 'cos I dint do nuttin' and that's a fact.'

'And you're not worried you're still a target for the Reaper?'

'I ain't no target for no Reaper. That geezer ghosted me family, but he ain't touch me two times now.'

'But the Reaper *is* still at large,' said Brian Burton.

Jason spied Brook in the crowd and pointed. 'And there's why?'

Reporters and cameras swung towards Brook and hurried across to him, sweeping Jason along in their slipstream.

'Inspector, care to comment on Jason's release from custody?' barked Brian Burton.

'Jason, if you ever had any respect for Denise Ottoman, go home now,' said Brook, staring at the grinning youth. 'This isn't a circus.'

The Resurrection

'I can go where I like, innit?' snarled Jason. 'It's still a free country, yo.'

'You're not going in that church,' said Brook.

'Hear that?' shouted Jason. 'That's me civil liberties bein' took.'

'It's not about civil liberties, it's a public order issue,' said DCI Hudson. 'Mrs Ottoman's family and friends don't want you here.'

A large corn-rowed black teenager in a dark suit squeezed himself to the front of the throng. 'Whyn't you leg it, wigger? This is a funeral, man and you dissing Mrs O.'

'What you say, nigger?' said Jason.

The black teenager tensed and Brook prepared to step between them but Hudson beat him to it.

'Jason Wallis, you have just committed an offence under section eighteen of the 1986 Public Order Act. Incitement to Racial Hatred...'

'No, I never,' snarled Jason.

'Unless you leave immediately,' continued Hudson. 'I'll have no alternative but to arrest you.'

Jason's face hung tough but a placatory grin broke through. 'Didn't mean nuttin' Winston, just chattin' shit, yeah?' He held out a fist to be knuckle tapped.

Winston ignored it and his eyes burned into Jason. 'You ain't no shine, white boy. Whyn't you take your faulty shit and chip, while you still can?'

Jason had a limited ebonics vocabulary but got the gist and, as though it was his idea, he turned to go. At that moment John Ottoman emerged from the church, pushing past his fellow mourners.

'How dare you come here, you filthy animal,' he screamed, pushing harder against the crowd who began to hold his arms to slow his progress. 'You attack my Denise and now you have the gall to dishonour her memory. Get away from here you twisted little pervert.'

'You heard that,' Jason announced to the reporters, holding up a finger. 'I've just been threatened. You heard that.' He grinned, advancing towards Ottoman then grabbed his crotch. 'You want some granddad, come and get it.' More hands grabbed at Jason and the two were held just feet apart. Ottoman was apoplectic in his sudden fury and Jason grinned the harder for it.

A second later, Ottoman wriggled free and got his purple face closer to Jason's. 'I should've finished you that night in Elvaston, when I had the chance,' he hissed. Flailing arms got a stronger grip on the middle-aged man and began to haul him away and, as they turned him back towards the sanctuary of the church, he seemed to stumble and collapse as though his legs could no longer bear him. His shoulders shuddered and the tears began to flow and he was helped away, head down.

The few who heard Ottoman's words failed to understand them. All except Brook, Noble and Hudson, who were well aware that Ottoman had donned a ski mask to stalk Wallis after Jason's assault on his late wife. They also knew that a terrified Jason had mistaken Ottoman for the Reaper and had flung himself down to beg for mercy, emptying his bladder and bowels in the process.

And now, for the first-time, Jason knew too. The grin froze on Jason's face and his eyes darted about in confusion as he realised that John Ottoman - a lightly-built, middle-aged teacher - had been the man who'd terrorised him.

Brook watched comprehension creep over the teenager's pale features and waited, planting himself against the tide of mourners returning to the church.

Jason's eyes flashed towards Brook and Hudson in turn. One glance at the grim smiles on their faces confirmed what he'd just learned from Ottoman and Jason lowered his eyes to the ground, humiliated.

Managing to resurrect a little aggression, Jason shouted in Ottoman's direction. 'I'm glad I...' He managed to stop himself. Balling his knuckles, he turned on his heels and dragged himself away.

∼

AFTER THE SERVICE, the congregation trooped from the church. The weather had worsened which was no bad thing as the crowd dispersed quickly to cars and minibuses. The hearse appeared from the back of the church carrying Denise Ottoman's coffin for the journey to the crematorium and waited by the gate, an empty black limo behind.

Hudson hung back inside the entrance and Brook joined him. 'Are you going to the crematorium?' Brook shook his head so Hudson held out a hand. 'Then I'm heading back to Brighton. Good seeing you, Damen.'

'You too.'

'And best of luck with you know what.'

'Thanks,' said Brook. 'Say hello to DS Grant for me.' Hudson arched an eyebrow. 'Laura.'

'I will. Watch your back.' He stepped out into the downpour, heading for his car.

At that moment, the last of the mourners pushed through the inner doors. John Ottoman and relatives walked with heads bowed, barely registering the professional soothing of the priest. A moment later, Ottoman ushered his relatives towards the limo, thanked the priest then hurried over to Brook. 'Inspector! Can I have a quick word?'

'Of course.'

Ottoman took a deep breath. 'I know you won't believe what I'm about to say, Inspector, but I believe my Denise was murdered.'

Brook was taken aback. 'Mr Ottoman, your wife had a heart attack.'

'Her heart stopped, yes. But she was murdered just the same - literally frightened to death - and I want you to look into it.'

'Sir, I'm sorry you were in custody when your wife died but, at the time, there was solid evidence to suspect you. The timing was...'

'Don't apologise,' said Ottoman, hands up to placate. 'I hold no resentment towards the police. It was my fault I wasn't with my wife. It was my decision to hound Jason, my decision that took me to the Ingham house that night and my fault I became a suspect. If I hadn't done any of that, my Denise...' Ottoman bit down on the rest. 'I know you'll think grief is driving this but you didn't see her. I found her the next day and the look of sheer terror on her face is something I will never ever forget.'

'Sir, with respect, I don't know how many dead bodies you've seen but...'

'Please!' interrupted Ottoman. He stared, glassy-eyed, into the distance to conjure up the memory. 'You didn't see the way her body was hunched up against the wall like she was trying to push through the very bricks to get away from something. Or someone.' He took a set of keys from his coat and held them out. 'I've not been able to go back so I'm staying at my sister's. Please. You were kind to Denise before all this happened. Do this one last thing and have a look at the bedroom in which she died. That's all I ask. If *you* say everything is normal and she died of natural causes, then I'll accept it and move on.'

The funeral limo's horn sounded and Ottoman leaned into the rain to hold up a single digit in its direction. He turned beseechingly to Brook, waiting for a response.

'The coroner...there was never any suggestion of foul play.'

'I'm aware of that,' conceded Ottoman, holding his ground.

Brook sighed, held out his hand, allowing the grateful Ottoman to drop the keys onto his palm.

'Thank you. This means everything.' Ottoman shook Brook's hand and hurried away towards the hearse.

∽

JASON SAT ON HIS BED, staring at the wall. 'Old man Ottoman,' he muttered, remembering that terrible night, running along the river path, running for his life. And all the time it was...

'Old man Ottoman.' It all made sense except for one thing. 'How does an old bastard like that get the balls to go up against me? Stalking me, chasing me down and laughing while I...' He couldn't bring himself to say the words. *While I pissed myself and dumped my sack into my Calvins.* He shuddered at the shame of it.

Another chink of light penetrated his brain and his mouth tightened with fury. 'Brook and that other fucking fossil, Hudson... they knew. They were all in it together. They knew what Ottoman done and they were laughing at me. The old fag must have coughed to it and they gave him a free pass. The cunts were laughing. At me!'

His sudden anger gave way to a grim smile of satisfaction. 'I'm glad I was there to watch your ugly old bitch croak,' he snarled, finally finishing the sentence he'd started at the funeral. 'I'm only gutted her ticker packed in before I could cut her open.' His smile broadened. 'Imagine your face when you found the stiff twat.' His expression hardened. 'Why am I pissing about croaking moggies? That's for kids. Time to get in the game.'

He jumped off the bed and padded downstairs to pull on his rucksack before heading out to the garden to mount his Kawasaki. With his helmet on, he turned the ignition.

14

Brook knocked on Chief Superintendent Charlton's door later that evening.

'Inspector,' said Charlton, not bothering to hide his displeasure. 'I'm just leaving for a meeting...'

'I've come to ask for a return to full-time duty,' said Brook, standing in front of his desk.

Charlton nodded but didn't answer, instead interlacing his fingers on the desk and staring down at them. After nearly a minute, Brook began to feel uncomfortable but resolved not to repeat his request.

Charlton still hadn't forgiven him for his off-the-record briefings during the Ingham investigation. Having chaired the press conference announcing John and Denise Ottoman as prime suspects, it was a personal humiliation for Charlton when Brook's belief in their innocence - communicated to a local journalist - had hit front pages the next day. If anything, the fact Brook had been proved right, only made matters worse.

'My hands are tied,' said Charlton, finally. 'The panel are still weighing the evidence and I can't approve a return until I've had the psychologist's report.'

'Sir, I'm not a novice. I really don't need...'

'How many sessions have you had?'

'Two.'

'Stick with it,' said Charlton, affecting concern. 'You endured a traumatic incident and could've been killed. Symptoms of PTSD don't always present straight after the trauma and, without adequate counselling, you're at risk of flashbacks, nausea and sleep deprivation.'

Brook stared back, granite-faced. 'I sleep like a baby,' he lied. 'My conscience is clear.'

'Good to hear. The science and the GSR test support you,' said Charlton. 'But there were three people present and three guns. You see the problem. Without corroboration, the board feels they cannot yet say, *officially*, that you were an innocent bystander.'

'I've never fired a gun in my life.'

'Your unsupported testimony has no bearing on the panel's deliberations, I'm afraid,' said Charlton. 'Be patient, Inspector. When your statement is confirmed, the Board will sign off on it and, *if* you've completed the required counselling, you'll be back working cases. You've been co-operating fully with investigating officers, I trust?'

'Yes, sir.'

'Good.' Charlton's smile could have frozen water. 'I hope that's clarified the situation for you.'

Brook headed for the door and turned. 'I'm not resigning.'

Charlton stared coolly. 'If you have any more questions about the process, please don't hesitate to ask.'

∼

NEARING MIDNIGHT, Brook sat in the dark, deserted incident room sipping at a vending machine tea and gazing blankly round the display boards filled with photographs. His eye fell on the cluster of pictures recording the Asian wedding reception on the Drayfin Estate, taken in the back garden of a house a few doors down from the Ingham property, just days before it became a crime scene.

His gaze fell on the blurred image of the unknown woman gazing down from the bedroom of Mrs North's empty home, a question mark captioning the photograph. Only Brook knew it was the spectral figure of Edie McQuarry, staring down at the backyard of the Ingham house as she prepared the attack on the family. And now she was dead too.

In another shot, the youngest member of the family, D'Wayne Ingham, sat astride a fence, flicking a V-sign towards the photographer and, according to the bride's testimony from that day, shouting racist insults at the wedding party. Within days, D'Wayne had died at the end of a rope, the two offending fingers of his V-sign removed with a scalpel and placed in his pyjama pocket. He was nine years old.

Brook looked at images of the other victims, their eyes frozen in shock for eternity. Stephen Ingham, D'Wayne's elder brother, sprawling on an old sofa in the yard, throat cut in identical fashion to Ben Anderson and David Gretton. The three friends had gathered to celebrate Jason Wallis's release from a young offender's facility.

Jason had survived, immobilised at the scene without a scratch on him. No, that was inaccurate. Jason hadn't survived, he'd been spared - left for Brook to apply the final cut as an initiation into the warped crusade of Sorenson's Disciple network.

And, after Denise Ottoman's funeral, he had once more been forced to ask himself whether it would have been so wrong to cut the vicious thug's throat and end his toxic existence, instead of granting him another undeserved reprieve? He trudged out of the station, hating himself for even entertaining such a notion.

~

JASON SAT SHIVERING on the groundsheet, in the thick bushes at the back of John Ottoman's overgrown garden, the cold ground under the canvas permeating his young bones. After a vigorous rub of his lean frame to generate warmth, he picked up his aunt's cheap binoculars and did another sweep of the property. The Ottoman house was in complete darkness and the drive stood empty. Prepping to kill Ottoman's bitch had been a lot easier because the pair had bunked off to France for a week to avoid arrest and the entire country knew when they'd been captured and returned to Derby. Jason only had to lie in wait for a couple of hours in the relative warmth of the roof space. Even better, Denise Ottoman had arrived back at the house alone and defenceless.

Jason smiled at remembered pleasures but, thinking of her death throes, he was immediately reminded of the funeral that very morning and old man Ottoman boasting about his campaign of terror.

I should've finished you that night in Elvaston...

Jason scowled at the memory of the night he'd begged

Ottoman for his life, crying like a baby and soiling himself. A volcanic anger swept through him.

'Teachers who fuck with me get fucked up double.'

∼

Outside the station, Brook buttoned up his coat against the elements. Something rattled in his pocket and he pulled out Ottoman's house keys, recalling his foolish promise to the stricken widower. Realising it was one more thing to prey on his mind, Brook drove to the Drayfin Estate and, fifteen minutes later, parked outside John Ottoman's semi-detached home. Stepping out into the cold night, he fixed his gaze on the dark building.

Three years ago, Jason Wallis had sexually assaulted Denise Ottoman in front of a classroom full of pupils and her withdrawal into the prison of victimhood had begun. Since then, the Ottoman's home had been allowed to fall into disrepair where once it had been pristine. Lawns and hedges grew unchecked, paint peeled from dirty window frames and, in case the dirt on the glass wasn't enough, fading curtains shrouded the damaged occupants from the gaze of neighbours.

Brook dragged himself reluctantly up the overgrown path to the front door and unlocked it. Inside, he flicked at a light switch and took a cursory tour of the ground floor. Windows were intact and the house secure with none of the disorder to suggest an intruder had been in the house.

He trotted upstairs to the master bedroom and, from the door, could see little had changed since that night, even by the faint light of a concealed moon. The bed was now bare and the rugs had been removed from the polished floorboards but everything else was the same. He stared at the window beneath which Denise Ottoman had been found. Sensing a problem with her heart and, fighting to breathe, she had dragged herself to the wall in her final moments for no apparent reason. Panic, probably.

The moon appeared from behind a cloud and the room was suddenly bathed in its pale radiance so Brook stepped onto bare boards without switching on the light. In the gloom, he advanced to the bed and sat on the mattress, imagining the poor woman clutching her chest as she felt her breathing shorten. To die alone like that…

The moon disappeared behind clouds and the sudden darkness blinded Brook. It took a moment for his vision to adjust and be able to pick out features in the room.

'Enough,' he mumbled, reaching over to the bedside lamp on a small cabinet to flick at the switch. It didn't work. Pushing himself off the bed, he made his way to the door and felt for the main light switch, flooding the room with its harsh brilliance.

Returning to the lamp, he saw the bulb was missing. Brook sat on the bed, thinking. He pulled out the drawer of the cabinet and found the light bulb. Puzzled, he extracted a pair of thin latex gloves from his coat and snapped them on, before picking up the bulb and examining the filament. It seemed intact. He held the bulb to the light and examined the glass for fingerprints but couldn't detect any with the naked eye. Finally, he fixed the bulb back into the lamp fitting. It worked.

Brook pulled an evidence bag from his pocket and placed the lightbulb inside. Next, he scanned the bare room for potential hiding places where an assailant might lie in wait, moved across to the walk-in wardrobe but stopped in his tracks when the crunch of something dry and dusty cracked under his leather sole.

Stepping back, he knelt to examine the offending grit on the floor which seemed to be a small area of fine debris, scattered in a thin line across the boards. Brook moved his foot over the area to hear the crunch again. A second later his eyes widened and he stood, slowly tilting back his head to look up at the ceiling. Directly above the line of grit was a small hatch allowing access to the roof space.

~

Jason Wallis watched Brook with an increasing dryness in the throat. At the first sign of life in the house, Jason had moved into position, relishing telling Ottoman every detail of his wife's death and embellishing the ebbing of her life for maximum distress. But when he saw Brook standing in the bedroom, his heart almost stopped and he shrank back to watch, a growing dread pulling on his gut.

Eventually, Brook stared up at the trapdoor and Jason could see the grim smile on his face.

'He's fucking sussed it,' Jason panted, his face ashen.

When Brook's face turned from the window, Jason gathered up his groundsheet and scampered out of the bushes, vaulted over the fence into next door's garden and jogged back to his Kawasaki, parked on the adjoining street. He dropped the helmet onto his head, stuffed the groundsheet into the rucksack and straddled the bike, fumbling for his keys. Hand shaking, he started the engine but, a second later, turned it off.

'Brook might know how I done it but he can't know it were me. Not for definite. I was proper careful. Kept my gloves on. And what can they actually do me for? B&E maybe. It's not like I cut the bitch. All I done was jump down out the roof. They can't do me for murder even if they could prove I was there, which they can't because the cunt croaked cos she were fucking ancient.'

Calmed, he reached for the ignition but then an incredible idea occurred to him. He thought it through several times, his features finally creasing with childlike pleasure at the brilliance of it.

∼

LEAVING DRAYFIN, Brook drove through the city towards the A52 and home. The twin emotions of excitement and trepidation rose within him. There *was* something suspicious about Denise Ottoman's death. Somebody else had been in that bedroom, somebody who'd removed the light bulb from the lamp before she got home, somebody who'd hidden in the loft space, waiting for her to fall asleep. Brook remembered the sentence Jason had left unfinished at the funeral when trying to goad John Ottoman.

I'm glad I killed your wife.

But he hadn't killed her. She'd died of a heart attack.

I'm glad I saw the bitch die.

Brook nodded. Better. Jason had attacked Denise Ottoman. The fact that she'd been so terrified that her heart had given out before he could strike, didn't diminish Jason's guilt, in Brook's eyes, at least. A court of law might disagree but Brook didn't doubt Wallis was responsible for Denise Ottoman's death.

Brook pulled up at a red light and yawned deeply and shook himself to concentrate. This was stupid. His cottage was forty-five minutes away and he could barely keep his eyes open. The lights turned green and, after opening a window to freshen the air, Brook hung a right towards the town centre.

Moments later, he parked beneath Magnet House and jogged quietly up to the top floor and let himself in, threw off his coat and went straight to the small bedroom where exhaustion overwhelmed him and he fell into a deep sleep.

~

Jason was home to Borrowash even later and glad to see his aunt had already left for her night shift at the hospital. She'd left him a strongly worded note about his responsibilities towards Bianca, even though she was fast asleep in her cot. He crumpled the note and tossed it on the kitchen floor so the nagging cow would see what he thought of her notes.

'Ain't no babysitter, bitch.' He opened the fridge to take out his meal but couldn't see anything plated up and nothing in the oven either. 'The fuck am I supposed to eat?' he seethed, slamming the oven door shut. He returned to the fridge, empty except for a half dozen bottles of his aunt's favourite lager and a carton of milk. He dragged a couple of Stellas from the shelf and opened them both.

In the lounge, he sat watching TV and chugging on his beer but with only sixteen channels to surf, he was soon bored. He drained the second beer and left the bottles on the floor before hauling himself across the room to see if there was any vodka left in the drinks' cupboard. He could see it through the glass, padlocked by his aunt to put a stop to his nocturnal foraging.

He smiled, pulling out a drawer from above the cabinet. The key was blu-tacked to the underside of the drawer and, without her knowledge, he'd been swilling her vodka for weeks and replacing the missing liquid with water from the tap. And because she drowned her vodka in tonic, she never even twigged.

Jason felt around the underside of the drawer for the key. While he groped, his eye was drawn to the document on top of a pile of papers. It was a receipt for the Kawasaki. Jason pulled out the drawer and placed it on the cabinet and picked up the document, an unfamiliar emotion tugging at him - guilt.

The bike had cost £1,995 nearly new from the dealer. 'Two grand,' he said, whistling. He was touched. Despite her nagging, his aunt must think a lot of him if she'd splashed out two grand to make his eighteenth special. He went to put the receipt back in the drawer, all thought of raiding the drinks cabinet forgotten.

About to drop the paper onto the pile, he caught sight of the document below and, as he read it, his face turned to granite. The letterhead was that of the Criminal Injuries Compensation

Authority. And there were other papers below which further soured Jason's mood - insurance papers. He read through them, his mood darkening. Angrily, he yanked the padlock key from its berth and took a long draught of the half bottle of watered-down vodka while he skimmed the documents.

'What the absolute...'

15

December 13th 2010

Brook woke early the next morning feeling refreshed but knew he shouldn't have slept in the flat. It had been a stupid risk and one he wouldn't repeat. Sooner or later, the Disciples were going to investigate McQuarry's death and when that time came, the flat would be their first port of call. Bad enough that he was inextricably linked to McQuarry's demise but spending time at the epicentre of the Reaper's activities in Derby was pure folly.

So, he pulled on latex gloves and retraced all his movements around the apartment, wiping down any objects or surfaces that he might have touched. When finished, he took out the phone Laura had sent him. It had a built-in camera so, when he'd worked out how to use it, he spent ten minutes photographing the apartment's contents, assuming that at some point the Disciples would purge the flat.

Finally, he pocketed Laura's confession and, when satisfied he'd removed all traces of his presence, fired up the computer to key in the password again. Moments later, the encrypted webpage had loaded its melodramatic countdown. Brook took a few pictures, moved the mouse around until the cursor indicated a link then pressed enter. A prompt flashed in a dialogue box and Brook flicked randomly at the key board.

As soon as Brook's finger had tapped the return key, cyber flames began to burn at the edges of the screen and the image began to degrade. A firewall had been activated and the laptop's secrets were being consumed by a virus.

'If only that could be the end of it,' he mumbled, wiping the keyboard clean before locking the flat and leaving.

∾

JASON WALLIS WATCHED from beneath the anonymity of his motorcycle helmet as the electric gate of Magnet House slid smoothly back. A second later, a black BMW emerged from beneath the building and turned towards the city. Jason couldn't make out the driver but having followed the same car from the Drayfin Estate the previous night, he already knew Brook was behind the wheel. Better yet, Jason had seen Brook turn on a light in an upstairs flat and knew exactly which property it was and now, having returned to the building properly tooled up, he was ready to go to work.

∾

BROOK WALKED through the main entrance of St Mary's Wharf clutching a bagged bacon sandwich, a cup of tea and the evidence bag with the light bulb removed from Ottoman's bedroom cabinet. He marched into the Incident Room where half a dozen CID officers were working, Noble among them. Seeing Brook, the low hum of activity dropped as he opened his bacon sandwich and took a generous bite, ignoring the six pairs of eyes flicking between Brook and DI Robert Greatorix.

Brook approached, swallowing a mouthful of sandwich. 'Bob, good to see you back. You look fit and well. Sorry we didn't get a chance to speak at the funeral.'

'Brook?' Greatorix considered him coldly. 'You do know this is the Incident Room for the Ingham enquiry, right?'

'It's like a second home,' said Brook. 'Just popped round to book in some Forensics.' He pulled the bagged light bulb from his pocket.

'You shouldn't be in here when you're under suspension,' said Greatorix.

Brook smiled as the silence deepened. 'I'm not on suspension, Bob. Somebody tried to kill me so I'm on light duty until I stop crying myself to sleep.' A snigger rippled round the room.

Greatorix glanced round, miffed at Brook's apparent rise in popularity. 'Well, until you get a clean bill of health on the McQuarry shooting, this enquiry and *this* room are off-limits. This is my case now so, if you don't mind, I have a murderer to catch.'

'And my Forensics?'

Greatorix flicked a glance at the bagged light bulb. 'I don't want it in here.' He grinned suddenly. 'But if you're struggling for something to do, there *is* a case that could use your immediate attention.'

'I'm all ears.'

'The Borrowash Cat Strangler,' laughed Greatorix, surveying his colleagues for appreciation. He cast eyes around his desk before picking up a piece of A4 and thrust it at Brook. 'Here. This is more your level.'

'Sir...' warned Noble.

'Seems someone's been killing local moggies out in the sticks. Maybe you'll have more luck with that than you do with real killers.' Greatorix beamed at Brook, puzzled at his sombre expression and surprised when he accepted the sheet and began to read it.

'I'll get right on it, Bob,' said Brook. 'Thanks.' Brook stabbed a glance towards Noble and headed for the door, clutching the evidence bag and the rest of his sandwich.

'Don't mention it,' snorted Greatorix. When Brook had gone, Greatorix turned to the room. 'The poor fucker's finally lost it.'

∼

IN HIS OFFICE, Brook slid the bagged light bulb into a drawer, while he reread the report about the strangled cats of Borrowash. The door opened.

'You should've told me, John,' said Brook.

'I was going to but I thought you might do something you shouldn't.'

'This is Jason Wallis, isn't it?' said Brook, waving the paper.

'You don't know that.'

'Don't I? He lives in Borrowash with his aunt on the same road this cat was killed.'

'You've no proof he's involved.'

'No, but I will have. It was only a matter of time. The Jasons of this world don't change their spots.'

'What are you going to do?'

'I'm going to bring the vicious little sod to book before he becomes a full-blown psychopath.'

'For strangling cats?' said Noble.

'Chapter one of the serial killer playbook - experimenting on household pets and animals is how their psychosis develops. This is how they express their need to kill and history tells us he won't stop there.'

'You're being over dramatic.'

'Jason is a violent criminal, John. He's got to be stopped.'

'In your situation...'

'My situation?'

'Your position with Charlton. Your career...'

Brook laughed. 'When have I ever cared about that?'

'Not nearly enough,' said Noble. 'But, when you can't put bad people in prison any more, you *will*.'

'You saw Jason at the funeral,' said Brook. 'And what he did to *my* cat.'

'You have no proof...'

'I'll find it, John.' Brook considered him. 'There's something else. Jason killed Denise Ottoman.'

'What? She died of a heart attack.'

'She died of fright.'

'You're not serious.'

'Jason was there, *in* the bedroom, when Denise died. I know it. He went there to kill her but she had a massive coronary before he could strike.'

'Which would make it manslaughter, at best, even if by some fluke you could ever prove it. Is there any evidence he was there?'

'Somebody was,' said Brook. 'Look, I was sceptical too but Ottoman gave me the key, made me promise to look over the property.'

'And you went?'

'I didn't feel I could refuse after everything he's been through and I only agreed to put his mind at rest. But when I got there, I realised he was right - someone was hiding in the roof above the bedroom. Grains of debris had fallen on the floorboards when the hatch was moved...'

'Is this a joke?'

'Denise went home alone while we interviewed her husband,' said Brook. 'Someone removed a working light bulb from a bedside lamp so that when he made his move, she was in the dark and helpless.'

'And you think it was Jason?' said Noble. 'Pure speculation.'

'Doesn't mean I'm wrong.'

'Okay, say you're right. What are you going to do?'

Brook hesitated. 'Something.'

'No, you're not because there's nothing you can do. And why is it even up to you?'

'Because I'm responsible,' shouted Brook. 'Twice now, I've...' He looked away.

'Twice now you've what?'

Brook took a breath. 'Twice I've watched him walk away from the Reaper's knife and now he thinks he's invincible. He's got to be stopped.'

'How?'

'I'll find a way.'

'This is a very bad idea. Greatorix should never have given you that report.'

'No, you should.'

'This is exactly why I didn't. Promise you won't do anything stupid.'

'Do I ever?'

'All the bloody time.' Noble sighed, held out a hand. 'Give me the light bulb.' Brook raised an eyebrow, retrieved it from the desk and handed it over. 'If I walk it through the lab and it's clean, will you put this nonsense to bed?'

Brook smiled but declined to answer.

~

JASON STARED through the glass-fronted entrance hall of Magnet House. After a few minutes, he saw a young woman descending the stairs so he leaned into the intercom to mime pressing a button. When the girl opened the door of the building, Jason shouted at the speaker, 'No problem. Second floor, yeah?' He stepped smartly inside before the security door closed.

A minute later he was on the top floor, looking at the doors deciding which was the right flat. One of the doors on the west side had the initials PH on the nameplate. Jason hesitated. Maybe Brook had been to a different flat. He trotted quietly to the top of the stairs to check his bearings again. It was the right door.

'Brook don't live here,' he said. 'So, maybe he's got some little squeeze on tap, the dirty old fucker.' He grinned maliciously, rapping on the door. 'Well, if he can get some, I can get some.'

After waiting in vain, he swung his rucksack to the ground and took out a key ring with a dozen different bump keys. He looked at the five-pin lock and selected the appropriate key before easing it into the cylinder then took out a hammer head and tapped the body of the key, turning it sharply at the same time. Jason felt the lock give and pushed the door back, stepping quickly inside and closing the door behind him.

'Anyone home?' No reply. In fact, there didn't seem to be anyone living there and the whole place seemed like it was for storage. There were no chairs and no TV, just a load of stacked boxes and crates. Nice mountain bike though.

'I'm having that,' he said, not immediately thinking how he'd get it home with his Kawasaki in the street below.

He put his helmet on one of the boxes and pulled on his aunt's marigolds from the rucksack then put his hand in a large cardboard box to lift out a demijohn of a colourless liquid. He unscrewed the top and took a sniff but it didn't smell like booze.

He opened another box and pulled out a bottle of red wine. *More like it.* He looked at the label. It had foreign writing on it, French probably, but it was called St George. Didn't make sense.

He put two bottles of wine in his rucksack and inspected the mountain bike but realised he'd have to leave it behind. He could always come back for it on foot but it wasn't like he needed it now he had the Kawasaki.

Moving into the small bedroom, he saw the computer. Too big to carry but that was something else he could come back for. Next, he examined the shelf of CDs without seeing anything he liked. It was all classical shit. Beethoven, Wagner, Mahler. Jason picked up the Mahler CD and opened it. The case was empty. He stared at the cover - Mahler's Ninth - and felt there was something familiar about it, without really knowing why.

Replacing the case, he moved into the kitchen and opened the fridge. There was nothing to eat and only a small bottle of spring water in the door. He opened the freezer compartment and found several packets of what looked like burgers and sausages from a butcher in Normanton. Again, Jason stared, knowledge that wouldn't surface tugging at him as he picked up a packet of sausages and dropped them into his rucksack.

Finally, rummaging through the kitchen units, he was confronted by an open box of scalpels and the elusive knowledge poured into Jason like a litre of Diamond White on a Saturday bender. 'Fuck. Me. This is...'

He picked up another bottle of the wine from the case and studied the label. 'That was on the mantelpiece in our house, the night the Reaper done Kylie and my parents...' He ran into the bedroom and pulled the CD case from the shelf. Mahler's Ninth. 'That was playing on the CD when the bastard cut their throats. And he done it with one of them scalpels.'

He wrenched open another drawer to find a box of bagged hypodermic syringes then ran into the living room and glared at the large demijohn of colourless liquid. 'And I bet this is the drug that put Stinger's mum under. Mine too. And my dad.' He stared, open-mouthed, rooted to the spot, heart pounding like a jackhammer. 'Fuck. Me.'

He hurried back to the kitchen and threw open the freezer. 'Them packets of meat are what we had at Stinger's barby, the night the Reaper done him, Banger and Grets.' Jason put a hand to his brow. 'Shit! Brook is the fucking Reaper! No wonder he hasn't made an arrest.' His expression turned to anger. 'You killed my parents, you smarmy cunt. You killed my sister and my mates.' His breathing was harsh and laboured and he took a few moments to calm down.

His breathing back to normal, he began to piece it together and when he'd finished, he pulled out his mobile to dial 999 and blow the place wide open. He tapped the first key then paused, pocketing his phone when an even better idea occurred. After thinking it through, a smile cracked his features and, decided on his course, he set to work.

He replaced the pack of sausages in the freezer but helped himself to a brand-new scalpel. He emptied the small water bottle from the fridge then filled it up with some of the colourless liquid from a half empty demijohn. He tightened the cap, put the water bottle into his rucksack and replaced the demijohn in the box. Next, he helped himself to a brand-new syringe, still in its plastic wrapper before, in the bedroom, he selected a CD from someone called Wagner and dropped the case into his rucksack, after checking the disc was inside.

Exploring further he examined under the kitchen sink and pulled out a large bin bag full of protective suits, gloves and masks - the kind used by CSIs at crime scenes. *Result.* He picked one close to his size and replaced the rest.

Finally, he returned one of the bottles of wine, retaining the other, then stood at the door to survey the scene. Everything looked the same as when he arrived. Confident his visit would go undetected, he grinned with anticipation, donned his helmet and left the flat.

∽

BROOK SAT in his car with the phone he used for contacting Laura. Instead of selecting her number on speed dial, he entered one from a scrap of paper and was connected seconds later.

'DS Tyson.'

'DS Tyson, it's DI Brook.'

'Brook?' exclaimed Tyson. *'What the hell are you doing? How did you get this number?'*

'I'm a trained detective.'

'That doesn't excuse...'

'I need to see you. Alone.'

'Is this a joke?' exclaimed Tyson. *'Speaking to me outside an interview suite would be completely inappropriate.'*

'This has nothing to do with the shooting,' said Brook. 'It's about the Reaper.'

There was a brief silence at the other end of the line. *'What about the Reaper?'*

'Your cold case review with DCI Fulbright. I need details.'

'You've got a nerve. Goodbye and don't ring this number again.'

'Wait, Kelly! Listen.' Brook wasn't sure how to proceed but opted for honest supplication. 'The Reaper was *my* case and it nearly killed me. Every copper has a case they can't forget, one that will haunt them to the grave unless they close it. I need to know what happened two years ago.'

'Look. We were just asked to go over case notes and maybe do a re-interview where possible. We didn't find anything new.'

'It didn't strike you as an incredible coincidence that the Reaper struck in Derby shortly afterwards?'

'*Perhaps, but I don't know what I can say that's going to change anything.*'

'Will you let me be the judge of that?'

'*No,*' she replied. '*Given our current relationship, if anyone found out we spoke, I'd be completely compromised. There's no way I could justify...*'

'The Reaper is still killing people!' said Brook. 'That's your justification.'

'*I don't see how talking to me can help,*' said Tyson, in the tone of someone persuading herself.

'No detail too small,' said Brook. 'Please. I won't mention the shooting or breathe a word about our meeting to a living soul. You have my word.'

A pause followed by a sigh. '*Where?*'

'Wherever's best for you.' Brook listened while Tyson selected a time and location. 'I'll be there.'

16

Same day - Brighton

Detective Sergeant Laura Grant adjusted her baseball cap and walked up the beach towards the promenade steps. Behind her wraparound sunglasses, she trained her gaze on the double fronted window on the second floor of the sturdy apartment building, facing out across the English Channel.

She had to know. This was no way to live, always looking over her shoulder, waiting for her past to catch up with her. For the second time in her thirty-years on this planet, Grant had resigned herself to the end of her life. Not raped, murdered and buried in a shallow grave in a remote Californian forest but incarcerated for decades, her career as a police officer in tatters. As Nicole Bailey, Victor Sorenson had saved her from her fate in California. As Laura Grant, her second demise had been averted by Damen Brook - a policeman Edie McQuarry had insisted was weak and corrupt.

She hadn't asked for the chance Brook had given her and, honestly, she knew she didn't deserve it. But, as Brook had risked his own future to save hers, there was no going back. She'd left Derby the same day, never to see Brook again and, in some ways, that was the hardest part. She'd finally found someone who could take Sorenson's place, a mentor who carried the same submerged pain and whose battle against the darkness, she found profoundly compelling.

Jogging up the smooth, damp steps, she sat on a bench facing the sea, kicked off her training shoes and casually knocked out the sand. Her shoes refastened, she stood, her course decided and looked over her shoulder again.

'Stop. Doing. That.'

She crossed the road, heading for McQuarry's apartment building which, like the Derby flat, had been acquired by Sorenson as a safe harbour for members of the network and a home for any equipment they might need for projects like Tony Harvey-Ellis. When McQuarry's fate was known, the Disciples would have a simple choice - purge all evidence from the apartment *or* contact her to find out what had gone wrong in Derby. As no communication had been attempted, Grant had drawn her own conclusions.

At the entrance hall door, she held a key card to the sensor and the door buzzed her through into the lobby. Inside, she marched, head-down, to the carpeted stairs and sprinted up to the second floor. At the door to the apartment, she extracted a second key card and pushed it into a slot next to the handle. Panting, she pushed the heavy door open and stepped quickly inside, closing it behind her.

She saw at once the apartment had been completely gutted. There was no computer, no furniture, no bed, no boxes of hypodermics, drugs, scalpels, nothing. Even the carpet and curtains had been removed. The place where she and McQuarry had planned the murder of Tony Harvey-Ellis was a shell.

She checked other rooms but it was the same story. In the bathroom, she detected the odour of a chemical agent, something to eradicate hair and skin samples and deep clean the sink and shower trap. All evidence of occupation had been painstakingly erased.

She took out her burner phone and thumbed out a text to Brook.

They know. EMs flat cleared and cleaned. They're not coming back. L.

A moment later, Brook replied. *You shouldn't be there. Dangerous. Get out and never return. You're in the clear. Live your life. D.*

Absolving myself not top priority. U know that.

It should be. Find a balance and take care. D.

Grant smiled, wishing she could see Brook's craggy features. She pocketed the phone, left the apartment and hurried down the stairs and out onto the busy Brighton seafront, dropping both key cards into a bin. The breeze blowing in from the channel carried a cold bite so she jogged away from the building to keep warm. She didn't see the man in the mirrored shades sit up in the driver's seat of a dark Mercedes and didn't hear him start the car and set off in leisurely pursuit.

∼

'You'll get the hang of it, Laura,' said Brook, pocketing his phone. 'Says the man who's spent twenty years trying.'

With time to kill before his meeting with Tyson, Brook locked his car and strolled along Station Road in the village of Borrowash, a few miles east of Derby. Approaching Jason Wallis and baby Bianca's new home, Brook stared at the dark house but kept moving.

A hundred yards further on, Brook opened the gate onto an overgrown front garden and knocked on the door of the house after a sensor illuminated his arrival. A woman, forty years old, with short black hair and red-rimmed eyes, answered.

'Amanda O'Neill?' asked Brook, brandishing his ID. She stared in disbelief. 'I'm here about the death of your cat.' Saying the words made Brook feel ridiculous and, despite her grief, he could see that O'Neill experienced the same frisson of comic absurdity.

'A Detective Inspector?' she said. 'For my Percy. And the Reaper man, at that.' At Brook's raised eyebrow, she added, 'It is you, isn't it? From the news. That serial killer taking out families on the Drayfin Estate.'

'It's me,' he said.

'This is a bit of a comedown, isn't it?'

'No. Just a different kind of serial killer.'

'So, he's done this before, has he? Killed other cats?'

'He has. And not just in Borrowash.'

'You'd better come in.'

Brook followed her into the neat red-bricked semi-detached house, too fussily furnished for his liking but then so was a monk's cell. In the front room, Brook refused a chair but accepted the offer of a hot drink.

While she was out of the room making tea, Brook wandered

around, noticing all the cat paraphernalia - the padded basket in front of a small wood burner, brightly-coloured balls with bells on, scratching posts. On the mantelpiece, Percy pictures proliferated. Percy in her owner's arms, Percy sniffing at the camera, Percy asleep upside down, paws in the air, in front of a roaring fire.

O'Neill returned with two cups. 'Thank you,' said Brook, taking a sip. He nodded towards the mantelpiece. 'I'm sorry.'

'You have no idea.'

'Actually, I do. My cat was killed too.'

'Well, my Percy was murdered. Then left by the front door for me to find so the little shit could watch my reaction and enjoy my torment. I swear if it's the last thing I do, I'll get even with that vicious fucker.'

'So, you know who did it,' asked Brook.

'Oh, yes.' O'Neill's face soured at the mere thought of him. 'Jason Wallis. He lives down the street.' She noted Brook's placid reaction. 'You don't seem surprised. No, why would you? You must know all about him. That was him involved in those killings a few weeks back, wasn't it?'

'It was.'

'Shame he didn't get his throat cut too.'

'How do you know he killed Percy?'

'I just do, okay.'

'Please. Any insight could help us build a case.'

'A case?' she scoffed. 'Yeah, right.'

'Please,' persisted Brook. 'I *will* pursue this.'

O'Neill took a deep breath. 'Shortly after he moved in with his aunt, I caught him having a piss in my garden - literally spraying his scent over the neighbourhood. So, I went out to show my disapproval and he looked at me like I was insane. Told me to go back inside before I got hurt. I mean his aunt's house is fucking yards away and he pisses in my garden.'

She shook her head. 'What's happened to people, Inspector? When you so much as suggest they treat you and your property with a bit of respect, they look at you as if you're mad. Like any attempt to curb their behaviour is an infringement of their human rights or something.' She laughed again but reached up her sleeve for a balled-up handkerchief and dabbed it against the corner of an eye.

'According to the report, Percy's neck was broken.'

'Yes,' said O'Neill, croaking out the words. 'So, what are you going to do about it?'

'Whatever I can,' said Brook. 'Unfortunately, there's only so much we can do without the body.'

'That's what I figured,' said O'Neill, gesturing Brook to follow her. In the kitchen she gestured towards the utility room. 'In there.' She folded her arms, before turning away, distraught. Puzzled, Brook stepped into the utility room and glanced back at O'Neill. 'He's in the freezer.'

∽

NOBLE STARED at Brook then back at the bag-for-life containing Percy's frozen corpse then at the astonished faces of DI Greatorix and the rest of the squad.

'Are you completely off your fucking trolley, Brook?' laughed Greatorix.

'If I am, what does that say about your judgement?' said Brook.

'Beg pardon?' snorted Greatorix.

'You gave me the case, Bob,' said Brook. 'I've done what you asked, interviewed the victim and gathered the evidence. Isn't that what you wanted?'

'What I wanted?' repeated Greatorix, as though unable to grasp Brook's meaning. 'This is a joke, right?'

'Far from it.'

'You expect me to sign off on forensics for a dead cat?'

'His name was Percy.'

'Do you have any idea what tests on *Percy* would cost?' said Greatorix.

'There's a price on justice now?'

'You're damn right there is,' snarled Greatorix. 'And the Chief Super would blow a gasket if he knew you were even *thinking* about putting a cat in for tests.'

'That's because he's a bean counter,' said Brook. 'But we're seasoned detectives who know a bit about the sharp end of the job.'

'The budget only stretches so far, Brook.'

'Not far enough to catch a killer?'

'What killer?'

'Jason Wallis killed Percy,' said Brook.

'Wallis?'

'After his parents were killed, he moved to his aunt's house in Borrowash,' chipped in Noble.

'Percy was killed a few doors up from her house,' said Brook. 'By Jason Wallis.'

'How do you know?' said Greatorix.

'He's local and he's got previous.'

'That doesn't prove anything.'

'This might,' said Brook, holding up the shopping bag. 'Now if you'll just...'

'I am not authorising forensics on...that,' said Greatorix. 'I suggest you get it out of here and stop wasting my time. I've got a proper killer to catch.'

Brook stared at Greatorix then picked up the bag. 'You don't get it, do you, Bob?'

'What?'

'What the public out there want from us.'

'Enlighten me,' snarled Greatorix.

'Haven't you ever wondered why the Reaper is so popular amongst law-abiding citizens?'

'Are you serious?' exclaimed Greatorix.

'Scum in fear, the Reaper's near!' said Noble.

'Come again?' said Greatorix.

'It's a slogan,' chipped in DC Cooper. 'On a sign carried by a neighbour picketing outside the Ingham crime scene.'

'The Reaper had just wiped out the family and the locals were celebrating,' added Noble.

'You see, Bob,' continued Brook. 'Ordinary people don't worry about what the Chief Super or the Home Secretary worry about. Armed robbery? Blaggers coming up against us or professional security guards. Murder? Very unlikely to happen to most people. No, what taxpayers who pay our wages worry about is the small stuff that never crosses our desks. The stuff that, if it fell into your lap, you'd be asking how it got there - a scratched car, a smashed window...'

'A dead cat?' scoffed Greatorix.

'Percy,' insisted Brook.

'You're nuts,' said Greatorix.

'We covered that.'

'You don't know what you're talking about, Brook,' sneered Greatorix.

'Don't I? Ask the people forced to live on the same street as

Wallis and the Ingham kids. People forced to put up with yobs urinating through their letterbox or slashing their tyres or torching their bins. People who don't dare go out at night because they might get abused and, if they protest, get a broken window or take a beating. I'm talking about people affected by crimes *we* don't even want to record, Bob - people like Amanda O'Neill who have their cats killed for fun, for the thrill of seeing the owner suffering.'

'This is ridiculous...' said Greatorix.

'Jason Wallis killed Amanda O'Neill's cat because she disrespected him,' said Brook. 'His DNA may be on the cat's body. I found cigarette butts in the garden where he hid to see her reaction. His DNA may be on those too.'

'So, we put him away to protect the neighbourhood cats?' laughed Greatorix.

'We do our job, yes,' said Brook.

'Wasting time on petty offences?'

'They're not petty to those on the receiving end,' said Noble. 'They make people feel vulnerable.'

'You're defending this shit, Johnny?' demanded Greatorix. 'Why am I not surprised? Far as I'm concerned, this...crap shouldn't even be in the stats. It's not important.'

'Not to you,' said Brook. 'But because it matters to ordinary people, it matters to the Reaper so, *if* you're in charge of hunting him, you need to remember that.'

'Fuck off, Brook!' snapped Greatorix. 'You had your chance and you blew it - more than once.'

'Sir, that's unfair...' began Noble.

'Tough,' said Greatorix, turning a baleful eye to his sergeant. 'Now get out of my incident room, Brook. Feel free to worry about petty slags like Wallis until the cows come home. Just keep out of my way so the grown-ups can catch the real criminals.'

There was a crackling silence as officers in the room smelled blood, their eyes darting between Brook - his face expressionless - and the sneering Greatorix.

Finally, Brook's visage broke into a mocking smile and he carried the bag containing Percy's frozen remains towards the door. Breaths had just started to be taken when Brook turned.

'If you were a decent detective, Bob, you'd know that most serial killers are petty criminals first. In fact, they're serial offenders *before* they kill. Look at any convicted serial killer's jacket and you'll find violent acts committed against animals and smaller children. That's how they warm up.'

'Fuck off,' seethed Greatorix, pointing the way.

'I'm going,' replied Brook softly. 'But just so you know, if you ever swear at me again, I'll punch your lights out.'

∼

'IT WAS ALL I could do not to applaud and the rest of the squad feel the same,' said Noble, clutching an unlit cigarette. 'Useless fat prick.'

Brook raised a finger to Noble. 'John. Controlling your mind is...'

'Says the man who threatened to punch a DI's lights out.'

Brook's expression soured. 'I did, didn't I? That wasn't too clever. I suppose he's filing a complaint in Charlton's office right now.'

'I know for a fact he isn't.'

'How come?'

'Because not a single member of his team heard it,' said Noble. 'Shocking acoustics in that room, don't you think?'

Brook stared at Noble before breaking into a smile. 'The worst.'

'So, what will you do now?'

'Greatorix gave a me a case to investigate...'

'I'm serious.'

'So am I.'

'You didn't seriously expect him to approve forensics on a dead cat, did you?'

'Not for a second,' said Brook. 'But I thought I'd give him the chance to make it official and save me some money.'

'You're going to pay for the tests yourself?'

'You bet I am. You saw Wallis at the funeral. The boy's a cancer on decent society and I intend to cut him out.'

Noble's features hardened. 'You shouldn't be talking like that.'

'Why?' demanded Brook. 'Jason Wallis has blighted too many lives and one day soon he's going to put himself in harm's way.'

'And when he screws up, we'll be there to put him away.'

Brook shook his head. 'I'm not prepared to wait until someone dies.'

'You're starting to worry me.'

'Maybe I'm having another breakdown.'

'Not funny.'

'Not laughing.'

Noble frowned. 'Look, if I sign the moggy through forensics will you ease up on this apocalyptic avenger stuff?'

Brook grinned and handed over the plastic bag. 'Thought you'd never ask.'

Noble sighed. 'Played like a fiddle.'

17

Brook sipped his Flat White and looked around the near-deserted Costa Coffee section of Trowell Services. M1 service stations weren't the cheeriest places to linger on a cold winter's night and Tyson was late - nearly twenty minutes. As motorway traffic was light at this late hour, he wondered if she'd had second thoughts.

Ten minutes later, as Brook prepared to leave, he saw her pacing across the empty car park, heading for the coffee shop. She managed a frosty nod in his direction and he sprang up to take her order as she pulled up a chair.

'You found it then,' she said, when Brook carried over a huge mug of frothy coffee.

'I'd almost given up on you.'

'I nearly didn't come,' she said.

'I understand. I assure you this meeting stays between the two of us. I'm only interested in the Reaper.'

'Mention anything related to the shooting and I'm out the door and straight to my boss to report your approach,' said Tyson.

'You have my word.'

She took a sip of coffee. 'You do realise what I know about the Reaper is a drop in the ocean compared to you.'

'Every detail I can get is important if we're ever going to stop the killing.'

'I thought a copycat killed the Ingham family.'

'Maybe. But the crime scene, MO, location and victimology

were all suggestive of previous killings so there's a strong link to the Reaper.'

'As there would be if it was a copycat.'

'You can never be sure of anything where the Reaper's concerned. He's endlessly adaptable to different surroundings, different circumstances...'

'Whereas other serials put their faith in the ritual,' said Tyson. 'I know the drill. You sound like you're still on the case.'

'Every hour of every day,' said Brook.

'If it weren't for your disciplinary problems...'

'I thought we weren't going there.'

'Sorry.'

'Don't be,' said Brook. 'If you're ever going to be a half-way decent detective, disciplinary problems are part of the landscape.' He studied her. 'Are you recording this conversation?'

'Seriously?' demanded Tyson. 'Why would you even think that?'

'Because you've taken a chance meeting me but now you seem to be avoiding the subject.'

'I've got a lot to lose,' said Tyson.

'I understand but if you won't accept my assurances...'

Tyson slammed her mug on the table and got to her feet. 'This was a mistake.'

'Fine,' said Brook, making no move to stop her. 'Go. But if you leave now, whatever questions *you* have about the Reaper will go unanswered.'

Tyson hesitated. 'Questions?'

'Yesterday you threw your case review at me like a javelin, hoping for a reaction,' said Brook. 'It's why you agreed to meet. Everyone who goes up against a killer like the Reaper ends up every bit as hooked as I am.'

Tyson studied him. 'It's a fascinating case.'

'I know,' said Brook. 'The crime scenes stay with you and the way the victims die. I could retire on a fat pension tomorrow but I'd only spend my days dwelling on the case. Catching the Reaper is the only way to avoid that.'

Tyson nodded and eased back into her chair. 'And whoever catches him becomes a legend.' She hesitated over her next utterance.

'As does whoever *fails* to catch him,' said Brook. 'It's okay to say it. I won't burst into tears. The Reaper has beaten me more than once and every detective who gets close thinks they can do better.' He smiled. 'But they never do.'

'You're famous at least,' said Tyson.

'Famous for failure,' said Brook. 'And nowhere more so than in the job. There's a long line of coppers who'll tell you I was never up to the task, DCI Fulbright among them.'

'How do you know that?'

'Because he told me so, when I went back to London.'

'He wasn't your biggest fan, it's true. I gather you had history, all the way back to the first attack in Harlesden.'

'What did he say?'

'Just that. Care to enlighten me.'

Brook considered his options and decided talking about the old days might loosen Tyson's tongue. 'Twenty years ago, Fulbright was in uniform, on crowd control in Harlesden when I was DS to Charlie Rowlands. When the Wallis family went under the knife, two years ago, I went back to London to check out old leads...'

'You mean Victor Sorenson,' said Tyson.

'Amongst others,' said Brook. 'Fulbright accused me of pursuing a vendetta, suggested I'd gone off the deep end, that I'd staged Sorenson's suicide to close a case I couldn't solve.'

'You *did* stalk him for a year after the Harlesden killing.'

'You know about that?' said Brook.

'I became aware of it though not from the case files.'

'So, Fulbright got hold of my personnel file.'

'Sorry.'

Brook shrugged. 'I'd have done the same.'

'So, what about it?'

'Sorenson was the Reaper. I couldn't prove it so, yes, I stalked him. I had no complaints about Fulbright suspecting me. It was a fair line of enquiry - obsessed copper seeks vengeance against an old foe.'

'And, did you? Stage his death, I mean.'

'No,' said Brook. 'And Fulbright couldn't prove I had.'

'Especially as Sorenson's deathbed confession exonerated you,' said Tyson.

'Fulbright and his attack dog, Ross, gave me a good grilling just the same.'

'He said you were very sure of yourself,' said Tyson. 'The word he used was unreachable.'

'I wish. The London killings cost me my marriage and very nearly my sanity.'

'But not your career.'

'I managed to salvage that,' said Brook. 'They cobbled together a transfer to Derby to a chorus of disapproval from local officers.' He smiled at the memory. 'I can't say I blame them. A mentally unstable officer, unfit for the Met, transferred to another division - what message does that send?'

'What's always intrigued me is why the Reaper followed you to Derby to kill on your new patch, eighteen years later, yet you went back to London to revisit ancient history.'

'Leads in Derby were scarce so I returned to the original killing ground.'

'And your original prime suspect,' said Tyson.

'London spawned the Reaper. I followed first principles.'

'But Sorenson was terminally ill. He barely had the strength to stand, never mind commit multiple murder.'

'Maybe.'

'Definitely,' said Tyson. 'As for first principles, you made a couple of calls to Hammersmith nick then dropped off the grid for days then resurfaced, drugged and unconscious in Sorenson's study. A man you claim was a serial killer, had you completely under his control yet cut his own wrists and confessed to murder on film. Why would he do that?'

'He didn't confess to being the Reaper,' said Brook.

'True, but there was no proof of him ever killing anyone until his confession,' said Tyson.

'Like you said, he was terminal. He took the easy way out.'

Tyson nodded. 'So, what happened in those missing days? Where did you go? You spent time with Rowlands before he died, I know that much...'

'Quid pro quo, Kelly. So far, all we've talked about is me.'

'But you're so fascinating,' said Tyson.

Brook frowned. 'Look, you're young, ambitious and smart. Catching the Reaper would be a huge feather in your cap but either we pool information or *I* leave.'

Tyson studied Brook while she drank another mouthful of froth. 'DCI Fulbright only gave me the Harlesden file to review. Ross had Brixton.'

'But you reviewed the Brixton file just the same.'

Tyson laughed. 'How did you know?'

'I'm a trained detective. Who else was on it?'

'Me, Ross and the guvnor.'

'Just the three of you?'

'Until the Wallis killing, the Reaper was ancient history. Fulbright said the review was a waste of time and he didn't want to divert other officers.'

'When did you start?'

'Two, maybe three weeks before the Wallis family died,' said Tyson.

'And Chief Superintendent Kerr initiated.'

'Fulbright said he had a real bee in his bonnet about it.'

'Do you know why?'

'I know Kerr went to see your old guvnor, Charlie Rowlands, in the hospital...'

'Do you know what was said?'

'No. And if Kerr told Fulbright, he didn't tell me.'

'Interesting you were given the Harlesden file and Ross got Brixton,' said Brook. 'The first murder in a series is crucial...'

'It carries the original hallmarks of the killer's psychopathy before refinements creep in. I've read the textbooks. What's your point?'

'You were only a DC, raw and untested...'

'None taken,' sneered Tyson.

'I'm not questioning your ability, Kelly, but Ross had seniority. By rights, he should have been given the Harlesden file.'

'I think Fulbright thought I'd do a better job. Ross isn't what you call a thinker and I brought a fresh perspective.'

'So, tell me about Harlesden. What did you see?'

'Nothing you hadn't seen before me and I went over it enough times,' said Tyson. 'As for the killings, the SOCO photos and videos were...mesmerising. Not the sort of thing you forget easily. And my conclusions were your conclusions - the Reaper is or was a cold-blooded, well-organised killer. No anger, no frenzy, no hint of a personal motive. I realised then the Reaper was no ordinary killer. What I couldn't get my head round was how Victor Sorenson could be a suspect. A wealthy businessman, a successful industrial chemist with interests all over the world and homes to match...'

'You did the background?'

'Enough to tell me that a connection to Sammy Elphick was comical. Yet there it was in the reports. What there was of them.'

She snaked a glance at Brook. 'I mean, a VCR recovered from the Elphick flat, reported stolen by Sorenson who just *happened* to have a record of the serial number so you could match it to the one at the crime scene. Who does that?'

'Nobody,' mumbled Brook. 'So?'

'So, yes, Sammy Elphick could have been the burglar of Sorenson's home, despite a long record of blagging in which he never once strayed outside Harlesden or Neasden.'

'But you didn't buy it.'

'Not without a lot more digging. Then I found out Sorenson had a brother, Stefan, beaten to death in 1989, the year *before* Sammy Elphick and his family were executed, in what appeared to be a home invasion gone wrong. The killer was never identified until Sorenson's phoney confession the night he died.'

'How do you know it was phoney?'

'Please,' scoffed Tyson. 'They looked into it. That girl, Laura Maples, Sorenson claimed to have raped and murdered...he wasn't even in London when she was killed.'

'Forensics couldn't put an exact date on her death,' said Brook.

'But they could estimate it to a few days either side and Sorenson was in Sweden that whole month. He couldn't have done it.'

'And his brother?'

'There was no evidence to put Sorenson at his brother's house on the night of Stefan's death. He even had an alibi. The whole confession was a crock. Sorenson didn't kill his brother.'

'Then why make the tape?'

'Know what I think?' said Tyson. 'I think he did it to get you out of the doghouse.'

Brook raised an eyebrow. 'Is that where I was?'

'You know you were. You were off the grid and in the shit and Sorenson's confession to two Unsolveds bought you a free pass from Brass and saved your career.'

'Sorenson did all that just for me? Why?'

'Maybe he liked having you around, feeding his ego, lapping up his Reaper bullshit.'

'I thought you said you had Sorenson down as the Reaper.'

'In the nineties, maybe. But not on the Drayfin two years ago. He didn't have the strength to kill the Wallis family.'

'But you like him for Harlesden and Brixton.'

'Hard to say,' said Tyson. 'But, suppose Sorenson found out

that Elphick was the intruder who'd killed his brother. It might then make sense for him to slaughter Sammy and family.'

'And the burglary of Sorenson's home?' said Brook.

Tyson shrugged. 'Never happened. Sorenson took the VCR with him, in a phoney attempt to fence it and get himself inside. But...'

'What?'

'But if it's revenge for his brother, where's the anger?' she said. 'And how does Sorenson manage to kill a whole family without leaving trace? The killings were cold, efficient. A revenge attack should show frenzy and rage but it's not there.'

'The blood writing on the wall was pretty nasty.'

'Pure theatre,' said Tyson. 'And not done in anger. Just phoney religious claptrap to suggest a fake motive. The whole thing was planned and carried out with incredible precision, the crime scene staged and the vics despatched without fuss or any of the physical abuse you'd expect from a revenge killing.'

'But the VCR was left behind,' said Brook. 'Isn't that a carelessness born of powerful emotions?'

'You don't really believe that,' said Tyson. 'Rage doesn't explain leaving a VCR at the scene having *already* reported it stolen. I mean, why tell us he was burgled in the first place?'

'A burglary you claim never happened.'

'It didn't,' said Tyson. 'And the VCR wasn't the only thing the Reaper left behind. The poster on the wall...'

'Fleur de Lis,' said Brook. 'We could never prove the Reaper brought it.'

'No, but he did,' said Tyson. 'And it had no business being in that shithole. But there it was, directly in the eyeline of Sammy and his missus as they were having their throats cut. That got my interest.'

'Another message?' said Brook.

'It absolutely was.'

'For us or the victims?'

'You tell me. Quid pro quo.'

'I think a bit of both,' said Brook. 'The Reaper wanted to bring a little beauty into their ugly world. For himself. For them. Show them what the human race can achieve.'

'And what did it say to us?'

'That the killings were part of some higher purpose,' said Brook.

'Another black mark against the revenge theory,' nodded Tyson. 'And the tears? Sammy and his missus cried buckets before they died. The Reaper toyed with them. Why?'

'Because he wants them to suffer.'

'But they don't!' said Tyson. 'All the vics die quickly.'

'The mental agony is worse,' replied Brook. 'You see, he's not just taking their futures, he's taking their past and their present as well. That's why he revives them, so they can see the consequence of their wasted lives...'

'Their dead son hanging from a light cord.'

'Exactly. And to make sure they know he's dead, he cut off two of the boy's fingers. That's when they know what they've done and there's no chance to make things right.'

'You didn't put *that* in the files,' said Tyson.

'Idle speculation,' said Brook.

'You're allowed to theorise on the record.'

'You're right. I didn't write down everything I should have but there was no proof and my boss, Charlie Rowlands, was sceptical. Also...' Brook hesitated. Tyson raised an encouraging eyebrow. 'I was heading towards a personal crisis. It was a chaotic time - in my career, in my marriage...'

'Convenient.'

'I didn't think so.'

'No?' said Tyson. 'Thanks to your *crisis,* there's barely a fag paper's worth of stuff on Victor Sorenson. And if you were struggling to keep it together, your SIO should have taken up the slack.'

'Charlie told me Sorenson was a dead end,' said Brook. 'And when I couldn't prove otherwise, I either l had to let it go or...'

'...or park outside Sorenson's house for a year, waiting for him to slip up.'

'Yes,' Brook conceded. He sipped his coffee. 'You did well in the short time you had.'

'Don't play me.'

'I'm not,' said Brook. 'Considering how little you had to go on...'

'No different to you. There's never been a shred of evidence. No fingerprints, no skin, saliva or hair. And this before we had full-blown DNA tests in our forensic armoury, when perps didn't worry about a loose follicle or a drop of sweat. Somehow the Reaper knows to leave us nothing so, either he's a ghost or he knew about developing crime scene tech and the future of DNA.'

Brook smiled. 'Someone like Sorenson.'

'Exactly like Sorenson. Several of his companies were involved in developing DNA profiling...'

'I'm impressed.'

Tyson had a flash of anger. 'Don't. Play. Me. You knew all this.'

'I've had longer than a couple of weeks to work it out.'

'I've had an extra two years to mull it over, don't forget.'

'Even so.'

Tyson shook her head. 'It's academic, anyway. The Reaper is still killing and Sorenson is dead. It couldn't have been him. Maybe the burglary of Sorenson's house was real and someone else killed the Elphick family.'

'That's Fulbright talking,' said Brook. 'And it doesn't explain Brixton.'

'Another reason it can't have been Sorenson,' said Tyson. 'Brixton makes the Reaper a serial killer. All that guff about the burglary and avenging his brother goes out the window. Plus, Sorenson has *no* connection to the Wrigley family and no earthly motive to put them in the ground. It can't have been him.'

'*Plus* is a mathematical symbol,' said Brook.

'I'll make a note,' snapped Tyson. 'Speaking of notes, there was nothing in the files about running down Elphick's KA's either.'

Brook's eyes narrowed. 'Known Associates? Why would there be? Elphick worked alone.'

'But he knew other blaggers.'

'So what?'

'So, maybe he changed his method and burgled Sorenson's house with one of his lowlife friends.'

Brook laughed. 'And what? Had a falling out over sharing the spoils? Seriously? An attack of *that* sophistication and ruthlessness carried out by one of Elphick's fellow burglars? Whose crazy idea was that?'

'DCI Fulbright seemed keen on it for a while.'

'More fool him,' said Brook. 'Did he look into it?'

'For a day or two. We were coming at it cold, remember.'

'Even so, Fulbright...'

'What?'

'Forget it. I shouldn't speak ill of the dead. I'm sure he had his reasons. Another coffee?'

Tyson declined and there was silence for a few minutes.

'So why *did* you visit Sorenson two years ago?' said Tyson. 'He was riddled with cancer. You didn't seriously think he got off his deathbed and dragged himself to Derby to commit multiple murder, did you? Or did you not know Sorenson was dying when you went?'

'I knew.' Brook paused. 'But Sorenson was Sorenson.'

'What does that mean?'

'It's hard to explain the power of the man. And I mean personal charisma not just financial muscle. And even though he was dying, I...thought it was worth asking the question.'

Tyson's eyes narrowed. 'You went to London for his confession.'

'And I got one.'

'But not the one you wanted.'

'More fool me,' said Brook.

Tyson sat back, studying him. 'You're lying to me and pretty good at it you are too.'

'I'm not lying, Kelly.'

'Everyone lies and you've had years of practice. Despite all evidence to the contrary, you still think Sorenson came to Derby to kill the Wallis family, don't you? That's why you went to London.'

'You never met him, Kelly. If you had, you'd know that if Sorenson wanted to do something, no disease in the world could stop him.' He watched a smile spread across Tyson's face. 'What?'

'But I did meet him. I interviewed him with DCI Fulbright shortly before the Wallis family died.' Tyson couldn't suppress a grin at Brook's expression. 'Looks like I'm having that second coffee.'

18

December 5th 2008 – Kensington, West London

Tyson looked up at the front of the plush house in Queensdale Road, while DCI Fulbright worked the old-fashioned brass bell-pull. Well-pruned ivy clung to the stone and everything she could see reeked of money and taste - the lacquered wooden door with its gleaming brass knocker, freshly painted windows, glossy wooden floors, at least in the basement room below ground. A four-storey house in an exclusive part of town wasn't the usual abode of serial killers.

She heard a bell chime deep inside the house. 'Nice crib, guv. What do you reckon it's worth?'

Fulbright shook his head. 'Three, four million, even after the crash. This is Kensington - prices at a premium.'

'In Leicester, you could get ten of these for that money.'

'Yeah but who wants to live in Leicester?'

Tyson raised an admonishing eyebrow but, at that moment, the door swung open and a handsome woman in her fifties peered out at them. She had short blonde hair - tinted to offset the grey - a soft, unwrinkled complexion and cool grey eyes.

'Can I help you?' Her voice carried a Scandinavian inflection and Tyson guessed she must be Swedish like Sorenson. Fulbright made the introductions and the pair brandished warrant cards to seal the deal.

'He'll be glad of visitors,' said the woman, ushering them inside. 'Victor doesn't get out much these days.'

'He's unwell?' asked Fulbright.

'Cancer. He only has a short time. Months, maybe weeks.' Her lip began to wobble and she bit down on the emotion.

Tyson touched her on the arm. 'If it's a problem we can see your husband another time.'

The woman narrowed her eyes then smiled. 'Oh, I'm not his wife. Victor isn't married. I'm his sister-in-law, Sonja.'

'Of course,' nodded Fulbright. 'His brother's wife...widow.'

A frost descended on Sonja's features. 'I hope I'll be remembered for more than that.' She turned away, heading for the staircase. 'It's a couple of flights.'

The two detectives followed her into the dark wood-panelled hall, past an iron coat rack and up steps covered in plush carpet. As they walked, Tyson took in her surroundings, especially the many fine paintings adorning the walls. She raised an eyebrow in Fulbright's direction and he nodded. Expensive art was far higher in value than bulky VCRs and much easier to carry.

At the top of the house, when they could climb no further, the two officers heard faint strains of classical music coming from behind a door at which Sonja Sorenson halted, holding a finger to her lips. 'He may be napping though it sounds like he's with us. Wait here.'

The door opened briefly and Sonja went inside, closing it behind her. For a split second, they caught sight of low winter sun illuminating the room beyond, a round porthole window transmogrifying the sun's rays into a celestial searchlight.

'Sorenson's a multi-millionaire and serious art collector,' whispered Tyson. 'Why wander off your patch to break into a house like this just for a VCR? Another thing. The Elphick crime scene had a single piece of art on the wall.'

'Remind me,' said Fulbright.

'A poster of a painting. *Fleur de Lis*. Can't remember the artist but it's in the inventory and on the SOCO film. Brook and DCI Rowlands thought the Reaper likely brought it because it was the only piece in the flat.'

'Did they say why?'

'No. Also...' She nodded at the door, behind which a dramatic piece of muffled music reached a temporary crescendo.

'Classical music,' said Fulbright, nodding.

'I peeked at the Brixton file,' said Tyson. 'There was classical music playing as the vics were killed.'

'Brought by the Reaper?'

'That was the thinking. Not only that, either Brixton CID or Brook - can't remember which - speculated the Reaper had brought the actual CD player with him, just to be sure he could play his music while he cut their throats.'

'And like the VCR, a good way to blag your way into a petty criminal's home,' said Fulbright.

'Offering something Wrigley could fence to feed his habit.'

'What music was it?'

'Mozart, I think.'

Fulbright pointed at the door. 'And this?'

'Not sure. I don't think it's Mozart though.'

'Something to ask our host,' said Fulbright. 'Okay, I see avenging his brother's murder as motive for offing Sammy and family but I still don't get how that sets him out on this crusade. I mean what's in it for him in Brixton and Leeds?'

They heard footsteps approach on bare boards. 'Hard or easy, guv?' said Tyson.

'Easy,' said Fulbright. 'We've got a pile of ifs, buts and maybes from an ancient cold case. Even if Sorenson falls to his knees and confesses, sounds like he'll never make it to trial. Just put the questions and see what we shake out.'

The door opened and they were ushered in. Sonja left, closing the door behind her.

The two officers stepped towards the upright figure in a chair by the fireside, a tartan blanket covering his legs. The man was completely bald and the skin on his scalp carried a jaundiced hue. His eyes were closed but only to better appreciate the music as his feeble arm cut the air in time to the piece, flowing from the speakers.

While they waited, Tyson and Fulbright admired the floor-to-ceiling, wall-to-wall bookcases, the opulent leather-covered desk, the expensive stereo off in one corner and the three leather chairs arranged around a small grate in which the embers of a coal fire were dying. The smell of fresh coffee permeated the air.

The music faded to a close and Professor Victor Sorenson

opened his eyes, a welcoming smile creasing his weathered face. Fulbright and Tyson gazed back at the blackest eyes either of them had ever seen and both were momentarily transfixed.

'Forgive me for not standing, officers. Terrible manners but I'm sure Sonja must have explained my difficulty.' Sorenson waved an arm at the two chairs facing him. 'What can I do for you?'

Fulbright and Tyson stepped round a small table on which sat a steaming coffee pot and a pair of empty coffee cups. 'Were you expecting us, Professor?'

'The only visitor I'm expecting is the Grim Reaper,' said Sorenson. 'But Sonja is very obliging and I have a small kitchenette adjoining my study where she made us a fresh pot. Please help yourself.'

Fulbright nodded faintly at his junior officer's glance and Tyson poured two cups of inky black coffee before continuing her visual sweep around the room. She spotted the door to the kitchenette at the back of the room almost hidden by bookshelves framing it on either side.

'We're sorry to trouble you, sir,' said Fulbright. 'We had no idea you were ill.'

'Why would you?' smiled Sorenson. 'Trust me, if it were any trouble, Sonja would have turned you away.'

'You seem reconciled,' said Tyson, before she could stop herself.

'I wouldn't say that exactly,' said Sorenson, turning to look at her. 'I have much I want to achieve in my remaining time. But I think that's the case for everyone facing the end, isn't it?'

'*So much to do, so little time,*' said Tyson, blushing. 'Sorry.'

Sorenson beamed at Tyson as she reddened. 'The last words of Cecil Rhodes. Odious man.'

There was silence for a moment as the two officers considered this slight old man in the chair before them, advanced age and infirmity mocking the idea of him as a serial killer.

Tyson made a final sweep of the room. 'You don't have a television.'

'I've never owned one,' said Sorenson with pride. 'Music and books are my companions to the underworld.'

'That was nice,' said Tyson, nodding to the stereo.

'Mahler's Ninth,' said Sorenson. 'Written when he knew he was dying. What an achievement at the end of a life. If only we could all sign off with such a work of genius.'

Fulbright took a sip of his coffee. 'Genius like that means you never die, I suppose.'

'Very astute, Chief Inspector,' replied Sorenson. 'I hope when I succumb to the tumours growing inside me, I can leave some work of note behind and listen to a wonderful piece of music as I drift away. Marvellous.' He threw out his hands in enquiry. 'Forgive my musings. What brings you to my humble home?'

'We're reviewing the burglary of your house, eighteen years ago,' said Tyson, aware of the absurdity of her words.

'Indeed?' said Sorenson slowly, picking up a small hand towel from the arm of his chair and dabbing his brow. 'How can I help?'

'You're not surprised to be asked about it after all this time?' said Tyson.

Sorenson's black eyes bored into her. 'Once you peer into the abyss, my dear, nothing shocks or surprises any more. Do you have a question?'

'We'd like to hear your version of what happened,' said Tyson.

'Version?' quipped Sorenson, with a first hint of acid in his tone.

'As well as you can remember.'

'I remember like it was yesterday,' answered Sorenson. 'A sobering business to discover an untalented burglar has robbed you. And worse to learn the burglar and his family were murdered soon after. Shocking.'

'Some things do surprise you then?' observed Tyson.

'Perhaps. But I really don't know what I can add to the statement I gave DI Brook at the time.'

'*DI* Brook?' said Tyson. 'Brook's a serving DI now but he was a Detective Sergeant back then.'

'So, he was,' agreed Sorenson. 'He was promoted when he transferred out of the Met, wasn't he? Derbyshire, wasn't it?'

'Are you in contact with him?' said Tyson.

'Sadly, no,' replied Sorenson. 'A very troubled young man. I hope he's put his past behind him. I do miss our little chats.'

'Chats?' said Fulbright.

'You saw him often back then?' said Tyson.

'Regularly,' replied Sorenson. 'You might not know this but DS Brook was once quite fixated on me as a suspect for the Elphick killings.' The two detectives exchanged a glance. 'He was quite obsessive about it. In the absence of more viable leads, obviously.

He sat where you're sitting now and we often talked things over in front of the fire, a glass of whisky in hand.'

'What things?' asked Fulbright

'The case. This serial killer he was hunting. The Reaper's deeds troubled him greatly and contributed to his breakdown, I believe.'

'Why would Brook have considered you a suspect, professor?'

'The juxtaposition of my reporting the burglary and the execution of Elphick and his family,' said Sorenson.

'So, he actually accused you of murdering them.'

'Oh, yes.'

'Because Elphick burgled your home?'

Sorenson couldn't resist a smile. 'Something like that.'

'And stole a VCR you'd purchased to record programmes from a TV you've never owned?' said Tyson, raising an eyebrow at him.

Sorenson was quiet for a moment though he didn't appear to be flustered. 'That's right. I bought it as a gift for a friend.'

'The name of this friend?' asked Tyson, preparing her notebook.

'It was a long time ago,' said Sorenson.

'So, not remembering things like it was yesterday then?' observed Tyson. 'Sir.'

'Evidently not,' replied Sorenson, with no apparent diminution of humour. 'Old age and vanity are unreliable bedfellows, I'm afraid.'

'So, Brook considered Elphick stealing this item sufficient motive for you to kill him and his family?' prompted Fulbright.

'Oh, that's not why I killed them.' Sorenson's smile faded to lips only and his eyes shone like polished coal. 'According to Brook.'

'We're all ears,' said Tyson.

'DI...DS Brook thought the burglary was a fabrication, that I took the VCR to Harlesden to gain entry to Elphick's flat, allowing me the chance to kill his family - revenge for the death of my brother, Stefan. I'm sure it's all in the files.'

'We'd prefer you to tell us,' said Tyson. 'If it's no trouble.'

Sorenson conceded with a shrug. 'You know about Stefan's murder?'

'Killed in a home invasion the year before,' confirmed Fulbright.

'Tied up and beaten to death,' added Tyson.

'Correct,' said Sorenson. 'As Brook saw it, using my extensive wealth, I *discovered* that this Sammy Elphick was Stefan's killer and instead of informing the police, I tracked him down and extracted my own vengeance.' Sorenson found his grin again. 'Fanciful in the extreme, you'll agree.'

Tyson refused the invitation. Sorenson seemed to be deliberately fanning the flames of suspicion like it was all a game. The prospect of impending death and the knowledge there were no meaningful punishments for a terminally ill killer, were loosening his tongue.

'Elphick's wife and ten-year-old child also died,' said Tyson. 'As revenge, that seems disproportionate.'

'It's one thing to rationalise these matters from afar, Detective Constable - quite another when you are caught up in the moment.'

'But their deaths weren't savage or spur-of-the-moment, sir. There was no frenzy at the scene. The Reaper was cool, clear-headed, meticulous.'

'Then your killer must have had a different motive,' said Sorenson.

'Did you discuss his motive with Brook during your...chats?'

Sorenson's black eyes continued to drill into her as though reaching into her essential core. 'Elphick was a habitual criminal. His existence served no purpose. Motive enough.'

'And his son?'

'His son paid for the sins of the father,' replied Sorenson. 'His death was merely a component of Sammy's punishment.'

'Component?'

'Of course. I know, in your profession, officers rationalise the harm that the Elphicks of this world inflict because the driving force of the justice system is compromise. You look at the bare facts of an offender's criminal history and you trade them off. You wrap them in a sentence, sometimes custodial, then draw a line through them and move on.

'But between the lines we both know that a criminal's CV represents only transgressions that can be evidenced in court. You ignore the casual violence of intimidation, bullying, verbal abuse, petty theft, graffiti, littering, noise pollution, vandalism - they don't even rate a mention in the courts and some offences are barely even covered by law.'

'You exaggerate,' said Tyson.

'Do I?' said Sorenson. 'Then I suggest you *really* listen to the people you claim to serve. If you do, you'll hear a deafening chorus of pain and anguish about what really worries ordinary people - the hooligan who slashes their tyres or throws a brick through their window or kicks their dog. Those are the crimes that kill. Not physical or biological death but mental degradation, inch by inch, day by day, narrowing people's minds, dulling their lives, spreading misery and fear.

'And when people ask that justice be meted out to those who blight our lives, who listens? Not the police. Not the courts. The petty offenders get little or no punishment for their crime and have no fear of consequences. And, without fear there is no restraint and there can be no order.'

The two detectives stared at Sorenson while he ran the small hand towel over his face, panting with the effort of speech.

'So, you think the Reaper is doing what the people want,' said Tyson. 'That the Elphick family died because they were a public nuisance.'

'It's a theory Brook subscribed to at one point.'

'What was his take on you *deliberately* leaving behind the VCR to flag up your involvement?' asked Tyson. 'I'm assuming he didn't think somebody as intelligent as you would do that unintentionally.'

'Of course not.' Sorenson found his smile again. 'Sergeant Brook had some notion that I wanted to draw attention to my involvement and show off.'

'As if the Reaper were arrogant and condescending, you mean?' replied Tyson.

Sorenson's black eyes creased with amusement and he leaned forwards to impart a confidence. 'Astonishing, isn't it?'

'And how did you like his theory?' asked Fulbright.

'I could see a logic behind it,' said Sorenson. 'It can't be easy in your work, having to deal with lowlifes, screaming about their human rights while trying to provoke you into giving them what they deserve.'

'And what's that?' asked Tyson.

Sorenson grinned. 'A shock. A reminder that they're mortal and that someone, somewhere has their measure.'

'Like the Reaper.'

'Exactly like the Reaper,' said Sorenson. Tyson's expression hardened but this only served to enhance Sorenson's pleasure. 'Please don't tell me you don't get a glimmer of satisfaction when a junkie takes an overdose after robbing a pensioner to buy heroin. Or smile when gang members kill each other over a disrespectful glance. I put the same point to Brook eighteen years ago, asked him to name a single person who had mourned the departure of the Elphick family. Of course, he couldn't. You see, those families were already dead, their souls corrupted, even before the Reaper took their lives. And once they'd departed, decent people got the chance to welcome a little beauty into their lives.'

'Like a painting.'

'Or a piece of music,' added Fulbright.

'Or an autumn walk or a sip of malt whisky or the embrace of a partner,' continued Sorenson. 'Any one of a million things. But if you can't appreciate any of them, or allow others to do so then you might as well be dead.' Sorenson's emphasis on the final word gave him pause. 'That seems to be his message. Elegant, don't you think?'

'So, the Reaper exists to promote the search for beauty.'

'And eliminate those whose ugly lives make beauty impossible. Go out into the streets and speak to harassed residents, drawing their blinds against the slum household. Speak to the teachers taunted and abused in their classrooms. Listen to your colleagues facing the hatred of drunken thugs on a Saturday night...'

'That's the price of freedom,' interrupted Fulbright. Sorenson looked sharply across at him. 'Would you prefer the tyranny of a totalitarian state, professor?'

'I would not, Chief Inspector. But it is those that deny those freedoms to others who are subject to the Reaper's justice.'

'Isn't that what the law is for?' said Tyson.

'That's what it *should* be for,' answered Sorenson. 'But how many petty offences are committed before the law catches up with the Sammy Elphicks of this world. Ten? Twenty? Thirty?'

'We can only act on evidence,' said Tyson.

'And in retrospect,' agreed Sorenson. 'Meanwhile each unacknowledged crime is an act of violence against someone's peace of mind. And that assault, that fear corrupts our schools, our estates, our public spaces...'

'And the dead children?' interrupted Tyson, trying to provoke a scintilla of guilt. 'What was their crime?'

'They are the fruit of the poisoned tree,' said Sorenson. He held up his hands in self-defence. 'DS Brook's theory, you understand. How is he, do you know?'

'In a peaceful backwater winding down his fading career,' said Fulbright.

'Is he?' Sorenson smiled at a joke he chose not to share.

'How much do you know about DNA profiling, Professor?' asked Tyson.

'More than most,' said Sorenson, without hesitation. 'I've taken a great interest in DNA profiling since the process was developed.'

'And you own several biotech companies, including three that were involved in DNA sequencing research and one that the FBI uses for profiling offender samples.'

'You've been very thorough,' said Sorenson. 'It's a fascinating area and, yes, I've been involved for some twenty years.'

'So, before the first patents were issued,' said Tyson.

Sorenson splayed his thin arms to accept her observation. 'Another piece of the jigsaw?'

'Sorry?'

'Offender profiling for the Reaper,' smiled Sorenson. 'Art lover, personal motive, DNA expert with resources to match. As a suspect, I realised immediately I was a good fit. And if you had any direct evidence against me, I'd be a worried man.'

'We're just talking here, sir,' said Tyson.

'And a most enjoyable conversation too,' grinned Sorenson. 'It gladdens my heart to support the forces of law and order but, as you know, I'm not in robust health and tire easily.'

'Then we'll only take up another moment of your time,' said Fulbright, extracting a thin envelope from his jacket and pulling out three photographs to hand to Sorenson. Tyson looked quizzically over at Fulbright. 'Have you ever seen any of these men before, sir?'

Sorenson stared disdainfully at Fulbright then down at the photographs. 'Why am I looking at these?'

'These are known associates of Sammy Elphick,' said Fulbright.

'Alternate suspects,' said Sorenson, nodding. 'Associates that you think may have been with Sammy when he burgled my home...'

'I can't speak to that, sir,' said Fulbright, gesturing at the photographs. 'But if you wouldn't mind.'

Sorenson thumbed through the mugshots, discarding the first two quickly but lingering over the third for a beat. In it, Vinny Muir, with his thin reddish-grey hair and dark eyes, stared

The Resurrection

vacantly back at the custody suite camera. Sorenson glared at the mugshot before placing it on top of the pile and handing them back to Fulbright. 'I've never seen these men before.'

Two minutes later Fulbright and Tyson were out on the pavement.

'Wow,' said Tyson. 'Did he just confess to us?'

'He's dying, Kelly. He probably just wanted a bit of fun at our expense.'

'I'm not so sure,' said Tyson. 'I say we dig deeper.'

19

'And did you?' asked Brook.

'No,' said Tyson. 'We had nowhere to go with it and the review fizzled out. Then the Wallis family were killed in Derby. Game over.'

'At our first meeting you said you'd have staked every penny you had on Sorenson being the Reaper.'

'Two years ago, maybe. I only met him that once and, even riddled with cancer, the power of his personality was incredible. I could see a healthy Sorenson as a serial killer and, if I'd had my way, we would have dug deeper.'

'But you didn't.'

'Like I said, there was nowhere to go,' said Tyson. 'He was dying and there's never been a shred of evidence to put him at the scene of either London killing let alone Derby.'

'I'm glad you met him. You describe the interview as though it was yesterday.'

'He made his mark,' said Tyson. 'And, even if he wasn't the Reaper, after speaking to him, I began to think the motive for the killings wasn't personal but something bigger, something universal in scope. I'm not making much sense.'

'You're coming as close as anyone.'

Tyson studied Brook. 'You still think it was Sorenson, don't you? All of it. Despite his illness.' Brook remained silent. 'So why *are* the files on him so thin? What are you hiding?'

'Sorenson's dead. What is there to hide?'

'But you thought he was guilty two years ago or you wouldn't have gone back. And, if he did come to Derby to kill the Wallis family, you also know he must have had help. So why not for the Ingham killings? A partner, carrying on the tradition.' Brook was impassive. 'Give me something.'

'Like what?'

'You were in his study all those years ago, kicking this around at his fireside. You tell me.' No response. 'The Reaper killings configured as a positive contribution to society, like a work of art, making the world a better place. You heard what Sorenson said - it was *your* theory.'

'And you believed him?'

'He was a damn sight more truthful than you've been. Why won't you share? Is it something to do with your mental problems?' Brook said nothing. 'And there it is again.'

'What?'

'When their mental health is questioned, most people would get angry and tell me to mind my own business. But you? It barely registers.'

He shrugged. 'Maybe I've...'

'Yeah, yeah. You've seen too much and it's left you bereft of emotion,' she said, draining her mug and preparing to leave. 'Pull the other one.'

'Before you go, I'm going to need the names of those known associates, Kelly.'

Tyson stood. 'You give nothing and expect everything.'

'We want the same thing.'

'What's that?'

'An end to the killing,' said Brook. 'And every detail counts.'

'Even the ones you pour scorn on?'

'I'm a big fan of ticking off unproductive leads,' replied Brook.

Tyson hesitated. 'Apart from Vinny Muir, I don't have the names off the top of my head.'

'Can you text them to me?'

'Seriously? I can explain away you ringing me but if I text you back...'

'It's okay. I have an unregistered phone...'

'Is that a fact?' said Tyson, a thin smile playing around her lips. 'A burner, eh? What the hell are you hiding, Brook?'

'My propensity for misplacing my phone.'

Tyson pulled a face. 'Sorry, but you seem a bit tightly wound for that sort of carelessness.'

'Do I get the names?'

'I'll think about it.'

~

JASON LAID the SOCO suit across his bed, having tried it on for size. It was hot and sweaty but it fitted like a glove and he wouldn't be in it for long. Perching on the bed, Jason pulled on the protective gloves, removed the packaging from the hypodermic syringe and carefully inserted the detachable needle. Placing the needle in the colourless liquid from the flask, he drew back the plunger to fill the barrel to the top.

Next, he took the Wagner CD from his rucksack. 'Who listens to this shit?' He shrugged. 'Still, if it's part of the Reaper's schtick...' He reached in for the wine, examined the bottle and left it by the bedroom door.

Finally, he unpacked the scalpel and marvelled at its thin blade. He placed the plastic wrappers from both scalpel and hypodermic in an ashtray and reduced both to a blackened ball with a cigarette lighter.

With nothing left to occupy him, the nerves began to bite so he spent another ten minutes moving his fingers expansively around the bedroom wall until he was satisfied the lettering was right. His life might depend on it.

'I'm ready,' he said, sitting quietly on the bed.

~

LEAVING THE M1 SOUTHBOUND, Tyson pulled into Donnington Services and parked. She extracted a recorder from her bag and replayed the conversation with Brook. As it was finishing, her phone vibrated.

'Well?' said DI Campbell.

'Not a dicky-bird,' she said. 'Brook is unreachable and whatever he's hiding, he's on message. He gave me nothing.'

'You dangled the carrot?'

'Yes and no.'

'What does that mean?'

'Connor, Brook's been around since the dinosaurs. If I'd steered him towards the shooting, he was bound to get suspicious.'

'But you asked him the question.'

She hesitated. 'Actually, I told him it was off-limits.'

'You did what?'

'Reverse psychology, forbidden fruit and all that.'

'How'd that work?'

'Like a charm. He didn't go near the shooting.'

'So, it was a bust.'

'No, I did get something. An insight into what's driving him.'

'And what's that?'

'The Reaper. Everything else is secondary. Brook doesn't care about the shooting and he's ambivalent about saving his career. His only interest was in grilling me about the Reaper case review in London.'

'Which gets us where?'

'For now, nowhere. Instructive though. Plus, he wants something from me so I have another card to play.'

'Make that two,' replied Campbell. *'Mike Drexler's conscious. I'm heading off to QMC to see if he's speaking.'*

'On my way. Anyone with him?'

'DC Holdsworth. He has a notebook and a standing order to keep Brook out of the room. With any luck we'll have what we need before Brook even knows Drexler's awake.'

'And if we get corroboration of Brook's account, we can put this to bed and get on with our lives.'

'What? You were the one who said he was lying.'

'He's still one of ours.'

'Don't go soft on me, Kelly. These things have their own momentum. If Brook's dirty, I want him off the Force.'

Tyson rang off and, after a moment's consideration, thumbed out a text. She hesitated at the end of it before sending it into the ether.

∽

BROOK ARRIVED at his Hartington cottage well after midnight, the growling sky reflecting his mood. He carried a mug of tea and a blanket out to the garden before lighting a much-needed cigarette then gazed up at the black sheet covering the heavens.

Bobbi skittered smoothly across the cold grass and jumped onto an arm of the bench, staring hopefully at him. Brook scratched his head and the cat careened around his fingers until Brook's phone vibrated and it hopped to the ground. A text from Tyson.

Elphick's KAs irrelevant but for one I told you. Vincent "Vinny" Muir. Sorenson looked hard at his pic. Not sure why but think S may have recognised him. One possibility. Will share when you GIVE me something. Don't text or ring me again ever. KT

Following her instruction, Brook resisted sending an acknowledgement, took his tea indoors to his cramped office and fired up the computer to log onto the PNC database.

After entering his passwords, he searched for Muir's record. When it loaded, Brook stared long and hard at the mugshot, probably the same picture Fulbright had shown to Sorenson two years before. Muir presented as a defeated old man, in his late sixties with thinning red hair, turning grey, delicate, almost bird-like features and furtive eyes, dark brown according to his sheet, though they looked black. Brook wondered if he'd ever nicked Muir back in the day. Checking his arrest record, it appeared not.

One possibility? Brook smiled. Tyson was new at this. 'Sorry, Kelly. You're two or three possibilities short.' He skimmed the information on the career misadventures of Vinny Muir, small-time thief from West London, incarcerated for more than half his adult life for a series of low value burglaries.

Muir was the kind of mediocrity who wouldn't cross Sorenson's path in a million years unless by design. Of course, it was possible Sorenson had recognised Muir as an associate of Sammy Elphick. After all, the professor must, at some point, have done some reconnaissance on Elphick's Harlesden flat before butchering the family. Could he have seen Muir going into Sammy's place? It seemed a slim prospect when Brook had a more compelling narrative, for which he read on in search of corroboration - it wasn't long in arriving.

During one of his rare periods of freedom, Muir had married a local stripper, Rosa. The union didn't survive Muir's next stint in prison but it did produce a daughter, Debra, born in the mid-seventies. Her name was hyperlinked so Brook clicked to see what she'd been up to.

Debra Muir - unmarried - had a longer record than her father and infinitely more varied. Theft, shoplifting, prostitution, drug-dealing, possession, fraud, deception, handling stolen goods. It was depressing reading.

Fortunately for Debra, bringing three children into the world, by three different partners, had saved her from the lengthy periods of incarceration her record of offending merited. Consequently, there were multiple links to a variety of public services at Hammersmith and Fulham Council - social care and health, children's services as well as council adoption services, when removal of Debra's children had been deemed appropriate.

Brook clicked on a few links to confirm his impression of a dysfunctional mother, mired in habitual criminality and in a tailspin of drug-fuelled decline. Worse, it seemed that Debra's two older sons, Liam and Jordan, were already violent local thugs, themselves heading for a lifetime of episodic confinement.

He was reminded of something Sorenson had said two years ago, during his last night on Earth, the night Brook had finally confessed his own sins to get the answers he needed. On that turbulent night, Sorenson had laid out everything, had talked about the roots of criminality and defined the principles that selected the Reaper's victims. Brook could still hear his voice, pontificating how all human behaviour was the product of either a person's genetic coding or their upbringing. Nature versus Nurture.

'When you're the child of a habitual criminal, your future is written. If the genes don't get you, the environment will. It's what the Americans call a slam-dunk.'

A slam-dunk indeed. Everything about Muir and his family matched the Reaper's victimology. Interestingly, Muir's last attended parole meeting was the tenth of December 2008 - the week before the Wallis family were murdered in Derby. A month later he was a no-show and warrants for his arrest were issued. The lack of violence in Muir's criminal history made the search low priority and he had never been located.

Brook wrote down a couple of last known addresses, logged off and padded through to the kitchen to make more tea.

On his return to the garden bench, his phone vibrated again. Answering the call, Brook smiled as he listened. 'That's great news. Thank you.'

~

DI CAMPBELL LOOKED up from his chair as Tyson entered the room. She gazed at the prone figure on the hospital bed, oxygen mask covering his face. Mike Drexler's eyes were closed.

'Anything?'

'Asleep since I got here,' said Campbell, standing to stretch. 'Coffee?'

Tyson nodded and sat on the warm plastic chair vacated by Campbell and inspected the various tubes transporting liquids into and out of the stricken patient.

Without warning Drexler's head moved slightly and his eyes opened, blinking at the ceiling for focus. Tyson leapt up and stood peering down at him and his eyes moved to her face. Through his oxygen mask, he tried to say something but it was inaudible. He tried and failed to move an arm, restrained by tubing.

'Wait,' said Tyson. After a quick glance over her shoulder, Tyson pulled down his oxygen mask. 'Welcome back.'

'Hello,' said Drexler, his voice little more than a croak.

'Do you know where you are?' said Tyson.

'Hospital, I guess. Are you a nurse?'

'I'm Kelly,' said Tyson, not wanting to lie or show ID.

'Kelly,' whispered Drexler, as though trying to memorise it. He looked up and down her face like a blind man, his sight restored. 'Kelly,' he repeated. When he had it nailed, his eyes darted back to her. 'Kelly?' he pleaded, a look of fear, invading his features.

'Yes?'

'What's my name?'

Tyson smiled at him, her heart sinking.

∼

'HE COULD BE FAKING,' said Campbell, sipping coffee outside Drexler's room.

'Come on,' she scoffed. 'Who comes out of a coma and starts lying?'

'An experienced FBI agent.'

'Ex-FBI.'

'The guy killed his partner,' said Campbell. 'If he's got something to hide, he's got the perfect excuse to lie and the longer we leave him alone to get his story straight, the harder it's going to be to nail Brook.'

'Nail Brook?' said Tyson. 'The only thing we want to nail is the truth.'

'That too,' said Campbell.

'What did the doctor say?'

'That there's no brain injury and his memory *should* come back in time,' said Campbell. 'But no guarantees, obviously. Problem now is, whatever Drexler *remembers,* Brook will have deniability. If it came to a disciplinary, any decent rep can point to Drexler's amnesia to taint subsequent recollections.'

Tyson shrugged. 'Then it's over and we've done all we can.'

'Are you serious?'

'Deadly. Brook's pushing fifty. How many more years do you think he has left even with a free pass on this?'

'Motherfucker,' snarled Campbell, under his breath. 'How the hell...?'

Tyson followed Campbell's angry gaze down the corridor. 'Brook!'

'You didn't...?' muttered Campbell.

'Don't even think it,' growled Tyson, her thunderous glance at Campbell leaving no room for doubt.

'Well, somebody tipped him off.'

'It wasn't me,' she hissed.

'What do we do?'

'What can we do?' said Tyson.

'Stall him,' said Campbell, moving to stand in Brook's path. 'Inspector, what are you doing here at this hour?'

'I've come to thank the man who saved my life,' said Brook, looking for a way past.

'He's in a coma, remember.'

Brook grinned. 'Another one?'

The colour drained from Campbell's face. 'How did you find out?'

'Does it matter?' said Brook.

'I wouldn't have asked, otherwise.'

'I bugged the room,' said Brook.

'Seriously?' said Campbell.

'No,' said Brook. 'So, do I get to see Mike?'

'Not a chance,' snarled Campbell.

'Why?'

'Oh, you know, witness collusion. That sort of thing.'

'Then come in with me,' said Brook. 'I've got nothing to hide.'

'Don't start that again,' growled Campbell. 'You are *not*...'

'He can't remember, can he?' said Brook.

'Wouldn't you like to know,' said Campbell.

'Don't worry,' said Brook. 'Amnesia is a standard reaction to trauma. The nurse told me there's no brain injury. It'll pass.'

'Doesn't mean you get to see him.'

'Then let Mike see me,' said Brook. 'Jog his memory. You'll have your statement sooner if you stimulate his brain functions.'

'He has a point,' said Tyson.

'Seriously?' said Campbell.

'Drexler knows Brook,' she said. 'We take him in with us and see what happens.'

'And if he remembers, what happens when Brook starts steering?' said Campbell.

'Then we call a halt,' said Tyson. She turned to Brook. 'But he won't say a word without say-so. Will you?'

Brook smiled and mimed pulling a zip across his mouth.

20

'Quite a delegation,' said Drexler. He put the plastic carton up to his face and sucked water through the straw then ran the moisture across dry lips with his tongue. His eyes fell on Brook. 'Who's the new guy?'

'Hi Mike,' said Brook. 'How are you feeling?'

'Tired,' replied Drexler, staring at him. After a few seconds, he said, 'I know you.'

Brook glanced across at Tyson who dipped her head in approval. 'Yes, you do.'

He stared some more before pointing a shaky finger. 'Damen?'

'That's right,' smiled Brook.

Drexler's face lit up. 'I live next door to you.'

'You do,' said Brook.

'Howdy, neighbour,' quipped Drexler, before confusion returned. 'But I'm American and this is England.'

'Long story,' said Brook.

'I got time,' said Drexler.

Brook glanced across at Tyson. 'I think my colleagues would prefer you remember in your own time.'

'Colleagues?' said Drexler. 'So, you're a cop like these guys?'

'For now,' sneered Campbell.

Brook smiled. 'What he said.'

'Are you in trouble or something?' enquired Drexler.

'Just getting older,' answered Brook.

'Me too,' said Drexler. 'Thankfully.' His brow furrowed when a revelation occurred. 'Wait, am I a cop? Is that why I got shot?'

'Something like that,' said Tyson, before Brook could speak.

Drexler nodded slowly. 'So, I'm a hero?' Nobody answered. 'If I'm a cop who got shot, I must be a hero, right? That's how it works in the States.' He frowned. 'But, if I'm in England, I can't be a cop.'

'Once a cop always a cop,' said Brook. Campbell gave him a warning glare.

'So, what happened to the guy who shot me?' demanded Drexler. No-one answered and Drexler looked suspiciously at each in turn. 'There are a lot of officers here and more outside.'

'It's complicated,' said Tyson.

Drexler nodded. 'Am I the bad guy?'

'Honestly, we're not sure,' said Tyson.

'You don't know what happened?' said Drexler.

'What do *you* remember?' asked Campbell.

Drexler closed his eyes to think. 'I'm not sure but...' He pointed at Brook. 'I have a mental image of you, Damen, and you were on your knees.'

Brook turned triumphantly towards Campbell and Tyson. 'Yes, I was.'

∼

'You're not out of the woods yet, Brook,' said Campbell, in the corridor.

Brook's grin was undimmed. 'Face it, Connor. The forensics supports me and I've given you the truth. I'm sorry it's not what you want to hear but it's not going to change just because you don't like it.'

Campbell's face flushed with anger. 'You smug...'

'It's been a long day!' said Tyson, sharply. 'Go home, get some sleep.' Campbell closed his mouth, nodded at Tyson then stalked angrily away towards the stairs.

'That went well,' said Brook.

'How do you do manage to aggravate people so thoroughly?'

'Honestly, I think it's a gift,' replied Brook. Tyson couldn't stifle a laugh. 'Think Connor will get over it?'

'You know, I'm not sure he will. No wonder your colleagues in Derby hate you.'

'Not the ones that matter,' said Brook.

The Resurrection

'How *did* you know Drexler was conscious?'

'I asked a staff member to phone me.'

'On your burner?' said Tyson.

Brook's only reply was a smile. 'So, am I out of the woods?'

'I'm not in charge but there's no science to contradict your statement and, although we'll need a fuller account from Drexler on McQuarry's motives, if your accounts continue to match...'

'And what happens to Mike?' said Brook.

'Somebody died,' said Tyson.

'He acted in self-defence.'

'He was carrying an illegal weapon...'

'...which he used to save our lives.'

'You can put the violin away,' said Tyson. 'He's not getting a medal but I can't see him doing any jail time, though no guarantees obviously.' Brook nodded, satisfied. 'Have you had time to think about the text I sent you?'

'Not yet,' lied Brook. 'But thank you.'

Tyson waited a beat. 'So, I still get nothing.'

'I've nothing of any use to you.'

'What does that mean?'

'It means, if you value your career, your sanity and any close relationships you might have, let it lie. The Reaper will chew you up and spit you out.'

'Like you?'

'Exactly like me.'

'What happened to *He's still killing people*,' said Tyson.

'Don't worry, I'm not giving up.'

'Just not sharing.'

'You've had a taster, Kelly. Be satisfied with that or it'll ruin your life and you'll end up chasing shadows.'

'You talk as though the Reaper's a ghost.'

'Worse than that,' said Brook. 'He's an idea. And an idea can't be put in prison or killed.'

'Then what's the point of hunting him?'

'To kill the idea. But it has to be his choice.'

'Wow,' she exclaimed. 'You know who he is, don't you?'

Brook was stone-faced. 'So, do you.'

She raised an eyebrow. 'Still betting on Sorenson? He's dead and the Reaper is still killing. It's not Sorenson. And if you think it is, you're nuts.'

'See?' said Brook. 'You don't want to end up like me. It's no way to live.'

'At least tell me where Vinny Muir fits in.'

'Nowhere,' said Brook.

'Have you considered that Sorenson might have recognised him coming out of Sammy Elphick's flat?'

'Briefly but I dismissed it.'

'What if Sorenson found out Muir and Sammy Elphick broke into Stefan's house the night he was beaten to death?'

'It didn't happen.'

'How can you be so sure?' said Tyson. 'Muir broke parole a few weeks after DCI Fulbright interviewed him about Elphick and hasn't been seen since.'

'But Muir's family has,' replied Brook. Tyson raised an eyebrow. 'Okay, I did a little background.'

'Just enough to dismiss my ideas out of hand.'

Brook strove for a way to soften the blow. He failed. 'Yes. Look, if Sorenson thought Elphick and Muir killed Stefan, he would have dispatched Muir and *his* family, in similar fashion. It didn't happen because they didn't burgle Sorenson's house and they didn't beat Sorenson's brother to death.'

'Then you must know who killed Stefan.'

Brook's blue eyes were unblinking. 'So, do you,' he repeated.

'Sorenson?' Tyson's mouth twitched.

'He told me the night he died,' said Brook.

'He told everyone, remember? But his confession was a pack of lies.'

'That bit was true.'

'Stefan's wife alibied Sorenson in '89. Why would she lie to protect her husband's killer?'

'Because Stefan was a monster and she was in on the cover-up. There. You wanted me to give you something. You're the first person I've ever told that. Only two people in the entire world know beyond a doubt that Sorenson killed his brother - me and Sonja Sorenson. You're the third.'

'Then why haven't you put it on record?'

'What good would that do?' demanded Brook. 'The only evidence was a confession that couldn't be corroborated.'

'Your opinion would carry weight extra weight,' said Tyson.

'Sorenson's dead. What would be the point?'

'Isn't the truth reason enough?' said Tyson.

'Not if it damages Sonja and her children.'

'Her children?'

'Stefan was a sadist,' said Brook. 'He terrorised his wife and sexually abused his daughter. Sorenson killed him to protect them from further harm.'

'And you believed him?'

'Not without corroboration.'

'From who?'

'Stefan's daughter.'

Tyson's eyes widened. 'You know Victoria Sorenson?'

'We're acquainted,' said Brook. 'She's mentally scarred. Her brother Petr too. Putting the abuse on record would hurt them both. You were at his house…'

'I didn't meet either,' said Tyson.

'But you met Sonja.'

'Briefly,' said Tyson. Brook raised an eyebrow. 'Okay, she did give the impression she was carrying some deep-seated burden, like a pain she'd become accustomed to controlling.'

Brook nodded. 'I shouldn't have told you any of that.'

'Yes, you should. What else haven't you told me?'

'I've already given you too much food for thought. When you've gorged on it, move on to your next meal and don't look back.'

'You still haven't explained how Sorenson recognised Vinny Muir's mugshot.'

'Haven't I?' said Brook. 'Look at Muir's family history and think about the sorts of people the Reaper exterminates. If you ask me, Muir and his family had been lined up for a visit.'

'Then why not slaughter the Muirs instead of traipsing all the way to Derby to kill the Wallis family?' said Tyson. Brook was silent. Tyson nodded. 'To get your attention.'

∼

DESPITE ARRIVING BACK at his Hartington cottage near five in the morning, Brook had too much on his mind to sleep so he made tea, lit a cigarette and stood at the kitchen door, blowing smoke rings into the darkness, cheered by Drexler's recovery and pleased Mike's limited recollections had supported his account of the shooting.

But all that could change. There was still the *Laura* situation.

Mike hadn't mentioned her but if her presence that night ever came to light, there would be impossible questions to answer. His and Laura's careers would be over and it might not end there. If it came to loss of liberty, Brook had no doubt Laura would make good on her promise to confess everything but even that wouldn't salvage his career. Brook had lied to investigating officers.

'Don't worry about what you can't control,' he said, tapping out a text to her. *Mike awake and no memory of you that night. So far so good.*

Draining his tea, he trooped into his tiny office, switched on his computer to scour the internet. Over the next hour, he read several accounts of DCI Fulbright's death and all agreed on the basic facts. Richard Fulbright was a passenger in a car which veered out of control on Interstate 5, in Orange County, south of Los Angeles, last year.

On the day of the crash, his younger brother Andrew had driven the pair out to nearby Huntington Beach for lunch. After the meal, Andrew had lost control of the vehicle, hurtling into a concrete barrier at sixty miles an hour, after apparently swerving to avoid a dog. There were no witnesses to the crash and the dog was never found though road conditions were dry and the car's steering was found to be in perfect working order.

Richard Fulbright suffered massive head injuries and was killed instantly. Andrew sustained minor cuts and bruises and walked away from the wreckage. Blood tests confirmed Andrew hadn't consumed alcohol but the autopsy on Richard showed him to be well over the limit. Testimony from restaurant staff established that Richard had consumed three glasses of wine.

After a full investigation, no evidence could be found to dispute Andrew's account, no charges were filed against him and the crash was declared a tragic accident.

Depressed at such a pointless death, Brook logged off and dragged himself to bed.

21

In the dimly-lit kitchen, Jane Harrison finished the last of her chicken sandwich, leaving the dry crust on the plate. Despite the blanket round her shoulders, she shivered, the heating having knocked off hours ago. It had been a tough shift and she was exhausted, cupping her chin on her hands and jamming elbows onto the table for support. Sunlight was a few hours away so she dragged herself to bed, stealing a peek into little Bianca's room on the way.

The little mite seemed content, her young frame contorted around the ginger teddy bear. Jane smiled, kissed her fingers and blew towards the infant's cot.

Outside her bedroom, she was surprised to see a light under Jason's door. She took a step towards the handle but the light went out a second later. She listened for a moment before turning into her own bedroom.

Closing the door, she set her alarm, undressed then collapsed onto the bed with a weary sigh. Her shift had overrun and she was due back on the ward in only eight hours, most of which she hoped to spend unconscious.

As sleep hurtled towards her, she drifted back to pleasurable thoughts of free money and the things she would do with it. A mixture of compensation schemes, insurance policies and the sale of her sister's house had dropped a windfall in her lap which would be hers in a matter of days.

The Drayfin house sale had disappointed, fetching a third of the price of similar properties on the estate but that was to be expected after her sister, brother-in-law and niece had met a violent death there at the hands of an infamous serial killer. Only Jason had survived the attack, after which the property had lain empty for two years. Lucky to sell it at all...

The noise of a door opening failed to penetrate her drowsy state and she sank down onto the mattress, drifting off to sleep a second later.

~

JASON SHIVERED as he slid the latch key into the front door lock at the third attempt. His hands were blue with cold but finally he pushed in the key and opened the door onto the dark maw of the house. With a furtive look round at Station Road, he stepped across the threshold, making sure to avoid the bloody footprints leading from the bottom step of the staircase, across the welcome mat and out into the cold night where they quickly disappeared on the damp path.

Closing the door behind him, Jason removed his sopping underpants, grabbed the towel from the coat hook and dragged it vigorously over his wet hair, naked torso and legs until the blood began to warm frozen muscles and his hands and toes returned to full function.

The pair of dry socks, left by the door, were pulled over his cold feet but otherwise he stood naked in the early morning murk, the wet towel folded around his underpants and tucked under his arm.

He stepped carefully into the hall, glancing towards the dark lounge on his left. The CD player's lights shone out like a distant ship on the horizon, the Wagner disc inside, ready to go. The opened wine bottle sat on the mantelpiece, a clean glass either side of it. All was prepared.

Jason snapped on the hall light and gazed up the staircase, eyes following the bloody footprints against their direction of travel to the upstairs landing. He nodded with satisfaction. They looked good.

He skipped over the bloody trail, scarring the worn carpet in the entrance hall, and made his way to the kitchen. Opening the back door, he peeled off the clean socks and washed his feet thoroughly in the bucket of warm water he'd placed in the back garden before his sprint down to the river. His feet were clean but he couldn't risk Five-O finding even microscopic blood samples on the soles.

Once again, he dried his feet, then popped the towel, his underpants and socks into the empty washing machine and started the most intensive wash cycle. He was certain everything was clean but even a droplet of blood might unpick his story.

After washing and drying clean hands on a tea towel, he tipped the bucket of water onto the garden and returned to the bottom of the stairs. On the unstained carpet, just inside the doorway, the remote was aimed at the CD player. With a knuckle, Jason pressed PLAY then REPEAT before slowly increasing the volume until Wagner's dramatic pulse began to beat through the speakers.

Finally, he kicked the remote control across the room towards the CD player then climbed the stairs naked, alternately placing his feet on the bare wood at each edge of the skirting board to ensure the bloody tracks were uncorrupted.

He paused at Bianca's bedroom door for a second, listening for the noise of disturbance but the music hadn't woken her so he stepped inside and closed the door to lean over her bed.

'You're gonna be a little smasher in ten years,' he said, brushing her ruddy cheek. 'Yes, you are.'

He left Bianca to sleep, closed her door and continued along the landing, avoiding the last of the bloody footmarks emanating from his aunt's bedroom where the tight old bitch lay dead. He stared at the blood-drenched handle of her bedroom door, a dramatic foretaste of what Five-O would encounter inside - his aunt with her throat slashed by the Reaper.

His nose puckered at the memory of the old fossil's dying moments as her bladder and bowels emptied and her lifeblood seeped out of her.

'Dirty old cunt! No fucking shame.'

Fleetingly, he remembered his Kawasaki, now hidden under a tarp in the back garden of an empty house, two streets over. It was the best birthday present he'd ever had and a pin prick of guilt troubled his conscience for a second.

But his expression hardened at the memory of the documents and deeds he'd found in the cabinet drawer. The money-grabbing bitch was set to make a fortune out of his misery, money that should be his and, if things went to plan, soon would be. Had the bitch worked all hours at the hospital to pay for his bike instead of stealing money that was rightly his, she'd be alive now. Instead she was just a dead thief and Jason steeled himself against remorse.

'Last lap,' he mumbled, padding into his bedroom, nervous at the prospect of self-harm but propelled by the promise of impending wealth and a life of ease. He'd covered all bases and everything had gone smoothly. There was nothing, and no-one, to point the finger.

No witnesses had seen him leave the house in the blood-soaked SOCO suit; no neighbours had been showing a light on his sprint down to the river. No car had passed him on the road, there or back, so no need to slip into darkened driveways and hide behind hedges. Only the hum of streetlamps had escorted him on his short journey to the cleansing waters of the Derwent and back.

In a couple of hours, houselights would go on and car engines would cough into life, belching fumes into the crisp, cold air as the community stirred. Half an hour after that, the milkman and postman would make their rounds, the alarm would be raised and Jason would be saved all over again, the world gathering him into its arms, sorry for his loss.

'Let's do this,' he muttered, his teeth chattering with cold. Not wanting to be carted off to hospital with his knob out, he pulled on a pair of fresh Calvins and lay on his bed. The filled hypodermic sat on his T-shirt, ready for use, and he fought back the nerves with a few deep breaths.

By the light of his bedside lamp, Jason massaged the muscles in his left forearm searching for a vein. Once located, he flexed a fist to keep the blood pumping, tapped the vein to raise it then gathered up the hypodermic in his T-shirt and steadied his grip under the cloth. It wasn't easy but after a few moments of fumbling, he held the needle above his vein and eased it carefully into his bloodstream before depressing the plunger.

∼

You are me, Damen. I came to Derby for you.

Sorenson's words echoed around Brook's head as he felt the jolt of the stretcher banging against the desk. Looking up, Fulbright mouthed something at him but Brook heard only the blood pounding in his ears as he turned to see Sorenson slumped over his antique desk, bald head turned to the window, scalp and neck sporting the snow-white pallor of death. The blotter beneath his head was a puddle of crimson.

Sorenson's left arm stretched across the desk as though reaching out to someone. The skin and sinew of the wrist was hacked and torn, the clenched fist and marble knuckles spotted with blood. He was clutching a necklace with tiny silver hearts on the chain.

Brook took it all in. Just feet away, Sorenson was dead. It was over. The blanched head of his nemesis told him so. About to sink back into unconscious, a languid movement drew Brook's eye and Sorenson's head lifted slowly from the desk, the slashed wrists levering him away from the tacky surface.

Startled and panicked, the paramedic at the rear lost his grip and Brook's feet dropped to the ground with a thud. Unable to move, he stared as the professor turned his head towards him, his demented, grinning, blood-coated lips parting in amusement. The old man's dusty cheeks creased around the eyes but the sockets were empty black orbs, from which twin columns of bloody tears streaked down his face.

Brook woke, panting hard, palms planted on the mattress for ballast. Sweat dotted his brow and he fumbled for the bedside lamp, the sudden illumination scattering the cloaked beasts of the night. Breath back, Brook sank onto his pillow with a jagged sigh.

∾

LATE MORNING FOUND Brook striding out across a white blanket of frozen ground that dropped down to the footpath beside the River Dove. The tough grass in the meadow crunched beneath his boots. In the distance, pockets of condensation rose from the earth as the rising temperature did its work on the ground.

After twenty minutes of brisk walking in the pale winter sun, Brook pulled off his rucksack, rested it on a large boulder and poured a mug of tea from a flask to warm his hands. As he sipped, he watched a large heron wading through the fast waters of the river, its bill exploring the rocks beneath its breadstick legs, rooting for tasty morsels.

A vibration from his backpack disturbed the peace and Brook extracted his phone.

'John. What's up?'

'There's been another.'

'Another what?'

'*What do you think?*' said Noble. '*The Reaper. He's struck again.*'

Brook was stunned. 'That's impossible.'

'*I've seen the body.*'

'But it's too soon.'

'*I wasn't aware there was a cycle.*'

'There isn't but it's still too soon.'

'*Serials chase the high, you said. That's why their timeline shortens.*'

'The Reaper's different.'

'*Not this time. All the evidence points...*'

'Where are you?'

'*I can't tell you. I shouldn't even be talking to you.*'

'Tell me or ring off.'

A hesitation. '*Station Road.*'

'Station Road, Borrowash?' said Brook, slowly.

'*The same.*'

'Where Jason lives?'

'*Yes.*'

'Is he dead?' said Brook, ditching the rest of his tea and slinging his rucksack over his shoulder.

'*No. He survived.*'

Brook narrowed his eyes. 'Of course, he did.'

'*Don't get too downhearted, he's critical. He was heavily drugged and might yet die.*'

'And the girl?'

'*Bianca? Alive. Dehydrated and distressed but she'll be fine.*'

'Then who...?'

'*Jason's aunt - Jane Harrison. Her throat was cut.*'

'Who else?'

'*Just her.*'

Brook shook his head. 'No. Impossible.'

'*I've seen her.*'

'I mean, it can't be the Reaper. She's a nurse.'

'*Trust me. It's the Reaper or a damn good copy.*'

'But the victimology...'

'*I know.*'

'And a single target. It's not the Reaper's style. He kills families.'

'*I know that too but you're not here, looking at all the signatures.*'

'Such as?'

'*Jason surviving, for one. Look, I've got to go.*'

'John!' exclaimed Brook. 'It's not the Reaper. Bear that in mind.'

'You're not seeing what I'm seeing.'

'I soon will be.'

'That's not a good idea.'

'Neither is trying to stop me,' said Brook, ringing off and yomping briskly back upriver towards Hartington.

~

Laura Grant pounded along the Brighton seafront in the dark, relishing the early morning breeze from the channel. The cold air nipped at her cheeks but hands and feet were glowing from the heat of exercise, adrenalin taming the fatigue of another sleepless night.

After upping her pace for a couple of hundred yards, she slowed through the gears and came to a halt to regain her breath. She tried not to look at the bench to which she'd followed Tony Harvey-Ellis on a similar morning only a couple of months before; or recall the look of surprise on his face as she pushed the needle into his neck. It was the last animated expression his face would ever hold. The drugs had taken effect within seconds and leading him down to the water's edge before stripping and pushing him into the sea, had been straightforward.

Of her first solo kill as a Disciple, Laura felt little regret - Tony Harvey-Ellis was a sexual predator and deserved his fate. But his murder had propelled her to Derby and a voyage of self-discovery that had exposed unpalatable truths about her chosen course. And living with those truths was proving the hardest test.

She jogged back to Lansdowne Road as Brighton was coming to life. Crossing the road to her apartment building, a movement registered in her peripheral vision. Reaching the other side of the road, Laura began her warm down stretches, glancing covertly at a man in a blue Mercedes, sipping on a hot drink, a light-blue baseball cap pulled low over his eyes, his head bowed to convey the impression that he was paying her no heed. After a final stretch, she made a mental note of the number plate and turned into her building.

Inside her flat, she ran to the window overlooking the street but the Mercedes was gone.

22

Brook pulled off Brian Clough Way and crossed the bridge over the A52 into Borrowash. A barricade had already been erected across the top of Station Road and a knot of interested onlookers had gathered. Brook parked in the nearby supermarket car park and set off on foot.

At the barrier, he could see the Harrison house, another hundred metres away, betrayed by the tangle of stationary vehicles, lights flashing - squad cars, ambulance and scientific support vans, parked haphazardly across the road.

Brook flashed his ID to the PC on duty and the constable waved him through. A second barrier of crime scene tape was strung across two approach roads and more onlookers stood dutifully behind the tape or at the gate of a neighbouring property - residents trapped inside the blockaded area. Brian Burton was on the tape, talking to a uniformed officer.

A couple of houses before the tape, Brook spotted Amanda O'Neill leaning on her gate and she hailed him as he approached. 'Inspector! Is Jason Wallis dead? Nobody will say. Please tell me he's dead.'

'I can't comment on that.'

'He's alive, isn't he? Fucking typical. Why doesn't this Reaper do the right thing and finish the little bastard?'

'It's too early to...'

'Spare me,' she snarled. 'I already clocked the front window before the first squad car got here. What the hell's happening,

Brook? The papers say this Reaper kills criminals. I didn't know his aunt but she was a nurse, wasn't she? Why kill a nurse, when that little shit was in the house?'

'I don't have an answer for you,' said Brook, turning towards his destination.

'What about my Percy?' she called after him.

Brook glanced towards Burton who had spotted him and was marching over. 'We're still doing tests...'

'Fat lot of good that'll do. I want him back to scatter his ashes.'

'You have my word,' said Brook, ducking smartly under the tape as Burton tried to buttonhole him.

'Thought you were off the case, Brook,' shouted Burton, from the other side of the tape, raising his phone to take a snap. Instinctively, Brook placed an arm over his face. Burton lowered the phone, grinning. 'Defensive pose. One for the front page.'

'Crawl back under your rock, Brian,' said Brook, continuing towards the house.

'And there's my headline,' crowed Burton.

As Brook neared the house, he saw a canvas tent, erected to shield the front of the property from inclement weather and prying eyes. Beyond the canvas, along the garden path to the pavement, half a dozen booted and suited SOCOs worked along a roped-off area, measuring, sampling and putting down evidence markers before photographing results. A SOCO with a video camera emerged from the house, still filming. For some reason he was straddling his legs as if to avoid something on the ground.

When he was near enough to see the large bay window, Brook stopped in his tracks. The word SAVED had been daubed in large capital letters across the glass. Red capitals.

'Sir?'

Brook looked round to see DS Morton in protective suit. 'Rob. Is that blood?' he said, nodding to the window.

Morton looked nervously over his shoulder. 'The victim's.'

'The killer wrote it on the outside of the glass?'

'Inside,' replied Morton.

Brook raised an eyebrow. 'Inside? So, he...'

'...wrote it on backwards, yes,' said Morton. 'Sir, you shouldn't be here.'

'Why write it on the inside?' mumbled Brook.

'We're not sure but DI Greatorix doesn't think it's important.'

'DI Greatorix doesn't think, Rob.'

Morton managed a smile. 'Sir, if he...'

'Footprints?' asked Brook, nodding at the posse of SOCO's on the path.

'Bloody ones,' said Morton.

'Leading where?'

'From the vic's bedroom out to the pavement, heading towards the bridge but they peter out on the pavement,' said Morton. 'We assume a waiting car.'

'Big assumption,' said Brook. Noble appeared. 'John. I hope you're trawling the Derwent.'

'Good to see you too,' said Noble. 'You need to go. Now. The Chief Super's on his way.'

'You'll need sick bags then,' said Brook.

'Are you listening?' insisted Noble. 'You can't be here.'

'I'm in the clear on the shooting,' lied Brook.

'Great,' said Noble. 'Working cases?'

'I'm here, aren't I?'

Noble shook his head. 'The Reaper isn't your case.'

'It's always been my case, John.'

'Not officially and you have to leave.'

'What are you going to do?' asked Brook. 'Arrest me.'

Noble took a breath. 'Sir, please go or we'll both be in deep shit.'

'Have you trawled the river?'

'Why?'

'Because the killer was covered in blood,' said Brook. 'He'd need to discard clothing and get himself clean.'

'We've worked cases before...'

'So, you'll trawl the river.'

'DI Greatorix...we think there was probably a car...' Morton left the sentence hanging after a sharp glance from Noble.

'Any witnesses to that?' asked Brook.

'Early days,' replied Noble.

'And not much CCTV round these parts, if memory serves,' continued Brook. 'So, the river...'

'Yes,' snapped Noble. 'We're checking the river.'

Brook nodded at the defaced bay window. 'And check the waste traps in the bathroom for blood trace. After killing his aunt, Jason might need a shower.'

'Jason?' exclaimed Noble.

'Who else?' said Brook. 'This farce has been staged. The Reaper doesn't kill nurses, John. That's not his narrative.'

'But it couldn't have been Jason,' said Noble.

'He was out cold when first responders broke in,' said Morton.

'But he's alive, you said,' said Brook.

'Barely,' said Noble. 'He's in intensive care and could still die.'

'Might be the best outcome,' said Brook.

'It's not Jason,' said Noble, gesturing at the window. 'That's a Reaper signature, right there.'

'Signatures can be copied,' said Brook. 'And it's written on the inside.'

'Where the Reaper would need to be to kill Mrs Harrison.'

'Then why not write it on an internal wall like he always has?' replied Brook, raising a finger. 'Why take the extra time *and* trouble to write it *backwards* onto a window that can be seen from the street.'

Noble stared. 'Does it matter?'

'It's crucial, John,' said Brook. 'I mentioned the bathroom...'

'SOCO are on it,' sighed Noble. 'We. Have. Done. This. Before. We know the drill. Bins, grates...'

'Bins?' said Brook. 'So, you haven't found the weapon?'

'When do we ever?' replied Noble. 'It's another signature. Apart from the Ingham murders, the Reaper has never left a weapon behind.'

'But Jason did this so the blade must be near.'

'Please...'

'Trust me,' said Brook. 'Jason knows enough for a rough Reaper mimic. And, if he was unconscious in the house, the weapon can't be far...'

'It's not Jason!' insisted Noble.

'The Reaper does not kill nurses,' repeated Brook. 'And he's not an extrovert who writes messages for passing pedestrians. You understand why Jason daubed his aunt's blood on a window instead of an internal wall, I hope.'

'I'm sure you're about to tell me.'

'Figure it out yourself,' snapped Brook. 'And when you do, you'll know Jason's your killer. What about the fatal wound? I'm willing to bet it's more kitchen knife than scalpel.'

'Then you'd lose,' said Noble. 'It's a single sharp cut.'

'John,' warned Morton.

'No, Rob,' said Noble. 'DI Brook needs to know so he can stop this nonsense. Doc Higginbottom says the wound was caused by a thin blade, likely a scalpel, maybe a Stanley knife, but very similar to the one used in the Ingham killings.'

'Then I've underestimated Jason...'

'Jesus!'

'Must be a Stanley knife,' said Brook, thinking it through. 'Although his aunt was a nurse so not impossible that she'd bring home a scalpel...'

'Then how do you explain the wine on the mantelpiece?'

'Wine?' said Brook, startled.

'Opened but not drunk and with the exact same label on the bottle - Nuits St Georges.'

'Impossible,' said Brook, eyes widening.

'It's the *same* wine,' said Noble. 'The *same* label.' He glanced over Brook's shoulder. 'Oh, great!'

'What the absolute fuck are you doing here, Brook?' shouted Greatorix, emerging from the house, peeling off disposable gloves and advancing towards them.

'There are journalists here, sir,' muttered Noble, gesturing beyond the police tape.

'I don't give a fuck if the Royal Family's here,' continued Greatorix, anger flushing his face.

'But the Chief will,' said Brook, as a sleek black car pulled up and Chief Superintendent Charlton emerged. He was in full uniform under his tan camel coat and, after locating the cluster of detectives, set off towards them, a solemn expression fixed to his face. The coal face of murder and extreme violence was not his preferred environment.

A malicious grin spread across Greatorix's face. 'How about that for timing, Brook? Better make yourself scarce. Oops, too late.'

'Brook, what are you doing here?' demanded Charlton, a few yards away.

'I'm helping DI Greatorix, sir,' beamed Brook.

'The hell you are,' spluttered Greatorix. 'Brook thinks he can gate crash my case, sir. And I'm guessing somebody in his old team tipped him the wink.' He glared at Noble who reddened.

'Then you owe your team an apology, Bob,' said Brook. 'I'm here at *your* request, following up on an interview.'

'Have you lost your marbles, Brook?' Greatorix grinned malevolently. 'Wait, don't answer that.'

Brook glanced over his shoulder towards another house.

'Amanda O'Neill lives on Station Road - her cat was killed and you asked me to look into it.'

Greatorix stared at Brook, trying to muster a rebuttal. Crestfallen, he glanced at Charlton's enquiring gaze before conceding with a shrug. 'Then why don't you do that, Brook?'

'While he's here, sir, he should do a oneover of the house,' said Noble, staring implacably at Greatorix. 'With his experience...'

'Experience of being a four time-loser,' snorted Greatorix, returning Noble's stare. 'Sir, we can generate our own leads.'

'I agree,' said Charlton.

'So, do I,' said Brook. 'I've seen enough. You should be able to make an arrest soon.'

'What are you talking about?' snarled Greatorix.

'DI Brook doesn't think the Reaper did this, sir,' said Noble.

'Another copycat?' said Charlton. 'Like the Inghams?'

'I'd bet against that too,' said Brook.

'What with?' growled Greatorix. 'Your reputation? I can't buy anything in a pub with what's left of that.'

'Inspector!' said Charlton, scowling at Greatorix. 'Brook, if there's something we need to know then tell us or leave. That's an order.'

Brook hesitated. 'Jason Wallis killed his aunt and he's passing it off as a Reaper copycat.'

There was silence for a second before Greatorix exploded with laughter. 'Impossible,' he snorted. 'Wallis was dosed up to the eyeballs. He's in intensive care.'

Charlton turned to Noble. 'Sergeant?'

Noble hesitated. 'Victimology is definitely wrong for the Reaper.'

'Wallis couldn't have killed his aunt, I'm telling you,' brayed Greatorix. 'He was out cold.'

'Then how do you explain the blood on the inside of the window?' said Brook.

A shout along Station Road halted the conversation and a Scene of Crime Officer jogged towards Morton, an arm of his protective suit dripping with sludge. Morton received the clear plastic evidence bag, held it up for inspection then brandished it to the huddle.

'Scalpel, sir,' he said to Charlton. 'Recovered from a grate half way to the bridge.'

'What kind of scalpel?' said Brook.

'It's a Swann Morton,' said DS Morton, squinting. 'Model number 60. See there?'

'The PM60,' said Noble, glancing ruefully at Brook, whose face had drained of colour.

'No, that can't be,' said Brook, dazed.

'It's the same brand of scalpel recovered from the Ingham crime scene,' confirmed Noble, lowering his eyes.

'Really?' crowed Greatorix, a big grin deforming his features. 'Remind me, John, didn't DCI Hudson and DI Brook clear young Wallis of the Ingham killings?'

'Yes, sir,' mumbled Noble.

'Yes, sir!' repeated Greatorix, so everyone could hear.

'So, if the Ingham murders were done by a Reaper copycat, Mrs Harrison was killed by the same copycat,' said Charlton.

'Unless it's a copycat of the copycat,' mocked Greatorix, leering at Brook. 'What do you think, John?'

'Seems unlikely,' muttered Noble.

'Seems unlikely,' repeated Greatorix, loudly. 'Thanks for your *experience*, Brook, but if you don't mind, the grown-ups have got work to do.'

Brook stared at Greatorix, a malicious grin fixed to his sagging face. He prepared to speak but thought better of it, instead turning on his heel and walking away, feeling the heat of assembled eyes on him and hearing the low rumble of Greatorix's scornful laughter.

23

Grant put her mobile number on the email to the car hire company that owned the blue Mercedes and sent it into the ether, having already decided against leaving a message on their answerphone.

DCI Hudson entered the office, carrying a Styrofoam tray of fish and chips and the sharp aroma of malt vinegar cut through the air. 'Are you working through lunch again, girl?' he said, chewing on a piece of batter. 'You need to eat.'

'I'll get something in the canteen.'

Hudson pushed the pungent tray towards her but she declined with a shake of the head. 'You work too hard, Laura.'

'One of us has to,' she replied, with an effort at levity.

'You wound me, girl,' said Hudson, grinning. 'I've got four months left. You want me running into burning buildings?'

'It'd be more of a shuffle, to be fair.'

'Ouch,' he said. 'I'm easing down gently, preparing for life in an armchair, shouting at the telly.'

'If you spend your lap of honour shovelling that crap into your mouth, you won't make it past Easter, guv.'

'Bollocks. My nan had a roast meal and smoked sixty Capstan Full Strength every day of her life...'

'...and she died when she was forty-two,' they said in unison.

Hudson smiled. 'At least, you won't miss my jokes.'

'Don't you believe it.'

Hudson studied her. 'Or my sermons.'

Laura caught his eye. 'Something on your mind, guv?'

'I was hoping I could help with whatever's bothering you.'

'What do you mean? I'm fine.'

'No, you're not,' said Hudson. 'Since we got back from Derby, you've been...different. Something happened there and you're trying to pretend it didn't.'

'Nothing happened, guv. I'm just tired.'

'I'm not senile, Laura.'

'I wouldn't put that to a jury,' she replied, grinning.

'Laugh it off all you want but something occurred and before I collect my carriage clock, I'm going to find out what.' He hesitated. 'I'm hoping it was a fling with Damen Brook...'

'Brook?' she exclaimed.

'Why not? A bit of lovesick pining is preferable to the alternatives.'

'And what are those?'

'You tell me.'

'Guv, I spent every waking minute in Derby on the case. How could I possibly have had a fling with Brook? Not to mention, he's almost as old as you.'

'Double ouch,' said Hudson, dropping the Styrofoam tray in a bin. 'I had a couple of days in bed with food poisoning, remember. Plus, I know what a night rake you are, walking around the streets at all hours...'

'Keeping fit for the job, guv. Helps me clear the mind.'

'Then why isn't it clear?'

'Because it's a tough job.'

'No tougher than you let it be. Talk to me.'

Grant stared at him, then broke into a smile. 'Damen Brook. Honestly.'

'Suit yourself. But I'm here a while yet, if you need me.'

She returned her gaze to the monitor but Hudson continued to stare. 'What?'

'I'm not sure I should tell you.'

'About the Ottoman funeral? You told me.' She clasped her hands together. 'And, oh, how my heart skipped a beat when you mentioned my one true love.'

'There's been another Reaper killing,' said Hudson.

Grant's expression slipped from mock to shock. 'What? When?'

'Last night. The copycat, by all accounts. Some poor nurse this time.'

'Copycat?' she croaked.

'The same ones that took out the Ingham family.'

'That's impossible,' she said, before she could stop herself.

'Apparently not. They found the same scalpel used on the Inghams and there were other signatures.'

'Who?'

'A woman called Jane Harrison.'

'The Reaper's never killed less than three.'

'Tony Harvey-Ellis was a lone kill,' said Hudson.

Grant stared into space. 'You said a nurse?'

'I did. She was also Jason Wallis's aunt and the little shit was *in* the house when she died.'

'He survived?'

'Barely. He's in the ICU. But his presence is another signature, in the Derby killings, at least.'

'Is he a suspect?'

'No. He was heavily drugged and completely comatose at the scene.'

'When did you find out?'

'About twenty minutes ago. John Noble thought we ought to know before it hit the wire. They're still working it and want to be sure before they go public.'

'A nurse,' repeated Grant.

'It gets better. Your *boyfriend* turned up at the house, unannounced and, without so much as a look-see, accused Jason Wallis of killing his aunt.'

'Brook said that?' mumbled Grant.

'He did.' Hudson shrugged. 'Who knows? I've learned to respect Brook's judgement so he must have had cause. I told Noble to bear it in mind.'

'It's hard to believe,' said Grant.

'I don't know why they bother hunting this Reaper. They should just put a surveillance team on Jason and wait for the next one.'

'It's not the Reaper,' said Grant.

'It's a quick turn-around, that's for sure,' conceded Hudson. 'And victimology is way off.'

Grant stood, gathering her car keys. 'I'll pack a bag.'

'What for?'

'It's our case, guv. You're SIO...'

'Hold your horses,' said Hudson. 'That's yesterday's chip wrapper. We're out. Charlton got himself a new lead.'

'I thought you said Noble...'

'John's still second chair but the new SIO is a DI Greatorix.'

'Do we know him?'

'I met him at the funeral. Been on the sick for a year.' He smiled to reassure, deciding against passing on first impressions. 'It's in good hands.'

'But why drop in another lead when we've got the background?'

'Greatorix is local and he's got Noble for continuity. Out of our hands.' Hudson chuckled. 'Brook, though. What's he like, blundering in there, pissing off management? Got to hand it to him.'

Grant snatched her jacket from the back of her chair. 'I'm going out.'

'Where?'

'Lunch. I work too hard, remember.'

'Then take the rest of the day, Laura. Clear your head. I'll hold the fort.'

Grant paused to consider. 'Actually, I think I will, guv. Thanks.'

∼

OUTSIDE THE STATION, Grant sat on the low wall and took out her *Brook* mobile. She was tempted to ring him just to hear his voice but settled for a simple text. *Is it true?*

After sending it, her eye fell upon a large blue car, parked behind trees in the Asda delivery yard, opposite the station. Pocketing her phone, she marched across the road towards the same Mercedes she'd seen outside her apartment building that morning. It was unoccupied so she pressed her face against the window. On the driver's seat was a large brown envelope and, even from outside the car, she could see her name written in large capitals. She yanked at the door, which opened. After a quick look over her shoulder, she snatched up the envelope, tore it open and pulled out a small wad of photographs. After a second to establish their content, Grant rammed them back into the envelope and marched back to the station to pick up her car.

∼

The Resurrection

LATER THAT AFTERNOON, as the sky darkened, Brook sat in his car in the car park of the Queens Medical Centre and tapped out a text to Noble.

Hope you didn't get flak from Greatorix. Developments? River? Bathroom?

The phone rang a few seconds later. 'John?'

A hesitation. *'They sprayed the bathroom for blood trace, including the trap - nothing on infrared. They'll do a thorough test, obviously...'*

'Then Jason must have cleaned up at the river before going back.'

'It's not Jason. You saw the scalpel. It's identical to the Ingham scalpel. How would Jason even get hold of one?'

'I don't know,' said Brook. 'But, to get away with this, he had to dump the weapon nearby before playing dead at the house.'

'Motive?'

'Isn't being a vicious thug enough?' said Brook.

'You know it isn't. You haven't got a shred of evidence. What would my previous DI have said to that?'

'He'd say look harder, John. Although it smacks of good planning, Jason's a novice killer. He's not smart enough to do this without missing something.'

'Like what? He lives there. We can expect his prints and DNA all over the house. Where does that get us?'

'His aunt was divorced with no children, right?'

'Apart from Bianca, Jason was her only living relative,' said Noble.

'He's the sole heir?' Brook smiled grimly. 'Did his aunt make a will?'

'Still checking! But it doesn't make him a killer.'

'And he'd have to be eighteen to inherit,' said Brook. No reply from Noble. 'John?'

'His birthday was three days ago.'

Brook let out a bitter laugh. 'The impatience of youth. How much? Ball park figure.'

'Are you American?'

'How much?'

Noble sighed. *'We found papers. Mrs Harrison received recent payouts. Criminal Injuries payments, her sister's life insurance. Also, it seems the Wallis house on the Drayfin is under offer, though it won't fetch more than forty grand, given its history. Throw in the aunt's house and her own life insurance and it should add up to about a quarter of a million.'*

'Motive enough for a low-rent scumbag like Jason,' said Brook.

'Speculation. Greatorix won't go for it and I have to agree. All the evidence points to the Reaper. Jason's in intensive care. He couldn't have functioned, never mind commit murder. And if he had, he'd have been covered in blood.'

'That's why he killed her, got himself clean *then* put himself under. What was the drug?'

'No results yet.'

'It won't be Twilight Sleep.'

'If it is, will you give up this nonsense?'

'It won't be. How was he drugged?'

'Needle in the arm. Responders found him unconscious on his bed.'

'Meaning he self-medicated.'

'You mean, after he cut his aunt's throat, trailed bloody footprints down the stairs, wrote SAVED on the front window then marched down the road to dump the scalpel down a grate covered in her blood?'

'Exactly. John, he's out in the sticks. Who's going to see him in the middle of the night? He cleaned up in the Derwent, weighed down the blood-soaked clothes in the water then went back to put himself under. Was the needle found next to him?'

'Does that matter?'

'Was it?'

'On the floor by the bed.'

'Prints?'

'None.'

'Anything close he might have used to wrap around his hand? A handkerchief, maybe?'

A pause. *'The needle was on the floor on top of a T-shirt.'*

'There,' said Brook. 'He kills his aunt, daubs blood on the window then leaves a deliberate blood trail into the street to make it look like an intruder. And if I were doing it, I'd make sure my bloody footprints were in the middle of the stair carpet so I could avoid them on the way back to my room.

'He dumps the weapon in the grate and gets clean in the river. Maybe he hid fresh clothes there earlier and changed into them.' Brook paused. 'No, he might get blood on them coming back. Better to come back virtually naked. It's not far.' Brook nodded at the simplicity of it. 'Yes. He comes back to the house near frozen, dries off, goes up to his bedroom, wraps the hypodermic in the T-shirt then injects himself. He's really thought it through and it looks like the perfect alibi, if you don't know what you're looking for.'

'Thanks.'

'Don't take it personally. He's been clever.'

'Not clever enough to understand the drugs might kill him,' objected Noble. 'No-one in their right mind would take such a risk.'

'He's not in his right mind, John. He's a fledgling psychopath. He kills cats for fun and his aunt for money.'

'So, you think he rolled the dice on dosage.'

'Why not? He doesn't have any prospects apart from his aunt's money. He takes a gamble. And with Greatorix on the case, it's liable to pay off handsomely.'

'Why the river?' said Noble, after a grudging silence.

'The bloodstains head in that direction and it's close. He strips off in the water, wraps the blood-soaked gear round a stone, then sprints back, avoiding all the bloodstains he's taken care to leave in the house. What about other clothes?'

'Other clothes?'

'He must have come back from the river in something. It's possible he picked up traces of his aunt's blood. Unless he dumped those as well, they must be in the house.'

'His bedroom is clean and so was he...'

'I sense a but coming.'

'There was a towel, underpants and a pair of socks in the washing machine. They'd been through an intensive wash cycle.'

'Tested?'

'No obvious blood on the fabric but they're still checking - the waste trap too.'

'Then that's all he wore and he used the towel to dry himself when he got back.'

'It's a theory, I suppose. If only you had proof.'

'Leave that to me.'

'We talked about this...'

'Have you checked his browsing history? He must have researched past killings.'

'He doesn't have a laptop but, yes, he's done plenty of browsing on his phone. But his family were killed by the Reaper - only natural he'd have a history picking over the details.'

'Or gathering information he needed.'

'Not all the information,' replied Noble. 'The brand of scalpel was never made public and there are no records of him buying one, even *supposing he knew what to look for AND had plastic, which he doesn't. He hasn't got a penny to his name.'*

'His aunt...' began Brook.

'...was never involved in post mortems and stock at hospitals is strictly controlled, that's assuming, for some unknown reason, she thought it a good idea to bring one home. Everything fits the Reaper, even Jason's survival. At both previous crime scenes, he was unconscious with no blood trail to connect him to the killing and nothing's changed. We know the Reaper - or his copycat - committed those crimes. We've got the same scalpel, the same wine, the same writing on the window...'

'John, it's the window that seals his guilt,' said Brook.

'What do you mean?'

'Think about it. If he gets the dosage wrong, he's taken a drug that might kill him. He needs to be sure help is coming. So, instead of daubing the blood on an internal wall, he writes it on the inside of the window to make *sure* someone sees it and raises the alarm. That's his insurance policy and he can't afford to let the rain wash it off.'

Noble was silent for a moment. *'Okay, I see the logic in that. But it's still supposition, unsupported by actual evidence. Besides, the music drew attention just as well.'*

'Music?' said Brook.

'When they broke the door down, Wagner was blasting out on the CD player and had been for a couple of hours.'

'How do they know that?'

'The neighbour was woken by it and stood it for a couple of hours then went round at seven to complain, saw the window and phoned it in - you know the rest.'

'Wagner,' said Brook, a terrible dread pulling on his gut. 'Which one?'

'I can't remember.'

'It's important.'

'Then I'll send you a picture. Now, remind me, isn't classical music another Reaper signature?'

'Sarcasm is unattractive, John.'

'I've got to find some way to get through to you,' said Noble.

'The music is more insurance - in case nobody notices the window.'

'It's not Jason! Okay, you asked for it. We did drag the river and found a carrier bag, weighed down with a brick...'

'And?'

'There was a garment in it with extensive bloodstaining. The lab techs are giving it a thorough going over.'

'Garment?' echoed Brook, picking up Noble's choice of words.

'Specifically, a scene-of-crime protective suit - overshoes, gloves and a mask too.'

'You mean...'

'No, I don't mean overalls and I don't mean a boiler suit. It was a specialised SOCO suit. Exactly like the one the Reaper copycat used to walk away from the Ingham crime scene, unchallenged.'

Brook's mind was racing. 'Are you certain?'

'Now you're being rude,' said Noble. 'So, I can accept Jason is cunning and vicious enough to kill his aunt and lay it all off on the Reaper. Far-fetched though it is, it's also just about possible his aunt brought home a hypodermic and an identical Swann Morton scalpel for Jason to get his hands on. I suppose, Jason could have found the identical bottle of wine to put on the mantelpiece but there's NO way he'd be able to get hold of specialised crime scene gear like a Forensics suit without leaving a paper trail the length of the M1. This is mail order equipment for forensic companies with an account.'

'You're checking?' said Brook.

'All over it like a cheap crime scene suit,' replied Noble. 'No record of him ever acquiring one. Not that he has any money. I told you, he doesn't have a credit card or even a bank account. He. Didn't. Kill. His. Aunt. Now, I've got to go. Put Jason out of your mind and pray he snuffs it and solves all your problems.'

Noble rang off and Brook got out of the car, trudging towards the hospital. 'How the hell did he get hold of a SOCO suit?'

He stopped in his tracks when a dreadful thought flashed across his mind.

24

Jason opened his eyes and his breathing deepened. He was alive. A woman he didn't know sat beside his bed and confusion warped his features until he realised it was a copper. He closed his eyes again, to take a moment to remember his lines then sat up as though just regaining consciousness.

'Who are you?' he croaked.

'I'm PC Banach,' said the officer, sitting forward. 'How are you feeling?'

Jason tried to move his arms and stared at his wrists when they obeyed. No handcuffs.

'Tired. Where am I?'

'Hospital. You were drugged.'

'Drugged?' He frowned. 'I don't understand.'

PC Banach produced a notebook. 'What's the last thing you remember?'

Jason's expression suggested bafflement. 'I went to bed and... that's it. Who drugged me? And why?'

'Jason, there's been an incident which somebody else will talk to you about. For now, you need to concentrate on getting some rest.'

A smile spread slowly across his face but he managed to turn it into a frown, as though trying to remember. He looked plaintively beyond Banach. 'Where's my aunt?'

'She...couldn't be here.' The PC smiled to reassure. 'I'll get you some water.'

As soon as she left the room, Jason grinned, thrilled that everything had gone so smoothly. Despite the ache in his guts, he was bursting to get out of bed and walk around the city, enjoy his freedom. He knew he couldn't but at least he could lay back and think of all the things he'd buy with his aunt's money.

'Correction. My money.'

∽

POURING TEA FROM HIS FLASK, Brook hunched forward on the unyielding plastic chair still processing his conversation with Noble and scrolling though the pictures from the Reaper flat on his burner phone, until alighting on the shot of the Wagner CD. He enlarged the picture with finger and thumb and turned his head to read the spine. It was a recording of Die Walkure - The Valkyrie. Loud and dramatic, perfectly suited to the task of disturbing the neighbours.

Disquiet spread through Brook's bones. Sorenson was not a man to inflict substandard beauty on the dying. To breathe one's last listening to anything other than humanity's finest musical achievements was to defile the entire Reaper project and Brook was confident the Valkyrie CD in the Reaper flat would have been the finest rendition ever.

But Sorenson was dead. Edie McQuarry too. And Laura Grant was safely back in Brighton. If the Wagner CD had been removed from the Reaper flat and taken to Jason's aunt's house since Brook's last visit, a different member of the Disciples must have collected it unless...

Unless Jason found the flat. And the only way he could've found the flat is if...

Brook drained his tea in dismay and stared through the open door of Drexler's room from his seat in the corridor. Access to Mike was restricted, Campbell and Tyson taking no chances on Brook coaching Drexler through some of the blanks in his memory. The plain clothes officer sitting beside the stricken American, nodded an acknowledgement and drained a plastic beverage cup before settling back into his padded seat.

'Fancy a refill,' shouted Brook, through the open door, shaking his flask.

'No, thanks.'

'Proper tea,' persisted Brook. 'Not that canteen muck.'

The officer smiled. 'Thanks, but I've done nowt but sup tea since I got here.'

Brook smiled, sensing an opportunity. 'If you change your mind.'

A text from Noble. *Confirmed Jason inherits all. Insurance policies, sale of Wallis house, Aunt's house. Jason only adult relative. £150k+ and Borrowash house clear. Lucky boy. Also, he's out of danger and conscious. Remembers nothing. No surprise. Drug ID soon.*

Brook's features set hard. 'Lucky boy.' He texted back. *Let me know.*

And if it's Twilight Sleep?

Cross that bridge...

Good thought about Jason as perp. If only. BTW your light bulb was dusted, had J Ottoman's prints on. No trace of Jason.

Brook had expected as much. He texted back. *Any news on Percy?*

?????

The dead cat.

Nothing yet.

Brook pocketed his phone and watched Drexler's minder start pacing around the room as much as the limited space allowed. It was beginning. 'Hated these duties when I was a DC,' called out Brook. 'How long have you been on?'

'Four hours. Another two to go.' The young man grimaced and returned to his seat.

'Long shift,' commiserated Brook, to be met with a shrug. 'Sure, you don't want another tea?'

'Certain.' He was beginning to cross and uncross his legs at regular intervals and shifted his weight in the chair every couple of minutes so, when he wasn't looking, Brook slid his thermos under the chair.

'Well,' said Brook, standing. 'Must be off. If Mike wakes up, tell him I called.' He left without further ceremony.

The officer watched him go then hurried to the door. With a backward glance at the sleeping Drexler, he peered out into the corridor. It was empty, Brook nowhere to be seen. A couple of seconds later, he stepped out, closing the door behind him before marching smartly along the deserted corridor, heading with some urgency to the nearest toilet.

As soon as Brook saw him pass by the safety glass, he opened the store room door and nipped into Drexler's room.

'Mike,' he said, laying a hand on his arm.

'Damen,' replied Drexler, opening his eyes. 'Has he gone?'

'You were awake?'

'About five minutes. I heard you talking and wondered if we'd get a chance to speak.' With fewer tubes now constraining him, Drexler manoeuvred himself into a seating position. 'Good to see you.'

'You too.'

'Is Laura okay?'

Brook stared. 'You remember.'

'How could I forget? Is she okay?'

'She's fine,' said Brook. 'She turned her back on the Disciples for good. She's back in Brighton, trying to live her life.'

'So, you gave her a pass?'

Brook braced for protest. 'You were at death's door and she helped get you to A&E. I think she earned it. Sorry.'

Drexler smiled. 'Don't be. You did good. She doesn't belong with the Disciples - never did. They got their hooks in when she was young and vulnerable. And, if you'd seen the cabin...she deserves another shot. How's she holding up?'

'Adjusting slowly, I'd say.'

'Must be tough. Campbell and Tyson haven't mentioned her.'

'I left her out of the narrative,' said Brook. 'Told them it was just you, me and McQuarry.'

'I figured. I've been doing the same.'

'Good. They're suspicious but so far it's holding.'

'What about earlier? I've said I can't remember details.'

'You asked me for a lift from the station, McQuarry pulled a gun on us and you drove the three of us to the field in her car - an Audi. I was in the back with McQuarry.'

Drexler nodded. 'Got it. There is *one* problem.'

'What?'

'I was careful about leaving incriminating evidence in the cottage, with you being next door and me thinking you were one of Sorenson's guys.'

'And?'

'Before I moved in, I was in London doing some digging on Sorenson and I *acquired* a photocopy of his post mortem report.'

'Why?'

'With Sorenson, I never believe what I don't see with my own eyes,' said Drexler. 'Crazy, I know, but Sorenson seemed indestructible like he couldn't die. Does that sound stupid?'

'No,' said Brook. 'I want to hear all about Sorenson and California when you're out of here, Mike.' Brook's head turned at the distant noise of a door closing and he hurried to the corridor. 'I have to go.'

'Wait!' said Drexler. 'The photocopy - I hid it in the cottage.'

'Where? I searched the place after the shooting.'

'It's inside the fabric on the underside of the armchair. If it falls into the wrong hands, they can link me to Sorenson. And, as I'm connected to you...'

'Just like that, they have a conspiracy,' said Brook.

'Exactly.'

'I'll see to it.' He peered into the corridor from the doorway.

'Damen! I've been painting you as the innocent bystander with Campbell and Tyson. Anything you want me to throw into the mix - a little heroism, maybe?'

'I'm fine, if you don't mind taking all the weight.'

'I pulled the trigger, buddy. Plus, if I'd trusted you from the get-go, I wouldn't be lying here.'

'If you're sure,' said Brook. 'And, you'll need some kind of motive for McQuarry coming at you like that.'

'Working on it,' said Drexler.

Brook nodded and stepped into the corridor, closing the door in the nick of time.

'Thought you'd left,' said the Detective Constable, suspiciously.

Brook crouched to root beneath the chair and brandished his alibi. 'Forgot my flask.'

~

RUSH HOUR HAD long since passed and traffic on Siddalls Road had eased to a trickle. Brook sat in the darkness of his car, smoking a cigarette, staring at a picture on his phone. Sent by Noble, a gloved hand held two see-through evidence bags containing the circular disc of Die Walkure and its case, both removed from the Borrowash crime scene. The recording was a performance by the Metropolitan Orchestra in Manhattan in 1987. It was the same edition as the CD in the flat.

Discarding his cigarette, Brook locked the car and trudged through a biting wind towards Magnet House. Once inside the building, he skipped up to the second floor and unlocked the Reaper apartment. Although in darkness, Brook listened before stepping inside and closing the door. Feeling his way to the small bedroom, he flicked on the bedside lamp and stood, glaring at the gap where the Wagner CD had stood.

He moved to the kitchen, opening the cupboard under the sink. The box of SOCO suits had been moved since he'd photographed them, the scalpels too. A bottle of wine was missing from the carton in the centre of the room. Brook didn't bother to check the flasks of clear liquid. He knew all he needed to know. Wallis had followed him from John Ottoman's abandoned home on the Drayfin Estate then broken into the Reaper flat, using the only skills he possessed.

Brook hung his head in dismay but it shot up at once. If Jason had been watching the Drayfin house…

He turned off the lights, locked the flat and hurried back to his car.

∽

JOHN OTTOMAN STIRRED from a fitful snooze in the armchair, his mouth dry, after a rare glass of red wine. Blinking, he looked around the tidy, dimly-lit lounge, located the remote and turned off the radio.

It was late - his sister had already gone up - so Ottoman dragged himself to his feet and padded to the kitchen, through the back door and out into the dark in his flimsy slippers. The street outside was deathly quiet and the pale streetlights made barely a dent on the night. Had he been on the Drayfin, he would never have put out the bins after dark but, here in leafy Oakwood, he had no such qualms and he wheeled the recycling bin down the path and onto the street for the morning collection.

As he manoeuvred the bin up against the hedge, he heard movement behind him and his heart leapt when a figure emerged from the gloom.

'Brook!' he panted. 'You frightened me.'

'Sorry,' said Brook. 'I didn't have a phone number for you.'

'Has something happened? I heard the news. Is it true? Has the Reaper killed again?'

'There's been an incident. That's all I can say.'

'But Wallis survived.'

'He's in hospital but, yes, he survived.'

'And the infant?'

'Bianca's fine.'

'Some comfort,' nodded Ottoman. 'Do you want to come in?'

'No,' said Brook, oblivious to Ottoman's shivering. 'I just popped by to warn you. Don't go back to your house in Drayfin. Not for a while at least.'

'Why?'

'It's too dangerous so, please, just do as I ask.'

'I definitely will go back unless you tell me why.'

Brook hesitated. 'When I went to the house a few days ago...I think I was being watched.'

'What? Who?' No answer from Brook. 'Jason?'

'I think so.'

'He killed Denise, didn't he?' Ottoman looked hard at Brook.

'There's no evidence, nor is there likely to be any,' said Brook. 'But, yes, I suspect he was there that night and played a part in your wife's death. That's why you need to stay away.'

'I had no intention of ever setting foot in the place again. It became a prison to both of us.'

'Good. Do you need the house keys back?' Brook made no attempt to hand them over.

'Keep them. I have another set and you may need them for the investigation.'

The investigation was dead but Brook decided against contradiction. 'I'm sorry I don't have anything concrete to tell you.'

'Don't be. Thank you for taking the time. I know you'll do right by my Denise.'

Brook's smile was thin. He looked over Ottoman's shoulder at the house. 'Nice house. Your sister's?'

'Yes.'

'It may be a long way from the Drayfin but keep a low profile just the same. Jason may want payback when he gets out of hospital. In fact, he may already be out...'

'Payback for what?'

'You stalked him, humiliated him. And, until the funeral, he had no idea it was you.'

'Really? I assumed you...'

'No,' said Brook. 'Not the sort of information we give out.'
'I suppose not. So, what do we do now?'
'*We* do nothing. I'll take care of it.'
'I mean Jason. He's a killer. He has to be stopped.'
Brook chose his words carefully. 'I'm working on it.'

25

Brook drove wearily back through the centre of Derby and headed for home, resisting the temptation to call in at St Mary's Wharf to check progress in the Harrison murder. Just as the fall-out from McQuarry's death seemed to be abating, the latest murder had thrown his life into fresh turmoil.

Forty minutes later, he arrived at his cottage and stepped onto the frosted tarmac. He padded next door to Rose Cottage, stepping over the police tape, blown to the ground by recent winds. At the side door, Brook took out the spare key given to him by the landlord after Drexler's hospitalisation, and scored through the seal.

Unlocking the door, he made a beeline for the one armchair in the tiny sitting room and turned it over. The fabric covering the wooden frame had been torn open and the cavity was empty, though a fragment of brown parcel tape still adhered to the frame. But, of the envelope Drexler claimed to have concealed, there was no sign. Brook righted the chair, locked up and returned to his cottage.

He lit a cigarette at the gate, pulled out his mobile and rang Kelly Tyson. Before she could speak, he apologised for ringing her.

'Don't worry, Inspector. I was going to ring you. We interviewed Mike Drexler an hour ago and filled in most of the blanks. He confirmed everything in your statements.'

'And?'

'We're signing off on the shooting so you're in the clear as far as McQuarry's death is concerned.'

'Outstanding,' said Brook, with no great enthusiasm. 'Campbell must be thrilled.'

'About the same as you, from the sound of it. Thought you'd be happy.'

'I've been kicking my heels under a cloud of suspicion for weeks, so forgive me if I don't do cartwheels.'

'Shit happens, Brook. That's why we clean the stables. I'd take the positives if I were you. You dodged a bullet in more senses than one. Don't you want to know McQuarry's motives?'

'My next question.'

'Seems she's been threatening and harassing Drexler for a while now, which is why he was armed. She's always been unhappy at how she was portrayed in his book and seemed to think she deserved some of his royalties.'

'So, what happens to Mike?'

'He committed a crime.'

'He was acting in self-defence.'

'Don't worry, he'll be given a caution and, when he's fit to travel, he'll be shown the door and never allowed back.'

'Fair enough.' Brook decided his enquiry about the search of Mike's cottage was ill-timed. 'Well, thanks for letting me know...'

'Was there something else?' asked Tyson.

'Like what?'

'I don't know. You rang me.'

'Did I? Yes. I was wondering what happened to Fulbright's brother after the crash.'

'Andrew? Still in California, as far as I know. He had a sales job of some kind, using his plummy accent to open doors and seal deals. At least that's how it played to Fulbright.'

'Do you have an address for him?'

'No, why would I?'

'No reason. Did Fulbright talk about Andrew much?'

'Not often. They didn't get on.'

'How so?'

'Something to do with their parents. Ross took me aside, early doors, in case I said the wrong thing in front of the guvnor. There was a home invasion a few years before and Fulbright's parents were attacked. His dad suffered severe head injuries. Died a week later. Soon after that, his mum had a stroke. Long story short, she never recovered and lapsed into a coma, unlikely to ever wake up. But the guvnor wouldn't give up hope and insisted she be kept on life support in a

private facility. Andrew disagreed and thought they should turn off the machines.'

'Is the mother still alive?'

'I've no idea. Why?'

'Just curious,' said Brook. 'They ever catch the attacker?'

'No. What are you after, Brook?'

'After?'

'Two-way street, remember.'

'Kelly, I have to ring off, I'm going through a tunnel.'

'You lying sod...'

Brook ended the call, turned off the phone and went into his kitchen. A lamp was on and the smell of coffee hit his nostrils.

'Damen!' Laura Grant was seated at the kitchen table, her hand gripping a mug.

'Laura. What the hell...?' Brook's enquiry was stifled when she came over and threw her arms around him, drawing him into a tight embrace. He pulled her arms down and gripped them to look into her eyes.

'I thought I'd never see you again.'

'That was the plan,' said Brook. 'What changed?'

Grant's gaze fell. 'I'm being followed.'

'Are you sure?'

'I'm still a copper,' she said, frowning.

'Who?' She shook her head. Brook removed his coat and draped it over a chair, took his empty flask to the sink to rinse out and switched on the kettle. 'Followed, here?'

'Of course not,' said Grant. Brook raised an eyebrow. 'I made certain.'

'Where's your car?'

'In the village, next to the pottery shop. No-one knows I'm here, not even Hudson. After the apartment in Brighton was stripped bare, I thought that would be it but there was a car - a blue Mercedes - outside my building. Later I saw it parked across the street from the police station.' Grant reached back to the table and handed Brook the envelope. 'And someone left me this.'

Brook pulled out around two dozen photographs of Grant running hard along the dark, deserted Brighton promenade, chasing down Tony Harvey-Ellis. One picture showed her injecting Harvey-Ellis in the neck, then leading him carefully down steps towards the beach. There was even a long shot of her guiding him into the sea.

'Who took these?' said Brook.

'I can guess.'

'McQuarry,' said Brook. He shrugged. 'So, they have something on you. That's how they operate - insurance to remind us there are costs to developing a conscience. They can't use it, Laura, any more than you can use what you know about them. If we want to live our lives, the only confession you or I can ever make is to a priest. And they know it.'

'I made my confession to you,' said Grant. 'Why didn't you tell me about Jason's aunt?'

Brook hesitated. 'I'm not on the case...'

'How does that stop you telling me?'

'I'm sorry. I thought it best to wait. I had no details.'

'Was she really a nurse?' Brook nodded. 'Then it can't be a Reaper killing.'

'I know.'

'What do we do?'

'*I* do what I can,' said Brook. 'And if I can't do anything, I do nothing. All *you* have to do is stay in Brighton and do your job.'

'How can I?'

'You don't have a choice.'

'But I can't stop thinking about Ed, about the shooting.'

'That'll pass,' said Brook. 'These things take time and you're handling it better than I did. I had a nervous breakdown, remember.'

'Right now, a nervous breakdown sounds like a breeze.' She stared hard at him. 'Did you think it was me?'

'What?'

'Jason's aunt.'

'Not for a second.'

'How about a split-second?'

'When I heard about all the Reaper signatures, there was a moment...'

'I didn't do it.'

Brook smiled. 'I know.'

'You read the letter I left you?'

'Yes, and I believed every word, Laura.'

There were tears in her eyes. 'DCI Hudson can confirm my alibi, if you need to ring him.'

'Feeling sorry for yourself won't help,' said Brook.

She plucked her car keys from the table and headed for the door. 'I shouldn't have come.'

'No, you shouldn't,' said Brook, blocking her way. 'But it's late and you're not driving around the Peaks in this state. The roads are dark and dangerous in winter, so I suggest you get comfortable.'

'Aren't you afraid to have a killer sleeping under your roof?'

'Back at you.'

'I have to go.'

Brook grabbed the hand holding the car keys and held her fast. 'You're staying.'

She struggled against his grip. 'Let me go.'

Brook opened his hands and she headed for the door. 'Don't you want to hear about the latest killing?'

'It's not your case.'

'It's always been my case, Laura. And, until I stop these people, it always will be.'

'But you're not on the investigation.' She narrowed her eyes. 'Noble?'

'He has the best seat in the house though he's drawing the wrong conclusions.'

'Did he tell you he asked me to find out if Mike Drexler spent time in Brighton?'

'No,' said Brook. 'But I'm not surprised. He knows I'm hiding something and he's dug deeper than anyone else. What did you say?'

'I told him I'd check it out then emailed a couple of days later to say there was no trace.'

'Lucky he asked you and not Joshua.'

'Wasn't it?'

'Sit down. I'll make more coffee.'

'I'd prefer something stronger.' Brook hesitated before pulling a bottle of Lagavulin from a cupboard and examining the two inches left in the bottom. 'Seriously?' said Grant. 'Uncle Vic's whisky?'

'What can I say? I developed a taste for it.' Brook poured a measure into a glass and handed it to her, then poured a smaller amount into an empty jam jar. He saw her looking. 'The Queen's borrowing my glassware for a state dinner.' Her smile heartened him. 'What did Joshua tell you?'

'Just that the MO suggested the Reaper and that you turned

up, accusing Wallis in front of the new SIO. Hudson said he's a safe pair of hands. Is that right?'

'Bob Greatorix couldn't solve a crossword puzzle in The Sun,' said Brook.

'I figured the boss wanted to stop me dragging him back up here. Why Jason?'

'Instinct.'

'Motive?'

'His aunt's life insurance money and the house.'

'Cold,' said Grant. 'Any actual proof?'

Brook hesitated. 'Yes and no.'

'What does that mean?'

'Jason found the Reaper flat,' said Brook. Laura stared. 'He must have followed me there and broken in...'

'And found everything he needed to step into the Reaper's shoes.'

'Exactly.'

'And he thinks he can get away with it because the only detective smart enough to know what he's done, can't say a word without incriminating himself.' Grant nodded, impressed. 'Neat. But why on earth would Jason be following you in the first place?'

'Long story,' said Brook. Grant looked at her watch and folded her arms.

26

16th December 2010

Just past five in the morning, Brook threw off the blanket and dragged himself from the cramped sofa to make tea, blanket round his shoulders, warming his hands on the kettle as it boiled. He hadn't slept well, customary while working on a case and the fact that he didn't really have a case to work on, made it worse.

Despite the early hour, he made a mug of tea for Laura and crept upstairs with it. Bobbi was stretched out on the top step and lifted a sleepy black eye to him.

'How did you get in?' said Brook, picking up the protesting cat and pointing him down the stairs. He knocked softly on the bedroom door.

'It's open,' was the muffled reply.

'Tea,' said Brook, leaving the mug outside the door.

'What time is it?'

'Ten past five,' said Brook. A groan followed. 'I have to go in early. Leave in your own time and put the key through. Which reminds me, how did you get in?'

'I hired a six-year old child to pick the lock,' she shouted back.

'I mean it,' said Brook.

'I forced your kitchen window,' shouted Grant. 'Though forced might be putting it strongly. Security measures around here, amount to little more than closing windows and doors and hoping no-one tries to open them. Your locks are a joke.'

'I live in the countryside,' countered Brook.

'Then don't be surprised when city folk break in.'

'Don't forget your tea,' called Brook, trotting downstairs to usher out the cat. Hearing the bedroom door open and close, he fired up the computer in his office, keyed in the appropriate passwords and loaded the files on Vinny Muir and family for another read-through. Learning nothing new, he loaded Muir's mugshot onto the screen and simply stared at it. He clicked onto the left and right profile pics for an enlarged view then opened another window and loaded Sammy Elphick's file onto the screen.

Switching to read a list of Muir's *Known Associates*, it didn't take long to find a possible connection. A supplementary note on the log suggested the pair had served time together in Wormwood Scrubs and a further entry claimed they even shared a cell for a short period in 1988, though there was no link to prison files or any document facsimile to support it.

Nevertheless, there it was on the log. Sammy Elphick and Vinny Muir had shared a cell in Wormwood Scrubs. Brook stared at the screen. Why would Fulbright pursue such a tenuous link? He checked the log entry. The information on Muir and Elphick had not been added until the beginning of December in 2008 - eighteen years after the first killing in Harlesden.

'Odd.' Then Brook remembered his conversation with Tyson, the previous night. 'You weren't interested in the Reaper, were you, Richard? You were still hunting the man who attacked your parents.' Brook played around with the idea and liked it except for one thing. 'But then why show Muir's mugshot to Sorenson?'

'Morning.' Brook turned to see Laura Grant in jeans and a T-shirt, clutching her empty mug, hair damp and dishevelled, her young face marked by sleep. 'Where are you going?'

'Work,' said Brook.

'At this time?'

'Early bird. When are you leaving?'

'Make a girl feel welcome, why don't you?'

Brook laughed. 'Sorry. Stay as long as you like.'

'I'll leave after breakfast.'

'Ah, about that...'

~

HAVING BADE LAURA A SOMBRE FAREWELL, including a tight hug at her instigation, Brook set off for Derby in freezing rain, arriving at St Mary's Wharf forty minutes later. Hurrying through the dark, flask in hand, he spotted Noble's car and frowned. He knew Greatorix wouldn't be around early but he'd especially hoped to avoid Noble. If anyone could see through his subterfuge, it would be him.

'Can't be helped,' mumbled Brook, vaulting up the steps to his office. Seeing no sign of Noble, he trudged down to the Incident Room where DC Cooper was pouring hot water into a mug.

'John not here?' enquired Brook.

Cooper gazed at Brook in surprise. 'Picking up a suspect.'

'Jason Wallis?'

Cooper smiled. 'Did you want something, sir?'

'Mike Drexler's cottage. There would have been a search after the shooting.'

'It was Nottingham's case, so they took a look but, being a shooting, the locals got first dibs and swept it for further weapons.'

'County searched it first?'

'Then Nottingham,' said Cooper.

'So, *we* didn't search the cottage because it was out-of-area.'

'No,' said Cooper.

'Did we get an inventory, at least?' said Brook.

'As we had a prior interest in Drexler, yes.'

'Prior interest?'

'You had John gather background about him during the Ingham investigation, so he asked Nottingham for an inventory.'

'Did he?' said Brook. 'Any chance I could get a copy? It's just that...'

'I'll print you one off,' said Cooper, leaning down to his monitor.

'Thanks,' said Brook, relieved not to have to trot out his unconvincing justification. 'How's Greatorix working out?'

Cooper's expression glazed over and he took a quick look over his shoulder. 'How useful is a chocolate teapot? Some of us were wondering when you might be back in the saddle, sir.'

'I hope to be back on duty soon,' said Brook, touched by this show of support. 'Though I doubt I'll be taking over the Harrison enquiry.'

'Shame.' Cooper handed over the warm printout.

Brook scrolled down the artefacts removed from Drexler's cottage. Amongst the passport, travel documents and other assorted papers, there was no mention of any document pertaining to Victor Sorenson's post mortem. At least, that made sense. Had such a document been recovered, Tyson and Campbell would have understood its significance and posed a very different set of questions.

'Find what you were looking for?'

'No,' said Brook, folding the sheet. 'But, thanks.' He left and marched down to the front entrance, shaking out a cigarette as a squad car pulled up. Noble emerged from the passenger seat to help the two uniformed officers extract a prisoner from the rear.

Between them, the two muscular constables cajoled a burly, unshaven man in his late thirties towards the entrance. Despite the uneven contest, the man struggled against his captors, unleashing a stream of Polish invective.

As the scrum drew level, the resistance ceased and the prisoner narrowed his eyes at Brook lighting a cigarette. Brook's heart sank as he realised the prisoner's identity and, worse, that recognition appeared to be mutual.

'I know you?' said the man, in a strong Polish accent. The two constables tried to jostle him along but, seeing the cigarette, the man planted his feet. 'Give me cigarette.'

Brook took the packet from his coat and dropped it in the handcuffed man's shirt pocket a second before he was hauled away towards the custody suite.

Noble watched the constables disappear into the building. 'In all the time we've worked together, I've not had that many fags off you, yet you dole them out to a slag like Grabowski without a murmur.'

'He looked like he needed cheering up,' said Brook. 'Grabowski?'

'You don't know him?' said Noble. 'He seemed to know you.'

'I'm famous, John,' smiled Brook.

Noble lit his own cigarette. 'Marek Grabowski. Derby's most wanted serial drunk driver, twocker and joy rider.'

'John Noble,' said Brook. 'Making Derby Safe.'

'Oh, it's more than a traffic collar,' said Noble, leaning in conspiratorially. 'We've found McQuarry's Audi, the one you drove to the hospital after the shooting. Marek must have boosted it from the car park after you carried Drexler into A&E.'

'You don't say.'

'The funny thing is, he kept the car quiet for weeks then got hammered on cheap vodka and torched the thing - wait for it - while it was sitting on his own drive.' Noble laughed but his gaze pierced Brook. 'Can you believe that?'

'Criminals are stupid, John.'

'Not Grabowski. We've been after him for two years.'

'Alcohol makes fools of us all.'

'True but he was drinking when he boosted other cars without ever getting pulled,' said Noble. 'And then he pulls this stunt. Even weirder, he had the presence of mind to remove the number plates before torching it. Go figure.'

'Are you American, John?'

'Yes,' replied Noble.

'How did you match the car without the plates?'

'A traffic bobby remembered the bulletin on make and model and checked the chassis number. It's the same Audi.'

'Sharp. Anything in it for Forensics?'

'Doubtful. It was completely gutted.'

'What a shame,' commiserated Brook. 'Grabowski doesn't seem to be taking it well.'

'Screamed his innocence all the way here,' said Noble.

'Maybe it's the truth,' said Brook. 'Nottingham's quite a hike if he lives in Derby.'

'How do you know where he lives?' said Noble.

'*Derby's most wanted drunk driver*,' replied Brook. 'Your words.'

'So, they were.'

'I wouldn't worry,' said Brook. 'I'm sure Bob will tear his story to shreds in interview.'

'Don't mock,' said Noble. 'Besides, his story's already in shreds. Swears on his mother's grave, he woke up to see some mystery man torching it before riding off on a mountain bike. I mean, who comes up with crap like that?'

'Have you checked if his mother's alive?'

Noble laughed. 'What are you doing in so early, anyway?'

'Come to collect my clean bill of health from Charlton.'

'Congratulations. But you know he won't be in for at least three hours.'

Brook splayed his arms. 'See what excitement does to you.'

'While I've got you, we had results back on that cat,' said Noble.

'Percy.'

'You were right. DNA on Percy's neck was a match to Jason Wallis.'

Brook nodded. 'But nobody cares because he just lost another relative.'

'I care,' said Noble. 'And I'll make sure we tackle him about it.'

'Say the word and I'll cuff him to his hospital bed.'

'Too late,' said Noble. 'He's being discharged today.'

'So soon?'

'He's young and fit,' shrugged Noble.

'Any word on what was in his system?'

Noble hesitated. 'It's too early to tell.'

'John,' said Brook. 'He wouldn't be released without doctors knowing what he'd had in his bloodstream in case of a relapse.'

Noble sighed. 'Then brace yourself. It was a mixture of Scopolamine and Morphine. Jason is innocent.'

Brook nodded. 'Twilight Sleep.'

'You're taking it well.'

Brook shrugged. 'Where's he going?'

'A hotel, for now. With a protective detail.'

'Which hotel?' Noble raised an eyebrow. 'Need-to-know basis, eh? Thanks for the vote of confidence.'

'Orders from Greatorix,' said Noble. 'And, given your current fixation on Wallis, I don't blame him. Jason didn't kill his aunt. You've had proof. Let it go.'

27

December 21st, 2008 - West London

Vinny Muir dried his hands on the grubby tea-towel and slipped through the curtain to the café and picked up the warm plate, its contents gently steaming on the hatch. 'All done, amigo,' he called out, as he picked up his free lunch.

'Bueno,' said Theo, the proprietor, who broke off cleaning the nozzle of his coffee machine and opened the till, pawed out a ten-pound note and folded it into Muir's top pocket.

'Gracias, Padron,' said Muir, collecting a knife and fork from the cutlery drawer. He made his way to an empty table with a view of the door for a heads-up on further unwelcome visits from DCI Fulbright.

Pulling an old copy of the Evening Standard towards him, he stared at the front-page headline - REAPER SERIAL KILLER RETURNS.

'Derby family's throats slashed, killing three,' he read, peering at the sub-heading in his under strength reading glasses. 'Is dormant London serial killer back from the dead?' He leaned back in his chair to think. Only days ago, Fulbright had told him a former cellmate had been the Reaper's first victim. Sammy Elphick. Some coincidence.

Remembering his cooling roast pork dinner, with extra gravy,

Muir began to devour his meal and every scrap of text on the latest killings.

'INFAMOUS SERIAL KILLER, *the Reaper, who killed two London families in the early nineties and another in Leeds in 1993, has been confirmed as the prime suspect in the home invasion and murder of three members of the Wallis family in Derby.*

Bobby Wallis, wife Rita and twelve-year-old daughter Kylie died in their home in the Derby suburb of Drayfin two nights ago. All three victims suffered fatal wounds to the throat, a signature method of killing from the Reaper's reign of terror in London.

Two members of the family survived the attack. Six-month-old baby Bianca was uninjured, having slept through the entire ordeal in her carry cot, and sixteen-year-old Jason Wallis was out of the house at the time of the killings.

Jason, who has a long record of petty juvenile offences, hit the headlines when he was excluded from his local school for an alleged sexual assault on a teacher during a lesson. He was still under suspension when his family were attacked.

All three victims had been drugged before being killed, another signature that police believe points to the Reaper. It is thought the drug, an unidentified narcotic used to incapacitate targets, was introduced onto a delivery of takeaway pizzas before they were consumed by the victims.

Initial accounts report that Jason was found unconscious on the kitchen floor. Police believe Jason must have returned to the house after the killer's departure and helped himself to leftovers of the doctored pizza. He is currently recovering in hospital.

"If this is the work of the infamous Reaper, the question on the lips of every detective and criminologist is, where has this man been?" said a Metropolitan Police Spokesman. "The Leeds killings in 1993, were the last documented Reaper attack, which leaves a fifteen-year gap between kills. One line of enquiry would be to discover whether the killer had been incarcerated or out of the country between 1993 and 2008 and detectives in Derby, Leeds and London are urgently trying to identify likely candidates who fit that timeframe."

According to Derby Chief Superintendent Evelyn McMaster, members of her Murder Investigation Team (MIT) are also not ruling out the possibility that the killings might be the work of a copycat, though local sources insist detectives are proceeding on the basis that the culprit is either the Reaper or someone familiar with his methods.

At yesterday's dramatic press conference, Derby Telegraph journalist Brian Burton revealed that the Reaper had used victims' blood to spell out the word SAVED on a wall of the crime scene.

In both London killings, the Reaper performed a similar ritual, using the same word in 1991 and the word SALVATION after his first attack in Harlesden, the previous year. Psychologists, criminologists and detectives have long believed that this points to some form of religious mania, though this has never been confirmed.

In a further twist, DI Damen Brook, Senior Investigating Officer on the Derby MIT, had previously been a leading investigator in the London killings when a Detective Sergeant in the Metropolitan force. His failure to catch the Reaper in London was cited as a contributing factor to a nervous breakdown, followed by a long period of convalescence, a divorce from his wife of five years and a subsequent move to the East Midlands force.

According to Brian Burton, Brook's transfer to Derby was controversial. "The notion that a mentally unfit Metropolitan officer could be foisted on a regional force has been a source of great irritation to local bobbies," he said, after a fractious press conference. "And given DI Brook's repeated failure to catch the Reaper, resentment about his move, and questions about his competence to head the MIT, will persist."

DI Brook refused to comment and it was left to Chief Superintendent McMaster to offer her full support. "I have every confidence in Inspector Brook. He is a dedicated and talented officer."'

MUIR'S EYE was drawn to a picture of DCI Charlie Rowlands, SIO of the Reaper killing in Harlesden. Their paths had crossed a few times and Muir remembered him as an old school copper - hard but fair. The sort of copper rapidly disappearing in the hunt for improved clearance statistics.

Another picture showed a file photo of DI Brook but Muir didn't recognise him. He also skipped past the helicopter shots of the murder house in Derby with its ghoulish labels, numbered to suggest a sequence of events.

The snapshots of Bobby Wallis and son Jason were both mugshots, as each had a long record of minor offences, with the son graduating to sexual assault at just fifteen years old.

'What you reading?' said Theo, plonking down a mug of tea

next to Muir and clearing away his empty plate. 'Ah, that Reaper bastard,' he said, spotting the headline. 'I remember him. Slicing up kids in Harlesden and Brixton...' He shook his head as though his point was made. 'Who do that? Ain't right.'

Muir shrugged, unable to dredge up much sympathy, given some of the little shits he encountered on the estate. 'Depends on the kids.'

Theo raised an eyebrow. 'Ten, eleven-year-olds?' He pulled a flat hand across his windpipe. 'Throat cut? You okay with that?'

'No,' agreed Muir, after a pause. 'You're right, boss.' He waved a hand at Jason Wallis's mugshot. 'I was thinking about this piece of shit.'

'Yeah,' said Theo, moving back to the counter to continue his cleaning. 'One lucky fuck, eh?'

'One lucky fuck,' agreed Muir, turning the page to see the same Sammy Elphick mugshot Fulbright had shown him a few days ago. He still didn't recognise him and, of an address in Kensington, there was no mention. Muir took a sip of tea and turned to a section subtitled, 'The Reaper in London'.

'THE REAPER'S first attack was carried out against a family in Harlesden, North London, in 1990. Career criminal, Sammy Elphick, his wife and ten-year-old son were killed in their first-floor flat on Minet Avenue. The parents had been incapacitated with chloroform and tied up on a sofa. Their ten-year-old son, James, had also been drugged, strangled to death then hung by the cord of a ceiling light in front of the parents. The parents were murdered after being revived to look at their dead son.

In a departure from subsequent Reaper killings, the boy had the middle and index fingers of his right hand removed while he hung from the ceiling. This required an extremely sharp instrument - probably the same scalpel or Stanley knife used to sever the windpipe and carotid artery of the boy's parents. Such post mortem defilement has never been repeated and the reasons for it never explained.

In Brixton, a year later, a similar scene greeted police officers. The bodies of eleven-year-old Tamara, father Floyd Wrigley and Tamara's mother, Natalie were found with their windpipes severed in familiar fashion. The weapon used at both crime scenes was never recovered and forensic examiners in Derby have yet to release details of the blade used against the Wallis family.

Investigating officers in the London killings believed the Reaper liked to spend time with his victims to "savour the unequal balance of power in their relationship". This often results in physical, mental and even sexual torture, though this appears not to be the case in the London killings, despite reports Mr and Mrs Elphick cried before their deaths. At the time, this was attributed to the anguish of seeing their son's corpse and its subsequent mutilation, according to DCI Charlie Rowlands.

A sexual motive was also discounted in Harlesden and Brixton by DI Brook, a serving Detective Sergeant in the 1990 enquiry. "The motive for these killings is unclear. Many serial killers are sexually aroused by their crimes. Indeed, killing is often the only act which gives them sexual pleasure and some are known to masturbate at the scene. More careful serial killers take trophies or revisit the crime scene to recreate the sexual thrill of the experience but the Reaper does not fall into either category and his reasons for killing remain a mystery," he said.'

MUIR DRAINED his tea and began to read a smaller piece about the third Reaper murder in Yorkshire. A shadow fell across the newspaper and a cheap mobile phone thudded onto the table.

'Merry Christmas.'

Muir looked up to see Fulbright standing over him. 'What's that?'

'You *are* behind the times.'

Muir gave Fulbright the skunk eye. 'I know *what* it is.'

'Excellent,' said Fulbright. 'Hang onto it.'

'Why?' demanded Muir.

Fulbright's amusement dissipated. 'Because I say so. Keep it on you day and night and I might be able to throw some work your way.'

'Work?'

'A job. Not hard but well-paid.'

Muir sat back and contemplated Fulbright. 'I'm not going back inside so, if you think I'm doing anything bent, you're mistaken.'

'Glad to hear it, Vincent,' said Fulbright, taking an envelope out of his pocket. 'The job's not bent and I wouldn't be offering if it was.'

'Then what? You want some dinner plates washing?'

'You have expert knowledge of housebreaking. People with security concerns are willing to pay for that. Think of it as a consultancy for which you charge a fee.'

'I'm not giving no pointers to no blagger,' said Muir.

'You won't have to.'

'Then what do I have to do?'

'Just talk about yourself, what you did, how you did it. Experiences.'

'Experiences?'

'The life. All the inside tricks and titbits...'

'Somebody writing a book?'

Fulbright dropped the envelope onto the table. 'You'll find out when you do the job. There's fifty quid in cash there. And another hundred and fifty after the job's done.'

Fifty pounds was a fortune to Muir but he let the envelope sit. 'Why me?'

'Because you're sharp. And because I've taken a liking to you.' Muir scoffed. 'I mean it,' countered Fulbright. 'I think you deserve a break.'

'So, it's not because I'm a broken-down old lag with few options when the law comes calling.'

Fulbright's manner chilled and he pointed a gloved finger. 'I can strong-arm you into doing it for nothing, if I want. Think about that.'

'Then why haven't you?'

'Let's just say your plight moved me.'

Muir hesitated before pocketing the phone then placed a hand over the envelope, dragging it towards him, exposing the newspaper. Fulbright's eye lingered on the Reaper story and Muir, counting the money, noticed. 'Looks like you're in the wrong town, Chief Inspector. Sammy's killer has moved up country.'

'So, it seems,' said Fulbright. He pointed his finger at Muir again. 'Day and night.'

28

Brook knocked on Charlton's door and entered on command.

'Inspector,' said Charlton, coldly. He rummaged on his desk.

'Morning, sir.'

'Sign this,' said Charlton, holding out a pen with one hand and indicating a blank space on a form. Brook took the pen and signed the form, after a cursory glance at the contents. Charlton gathered the paperwork without making eye contact and turned his attention to his in-tray to imply a return to work.

Brook stared at the top of his head. 'Do you have cases for me, sir?'

Charlton looked up, pretending to think about it. 'We discussed this. When you've finished the course of counselling, you can go back on the roster.'

'I see. Then I'd like to request a month's leave, effective immediately. I have the time owing and more, if you need to check.'

'A month? But you've just been...' Charlton broke off.

'Just been what?' enquired Brook, raising an eyebrow. 'Relaxing at home?'

'I didn't mean to imply...'

'Didn't you, sir? Then may I point out, in case it wasn't clear, that I haven't been relaxing and I haven't been on holiday. I've been summoned for questioning on several occasions and

The Resurrection

endured a period of great uncertainty and stress. So, with your permission, I'd like to request some leave. Sir!'

'If you're trying to play the stress card...'

'No!' said Brook, his voice like the crack of a whip. 'I need some leave,' he added quietly.

Charlton took a deep breath, Brook staring past him, face like granite. 'A month?' Brook nodded. 'Very well. I'll let HR know. Make sure you complete your counselling when you get back.'

Brook turned on his heel and left, feeling Charlton's eyes burning into his back. Pleased to have got that off his chest, he returned to his office and booted up the computer to search for the US Embassy site.

∽

'I'M COMING WITH YOU.'

Drexler stared at Brook. 'Back to the States?'

'Where else? You're injured and you'll need help getting around on the journey.'

Drexler laughed. 'That's nice of you, Damen, but I can manage.'

'I'm sure you can. But I've already taken the time off. It's settled. When can you leave the hospital?'

'The specialist said I should be up and around in another week.'

'Good. I'll book the tickets and pack your bags, if that's okay.'

'I'll need my passport back from Nottingham.'

'I'll pick it up for you.'

'And I can buy my own ticket...'

'Then I'll send you a bill but I'm buying them tonight. Where do you need to fly to?'

'Boston,' replied Drexler.

'That's a pity because we're going to Los Angeles. Will that be a problem?'

'LA? Why?'

'I've always wanted to see the Hollywood sign,' replied Brook.

Drexler smiled. 'Me too. And I'll be glad of the company. Did you...?'

'It wasn't there.'

'Someone took it?' exclaimed Drexler. 'Who?'

'Short answer - I don't know.'

'There's a long answer?'

'Well, we know who didn't take it.'

'Campbell and Tyson,' mumbled Drexler.

'If they had, they'd have been all over us, asking about Sorenson with a hot lamp shining in our faces. Especially Tyson.' Drexler raised an eyebrow. 'She was involved in a case review a couple of years ago.'

'Involved?'

'She was in London. A former colleague, DCI Fulbright, headed a team to look at Harlesden and Brixton. They even interviewed Sorenson.'

'And?'

'They gave it up after the Wallis family were killed.'

'Understandable,' said Drexler. 'Tyson's good. Gave me a hard time the other night. Campbell's a battering ram. She asked all the difficult questions.'

'I heard,' said Brook. 'Do you think they believed you?'

'It hardly matters,' said Drexler. 'They've got nothing but a weapons charge. What did Tyson make of Sorenson?'

'We have a lot to talk about, Mike. Let's save it for the plane.'

∽

'HELLO, CONNOR,' said Brook. 'I hope you're well.'

'Knock it off,' growled Campbell, as Brook approached. 'What do you want?'

Tyson walked in, carrying two mugs of coffee. 'Well, look what the cat dragged in.'

'I just came to thank you *both* for your diligence.'

'Don't make me heave,' muttered Campbell.

'I mean it,' said Brook. 'Somebody has to clean house and you did a thorough job.'

'Where's my fucking tambourine?' scoffed Campbell.

'Taking the positives, Inspector?' said Tyson. Brook smiled. 'Which involves us how? The paperwork was emailed.'

'Mike asked me to pick up his personal effects,' said Brook.

'I thought he had another week,' said Tyson.

'He does,' said Brook. 'And, assuming you're finished with him, he intends to fly straight home so I'm helping him get organised.'

'What a prince!' snorted Campbell.

'He saved my life, Connor,' said Brook. 'It's the least I can do.'

'I need some air,' said Campbell, gathering his mug of coffee. 'See you *very* soon, Brook.'

'Missing you already,' Brook shouted after him.

'Still pushing buttons?'

'He's a DI, Kelly. He shouldn't make it so easy.'

A few minutes later, Tyson tipped out the bag with Drexler's effects onto the counter. 'These were on his person - watch, keys, wallet and coins - these from the cottage. Passport etc.'

Brook picked up the exhibit officer's list, as though it were new to him. 'You did the initial search with Campbell?'

'No, I wasn't on the case then. After County swept the place, it was a Nottingham gig.'

'So, Campbell and his team did the duty.'

'That's DI Campbell's signature on the X.O.'s form, isn't it? No breaks in the chain. Something missing?'

'No, it's all here.' Brook showed no sign of moving away.

Tyson folded her arms. 'What?'

'Two years ago...'

'Here we go,' said Tyson. 'More free information.'

'Forget it,' said Brook. 'You probably won't know anyway.'

Tyson rolled her eyes. 'Two years ago, what?'

'I was wondering if you knew how Vincent Muir and Sammy Elphick came to be connected. There's no official citation in the log.'

'Why are you asking?'

'Because I checked the entry,' said Brook. 'The information alleging Elphick and Muir were known to each other wasn't added to the file until December, two years ago.'

'What?' said Tyson. 'Impossible. That's...'

'...after your case review had started,' said Brook, nodding. 'Did Fulbright ask you to enter it in the log?'

'I think I would've remembered. Are you sure about the date?'

'Check for yourself,' said Brook, picking up the bag of Drexler's effects. 'What about Ross? Maybe he did it.'

'I've no idea. Where are you going with this, Inspector?'

'To the truth, Kelly,' said Brook, heading for the door.

'I hope you recognise each other,' called Tyson.

JASON MARCHED between the two uniformed officers, through the foyer of the Hallmark Inn, to the stairs. A minute later, they'd located Jason's room on the second floor, checked it was secure and left him with a holdall of standard-issue clothes, toiletries and his bag of pill dispensers.

'Sweet crib,' said Jason.

'We'll be right outside if you need anything,' said one of the officers.

A big grin infected Jason's face when closed the door on them. From the window, he stared out at the blandness of Midland Road with the railway station across the street. His corner room overlooked Park Street and, looking down, he saw the flat roof of an outbuilding. It was a simple climb down to the road.

At his door, he peered through the spyhole. One of the officers was sitting on a chair in the corridor so Jason sat on the bed and turned on the TV. He'd have a sleep, take his tablets and wait until dark. Then, if he felt okay, he'd order a burger on room service before pretending to go to bed then leg it out the window and be back in his room before breakfast. No-one would even know he was missing. *Sweet.*

∽

ALTHOUGH IT WAS ONLY five-thirty when Brook pulled up outside the cottage, the sky was already bruised and black and a hard freeze was settling on the village. The light was on in the kitchen and Brook flicked on the kettle to make tea and placed his flask on the table where a brand-new bottle of Lagavulin sat next to a carrier bag containing a loaf, a packet of bacon and a carton of eggs. Laura hadn't left a note this time.

He made a mug of tea and carried it round to Drexler's rented cottage, this time letting himself in with Mike's own keys. He dropped Mike's passport and other effects on the table and jogged upstairs to the tiny bedroom, pulled down the case from the top of the wardrobe and packed Mike's clothes.

Brook's head turned at a noise from downstairs and he crept along the landing.

'Someone there?'

Brook recognised the landlord's voice and jogged down the steps. 'Evening, Tom.'

The Resurrection

'Thank god,' said Tom. 'I saw the light and wondered what were going off.'

'I'm packing Mike's things.'

A change of expression on the landlord's face. 'He's not...?'

'No,' said Brook. 'He's on the mend and he'll be pushing off back to the States next week, if you want to advertise the place again.' He handed Tom the spare keys.

'Thanks,' said Tom. 'He signed a six-month lease, you know?'

'He's not expecting a refund,' said Brook. Tom beamed like the cat that got the cream. 'By the way, did you speak to the police when they searched the cottage?'

'Oh, aye,' said Tom. 'Twice. Asked me what I knew about Mike, how long he was staying. The basics.'

'You didn't happen to mention I had a set of keys for the cottage, did you?'

'Why would I?' said Tom. 'You're a copper. Assumed you told them yourself.'

Brook smiled. 'You assumed right.'

Ten minutes later, Brook returned to his cottage, refreshed his tea and settled down in his office to do more research. After finding the hospital's address, he returned to the kitchen and broke the seal on the whisky, pouring a small measure topped up with water.

A noise turned his head in time to see Grant, damp hair streaming down her back, wrapped in only a bath towel, walking down the stairs from the bathroom. She had her mobile phone in her hand.

'I thought I heard you,' she said.

'Laura?' said Brook.

'Your eyes are working then.' At the bottom of the stairs, she grinned then turned to take a selfie with Brook in the background.

'There,' she said with satisfaction.

'Is everything alright?' said Brook.

'Couldn't be better, lover,' she said, waving the picture on her phone at him.

'What are you doing?'

'Something to shut down the guvnor.'

'Hudson?'

Her mirth subsided. 'I've been having trouble...you know...adjusting.'

'And Joshua noticed.'

'He's been nagging me,' she sighed. 'Trying to find out what's wrong.'

'And you think telling him we're…'

'Lovers?' said Grant. 'He already thinks that.'

'Seriously?'

'Seriously. He thinks we had a thing during the Ingham case.'

'After the way you tried to get me thrown off the case?'

'Crazy, isn't it?'

'And when did we find the time?'

Her amusement faded and she undid her towel and allowed it to fall to the ground, fixing her gaze onto Brook like a tractor beam.

Brook returned her stare, aware of her naked body, goading him into a longer examination. With an effort that shortened his breath, he maintained eye contact. 'What are you doing?'

'What does it look like I'm doing?' she said, walking slowly towards him. 'I'm offering myself to you.'

'Laura, this can't happen.'

'Hudson thinks it already has,' said Grant. 'And he's a good detective. He may need more evidence.'

'No, you…we can't. You're vulnerable. It wouldn't be right.'

She came closer and, for a millisecond, Brook shot a glance at her athletic frame, the smooth thighs, the flat stomach.

'How can two consenting adults having sex not be right?'

'Trust me on this, Laura.'

'I do trust you, Damen. That's why I want *you* to take my virginity.'

'Your what?'

'You heard me. I'm thirty years old and I'm still a virgin.'

'I'm…sorry.'

'Don't be,' she said, her eyes locked onto him. 'After what I went through, did you think I could enjoy a normal sex life?'

'I didn't think about it.'

'Yes, you did.'

'Alright, I did.' She tried to pull him towards her but he grabbed her arms to keep her at bay. 'Stop!'

'Come upstairs and fuck me, Damen.'

Brook's features hardened. 'No.'

'I need you to do this for me.'

'It's not happening.'

'Yes, it is,' she replied. 'I want to and you want to.'

Brook's mouth was dry. 'It wouldn't be right. You're very attractive but you're damaged.'

Her eyes blazed suddenly. 'Do you think I don't know that? That's why my first time *has* to be with somebody I trust, someone who understands me. I'm the wrong side of thirty, Damen. I'm a virgin, for fuck's sake. I'd be called a freak if people didn't know what had happened to me. Don't you see, you're the only person in the entire world that knows *who* I am and what I've done. It has to be you.'

'Laura, I'm sorry. I really am. But it won't make either of us feel better.'

'It'll make me feel better.' She reached up to kiss him, her mouth a couple of inches from Brook's.

'Stop,' said Brook, turning his head.

'Why?'

Brook stared into her eyes, weighing his response. He decided if Laura was ever to be properly fixed, he'd first have to break her. 'Because I'm not your father!'

The colour drained from Grant's face and she looked at him as though she'd been slapped. Tears filled her eyes and started to run down her face as she backed away. Goose bumps dotted her body and Brook whipped a blanket from a chair and draped it around her.

'How can you say that?' she began to sob, her body shaking.

'The loss you suffered left a gaping hole and, psychologically, it's natural to seek a replacement.'

'I...'

'I'm the age your father would be if he was alive. He was killed and it was a terrible thing but some day you're going to have to face it.'

'I have.'

'No, you haven't.'

'You're an expert, are you?' sneered Grant.

'More than you know,' said Brook. 'This isn't the first time I've been propositioned by someone nursing the same trauma, looking for a surrogate to keep her safe and secure. After Sorenson rescued you, he gave you all that and you responded like any daughter would - by doing his bidding.'

'No...'

'Yes. He gave you a father's authority and now he's gone and he's never coming back. Neither is your father. I can't take their place. I'll mentor you the best I can but the sooner you face the damage done to you, the sooner you can get on with your life.'

Grant's sobbing ceased, though she couldn't look at him. She pulled the blanket tighter and began to move towards the stairs. 'I'm sorry. I've made a fool of myself.'

'Please,' beseeched Brook. 'You've nothing to be sorry about, it's not your fault.' She padded slowly to the stairs as though lead weights were attached to her ankles. 'You're hurting and that's natural but it will get better, Laura. I promise.'

She turned suddenly and looked at Brook, her cheeks tear-stained, her eyes red. 'Not the first time?'

Now it was Brook's turn to cast down his eyes. 'I…Sorenson's niece. She'd lost her father, Stefan, in different circumstances.'

Grant's expression turned to confusion. 'Vicky Sorenson?' Brook nodded. 'And did you…?'

Brook remembered the night two years before, when another damaged young woman came to his bed, asking for comfort, and he'd held her tight until the morning, a strategic pillow keeping them apart. 'No.'

∽

AT NINE O'CLOCK, Jason turned off his room lights and opened his window. Thirty seconds later, he dropped to the ground outside the hotel, crossed to the railway station and took the first cab on the rank for the journey out to Borrowash.

Fifteen minutes later, the cab pulled over onto Victoria Avenue and Jason fumbled in his pocket while opening the door. Instead of drawing out a note, Jason showed the driver his middle finger and hopped out. 'Whistle for it, Paki.'

Cursing, the driver leapt out of the cab but Jason was already hurtling down a path through a line of terraced houses and after a few more choice words, the disgruntled driver returned to his cab and drove away, muttering undeliverable threats.

Moments later, Jason jogged onto Dovecote Drive. At the end of the cul-de-sac was an unoccupied property, guarded by wildly overgrown bushes which he squeezed past, onto the broken path of the unkempt garden. He followed the pebble-dashed wall to the back of a ramshackle garage where a riot of impenetrable brambles prevented further progress.

With some difficulty, Jason balanced on one foot and reached round to a rusty hook from which he lifted a damp groundsheet, under which was a rucksack. Unzipping a pocket, he took out his bike keys then moved round to the warped garage doors, forcing them apart to reveal the Kawasaki, motorcycle helmet on the saddle.

Five minutes later, he sat astride the bike, staring through his visor at the police activity outside his aunt's house. 'Correction, my house.' He giggled under the helmet, revved the bike, did a quick rear-wheel burnout and tore off down the road towards the city.

∼

THE GATE to Magnet House's underground car park swung open and the resident's car rolled down into the darkness and out of sight. Jason gunned the Kawasaki through the gate before it closed and killed the engine. He waited a few minutes for the resident to clear the car park before rolling his bike down the access road and under the building.

Throwing the groundsheet over bike and helmet, he climbed the stairs to the front entrance and out onto the road, grinning at the irony of parking his bike under Brook's apartment building.

'And when I need more gear to ghost that fucking teacher, I can boost it from the flat whenever I like,' he sneered. 'And you can't do nothing about it, pig.'

29

17th December 2010

In the dark, Brook dragged himself fully-dressed from the sofa and made a flask of tea. Composing a suitable note to Laura took longer but, fortunately, he'd done much of the heavy lifting during a sleep-deprived night. He knew he should wait for her to wake, make sure she was okay, but he was afraid of reigniting the emotions of the previous night and, if he was honest, it was a relief to ease the door closed and get in his car for the long drive to London.

It was still dark when he hit the M1 and Brook sped south through sparse traffic while he had the chance. At eight o'clock, rush hour congestion had slowed his progress to a crawl so he pulled off at Toddington Services for a leisurely breakfast, washed down by three acceptable cups of tea, setting off an hour later when traffic had eased.

Another hour saw him crossing the Thames on the South Circular and he headed for Putney. Ten minutes later, he steered the BMW through the gates of the Royal Hospital for Neuro-Disability. After a few words at Reception and a quick flash of his warrant card, Brook was directed to the PVS Unit.

'Help you?' asked a smiling nurse, when Brook presented himself at the desk.

'I'm looking for Lydia Fulbright.'

'Relative?'

Brook flashed his warrant card again. The nurse examined it without expression.

'This way.' She led Brook along the corridor. 'You're not expecting a conversation, are you?' she said, over her shoulder.

'I don't know what to expect,' answered Brook. 'Care to enlighten me.'

'PVS means Permanent Vegetative State and we keep them in what we call the vegetable patch.' She flushed. 'Staff humour, you understand. I wouldn't use that language in front of a relative. Anybody paying through the nose to keep a loved one alive in here doesn't need to be reminded.'

'Reminded of what?'

'That miracles are in short supply,' she said. 'They're not called vegetables for nothing.'

She pushed open a door into a private room and Brook's eyes fell on the shrunken figure of Lydia Fulbright, lying on her back, pillows hoisting her upper torso above the horizontal. She had tubes taped over her nose and mouth, feeding her oxygen and essential liquids.

'She can't breathe without a machine?'

'No, she'd asphyxiate. And, obviously, she can't feed or hydrate herself either.'

'Can she hear us?'

'Unknown. It depends on brain damage and Mrs F isn't so damaged that cognitive function is impossible but she doesn't respond to anything except extreme physical stimuli.'

'Such as.'

'Applying a needle to some areas will provoke a pain response.'

'So, some nerves are working.'

'Yes.'

'What about reading to her or playing music?'

'It can't do any harm and it certainly makes visitors feel better.'

'Does she have visitors?'

'Not for a couple of years now. Her two sons used to come, one of them every week. He died but I expect you know that.'

Brook nodded. 'What about the other one?'

'Moved to America, I believe.'

Brook switched his gaze to a magnificent bunch of fresh white roses next to the bed. 'The hospital?'

'Not a chance,' scoffed the nurse. 'Profit is everything in this place. There's a standing order at a local florist. A fresh bunch arrives every couple of weeks. It's not part of my job description but the flowers are lovely and the client is paying through the nose, so I make sure they get into a vase with some water.'

'And who exactly is the client? The surviving brother?'

'You'd need to confirm with the florist but that's what the labels say.'

Brook smelled the flowers. 'It's a nice room.' He read the printed inscription on the label. *'Get well soon, mum. Your loving sons.'*

∼

JOHN OTTOMAN FINISHED PACKING the few decent clothes he'd brought to his sister's house and left the suitcase on the bed. He placed the letter addressed to her on top. Having told her he was visiting an old teaching colleague in Ashbourne for the night, she was unlikely to read it until the deed was done. Apart from the clothes he was wearing, the items that even a charity shop wouldn't want he'd dropped into a bin bag. Hoisting it over his shoulder, he descended the stairs quietly, closing the front door with equal consideration.

He opened the boot of his car put the bag of clothes on top of the pile of boxes, purchased the day before. Jumping into the driver's seat, he drove the fifteen-minute journey to the Drayfin Estate, his heart rate climbing with every mile.

Pulling to the side of the road in Drayfin, he stared at the house he hadn't visited since discovering his wife's lifeless body in the bedroom. The place which had once been a sanctuary was now a mausoleum for his marriage and he was tempted to drive away and leave it like that.

Instead, he manoeuvred the car onto the crumbling drive and unpacked the boot. After dropping the bin bag into the empty dustbin, he carried the boxes into the house. Opening the front door, a musty odour greeted him so he set off around the house to confirm its integrity and open some windows. To his surprise, all the windows were intact and the house uncorrupted.

In the kitchen, he set about emptying boxes and carrying the contents into every room. Setting up the equipment, took another hour and when he'd finished, he made a cup of coffee and sat

The Resurrection

down at his laptop to check all the cameras were working properly. He clicked on the various views and made a mental note to adjust the camera on the stairs. The cameras in the living room, kitchen and bedroom were spot on.

∽

BROOK SAT at a corner table of the Greece-e-Spoon Café in Hammersmith nursing a mug of tea and turning the flower shop label around in his hand. The florist had confirmed a standing order for a dozen white roses, every fortnight, from a bank account in Los Angeles in the name of Andrew Fulbright.

'Theo?' said Brook, to the man passing his table, a plate of steaming food in each hand.

'I know you?' said Theo.

'No. Can I have a minute?' Brook's warrant card gilded the invitation. Theo rolled his eyes to the door, delivered his order and stepped outside to light a cigarette to be joined by Brook, who brandished Vinny Muir's photograph.

'Still looking for Vinny, eh?' said Theo. 'He's a good man. Leave him be. What he do so bad?'

'Have you seen him recently?'

'No. Couple a year, easy.'

'But he worked here, according to his parole officer?'

'Sure. I give him job. He wash dishes. He do good work. Nice man. No trouble. Then he leave, say nothing.' Theo shrugged. 'London. People come, people go.'

'Any hints about where he was going or why?' Theo shook his head. 'Trouble at home maybe?' Theo hesitated so Brook pressed him with silence. 'Only thing. One of your lot come see him the week before he leave and Vinny go quiet after. Like he was worried.'

'Uniform or detective?'

'Plain clothes,' said Theo.

Brook didn't have a picture of Fulbright so racked his brains to recall his features. 'Late forties? Tall. Thin face. Well dressed.'

'Sound like him. He don't smile much. I heard him say his name to Vinny but I forget.'

'Fulbright?'

Theo's face lifted and he pointed a finger. 'That's it. Chief Inspector. He tell Vinny and Vinny go quiet. Vinny don't like him.'

'What did he want with Vinny?'

'Just sit at table and talk. But he come two times and they talk plenty. First time Fulbright show Vinny a photograph but I don't know what it was but Vinny shook his head and give back.'

'And the second time?'

'Second time he offer Vinny a job, I think.'

'A job?' exclaimed Brook. 'What kind of job?'

'Don't know. But he pay Vinny with envelope and I see him count fifty quid. Also, he give him a mobile. He drop it on table, say hang on to it, wait for call.' Theo shrugged. 'Call for job I guess but Vinny still not happy. Something dodgy, I reckon.'

∼

BROOK TRUDGED THOUGHTFULLY towards the King Edward's Estate. What job could a DCI in the Met possibly offer an ex-con like Vinny Muir?

At the stairwell of Muir's tower block, Brook hopped over a large puddle of urine, bloated cigarette ends floating on the brackish surface. He ignored the graffiti-covered metal door of the lift and started up the stairs, even though Muir's flat was six floors up.

Five minutes later, panting heavily, Brook banged on the Muir family door. No answer. A door opening nearby turned his head.

'You won't get sense out of them at this time of day, dearie.'

Brook walked to the barely-opened door, behind which peered an old lady. 'Hello. Is that Vinny Muir's flat?'

'His family, yes. Not Vinny. And his brood won't stir for a while yet. They go down the pub most of the afternoon and evening. I'm Ursula. Are you Police?'

'That obvious?'

'Only because they're always getting visits from you,' she said. 'Nothing ever comes of it, more's the pity.'

'What about Vinny?'

'He moved across the block for a while but he's gone now,' said Ursula. 'That red door over there.' Brook turned to look. 'I could tell you stories if you've time for a cup of tea. I don't get much company these days.'

Brook felt a stab of pity. 'What are you doing six floors up, Ursula?'

'This is my home. I can't leave it after forty years. I manage well

The Resurrection 241

enough with a bit of help from my son. Patrick and me moved in when we got wed and...well, you're not interested in all that, I expect.'

Brook looked at his watch. He had questions. 'Is the kettle on?'

∽

Sipping tea and nibbling a biscuit in Ursula's neat little living room, Brook steered the conversation back to Vinny Muir.

'Not seen him for a long time,' she said. 'Nice man - for an ex-convict. Quiet and polite. Couldn't stand to be near his family. That's why he scarpered. Is that still a word?'

'It is,' said Brook. 'So, his family are difficult.'

'Awful people,' said Ursula. 'I don't like to speak ill...well, Vinny broke his parole to be away, so draw your own conclusions.'

'Is there another tenant in Vinny's flat now?'

'I've seen a man from time to time, smartly dressed like you, though he's hardly ever there.'

Brook set his face towards the window looking out across to the red door of Muir's old apartment. 'I'll knock on his door just the same. He may have seen Vinny or be holding letters for him.'

'He's not there now,' insisted Ursula. 'And even if he was, he never opens the door in daylight. Strange, he is. He doesn't belong here, that's for sure.'

'Why do you say that?'

'He's got money and dresses smart. And the hours he keeps. Comes to the flat gone midnight usually, quiet-like, and sneaks in, thinking I haven't seen him. But I see him. I don't sleep much with my arthritis. Next morning, he leaves before it's light or waits until it gets dark again. And do you want to know something else? He's never once put on the light.'

'Never?'

'Never. And I've never seen him bring anything to the flat except a plastic bag. No luggage, no furniture. Lord knows what he sleeps on. Vinny's old mattress, I guess, but he barely had two sticks to rub together and nothing has changed.'

∽

Brook knocked on the door to Vinny Muir's flat, the noise from his knuckle creating a hollow noise, a sound he knew well from attempting entry into squats and derelict houses. Carpets, soft furnishings and even wallpaper could absorb or soften a rap on the door. Only an empty apartment threw back such an echo.

He stooped to peer in through the dirty net curtains but could see only the bare floor beneath the sill. Kneeling at the letter box, Brook pushed open the flap and saw piles of junk mail spread across the rough concrete. Beyond, lay the living area and he could see all the way through to the kitchen. The flat was effectively unfurnished apart from a cheap plastic foam armchair in black leatherette pushed back against one wall, an ancient oval coffee table beside it and a stiff-backed wooden dining chair, near the middle of the room. In front of that sat the most interesting artefact in the room - a shiny black tripod capable of supporting a camera or a pair of binoculars. Presently, it supported neither.

∽

BROOK PULLED into St Mary's Wharf just after eleven that night. His journey up the M1 complete, the motorway rain had given way to a crisp, clear, Derbyshire night. Keen to be home to his bed, he was deterred by the thought that Laura might still be there and, as Noble had texted him about the return of Percy's remains, he decided to circumvent further awkwardness. His cowardice in intimate relationships shamed him but he knew intense emotions had a destabilising effect on his mental wellbeing and were best avoided.

In the Incident Room, Morton and Cooper were sifting through paperwork, an air of futility about their labours. The aroma of strong coffee was omnipresent.

'John?' enquired Brook.

Morton nodded to the ceiling, so Brook bolted up the stairs to what was still his and Noble's shared office.

'You're burning the midnight oil,' said Noble, looking up in surprise.

'Back at you.'

'But I'm not a gentleman of leisure, like you.'

'You heard then.'

'Greatorix was sounding off about it. You'd think after a year on the sick, he'd have developed a sense of irony.'

Brook nodded at the pile of papers on the desk. 'How's it going?'

'Where it always goes with the Reaper. Nowhere.'

'But it's *not* the Reaper,' said Brook. Before Noble could prepare a rebuttal, he held up his hands in mock innocence. 'I know. Not my case.'

'If only,' sighed Noble. 'We'd be getting nowhere a damn sight quicker with you as SIO.'

'Er...thanks,' said Brook.

'You know what I mean. You've come for Percy?' Noble opened a desk drawer and lifted out a polished wooden urn with a gilt trim.

'He's been cremated?'

Noble shrugged. 'The boffins had done a lot of cutting so I assumed what's-her-name wouldn't want her moggy back, resting in pieces.' He nodded at the blank gilt heart. 'Space there for an inscription.'

'I'm sure what's-her-name will appreciate your kindness. How much?'

'What for?'

'Lab techs toss unwanted parts in the furnace. This is your doing.'

Noble shrugged. 'I had a kitten when I was a boy.'

'Tell me how much and I'll get it from Amanda O'Neill.'

'Forget it. It was the decent thing to do.'

Brook took out a carton of two hundred cigarettes from his desk and threw it at Noble. 'Here.'

'You don't have to...'

'I owe you that many.'

'And the rest,' said Noble, dropping the cigarettes in a drawer. 'Thanks.' Brook was staring at the pile of papers on his blotter, Noble making no move to cover them. 'Mrs Harrison's financials.'

'I'm on leave,' said Brook, feigning disinterest.

'Going anywhere nice?'

'The States.'

'Seriously?'

'I've got the visa and booked the flights.'

'When?'

'When Mike's fit to travel,' said Brook. 'I want to make sure he's comfortable on the flight. The least I can do. Well?'

Noble looked down at the stack of paperwork. 'When the dust settles, Jason's going to be very comfortable, for a teenager with a criminal record and no prospects.'

'He'll need it for a decent lawyer.' Noble grunted in amusement. Brook tucked the urn under his arm. 'I'll see you when I get back from America.'

Noble pushed back his chair. 'I'll walk you out.'

'You look exhausted, John. Call it a night.'

'Would you?'

'No, but on *my* cases, I'm SIO. Where's yours?'

'Went home hours ago.'

'Well then.'

'I'll have a fag break and give it another hour.'

Brook nodded at the papers. 'You're leaving those there?'

'Have a look through if you want. Maybe you'll see something I've missed.' He headed for the door. 'Let me know though.'

'Scout's honour,' answered Brook, moving behind the desk to sit in Noble's chair.

Noble extracted a pack of cigarettes from his jacket. 'You were in the Scouts?'

'Nope.'

Chuckling, Noble left the office and Brook picked up the top document, a life insurance policy for Jane Harrison. Another policy - for £30,000 - had already been settled in the aftermath of her sister's murder - Jason's mother - slaughtered at the Wallis home on the Drayfin Estate two years before. The deeds to both the Drayfin house and her own home in Borrowash were also attached. Everything would soon belong to Jason.

Brook worked quickly through to the bottom document, an invoice for a Kawasaki motorbike, presumably the same one he'd seen Jason riding at Denise Ottoman's funeral. Interestingly, the bike was purchased just a few days before Jane Harrison's death.

∼

BROOK VACATED the chair and picked up the urn.

'Anything?' said Noble.

'Motive, John, and plenty of it. You need to convince Greatorix.'

'No point,' said Noble. 'He won't last much longer.'

'What do you mean?'

'I reckon he only came back to stick it to you and I think the novelty's worn off. He's doing shorter and shorter days and eating like he did before he got ill. I mean, really eating. If his appetite for the case matched that for bacon butties, we'd have cracked it already.'

'Then take the initiative. Focus on Jason.'

'He's due for a formal interview,' said Noble. 'So far, he claims to remember nothing.'

'Wouldn't you? Which hotel did you say he was in?'

Noble wagged a finger. 'I'm not that tired.'

'Worth a try,' said Brook. 'Who's babysitting?'

'Uniform have a body in the hotel corridor.'

'Just one?' exclaimed Brook. 'Pretty thin for protective detail.'

'Maybe. But the Reaper's had three chances to put Jason out of our misery and hasn't shown the slightest inclination.'

'I'm not concerned about attacks on Jason, I'm worried about him getting out and causing mayhem.'

'Why would he?' said Noble. 'He's about to come into money and he's got nowhere to go until his aunt's house is released.'

'He can't help himself, John. Are there ways he can get on the street?'

'It's a hotel. There'll be fire escapes and emergency exits.'

'Check!' said Brook. 'And if Jason skips, put a car outside John Ottoman's house on the Drayfin Estate.'

'I thought Ottoman was living with his sister.'

'He is but that's where Jason will go looking for him.'

'I wish you'd stop this...'

'You were at the funeral when Ottoman taunted him about the stalking. Jason was humiliated and he's going to want payback.'

'That doesn't mean...'

'He's a killer, John, and now he's got the Reaper method in his locker. If Jason can execute his own aunt for money, he won't hesitate to kill a middle-aged teacher who crossed him.'

∼

BROOK DROVE HOME through the freezing countryside, Percy's urn on the passenger seat. Half an hour later, he pulled up outside his cottage, relieved to find it in darkness.

Crunching along the frosty path, Brook experienced a surge of guilt. Laura Grant was an intelligent, yet profoundly damaged young woman and the fact she was the only person in the world who knew all his secrets, gave them a personal connection neither of them could replicate with anyone else. But therein lay the problem. With her mask removed, the traumas Laura had suffered were laid bare and guaranteed the kind of unsettling emotions that threatened his fragile peace.

Being an occasional mentor, he could handle. Being her lover was a whole other level of engagement though, he had to admit, Laura was right. She could never fully trust another human being the way she could trust Brook and, if he was honest, the reverse was true.

He pushed through into the kitchen, placing Percy's remains on the table. There was a note from Laura.

DAMEN,

I SEEM to spend half my time composing messages to you. Well, here goes. Thank you for last night and for thinking of me. You are too considerate, and I don't deserve you. But please understand, I DO know how much I'm a product of the traumas I've suffered. That said, I don't want you, of all people, to treat me as a victim. If I'm ever going to be a fully-rounded person, you must stop seeing me as someone controlled by the harm done to me. I know what happened set me on the wrong path but, thanks to you, I have another chance to lead a meaningful life. If I'm to start afresh, in future I want you to take everything I tell you at face value. And I mean EVERYTHING. Keep in regular touch and please let me know if you change your mind about my offer. My feelings haven't changed because, let's face it, it's us against the world. We are both alone but we can be alone together for as long as you might want me.

L

30

18th December 2010

Brook woke in the grey dawn to light snowfall, made tea and phoned Amanda O'Neill to arrange delivery of Percy's remains that evening. He then dressed for the outdoors, pulled on his walking boots and set off along the crisp tarmac of Reynards Lane and on towards Dovedale for a hard, two-hour yomp.

When he arrived back at the cottage, threatening clouds filled the sky and more snow seemed likely. After a shower, Brook busied himself packing a case for the trip to America and, having packed a few of his smarter clothes, made more tea and sent out more texts, one to Laura to check she was okay. He chose his words carefully, acutely aware of keeping the tone as neutral as possible to avoid offering the kind of encouragement he'd stifled during her visit.

He sent another text to Noble repeating his suggestion for a patrol car to be stationed outside the Ottoman house but received no reply. He then spent an hour fiddling around on the computer unsuccessfully trying to discover the name of the new occupant of Vinny Muir's flat in Hammersmith - if indeed there was one.

As darkness fell, he drove to Borrowash to face the unenviable task of reuniting a deceased pet with its grieving owner.

~

It was dark in Drayfin when John Ottoman finally finished packing his wife's remaining effects, his cheeks tacky from dried tears. His own meagre belongings were already sorted and packed in a case in the kitchen, ready for disposal. When everything had been done, he toured the house turning on every light and leaving all curtains open. In the stark bedroom where his wife had died, he took a few moments to compose himself. His best suit lay on the mattress and when Ottoman was sure there was no more heavy lifting to do, he changed into it, returning to the living room where he sat in an armchair to wait for his nemesis.

~

When Brook left a weeping Amanda O'Neill, he felt drained. It had been a tough few weeks and only now, having stepped off the insane Wurlitzer that was his life, did he realise how tired he was.

At least Amanda would be able to find some closure. She'd bridled, at first, that someone else had overseen her beloved Percy's cremation and selection of urn. But it was clear, moments later, when she'd pulled Brook into an emotional hug, that the care he'd taken of Percy had been above and beyond what was expected and a great weight had been lifted from her shoulders.

The conversation became trickier when she'd asked about the DNA tests and Brook forced himself to lie as convincingly as he could manage. It could serve no useful purpose telling the poor woman that, in spite of detecting Jason's DNA on her murdered cat, in all likelihood his crime would go unpunished. At least by the police.

Outside on Station Road, Brook's gaze gravitated towards the murder house a few doors away. The road itself was still cordoned off with police tape blocking traffic and pedestrians on either side of the property and, even though crime scene activity was minimal at this late hour, arc lights still pierced the darkness and SOCOs still went about their business, hunching over potential exhibits or trudging back and forth between the house and their specially equipped vans.

Brook approached the house with a confident gait and flashed an ID at the uniformed officer standing behind the tape. The officer nodded him past unchallenged and Brook stepped quickly across to one of the SOCO vans to tear open a sealed bag from which he plucked a protective suit and gloves. Properly attired, he followed the taped walkways into the house, his footfall exploding like gunshots on exposed floorboards.

At the door to the lounge, he paused to let his eyes wander, staring soberly at the scarlet message daubed on the inside of the window, now hidden from the street by a large canvas sheet.

He turned to climb the stairs to the murder room and stood, rooted, in the bedroom doorway, imagining the gruesome final moments of Jane Harrison's life. There was little to be gained from further examination as the room had been stripped of all artefacts, including the bed and the carpet. Only the blood spatter and extensive staining on the wall behind the bed suggested the violent death that had occurred there.

Returning to the ground floor, Brook entered the kitchen at the rear of the house, staring out at the small, overgrown back garden, its disarray exposed by more unforgiving arc lights. Another constable, feeling sufficiently alone to be smoking a cigarette, stood at the back gate which opened out onto an unsurfaced back lane.

There was no garage, just a compact shed so Brook went outside to take a look. The uniformed officer saw his approach and covertly dropped the cigarette, grinding it out under his shoe.

'Sir.'

'Everything quiet?'

'Yes, sir.'

Unable to drum up further small talk, Brook opened the shed door. Apart from a bag of charcoal and a stack of dry logs, it was empty. Puzzled, Brook stepped onto the compacted dirt of the back lane.

'Have you got a torch, Constable?' Brook accepted the offered torch and shone it up the unlit lane. Nothing. He walked the hundred-yard length of the potholed track, shining the torch into back gardens along the way. After giving back the torch, he marched through the crime scene out onto Station Road, and up and down the street, looking into neighbouring gardens. A few minutes later, he fumbled for his phone under protective layers.

'John. I'm at the house.'

'House?'

'Jason's house.'

'What? If Greatorix...'

'Never mind Greatorix. Where's the bike?'

'What bike?'

'The Kawasaki Jason was riding at the funeral. There's a receipt for it in his aunt's papers.'

A pause from Noble. *'It's not there?'*

'No.'

'Odd.'

'So, you didn't see it.'

'Come to think of it, no.'

'And no-one had it removed.'

'Not that I'm aware. Maybe it's at a friend's place.'

'His friends are dead, John. Think. Jason was taken to hospital from here, yes?'

'Yes.'

'Then his bike should still be here.'

'Have you tried neighbouring gardens?'

'I checked. Nothing.'

'Then maybe it's been stolen?'

'From a property crawling with police officers? I don't think so. I think Jason stashed it somewhere *before* his aunt's murder.'

'Why would he do that?' said Noble, in a voice that suggested the answer had already occurred.

'Because he knew the house was going to be a crime scene and he wanted to be certain he had access to it when he regained consciousness. He killed his aunt, John. He planned it, he carried it out and he moved his bike beforehand because he's going to need it for his next kill.'

'Ottoman,' said Noble.

'Please get a car outside Ottoman's house. And tell your protective detail to knock on Jason's door and ask him about the bike?'

There was a pause at the other end of the line. *'I can't do that.'*

'Why not?'

'Because he's not there. They knocked on his door earlier tonight and got no answer. It seems he climbed out of the window.'

'Brilliant.'

'He can't have gone far.'

'He can if he has a motorbike.'

Noble sighed. *'I'll put out a bulletin.'*

∽

The Resurrection

JOHN OTTOMAN WOKE from his nap and reached for his spectacles on the arm of the chair. Cold air blew in from the open window but instead of closing it, he rubbed his hands to get warm and got up to make coffee, gazing out at the dark, overgrown garden, wondering whether Wallis was out there, watching the house.

'Come and get me, you vicious scumbag,' muttered Ottoman, impatiently. 'I'm a sitting duck. What more do you want?' A thought occurred. Maybe he was going about things the wrong way. After all, thieves and murderers like Wallis operated in the shadows and when the bastard had killed Denise, he'd broken into a locked house. Maybe, being so visible in a brightly-lit house was counterproductive.

Deciding on a change of tack, Ottoman gathered up his car keys, turned off most of the lights then pulled the kitchen window closed before leaving the house to go for a short drive to give Wallis the opportunity to make his move.

∽

JASON WALLIS SHIFTED his weight on the groundsheet, eyes trained on the kitchen window. John Ottoman walked back into view, just yards away - so close he could almost touch him. Unfortunately, the house was lit up like a fucking Christmas tree and there was little sign he was turning in for the night.

With the cold seeping into his bones, Jason began to yearn for the warmth and comfort of his hotel room. He could be having it large right now, ordering a burger and chugging on room-service booze. Instead, he was here, freezing his nads off in Ottoman's garden.

But suddenly Ottoman began turning off lights, upstairs and down but, instead of going to bed, Ottoman emerged from the house two minutes later, locked the door and reversed his car into the road before pulling away.

'Game on,' mumbled Jason, gathering up the groundsheet and folding it into his rucksack. Moving quickly towards the darkened house, Jason removed a tool from another pocket of his rucksack and raised a hand, poised to prise open the kitchen window.

31

It was nearly two in the morning when Brook pulled up outside his cottage, having spent an unproductive couple of hours walking the streets around the Borrowash crime scene, searching for Jason's Kawasaki.

Yawning, he manoeuvred his BMW onto the small drive and was heading for the door, when he noticed a previous text from Noble.

Car stationed outside Ottoman house. Lights on but nobody home.

'Lights on?' Brook puzzled over this but then noticed a light from the next-door cottage and he went to peer through the kitchen window. The blind was pulled down so he moved to the door and turned the handle as quietly as he could then pushed quickly inside.

'Hello, Damen.' Mike Drexler was sitting at the kitchen table, smiling, a glass of water in his hand. He looked pale.

'Mike,' said Brook, stepping over the threshold to shake his hand.

'I waited up for you. You've been putting in the hours.'

'How are you?'

'I'm good. You look tired.'

'You too.'

'Yes, but I've been shot,' said Drexler, grinning.

'But you're okay. I mean they discharged you so obviously you are.'

'I'm okay. Officially, they wanted to hang on to me for a few more days but I'd had enough of the same four walls, so they let me go. You want to know the best bit? I didn't get billed.'

'Welcome to civilisation,' said Brook. 'How did you get here?'

'Taxi. And thanks for packing my gear. Did you...?'

'I looked everywhere,' said Brook. 'It's not here. Someone took it.'

Drexler's brow furrowed. 'The Disciples?'

'Why would they?'

'Leverage?'

'If they see you as a threat, they'd need something more compelling than a copy of Sorenson's post mortem. Your only connection to that document is the fact it was in your house.'

'And removing it breaks the connection,' nodded Drexler.

'Exactly.'

'Unless they hid it somewhere else on the property.'

'Why? You haven't been here for weeks. As far as you're concerned, anyone could have planted it.'

Drexler nodded. 'So, when do we fly to the States?'

'You're fit to travel?'

'Fit enough,' answered Drexler. 'I've got a holdall full of tablets and ointments, so I should be fine, though sitting on a plane for eleven hours won't be pleasant.'

'That's why we're flying Business.'

'We are?'

'I don't like flying, Mike. I want it to be as painless as possible, for me as much as you.'

'Bill me, Damen. I can afford it.'

'Not a chance. Besides, you'll be working your passage.'

'I figured that's why we're flying to LA. When?'

'Whenever you're ready,' said Brook. 'We have open tickets. We could fly tomorrow night from Manchester.' He checked his watch. 'Tonight, in fact.'

'On one condition.'

'What's that?'

'We check in early and have lunch in the business lounge. I've been eating cold mashed potato and yoghurt for too long.'

'Deal.'

∽

BROOK RETURNED TO HIS COTTAGE, made tea then jogged up the stairs to finish packing his suitcase. Bobbi was stretched out on the bed in the kind of unnatural body position only cats and small children can achieve. Ignoring the yowls of complaint, Brook carried the cat downstairs, turned out a tin of cat food onto a saucer then opened the door so he could leave when finished.

Back upstairs, he picked up the half-filled case from the floor, brushed dust from it and threw it on the bed before adding more clothes and some basic toiletries. He carried the case downstairs, threw in a large packet of tea bags, zipped it up and left it in the kitchen then stood, deep in thought, looking out into the cold night.

Bobbi had disappeared so Brook locked the door and padded through to his office to boot up the computer and confirm the tickets for the flight to Los Angeles. Job done, he pulled out a drawer of his desk and extracted a large padded envelope and carried it to the bedroom. He placed it under the chair, next to his bed, then fetched a glass of water from the bathroom and put it next to his bedside lamp. Yawning extravagantly, he stripped down to his underwear and threw his clothes onto the chair before turning off the light at the wall and slipping under the duvet.

∼

JASON SMILED when the light was finally extinguished, remembering with relish the shock on Denise Ottoman's face the last time he dropped out of the sky to kill. The wait in the attic had been uncomfortable but it was going to be worth it and he began flexing his torso, arm and leg muscles, to get the blood moving again.

Ten minutes later, he checked the hypodermic and the scalpel were securely capped, sheathed and taped to his forearm before carefully lifting the trapdoor from its wooden housing. It came up smoothly and Jason swivelled to his left to manoeuvre the piece of chipboard noiselessly onto waiting beams, letting go only when certain it was supported.

He took his first breath of fresh air for some time and moved his legs above the void then lowered his feet into the darkness. Then, bracing with his arms, he eased his body into the space and lowered himself through the trapdoor until he hung from the frame like a baboon.

The Resurrection

The sound of regular, restful breathing from the bed, filled Jason with an almost uncontainable glee. For all the humiliation he'd suffered, the old fucker was going to pay.

Measuring his descent in the gloom, Jason let go of the frame, dropping to the floor with barely a tremor to betray him.

Gettin' good at this, bitch.

He unfurled himself, feeling the exquisite ache in his muscles recede while his eyes acclimatised to the dark. He was at the bottom of the bed where he could just make out the sleeping form, crooked in repose, head in shadow, peeping above the duvet.

Jason peeled the tape from his arm and gathered the hypodermic into his right hand, removing the coloured cap from the needle, at the same time. He crept towards the head of the bed and, raising the hypodermic in his right hand, pulled back the duvet.

As the hypodermic closed on its target, Jason was blinded by a bright light and blinked in shock at the arrangement of pillows on the mattress below him. Brook sat on a chair, fully dressed in the corner, his left hand withdrawing from the lamp cord, his right hand holding a substantial-looking gun. Jason flexed to jump towards him but Brook pointed the weapon at his chest.

∽

'Don't!' warned Brook, tensing up. 'This thing will blow a big hole in you.'

Jason froze, scowling, panting hard. 'How the fuck…?'

'When you moved the trapdoor, you dislodged dust onto my case,' said Brook. 'Just like the night you attacked Denise Ottoman. When I saw the bulb missing from my bedside lamp, I knew. When I put out the overhead light, I felt for the bulb in the drawer and replaced it.'

Jason blinked. 'I never killed Ottoman's bitch. She had a heart attack. It was in the papers.'

'You were there,' said Brook.

'You can't prove that and, even if you could, that don't make me responsible. I never laid a finger…'

'And your aunt?' said Brook. 'She took you in, put a roof over your head and, in return, you slaughtered her like a cow in an abattoir.'

'Don't you read the papers, bitch?' grinned Jason. 'The Reaper done that.'

'It was a good imitation but you killed her.'

'Prove it!' sneered Jason. 'Can't, can you? Because *you're* the fucking Reaper and I got all the gear from *your* flat - needle, scalpel, drugs. Even the monkey suit.'

'So, you did follow me from Ottoman's house.'

'And there's nothing you can do about it without dropping yourself in the shit.'

'And John Ottoman?'

'That cunt stalked me and he's going to pay. He'd be dead now if it weren't for that fucking bacon cruiser turning up to his house. I had to leg it and give Ottoman a pass but seeing as how I was all tooled up, I decided to come straight for the main course.'

'You knew where I lived?'

'Course I did. Followed you last year after you threatened me. Don't you never sleep, pig? You're never here before midnight.'

'It's called work.'

'Never heard of it,' grinned Jason.

'How did you get in?'

'Please,' scoffed Jason. 'My sister could've broken in.'

'The sister you raped or the sister you've orphaned for a second time?'

Jason's grin vanished. He nodded to the gun. 'Does that antique work?'

'I'd love for you to test me,' said Brook, taking a firmer grip on the old Webley service revolver he'd inherited from Charlie Rowlands and, given the absence of bullets, exuding more confidence than he felt.

Jason removed his rucksack and dropped in the hypodermic and scalpel. 'Okay, pig, you win this round but I'll be back to finish this.' Brook raised an eyebrow. 'Well, it's not like you're gonna shoot me, innit? A copper? In your own gaff? Ain't legal.'

'You're armed, you broke in. If I shoot you, it's self-defence.'

'A shooter against a blade? Not gonna fly, pig. Besides, you ain't got it in yer, remember? You couldn't do it last time; you won't do it this time.' Jason took a backwards step, so Brook pushed himself off the chair to follow.

'This is good, as it happens,' continued Jason, staring at the gun. 'Now you know what's coming, you can be looking over your shoulder, bricking it like I done all those months, never knowing when I might get my throat cut.'

'I should have killed you when I had the chance.'

'You ain't got the stones unless your vics are whacked out like zombies. Like when you did my family.'

'I didn't kill your family,' said Brook.

'Bollocks. You're the Reaper. You've got a flat full of gear and a copper's ID, get you in any door. And you was in London when them other families got done - I read it in a book. Problem is, you're still a copper. You can't arrest me cos I know too much and you can't shoot me in cold blood and get away with it, even supposing that piece of junk works.' Jason took another backward step.

'That's far enough, Jason.'

'Or what?' he sneered. 'Go on, pull the trigger, pig.'

'Drop the rucksack and put up your hands.'

Jason laughed, slipped the rucksack back onto his shoulders. 'Fuck off. Shoot me.'

A few seconds passed and Brook lowered the gun. 'Get out of my house.'

'I'm going.' Jason stepped back through the doorway. 'But I *will* be back and you gotta sleep sometime. And when you do, I'll cut you open, like you done my family. That's a promise.'

At the top of the stairs, Jason placed one foot behind him to transfer his weight and landed on the cat reclining under the top step. The fur ball became a seething, writhing dervish, scratching and hissing before skittering down the stairs, aggrieved.

Unbalanced, Jason began wheeling his arms around to regain his equilibrium, the frantic whirling in direct contrast to the slow-motion arc the rest of his body described, as it plunged backwards down the stairs. On first contact, a scream of panic died in Jason's larynx, punctuated by a sickening crack as he came to rest in a heap at the bottom of the stairs.

∽

BROOK SAT IN THE SHADOWS, gaze fixed on the inert body of Jason Wallis, his thin frame a tangled mess, limbs splayed unnaturally. A cricket ball sized lump swelled Jason's forehead and blood leaked from his nose. Worse, his right leg was bent double and, tucked underneath his buttocks, the heel of his right foot jammed against his coccyx. Just above the knee, blood spotted the denim from the jagged protuberance elevating the fabric of his jeans.

Brook was no doctor but he knew what a compound fracture of the thighbone was and that the pain, when Jason woke, would be unbearable. To forestall his screams, Brook had placed a large sticking plaster over the unconscious boy's mouth. While he waited for Jason to come round, he carried his suitcase out into the dark morning and threw it in the BMW's boot.

On his return, Jason's breathing had become a little more animated and the teenager's struggle for oxygen intensified as consciousness neared. Brook stepped over to look down into the boyish face.

'Jason.' The eyes opened and Jason tried in vain to lift himself. 'Don't move,' insisted Brook. 'You're badly hurt.' Jason sank back down, eyes widening in terror at the sudden flash of pain. He began to yelp through the sticking plaster.

'I know,' said Brook. 'Here.' He lifted Jason by the shoulders, just enough for him to see the lump of bone angling up into the fabric of his jeans. The boy's eyes closed and his gasps for breath turned to serious panting as pain and panic took hold. 'It's not good,' continued Brook. 'And I wish I could say help was on the way.'

Jason tried to speak through the plaster, his face covered in sweat, his pallor chalk-white. 'Help. Me.'

'I've got a plane to catch,' said Brook, regretfully. 'But you should definitely call an ambulance. I couldn't find a phone in your rucksack. Did you leave it at your aunt's house? The hotel?' No answer from Jason. 'Not to worry. Feel free to use the landline.' He pointed helpfully towards the office. 'It's in there.'

Jason's eyes widened and he mumbled something through the tape.

'I can't hear you,' said Brook. Jason tried to lift a hand to his mouth, but Brook held it away. 'No, leave it. I couldn't bear the screaming.' Jason made a strange mewling noise and more tears began to well after he glanced towards the office.

'It is a long way, yes,' said Brook. More muffled sounds, for which Brook provided his own narrative. 'I do feel bad but then I think about your sister, raped without a care for her future. I think about your aunt taking you in and rewarded with a scalpel across her throat. I think about Denise Ottoman, living in fear and literally scared to death. I even think about the cats you killed for fun. Is that wrong of me?'

Another moan from Jason and tears cascaded down his cheeks soaking the fabric of the plaster. His body shuddered with the pain.

'I know it's hard but if you don't fancy dragging yourself to the office, take the plaster off and shout for help. The walls are pretty thick and next door will be empty, but the postman should be along in three or four hours.' More whimpering so Brook returned to the kitchen to retrieve a small packet which he guided into Jason's trembling hand. 'Some aspirins to help with the pain and I'll leave the front door unlocked so the paramedics can get in.' He stood up from his haunches. 'I think that's everything.'

In a sheer act of will, Jason managed to get his hand to obey and tore at a corner of the tape. 'Please,' he panted.

Brook pushed the tape back over Jason's lips. 'I've got to go but when I get back, we'll catch up like you suggested, yeah?'

Through desperate eyes, Jason watched Brook pull on a coat. He pulled the tape from the corner of his mouth again. 'Please,' he begged, though his throat was on fire and every pore of his body was awash with sweat, salt stinging his eyes when he blinked. 'Please.'

Brook studied him. 'You're getting more of a chance than you gave your aunt and were about to give me.' He turned off the kitchen light, plunging the cottage into darkness then leaned over Jason and ripped the rest of the tape from his mouth. The stricken teenager unleashed a torrent of abuse, interspersed with beseeching appeals.

Before he could change his mind, Brook tossed the door keys onto the table and left the cottage, closing the door behind him. He hesitated on the path, listening for more screams but, hearing nothing, marched next door.

At the gate, he hesitated. A car - a Nissan Micra - was parked on the lane. It seemed familiar so he ambled across the frosty tarmac for a closer look, pressed a hand on the bonnet. The engine was cold, though the car had yet to ice over like the other parked vehicles.

Probably day hikers setting off into the Peaks before sun-up.

He thought no more about it and strode round to Drexler's cottage to bang on the door.

~

'GLAD WE GOT HERE EARLY,' said Drexler, dabbing his mouth with a napkin and taking a sip of champagne. 'Are you okay?'

Brook looked up from his teacup. 'Sorry?'

'All this free food and drink and you're just having tea.'

Brook tried to smile. 'I'm fine. Nice food?'

'Are you kidding me?' said Drexler, moaning with pleasure. 'After hospital food, I could eat all day. I'm only sorry I can't go nuts on the booze. I shouldn't really be having this with all the tablets I have to take.'

'One glass won't do any harm.' Brook glanced up at the Business Lounge Departures screen to check their flight status. 'Better get another plateful, Mike. We board in an hour.'

~

AN HOUR LATER, strolling through the departure gate and onto the jetway, Drexler turned to speak to Brook and realised he was ten yards behind, reaching for his phone. 'Damen?'

'I'm a policeman, Mike.'

'That's some great memory you got there, fella.'

'It's coming back, thankfully. Give me a minute, will you?' Brook raised a placatory hand to staff and retraced his steps to the terminal where he rang Noble. His mobile was busy so Brook tapped out a text.

URGENT - At the airport with MD on way to States. A neighbour rang, thinks he heard someone moving around in my place. Could you check or alert local station to do same? Thanks.

He waited impatiently for a reply, deflecting appeals from staff for him to board. After what was only ninety seconds but felt longer, Noble's reply arrived.

Will do. Anyone nearby have a key?

Brook sighed, anticipating the mockery to come.

House unlocked. Couldn't find my key. Thanks again.

Noble's mockery was a line of laughing emojis and Brook took the ridicule on the chin before boarding the plane, a huge weight off his shoulders.

32

December 22nd, 2010 - San Francisco

Brook sat back from his empty plate of scrambled eggs and wheat toast to take a swig of the inky black coffee that never seemed quite hot enough in American diners. At least it was better than the tea. He gazed out of the window while Drexler spoke on the phone to an old FBI colleague, a finger in his ear to filter out the hubbub of the breakfast shift and the ever-present drone of passing traffic.

Brook hankered after a cigarette but even going outside to smoke was problematic in California, with its exclusion zones requiring smokers be a set distance from buildings before lighting up. This, in a city where four-lane highways snaked through local neighbourhoods, belching exhaust fumes around-the-clock. *Go figure.*

Drexler ended the call, his expression not inspiring confidence. 'I was right. It's a postal drop. Andrew collects mail there but that's it. And it's the only current address the bank has on him.'

'Is that legal?'

'As long as there are funds in his account to pay his bills, yes.'

'What about getting a look at his financial statements?'

'We could suggest applying for a warrant, but it won't be easy without showing cause, even assuming I can get my buddy interested. Plus, it's Christmas, so enthusiasm is in short supply. We could try again in a few days.'

'Surely the FBI must know where to find a foreign national in its own country.'

'Given time and a paper trail,' said Drexler. 'But if he's travelling around...this is a big country.'

'What about his employers?'

'They don't know any more than what they told us in LA. After the crash, Andrew was too traumatised to return to work and, as the apartment came with the job, he had to move out. Sounded reasonable.'

'With no forwarding address?'

'It's not a legal requirement.'

'No, but it doesn't help us find him.'

'Any relatives who can point us in the right direction?' said Drexler.

'None. Father dead and neither brother had children. So, how do we find him?'

Drexler shrugged. 'This is America, Damen. He's free to do as he pleases and go where he wants.'

'What about his green card? Wouldn't that be revoked if he leaves his job?'

'Sure. But if he has sufficient funds and isn't spitting on the sidewalk, tracking him down is going to be low priority. So, what now?' Brook raised an eyebrow. 'You seriously want to travel up to Tahoe in winter when there's so much to do in town?'

'I've seen the waterfront and the Golden Gate Bridge,' said Brook. 'What else is there?'

Drexler frowned. 'Damen, you could be here a month and leave stuff unseen. Pity it isn't spring, we could go see a ball game. AT&T Park is a sight to behold plus it's the home of the World Champions.' A pause to consider Brook's blank expression. 'It's a baseball stadium, right on the bay.'

'That's the one with the big glove, right?'

'It's a mitt,' sighed Drexler. 'And then there's Sausalito, Lombard Street, Coit Tower, the Presidio. Hey, we haven't been on a tram yet...'

'Mike, I'm sure it's great but I'm here for a reason.'

'It's winter. The roads to Tahoe may be closed.' Brook smiled patiently at the objection, waiting for Drexler to crack. 'So, maybe that's something I should check on and get back to you.'

'And if the roads are passable?' said Brook.
'We rent a car and take a trip to Tahoe,' conceded Drexler.

∾

BY ELEVEN O'CLOCK THE next day, Brook and Drexler had driven their hired Ford Taurus Sedan out of San Francisco, taking the Bay Bridge onto Interstate 80 and travelling north, towards Sacramento where they turned onto US50. Passing the sign for Folsom, Brook looked across at Drexler.

'Yep. *That* Folsom,' said Drexler, before Brook could ask. 'Want me to sing the song?'

'I'll...take a rain check.'

'Are you American?' laughed Drexler.

'When in Rome...'

Just past noon, Drexler pulled the Taurus off the highway in a town called Placerville and, without hesitation, swung onto a trading estate and parked in front of a Starbucks.

'You've been here before,' said Brook, when they were sat on a bench in the chilly sunshine, sipping their coffees.

'I stopped here with Ed in ninety-five on the drive up to Tahoe, after we took the Ghost Road call.'

'I'm sorry. You were friends once.'

'Friends don't try to kill you.'

'Did you ever find out how Sorenson turned her?'

'I never did,' said Drexler. 'Funny thing is, I was always the one with skeletons in the closet.'

'Your father and sister?'

'That's how Sorenson tried to get to me. You?'

Brook hesitated. 'Twenty years ago. A case I couldn't solve. A young girl called Laura Maples who ran away from home for a more exciting life.' Brook had a vision of her rat-infested corpse. 'She was raped and murdered in a derelict basement and left to rot for months. It was a bad one.'

'Laura Maples?' said Drexler. 'That's the girl Sorenson confessed to murdering before he killed himself.'

'The same,' said Brook. 'He even had her necklace in his dead hand.'

Drexler was sombre. 'That doesn't sound like Sorenson's style.'

'No.'

'He didn't kill her, did he?' said Drexler. Brook shook his head. 'Any idea who?'

'A guy called Floyd Wrigley.'

Drexler raised an eyebrow. 'The drug addict Sorenson murdered in Brixton?' Brook nodded. 'Floyd killed the Maples girl so Sorenson killed Floyd and his family?'

'Something like that.'

'Wow. So, Sorenson knew you were obsessed with Laura's murder.'

'I may have mentioned it to him.'

'One of your fireside chats?' Brook nodded. 'So, effectively, you set Wrigley up as a target.'

'Not intentionally,' said Brook. 'I had no idea Floyd had killed Laura until I...saw his body.'

Drexler was thoughtful. 'And Sorenson recycled Laura's name after he rescued Nicole Bailey to get your attention.'

'I suppose.'

'While flying under the radar himself.'

'He's good at that,' said Brook.

'Tell me about it,' laughed Drexler. 'The Reaper killings have been public property for twenty years but he gets barely a mention in any of the literature.'

'Your book being no exception.'

'I can't deny it,' said Drexler.

'I did wonder about that. I mean, you and McQuarry interviewed Sorenson as a witness. There was legitimate reason to put him in the book.'

'Sure, but nothing tied him to the killings. And, behind my back, Ed stripped his name out of the paperwork. When the dust settled and I was writing my book, it was too late to rewrite history or put Sorenson back into the mix, even as a minor player. It would have provoked awkward questions.'

'Which you couldn't answer because you were compromised.'

'Ed killed Jacob Ashwell with my gun and my prints were all over it. They had me over a barrel.'

'Sorenson always gets good leverage,' said Brook.

'Yes, he does,' agreed Drexler.

Brook was silent, unsure if there was an enquiry in Drexler's last utterance.

∽

AT DREXLER'S INSISTENCE, they crossed the retail park after their coffees and bought warm winter clothing and boots at a winter sports outlet.

Back on the road, they left behind the flat, featureless terrain of the plains as US50 began to climb through thickening forest. The road became sinewy and the weather deteriorated, light snow swirling around the car, affecting visibility. A low wall of snow and ice enclosed them on either side of the road, where previous deposits had been dumped by the state-of-the-art snowploughs operating in the area.

Like a tramp's teeth, the ice wall was holed by hardy residents, clearing drives for access to neat wooden houses set back from the road, every property with its own flagpole. Every occupied house flew the Stars and Stripes and belched out a grey plume of wood smoke. As a lover of solitude, Brook marvelled at these homes, far from civilisation. In comparison to this forested wilderness, the Peak District was like Trafalgar Square.

Half an hour later, the Taurus crested a rise and the road began to level out at an altitude where the snow had hardened into black ice, requiring an appropriate decrease in speed. There were no houses on this stretch.

Soon the road began its descent and rising temperatures cleared the packed snow from the road surface. Houses began to reappear and, after passing Echo Lake, Drexler turned onto US89.

'Welcome to Alpine County,' said Drexler. 'This is the Ghost Road.'

'It's so remote,' said Brook, in genuine awe. 'Easy to see how the Ashwells could indulge their lethal urges for decades.'

'How do you like the Californian wilderness, Damen?'

'It's...incredible,' said Brook, eyes glued to the terrain. 'Stunning.'

Fifteen minutes later, Drexler pulled the car onto the pot-holed forecourt of a disused gas station, his breathing suggesting an increase in blood pressure. 'This is it. Caleb Ashwell's gas station.'

The pair got out of the car and, in their new boots, walked tentatively towards the low slab of a building, their soles crunching through old snow with a layer of brittle ice beneath. The station was in an acute state of disrepair, the roof badly holed, windows smashed and walls blackened by fire.

Stepping through the ruins, Drexler pointed out the girder

from which Billy Ashwell had been hanged and, set back from the road, the derelict homestead where Caleb Ashwell had been handcuffed to a chair before his throat was cut.

Inside the cabin, Drexler kicked open a heavy door, sopping wet from winter rains and rotten shards of wood shattered under his boot. He stood, gazing at the room, remembering the horror of his first visit. 'After they killed the parents, this foul-smelling hellhole is where they kept Nicole and her sister, Sally.'

'I can't smell anything,' said Brook.

'You had to be there,' said Drexler.

Brook nodded, monitoring Drexler's thousand-yard stare - his quick breath and pale face. Brook was asking a lot of him and was tempted to abort the visit but the impulse was short-lived. The case was everything and, realistically, he was never coming back so this was his one chance to see it all, if only to better understand what had happened to Laura.

'Where was Sally killed?'

Drexler took a breath. 'When they got tired of her, they took her out back and shot her in the head then buried her. Nicole... Laura had been badly smashed up in the crash so she could legitimately pretend to be unconscious whenever they came through the door. She heard some of what they did to Sally before they killed her - the begging, the crying. When they took Sally out to kill, she would have heard the screaming and the Ashwells laughing - the shot too.'

'But they hung onto Nicole,' said Brook.

'Until the night Victor Sorenson came through the door to free her. He saved her, Damen. No doubt. He was a customer the night the Ashwells died. He bought gas, was given a free coffee and went on his way. That much we know from the film.'

'But he didn't go on his way.'

'There's an access road for the Forest Service that winds back from the cabin, through the woods and back onto 89, a couple of miles away. Sorenson used it to return on foot to kill Caleb and Billy. Though we could never prove it, of course. We?' He laughed without humour. 'Until we visited his house on the lake, I assumed Sorenson was just another passer-by. But the minute we started talking to him, I knew.'

'You found him on a license plate, right?'

Drexler nodded. 'Ashwell recorded all customer vehicles in a ledger so we had that much. But Ed wrote up Sorenson's interview as a routine vehicle check. By that stage, I'd become too immersed in catching him that I didn't check the record. By the time I discovered Sorenson had been airbrushed out, it was too late. He's untouchable, even beyond the grave.'

They walked on, crunching along the icy track to the enclosed natural rock bowl where all the victims' cars had been kept after their abduction, now long since towed away for evidence retrieval and then scrap. The clearing had been returned to the elements so Drexler described the scene.

Back on the road, both were sombre as the light began to fail. On the outskirts of South Lake Tahoe, Drexler broke the silence. 'There's something else not on the books, Damen.'

'What's that?'

'When Sorenson bought gas, he used your name.'

~

AFTER A PLEASANT MEAL in a pub crowded with skiers, some still in salopettes and ski gear, Drexler and Brook returned to their lake-view apartment and, on Drexler's iPad, watched the film of Sorenson's encounter with Caleb and Billy Ashwell at the gas station. There was no sound and the meeting seemed routine enough until Drexler pressed the pause button.

'There. We had a lip reader come in. Caleb asks Sorenson his name. His answer was *Brook*. Guess you were on his mind.'

'Nineteen ninety-five,' said Brook. 'I hadn't seen him for four years.'

'You obviously made an impression.'

'But why use a false name at all? He wasn't buying gas with a card.'

'Natural caution. He may not have planned to kill Ashwell but he *was* prepared. George Bailey was an employee and a friend and the professor was hunting his killer so he had a rough plan, in case he found his prey. Once he'd found the Ghost Road Killers, he dangled the carrot and showed Ashwell his fat wad of bills.'

'Which is why the victims were never traced to the gas station because they'd all paid for their gas with cash,' said Brook. 'If they'd used a card…'

'It would've generated an electronic record and Caleb would let them go on their way unmolested,' said Drexler. 'But if they paid cash and the prize seemed worth it, Caleb set the wheels in motion. Literally. He'd offer the driver drugged coffee, on the house, then send Billy after them in the tow-truck to haul back the wreckage and its passengers to the station.'

'But when Sorenson didn't drink the coffee, Billy drove back empty-handed.'

'And Sorenson came back a few hours later to kill them both,' said Drexler.

'How did he know about the access road?'

'Probably carried detailed maps and anything else he might need - like the bottle of wine for when the deed was done. It was expensive so we assumed he brought it with him. Same for the rose petals he placed in Billy's pockets - Zuzu's petals from *It's A Wonderful Life* - telling us the killings were connected to George Bailey. Sorenson *wanted* us to know.' Drexler laughed. 'The arrogance of the man. And was he ever ready for us when we called to interview him.'

'I've seen him like that,' said Brook. 'Not a word out of place. Confident, condescending. Did he play you music?'

'*Vesti la giubba* from *Pagliacci*. Followed *by Faure's Requiem*.'

'Lovely.'

'I made the mistake of recognising one of the pieces and he nearly fell over himself to confess.'

'As soon as Sorenson thinks you're smart enough to catch him, he starts reeling you in.'

Drexler allowed the rest of the film to play to the end. 'See the penknife he bought? Corkscrew attachment to open the wine.'

'I know it's fifteen years ago, but Sorenson was still an old, lightly-built man. How on earth did he pacify father and son?'

'Probably had a gun.'

'Hardly Sorenson's style.'

'When in Rome,' said Drexler. 'And, make no mistake, he could handle a weapon. Pulled one on me when I went for him one time after he started throwing my sister's name around. I lost my temper and was ready to squeeze the life out of him...'

'Even so, a gun.'

'This is America, Damen. He was an old man, I was an armed cop. What else was he going to use? And if that same man hunts a serial killer in the Californian wilderness, it's a fair bet the bad guys will carry guns, so he would too.'

After watching the footage of Sorenson leading a near-comatose Billy Ashwell to the rope, the pair stared out of their window at the mist rolling across the dark lake, sipping whisky from the minibar, comfortable in their silence.

'Seen enough yet, Damen?'

'I'd seen enough twenty years ago, Mike. One more day won't make a difference. But if this is bringing back painful memories, mark the locations on the map and I'll drive you to the airport tomorrow and you can head home to Boston. I'll be coming straight back here.'

Drexler smiled. 'And let you have all the fun?'

33

December 23rd 2010

The next morning, Brook and Drexler drove through South Lake Tahoe on US50, towards the state line. The garish high-rise hotels and casinos on the Nevada side of the line, rose up like shark's teeth beyond Stateline Avenue, where the conservatism of California ended and the brashness of Nevada took over, beckoning gamblers from all over America to part with their cash.

They drove along the lakeshore, past Elk Point and Zephyr Cove and on towards Glenbrook where the road headed inland towards Carson City.

Forty minutes later, Drexler directed Brook to an intersection on US395, then told Brook to pull over.

'There,' said Drexler, nodding to the opposite side of the highway. The Golden Nugget Motel was an unremarkable building with a low, brick-built outer office and beyond a standard parking lot, servicing a series of unappealing, one-storey wooden cabins.

'This is where Jacob Ashwell, alias TJ Carlson, was working as a night manager, keeping a low profile after we began digging up bodies at the gas station.'

'And the might and combined resources of the FBI couldn't find him,' said Brook. 'Yet Sorenson could.'

'Found him and led me right to him.'

'You said Sorenson hired *all* the cabins that night,' said Brook.

'Paid cash and gave a false name,' said Drexler. 'Also made certain Ashwell would be working the night shift. After Sorenson left, I braced Ashwell, not knowing who he was. Bribed him to tell me about the booking, as Sorenson expected I would.'

'And the trap was set.' Brook swung the Taurus across the road and drove onto the parking lot.

'Exactly,' said Drexler. 'As Tuesday night approached, I got more excited. I was so close. I'd phoned Ed and told her everything and, of course, she drove straight up from Sacramento to *help*.'

Getting out of the car, Brook didn't need to ask where Jacob Ashwell had met his death - Drexler's eyes locked onto the end cabin and he set off towards it, going no further than the stoop, where he stood quietly, head bowed. Brook hung back and left him to his memories.

Finally, Drexler lifted his head. 'I lost my friend here. She may not have died that night but this is where I lost her. She betrayed me to Sorenson and told me to execute Jacob. When I refused, Nicole injected me with some of Sorenson's magic potion and I woke up in his house on the lake. But the bird had flown and the place was mothballed. I resigned from the FBI within weeks and I never heard from Sorenson or Ed again. And then I came to Derbyshire and shot my friend.' He was sombre. 'I'd killed before, in the line of duty - ironically to save Ed's life.'

'The Reverend Hunseth,' said Brook. Drexler looked up, surprised. 'I read your file. Hunseth attacked your partner with a knife and you protected her. You were given a clean bill of health.'

'I put four bullets into him, Damen. Four.'

'I know that too,' said Brook. 'It may have been overkill but would he have been any less dead if you'd only fired twice?'

Drexler smiled. 'No.'

'Then give yourself a break. You saved her life.'

'And then I took it.'

'You had no choice. McQuarry was out of control. Sorenson would never have sanctioned the killing of police officers. He would have been appalled.'

∼

ON THE ROAD back to South Lake Tahoe both men were lost in their separate pasts, Drexler driving on auto-pilot, Brook staring out of the window, barely blinking.

'Mike,' said Brook, coming to a decision. 'There's something...'

'It's okay,' said Drexler, not taking his eyes from the road. 'I already know. Sorenson didn't kill Floyd Wrigley. That's not what he does. He gets someone...motivated to do it for him.'

'How did you know?'

'I'm a trained detective,' said Drexler.

'That's my line.'

'It's a good one,' said Drexler. 'Sorry. I didn't mean to spoil your moment.'

'I'd been wondering how to tell you.'

'You kind of already did. The night you came to the cottage and we squared up, you said Floyd Wrigley was a mistake and one you were never going to repeat. I figured Sorenson used the same tactic on you that he did when he set me up to kill Jacob. No surprise his Disciples are using the same playbook. I also figured Ed offered up the Wallis kid for you to finish off at the Ingham house.'

'She did.'

'Then give *yourself* a break,' said Drexler. 'You didn't waste Jason Wallis and God knows he's got it coming, especially if you're right about his aunt.'

'I am.'

'Well then. You made a mistake - one time. You have nothing to feel guilty about. What you said to me about Hunseth applies double with Floyd Wrigley. Hunseth may have been a violent drunk but he hadn't killed anyone. Wrigley was a rapist and a killer and there's no telling how many other girls he attacked. Hell, I even read a report about him pimping out his daughter for a fix. That true?'

'Yes,' mumbled Brook.

'Then you deserve a Gold Star, my friend. Wrigley's life served no purpose and you took it away. Boo fucking hoo! Okay, Sorenson manipulated you and, after doing his bidding, he had his leverage. Did you do it again? No. Did you kill Wrigley's girlfriend and daughter?'

'They were dead when I got there.'

'Then face it, Damen, you're one of the good guys. Put it behind you and move on.'

'Sounds like the advice I gave Laura,' said Brook.

The Resurrection

'Then take it.'

Brook looked over at him. 'You're the only person in the world, apart from Laura, who knows what I've done. After Sorenson died, I assumed that knowledge died with him.'

'What about your sergeant? He seems smart.'

'Noble? He knows there's something I'm not telling him but that's as far as it goes.'

'Or maybe he knows and doesn't care,' said Drexler. 'Like me.'

Reminded of Noble, Brook brooded about Jason Wallis and what had happened after his last-minute text from Manchester Airport. For the first time since landing in America, he allowed himself to fret over Noble's one-word reply, the day after.

Sorted.

What did that mean? What was sorted? How had Wallis explained his presence in Brook's cottage? And what had he said about Brook's conduct?

'Sorted,' mumbled Brook.

'Glad to hear it,' said Drexler. 'And while we're on the subject, what say we put the past behind us and leave now. We could be in San Francisco in four hours then out for a steak dinner. Tomorrow we wish each other a happy Christmas and go our separate ways, put the whole sorry mess behind us. What do you say?'

'It's not behind us, Mike. If we could leave it alone, we would. You flew to Britain to look for answers because they'll never leave us in peace. You know that, don't you?'

Drexler nodded. There was silence for several minutes. 'If we do this, you owe me one last story.'

'Which one?'

'You haven't told me about the night Sorenson died.'

∼

YOU ARE ME DAMEN. *You're ready. I came to Derby for you.*

A jolt and Brook woke on the stretcher. People around him, carrying him. He turned his head to the professor, seated at the desk, his bald head turned to the window, cheek flattened against the deep scarlet of the blotter. His scalp and neck were white. Sorenson was dead.

The paramedics adjusted their grip and lifted him again. A last look at his nemesis. The clenched fist dotted with blood, the necklace with little silver hearts, the roots of his hair, the bleached-white knuckles, the skin of his scalp, scarred like a glacier...

The blackness engulfed him again. Sorenson was dead, Brook was alive. He'd won.

∼

THE CAR DOOR opened and Drexler jumped in, breaking Brook's reverie. 'You asleep?'

'Just thinking,' said Brook, rubbing his eyes. 'You were a long time.'

'Couldn't find the washroom,' replied Drexler, avoiding Brook's gaze. He started the car and drove out of the shopping mall. 'You were telling me about Sorenson.'

'No more to tell,' said Brook. 'When I regained consciousness, I was on a stretcher, being carried out of his study.'

'And this DCI Fulbright came at you hard,' said Drexler.

'He wanted me to confess that I'd killed Sorenson and staged the whole thing.'

'And did you?'

Brook tilted his head. 'No.'

The American laughed. 'Sorry. Fair question though.'

'I wasn't complaining,' said Brook. 'My fixation on Sorenson was known. After a year on his trail, I was beaten and exhausted, my marriage wrecked, my career in tatters and on the cusp of a breakdown. It wasn't a stretch to imagine I could brood for years then, at the end of my tether, take the law into my own hands. It happens.'

'But the facts didn't support it.'

'Luckily for me.'

'I wouldn't have blamed you if you *had* stuck a needle in him and cut his wrists,' said Drexler.

Brook gazed at Drexler. 'Stuck a needle in him?'

'According to the post mortem notes, Sorenson had Scopolamine and Morphine in his bloodstream. You didn't know?'

'No, I didn't.'

'Yep,' said Drexler. 'I guess, when it came down to it, even the professor needed a little painkiller before cutting his wrists. Something to make it go easy. Makes him more human, don't you think?'

'I suppose,' replied Brook, deep in thought.

'And this Fulbright died a few months later?'

The Resurrection

'Car crash near LA the following summer,' confirmed Brook.

Drexler shook his head. 'What a dumb way to go.'

'I only found out from Tyson a couple of weeks ago.'

'Did she go to the funeral?'

'I didn't ask. The cremation was in LA, so I assumed not.'

'Odd that his remains weren't repatriated,' said Drexler.

'Is it?'

'It's a big thing in the States,' said Drexler. '*Coming home* in whatever condition - even a pine box.'

'There was only his mother left to care and she's in a coma,' said Brook. Drexler raised an eyebrow. 'She collapsed during the home invasion that killed Fulbright's father.'

'That'll mess with your head,' said Drexler.

'Especially as they never made an arrest. Tyson told me Fulbright never stopped looking for the killer.'

'Not something you forgive and forget. Any chance his mother recovers?'

Brook shook his head. 'She's a vegetable until the money runs out.'

'Christ. If I'm ever in that condition, put a bullet in me, will you?'

'Another one?'

Drexler chuckled, staring out at the leaden skies over the lake. The light was fading and a snowstorm was coming. 'Can we stop talking about death now?'

'What would you like to talk about?' asked Brook.

Drexler considered for a few seconds. 'How about those Giants?'

'I have literally no idea what you just said.'

34

Twenty minutes later, they were back on the Californian side of South Lake Tahoe's state line and snow began falling in fists. Ten minutes after that, Drexler pulled carefully onto Cascade Road, squinting through the snow-covered windshield and drawing to a halt outside an imposing pair of wrought iron gates.

'This is it!' said Drexler.

The two men pulled on heavy coats and scrunched across a mix of soft snow and ice to gaze through the locked gates at a tarmac drive which dropped down towards an impressive grove of trees, shielding the house from sight, three hundred yards away. Beyond the trees, the icy waters of Lake Tahoe lapped against the shore, driven by a stiff wind.

'A waterfront property in one of the most expensive real estate zones in the United States,' said Drexler, squinting through thick flakes at the white duvet of snow hugging the land. 'It's worth several million dollars.'

'I'd expect no less,' replied Brook. 'Do we know who owns it now?'

'Last time I looked, Falcon Fairway, a shell company in LA,' said Drexler. 'They've owned it for ten years. No record of any tenants or local business usage that I could find. Before that a subsidiary of a big pharma corporation.'

'With links to Sorenson?'

'Hard to tell,' said Drexler. 'The professor knew how to cover his tracks.'

'Speaking of tracks, no tyre marks on the drive. Looks like no-one's home.'

'Not unusual in Tahoe.' Drexler examined the chunky chain wrapped around both sides of the gates and padlocked in the middle. 'A lot of homes are boarded up for the winter. Only skiers and permanent residents stay behind.'

'All this way for nothing,' said Brook.

Drexler smiled. 'Maybe not.' He pressed the button of an intercom on the stone wall and waited for a response. Nothing. After another attempt, he looked down to the lake but was unable to see beyond the shoreline. 'It's getting dark and those clouds are carrying a lot more snow. We should go.'

'I've come halfway around the world...'

'Look!' said Drexler, touching Brook's arm then gesturing at a wisp of wood smoke curling towards the forbidding sky. 'See that? It came from behind the trees.'

Brook pressed the intercom. 'Hello,' he shouted. 'FBI.' No answer. 'Now what?'

'Have you never been to the movies, Damen?'

'You mean the one where the vampire hunters arrive at Dracula's castle just as it's getting dark?'

'There you go,' said Drexler, grinning. He clambered onto the top of the wall and dropped down onto the apron of the drive on the other side, grimacing with discomfort and holding an arm across his chest until the pain eased.

'Are you okay?'

'I'll live.'

After a brief hesitation, Brook swung himself down next to Drexler and the two men began to trudge steadily towards the lake, their footsteps and voices muffled by the deadening effect of the snow.

'Could we get arrested?' said Brook.

'Damen, this is America. We could be shot dead for trespass and the local cops would clap the owner on the back for saving them the trouble.'

'Good to know,' said Brook.

The wind whipped snow into their faces and the pair pulled their coats tighter. Nearing the house, they passed many fine trees

- mature white firs, lodgepole pine and aspen trees, lined up like a wind break to shelter the dwelling.

Drexler flicked his head towards a particular tree in the middle of a bark-covered flower bed, its deep-green leaves gleaming like the finest olive oil. 'The Borrachero - it means *drunken binge*. The seeds of the flowers can produce Scopolamine when processed properly. Combine it with morphine and you get Twilight Sleep, as you call it. Colombian gangs use it for rapes and robberies.'

'How did it end up here?'

'Caleb Ashwell used to fly cargo planes in and out of South America and we figured he brought back some saplings to grow - there was a line of them planted at Ashwell's gas station.'

'I didn't see them.'

'The bureau destroyed them. But not before Sorenson stole one and replanted it right there. Something else that didn't find its way into the paperwork.'

Brook stepped over the frozen, bark-covered soil, removing a glove. The leaves were large and oily and he could smell the sticky resin on his hand after touching them.

Nearing the lake, the large, ranch-style house came into view. Off to one side, stood a three-car garage, its pale doors sealed, snow piled high against them, and no sign of vehicles or recent tracks.

The house itself, built with natural wood and local stone, stood on a raised bank to protect it from potential flooding as well as affording residents a loftier view of the water, no more than forty feet away. At the edge of the water, a wooden pier, bleached by the seasons, stretched out towards the heart of the lake. No boat was moored though there was a boathouse beyond the garage.

'No car, no boat,' said Drexler.

'Locked away for the winter,' said Brook.

'Maybe. But, if there is anyone here, you don't survive a Tahoe winter without big wheels or a bigger larder.'

Brook glanced up at the roof but couldn't see anything coming from the chimney. 'Think we imagined the smoke?'

'Only one way to find out.' Drexler headed for the covered patio at which he and Ed McQuarry had been greeted by Sorenson fifteen years before. This time the patio was empty - no glass-topped table, no coffee pot, no empty cups waiting to be filled. There was, however, a security camera near the roof line and Drexler drew Brook's attention to it.

Brook nodded. A quick reconnoitre located two further cameras. 'Are they on?' said Brook. 'I don't see a light.'

'Hard to tell.'

At the patio doors, Brook and Drexler pushed their noses up against the glass and saw a large, unlit, sparsely furnished room with a vaulted ceiling, more like a small school hall. It was several times larger than Sorenson's study in London but, in Brook's eyes, that only served to amplify its austerity.

A polished dark-wood, mezzanine balcony, running along the far wall of the upper storey, was serviced by a magnificent wooden staircase which expanded generously into the lower storey and, despite the gloom, Brook could make out doors on the upper storey leading off to at least four other rooms.

On the ground floor, a large fireplace, framed in wood and stone, dominated the whole of one smaller wall and, arranged to face it, were an enormous polished oak coffee table flanked by two dark leather sofas. Beside both sofas, occasional tables supported two chunky lamps. The sparse furniture reeked of expense and restrained good taste.

'Is there a fire in the hearth?' asked Brook.

'I can't see but the rest is exactly as I remember it,' said Drexler, his hand shielding his eyes. 'The sofas, the lamps...it's the same.'

The pair locked eyes as the first ominous notes of *Vesti la giubba* by Leoncavallo, reverberated through the patio door.

'You hearing that?' said Drexler, his breath shortening. 'This can't be happening.'

'It's real, Mike,' said Brook. 'Looks like we're expected.' Drexler reached under his coat to pull out a gun. Brook grabbed his shoulder. 'Where did you get that?'

'At a gun shop when we stopped at the mall.'

'I thought California had strict rules.'

'That's why I bought it in Nevada,' replied Drexler, reaching for the door handle. Brook pulled his hand away.

'Mike, put it away. Guns kill people.'

'That's the idea.'

'I mean it,' insisted Brook. 'We're trespassing. Whatever's on the other side of that door, what better justification for executing us if we're armed?'

Drexler considered for a second then reluctantly holstered the weapon. 'I hope you know what you're doing.'

'So, do I.'

Drexler pulled open the patio door and a gust of heat hit them as they stepped inside. Clearer now, the first mournful words of lament left Pavarotti's mouth and, as they advanced, Brook's eye fell upon a large walnut cabinet in one corner. The cabinet door was open, revealing a music system that fed at least four speakers, placed discretely under beams at the four corners of the room.

'Nothing's changed,' said Drexler, stepping towards the sofas. Now he could see the dying fire, smouldering in the hearth. 'Nothing.'

'Some things have,' said a voice, from the darkness of an unlit alcove. A hand emerged to flick on one of the lamps and a figure stepped forward to face them, thin and tall, with greying hair, holding a gun in his right hand and a remote control in the left. He pointed the latter at the walnut cabinet to turn down the music. 'I'm guessing neither of you is Santa Claus.'

'Sir,' said Drexler. 'Put the gun down, we're police officers...'

'Mike,' warned Brook.

'We took a wrong turn on the highway and we came to ask directions...'

'Mike!' repeated Brook.

The man thrust the gun forward. Its elongated muzzle catching Drexler's attention. 'What's with the silencer?'

'Merry Christmas, Brook.' The man moved to turn on the other lamp, which made no more than a dent on the stygian gloom. Bizarre shadows leapt up onto the high walls and ceiling. His eyes locked onto the two intruders, though it was Brook who drew his interest. His lined face creased into a smile at their expressions, Drexler, confused and enquiring, Brook, sanguine and resigned. The man turned to Drexler. 'Mike.'

'I know you?' queried Drexler.

'No, but I know you,' said the man. He turned back to Brook. 'You don't seem surprised.'

'Mike, this is ex-Detective Chief Inspector Richard Fulbright of the Metropolitan Police.'

'The dead guy from the crash?' exclaimed Drexler.

'Reports of my death have been exaggerated,' grinned Fulbright. 'And you left out my new title. I'm the head of the Disciples.'

'Wouldn't that require leadership skills?' said Brook.

Fulbright's grin dimmed. 'Still not lost that happy knack of irritating people, I see. Are you armed, Mike?'

'Of course not,' said Drexler. 'We've only been in the country a couple of days and I'm not a California resident.'

'Those pesky background checks,' chuckled Fulbright. 'Whatever happened to freedom?' He gestured towards Drexler's feet.

'I'm not wearing an ankle holster either.'

'Forgive my lack of trust,' said Fulbright. 'I don't want to make the mistake others have.' Slowly Drexler bent down and pulled up his trousers, revealing his bare legs. 'Thank you.' Fulbright gestured them towards one of the sofas. 'Now, take off your coats but keep your arms in the sleeves then sit on your hands.'

When they were seated, Fulbright produced two plastic wrist ties from a pocket.

'Why the silencer?' said Drexler. 'Can't be anybody within a mile of the house.'

'Turn around, kneel on the sofa, hands behind your back,' said Fulbright. After Brook and Drexler obeyed, he pulled off their jackets and looped the ties around their wrists and tightened them, patting down Drexler and removing the gun from the holster. 'So much for trust.'

'With dirty cops like you around?' muttered Drexler. 'Would your father be proud?'

Fulbright grabbed Drexler's hair and jammed the muzzle of his gun behind his ear. 'He'd be proud my work avenges the innocent victims of people like Jacob Ashwell. Yeah, I know all about your record of failure, Mike.' He smashed the butt of the gun against Drexler's head, eliciting a yelp of pain then aimed the silencer at Drexler's head. 'And you have the gall to mention my father...'

'Richard,' barked Brook, trying to making eye contact. 'Calm down. Mike didn't kill your father.'

Fulbright eyed Brook, the brief flash of anger subsiding. He lowered his gun. 'Sorry, Mike. Touchy subject, fathers. You of all people should know that. Now, turn around but stay seated.'

Brook and Drexler did as they were told and Fulbright retreated to the fireplace to throw another log on the fading embers. Sparks leapt up the chimney.

'Where's Andrew?' asked Brook.

'Resting in peace,' said Fulbright.

'So, the crash was staged,' said Drexler.

'You *were* a detective once,' snickered Fulbright.

'You pulled a switch,' concluded Drexler.

'Swapping identities is Richard's speciality, Mike,' said Brook. Fulbright raised an eyebrow. 'Can't have been too hard. Strangers in a foreign land, a deserted road. IDs exchanged.'

'Throw in a friendly investigating cop and you're home free,' said Fulbright.

'All you need to do then is disappear so those few people in LA, who actually did know Andrew, don't cry foul,' nodded Brook.

'And who would question the inconsolable brother retreating from public life?' said Drexler.

'Not quite that simple but essentially correct,' said Fulbright.

'Neat.'

'Not neat enough to surprise you, Brook,' said Fulbright. 'You didn't turn a hair when you saw me.'

'Let's say I had an inkling,' replied Brook.

'How?'

'For one thing, your brother's opposition to keeping your mother alive.'

'My mother?'

'I see his point,' said Brook. 'It's an expensive hospital and she has no prospect of recovery.'

Fulbright's expression softened. 'You've seen her?' Brook nodded. 'How is she?'

'No change.'

'I know that, I meant what's her room like? Is she getting good care?'

'The best,' said Brook.

'Are my flowers delivered?'

'The flowers are beautiful and the room is peaceful. She has dignity.'

Fulbright blinked away a tear, threatening the corner of an eye. 'Thank you. That means a lot. The thing I miss most about home is visiting mum. And, you're right - my greedy little brother would have turned off the machines and squandered the money on women and cars at the first opportunity.' He stroked the barrel of the gun against his chin, a frown creasing his forehead. 'But now I wonder how you come to know about our fraternal argument over my mother's hospital treatment?'

'I'm a trained detective,' said Brook.

'Kelly Tyson,' concluded Fulbright. 'You quizzed her about the case review and it went from there, right? Careless of me, opening myself up like that. That's vanity, for you - a middle-aged man with an attractive young woman. Should have known better. What did you think of her?'

'Impressive.'

'I'm glad you liked her,' said Fulbright. 'She was sharp as a tack going through the Reaper files. Surprised me and put Ross to shame. You remember DS Ross?'

'Hard to forget a misfit, overcompensating for his lack of height with uncontrolled aggression.'

Fulbright laughed. 'I'd give anything to have him hear you say that. And, boy, how he lusted after Kelly. Unrequited, of course. Far too good for him. I only picked her for the review because she was raw. I thought we'd give it a week, just to please the Chief Super, then bury it for another ten years. Not a chance with her nose for a puzzle. She'll go far.'

'Who's we?'

'The professor and I,' said Fulbright. 'Kerr asked for a case review just as we were making plans for the Wallis family.'

'You and the professor...?' said Drexler.

'Partners in a great enterprise,' said Fulbright. 'And, to think, either one of you could have been standing where I am today.'

'And where's that?' said Brook.

'In a position to rid the world of scum, one unwanted family at a time.'

'Did Kelly feel the same way?'

'Is she a Disciple, you mean?' said Fulbright. 'Sadly, no.'

'So, her interview with Sorenson was on the level,' said Brook.

'Oh, yes. And Kelly was quite brilliant. Knew her brief inside out, when she was being misdirected or sweet talked. I just sat back and enjoyed the tussle. Sorenson was thrilled with her and, even though I'd warned him we were coming, she pinned him down a couple of times. She'll make an excellent recruit, in time.'

'Kelly's far too passionate about the truth for your jaded squad of angry losers.'

'Ah, but what does the future hold, Brook?' said Fulbright. 'Another Floyd? Another Caleb Ashwell? It's only when someone you care about is snuffed out for no reason that you start to understand the work we do. Innocent people deserve more than the handwringing of police and courts. They deserve justice, they deserve vengeance. Kelly will see that one day and, when she does, we'll be ready to accommodate her. Well done for seeking her out.'

'You can thank McQuarry for that,' said Brook.

'What do you mean?' said Fulbright.

'Tyson was on the team investigating Ed's shooting,' said Drexler.

'But Kelly works out of Leicestershire CID,' said Fulbright.

'The field where McQuarry tried to kill us was in Leicestershire,' said Brook. 'Just.'

Fulbright shook his head. 'Oh, dear. And McQuarry one of our senior people. Just goes to show. Still, Kelly back on the trail of the Reaper with you as her mentor. Bet you couldn't believe your luck. All over you like a rash, I'll wager - *the great Reaper detective*. How you must have milked it. Can't say I blame you. Pretty girl like that.' Fulbright leered. 'Eager to learn.'

'Sorry to disappoint. Until she mentioned the case review two weeks ago, I had no idea about her connection to you *or* Sorenson.'

'Must have been a shock,' grinned Fulbright.

'You've no idea,' conceded Brook.

'So, how is she?' said Fulbright. 'Did she mention me?'

'She was sorry you were so tragically taken,' said Brook. 'She enjoyed working with you.'

'She did,' said Fulbright. 'The Reaper really got under her skin.'

'He's still there,' said Brook.

'Unsolved serials will do that,' said Fulbright. 'Did she say anything else?'

'She mentioned how incredibly attractive you were,' said Brook. 'And, despite your advanced age, she could imagine bearing your children.'

Fulbright's features iced over. 'You know I've got a gun, right?'

'Then shoot me.'

Fulbright regripped the gun, smiling. 'Charlie always said you had a death wish.'

'His instincts were never wrong,' said Brook. 'About anything.'

Fulbright grunted. 'That old bastard never gave me a chance. Even when you went to the funny farm, you were still the golden boy, the genius detective. I never got a look-in.'

'I'm sorry,' said Brook. 'If it's any consolation, had Charlie known about the Vinny Muir wheeze you cooked up, he'd have changed his mind.'

Fulbright's good humour returned. 'You liked that?'

'It was quite brilliant.'

The Resurrection

'Who's Vinny Muir?' enquired Drexler.

'Did Kelly catch on?' said Fulbright.

'She thought it was fishy but no more.'

Fulbright shrugged. 'Yeah. It was a last-minute thing. Worked quite smoothly, considering. Did you lay it all out for her?'

'Certainly not,' said Brook. 'I wasn't convinced just from Muir's mugshot so I put her off the best I could. It's not healthy having wild theories about serial killers running around in your head. And, until the moment I saw you, that's all it was.'

'Who the hell is Vinny Muir?' said Drexler.

'You're better off not knowing, Mike,' said Brook.

'You might as well tell him,' said Fulbright. 'Mike killed one of my Disciples. You can't save him.'

'It was self-defence,' said Brook.

'He also knows I'm alive,' added Fulbright, raising the gun. 'I can't allow that either.'

'You can't kill us just like that,' said Brook.

'I can't shoot two housebreakers in America? Have you been on the Twilight Sleep, Damen?'

'I'm not talking about how it looks to the police,' said Brook. 'Killing us is against everything Sorenson stands for.'

'I'll risk it,' said Fulbright.

'Who is Vinny Muir?' demanded Drexler.

'Brook didn't tell you?' goaded Fulbright.

'Not a word,' said Drexler. 'Damen?'

'Until five minutes ago it was just a theory, Mike,' said Brook.

'What happened five minutes ago?' said Drexler.

'He confirmed I was alive,' said Fulbright. 'Tick tock, Mike.'

'I don't understand,' said Drexler.

'Fulbright was SIO that last night in Sorenson's study,' said Brook.

'So?'

'In charge of the crime scene,' added Fulbright, raising his eyebrows to encourage Drexler. 'In charge of taking statements,' he added, as though speaking to a child. 'Come on, Mike. You were a cop once. Impress me.'

Concentration furrowed Drexler's brow. 'I don't...'

'Time's up,' snapped Fulbright. 'On your feet, both of you.'

'You can't do this,' said Brook. 'We've served. You've got your leverage. We can't tell anyone.'

'You're a danger to the Disciples,' said Fulbright. 'McQuarry knew it. I know it. Up.'

'Sorenson will turn in his grave if you shoot us,' said Drexler.

'Shoot you?' said Fulbright. 'Waste two bullets and have all that cleaning? No, thank you.' He pointed to the patio doors. 'Outside.'

'What are you going to do?' asked Drexler.

Fulbright looked quizzically at him. 'Are you sure you were in the FBI, Mike?'

'The lake,' mumbled Brook, as they stood and shuffled towards the patio door.

'The great detective speaks,' said Fulbright, ushering them out. With Brook and Drexler's hands tied, he had to lean across to open the door. Brook saw his chance thrust his shoulder towards Fulbright's chest and body-checked him hard to the ground.

'Run, Mike.'

Drexler hurtled out onto the patio and slithered away in the vague direction of the drive, struggling to keep his balance with hands tied. Brook watched him go then hurtled towards the coffee table. 'Help!' he screamed at the top of his voice.

Unable to pick up Drexler's brand-new gun, Brook threw himself to the floor and jammed his chin onto the volume button of the remote control until the music could go no louder and the room shuddered under Pavarotti's soaring misery. Back on his feet, Fulbright strode angrily towards him, gun raised and Brook planted himself to block Fulbright's path to the remote control.

'Very clever,' shouted Fulbright, aiming the gun at Brook's head. 'I should kill you where you stand.'

'Then do it,' Brook shouted over the music, bracing himself, as certain as he could be that Fulbright wouldn't fire.

Fulbright raised the butt of his gun and tried to smash it down on Brook's forehead. Seeing it coming, Brook rolled backwards, away from the impact but that only enabled Fulbright to pounce on the remote control and turn off the music.

The sudden silence was punctured by the heavy panting of two middle-aged men.

Getting his breath back, Fulbright aimed the gun at Brook's head. 'Outside or die now.'

Brook didn't budge. 'Go ahead. I'm ready.'

'Suit yourself.'

'Richard! Put the gun down!'

Fulbright froze at the shout from the top of the stairs, his gun trained resolutely on Brook. 'Don't make me tell you again,' the voice commanded. With a grimace of defeat, Fulbright lowered the gun and both combatants turned to watch the figure glide calmly down the stairs towards them, eyes locked angrily onto Fulbright.

35

New Year's Eve 2008 – Hammersmith, London

Muir sat in his foam-cushioned chair, eyes closed in the dark apartment, listening to the shouts of faceless neighbours arguing beyond his door. It was early yet for the noise of struggle and strife, of sobbing and screaming, of furniture being thrown, doors kicked and even windows broken when things got heated. But, eventually, somewhere on the block, conflict would break out and those not too close to the action would hang off the railing to watch the free entertainment, the bravest offering advice or encouragement. And on New Year's Eve the free cabaret was likely to go on all night.

Accustomed to it, Muir opened his eyes to the rotating light show from other flats, the sporadic illumination filtering into his three rooms through shabby net curtains. He could afford to turn on the light but usually sat in the dark, until it was time for bed. Perversely, he'd then switch on a small lamp to discourage burglars while he slept.

Fortunately, most of the estate's lowlifes knew he was Liam and Jordan's grandfather and wrongly assumed breaking down Muir's door to steal his pathetic sticks of furniture might provoke retribution from his fearsome grandsons. To be left to his own devices, Muir was happy to encourage this assumption.

Not that he feared losing his possessions. His flat contained no TV, no oven, no washing machine, no fridge and no functional heating. In winter, the warmth from surrounding flats radiated a tolerable temperature and when it got bitterly cold, he sat in the chair under blankets, grateful for the roof over his head.

He had the luxury of a sink and an old kettle for making his morning tea so Muir considered he wanted for nothing. Best of all, he had a small bath and a flushing toilet instead of a metal pail and a communal shower - extravagance for an old lag used to the stench of a crowded cell.

And now, to gild the lily, he had a bit of spare cash - four crisp ten-pound notes and change, sitting on his smoke-damaged coffee table. The fifth note, plus his day's wages, had been converted into two packs of cigarettes, a tube of ointment for his aching hands and a half bottle of Scotch which sat unopened next to the ashtray.

The mobile phone disturbed his peace and Muir looked round the bare room to locate it. Padding across the bare concrete, he flicked at a button and gripped the phone to his ear.

'Meet me at The Castle pub, one hour,' said Fulbright. *'I'll bring the rest of your money.'*

'Where's that?' Muir listened. He knew it - a short tube journey. He threw on a coat and grudgingly left the flat.

∽

MUIR DRAINED his drink and followed Fulbright out of the pub, onto Holland Park Avenue, the street full of revellers heading out to celebrate the end of the year. Fulbright was dour and uncommunicative and Muir began to wish he hadn't agreed to this. He came to a halt.

'Where are we going?'

'You'll see.'

'Tell me now or I walk.'

Fulbright studied him for a few seconds. 'Then walk.' Muir licked his lips and turned to go. 'I'll have the fifty pounds back before you go.' Muir stopped cold and turned to face Fulbright, who reached into his overcoat and pulled out a rolled wad of notes. 'And, of course, you'll be foregoing the rest of your fee.'

Muir looked hungrily at the thick roll of ten-pound notes. 'Who are we going to meet? I want to know now.'

Fulbright's expression softened. 'A nice lady in a house that's been burgled. She needs your advice. Happy now?'

Muir wavered but thought of what he could do with the money. 'It's New Year's Eve.'

'You late for a party?' sneered Fulbright. 'She won't keep you long.'

Muir bowed his head and followed Fulbright.

∼

THE LACQUERED door of 12 Queensdale Road swung open and a middle-aged woman with short, tinted blonde hair and wide grey eyes, stared back at Muir. She glared icily at Fulbright and seemed unwilling to let them in.

'It's cold out here,' said Fulbright. 'Any chance of a drink for Mr Muir and myself before we start?'

Still the woman showed no sign of stepping aside until something fractured in her manner and she flattened herself against the door. 'Mr Muir,' she said, her Scandinavian accent causing Muir's eye to linger. 'I'm Sonja. It's nice to meet you.'

Muir managed a smile. 'My pleasure, Sonja. Glad to help.'

'Straight ahead and on your right,' said Sonja. 'There's a decanter of whisky. Help yourself.' She heard a muffled thank you as the old man shuffled arthritically towards the glowing warmth of a blazing coal fire in the adjacent room.

Fulbright stepped over the threshold, eyes glued to Sonja, expression like concrete. 'Problem?' he said, under his breath.

'You know there is,' she replied, her face set. 'This is wrong.'

'It's already been decided.' As Fulbright made to follow Muir, he extracted a hypodermic from his overcoat.

Sonja's hand closed around Fulbright's wrist. 'No.'

'What are you doing?'

Sonja's pale eyes stared up into his. 'Let the man have a drink and get warm.' Fulbright frowned and pulled against her hand but she redoubled her grip and from somewhere wrought out a smile. 'Then you won't have to carry him up.'

A second later, Fulbright relaxed his hand, dropped the hypodermic back into his pocket and answered with a smile of his own. 'Good thinking.'

36

Fulbright's gun arm fell and Brook watched the diminutive Sorenson descend the final step, his gaze firmly locked onto Fulbright, his slight frame enveloped by a white lab coat.

For Brook, the sight of his long-time nemesis stirred conflicting emotions. His intervention had saved his life but to see the man who'd led him a merry dance across two continents, and the same number of decades, descending calmly towards him with those unblinking black eyes, sent shivers through his spine. Twenty years gone and still Sorenson dominated the room.

But, as he advanced on Fulbright, Brook saw that Sorenson had aged. He was greyer, stooped and carried a slight limp. Victor Sorenson was mortal and, in his current situation, Brook didn't know whether to draw fear or comfort from that particular well.

Sorenson came to a halt inches from Fulbright and his black eyes drilled into him. The object of his gaze seemed paralysed. Then, as though it was the gentlest handshake, Sorenson's hand detached the gun from Fulbright's unresisting grip and, finally, his eyes broke off their silent rebuke.

'Damen Brook is my friend.' He unscrewed the silencer from the muzzle of the gun and dropped it, with the gun, into the voluminous pockets of his snow-white lab coat. 'You do not point a gun at my friend.'

'He broke in,' explained Fulbright.

'That's not a capital offence,' replied Sorenson.

'I know but...'

'We've been over this, Richard. There's nothing Damen can say or do that can stop our work - not without incriminating himself. We have nothing to fear.'

'And Drexler?' said Fulbright.

'Michael's here?'

'He was. He got away.'

'Do you blame him? I suppose you would have shot him too.'

Fulbright nodded at the coffee table. 'He brought a gun. It was self-defence.'

'Of course, he brought a gun. He's ex-FBI.' Sorenson's black eyes were hypnotic in their intensity. 'Michael is also a friend of this organisation and, no matter his feelings towards it, he is not to be harmed. Is that clear?'

'He killed McQuarry,' said Fulbright. 'She was your friend too, a loyal Disciple and, as head of that network, I demand...'

'You demand?' roared Sorenson. The two former Metropolitan Police detectives shrank back. Brook had never seen Sorenson angry before and had certainly never heard him shout. It didn't last and the cold smile returned. 'You demand nothing. Find Michael and bring him here before he freezes to death.'

'He could be halfway to Tahoe by now,' muttered Fulbright.

'Then go and look,' insisted Sorenson. 'Check the cameras, take a flashlight and follow the footprints.'

Fulbright dragged himself to a walnut cabinet and opened a door to reveal a CCTV monitor. 'I can't see him.'

'Car?' enquired Sorenson, without turning.

'It's at the gates.'

'Then go to the car and wait, force Michael back to the house.'

'It's below zero out there.'

Sorenson rummaged through Brook and Drexler's heavy coats on the sofa, pulled out the car keys, tossing them to Fulbright.

Fulbright hesitated. 'What if he tries to attack me?'

Sorenson took Fulbright's gun from his lab coat, ejected and pocketed the clip before holding the weapon out to Fulbright. He took it churlishly and stalked out of the room. A few seconds later an outer door slammed.

Sorenson breathed a sigh, finally fastening his gaze on Brook. He put a hand in his coat pocket, pulled out a scalpel and approached Brook, raising a hand to his shoulder to turn him before cutting the plastic cuffs from his wrists.

When Brook turned to face him, Sorenson's smile was warm. 'You turned up the music to get my attention, didn't you?' Brook didn't answer. 'You knew I was alive?'

'Not for certain. I suspected Fulbright was and, once that was confirmed, other possibilities suggested themselves.'

Sorenson shook his head in admiration. 'What I could have achieved with you by my side.' He nodded towards the patio doors. 'And look at the material I'm condemned to work with. Charlie was right about Richard.'

He gestured Brook towards the sofa, while he went to the cabinet and extracted three crystal tumblers, put them on a tray and poured large measures of whisky into each. Brook sat, accepted the offered glass and took a warming sip of the smoky golden liquid, unable to suppress the feeling that he was where he needed to be, for one last conversation.

'What made you suspicious?'

'The way things ended in London always bothered me,' said Brook. 'You, dead by your own hand, me on a stretcher, drugged and barely conscious, offered a final glimpse of your corpse to convince me. In hindsight, it seemed too convenient, your death too banal.'

'But you accepted it.'

'The police were there. It was official. That was the clever bit.'

'But you were uneasy.'

'I guess I always believed your demise would be more...operatic.' Sorenson chuckled. 'To die so meekly seemed incongruous after all that you'd been. Sometimes in my dreams, it bothered me. I'd see the back of your head, white as a sheet except for the roots of hair follicles dotting your scalp. But you lost your hair after the chemo. The head I saw had been shaved.'

'All that in a dream.'

'The unconscious mind can play tricks and I wasn't about to sound the alarm. But when I heard Fulbright had died, I realised the official version of events that night derived entirely from his authority. He was in charge of identifying the body, taking statements, gathering forensics. From there, I only had to accept that Sonja was in on the switch and I had a conspiracy theory that worked. My suspicions grew and other coincidences began to trouble me.'

'Such as?'

'Fulbright's car crashing in the same US state as your business empire and lakeside home. Fulbright's body being cremated in LA then his brother Andrew promptly disappearing. When I heard they'd argued about their mother's treatment, I was most of the way there.'

Brook took another sip of whisky. 'And then I met Kelly Tyson.' Sorenson raised an eyebrow. 'She told me about the case review, about Fulbright's death and how he'd pushed some ridiculous theory about Sammy Elphick and Vinny Muir. One look at Muir's mugshot sealed the deal - similar height, age, build and, of course, the eyes, black as pitch. The same photograph Fulbright showed you, during the interview with Tyson. To get your approval.'

Sorenson frowned. 'Richard thought it amusing to advance our agenda in the middle of an interrogation. Stupid. How often did I rail against the dangers of vanity, Damen? Our work is too important. I knew, if you ever got to hear of it, you'd be suspicious.'

'Muir was a good likeness.'

'One of the factors in his selection.'

'Selection?' said Brook, with a hint of censure. 'Muir was a human being and you killed him.'

Sorenson laughed. 'Still defending the recidivists?'

'Muir was a career thief but he was no killer and he didn't deserve to die.'

'Rubbish. Muir's life was a monument to malice and his death the only worthy act of his tawdry existence. His record of offending, and the delinquent family he bequeathed, sealed his fate.'

Brook looked away. 'You've researched his progeny, I see. What an assortment of ghouls. Pity those condemned to live amongst the Muir clan as they spray their noxious scent over the neighbourhood. There ought to be a law.'

'There is.'

'It's not working,' said Sorenson. 'How is young Kelly?'

'Apart from an unhealthy obsession with the Reaper, she's fine.'

'And why shouldn't she obsess? My deeds are the stuff of legend. Any detective worth their salt wants to pit their wits against the Reaper and Kelly may not be in your league yet but she wrongfooted me a couple of times. Reminded me of you. How did you meet her?'

'She investigated McQuarry's shooting.'

'And, on encountering the great Damen Brook, she became

ravenous for the store of Reaper knowledge you carry inside you.' He grinned. 'Did she offer herself to gain access to those insights?'

'That's beneath you, professor.'

'I'm serious,' said Sorenson. 'In spite of your years, don't underestimate the attractions of a man with intellect and integrity - a rare combination. You made a profound impression on my niece Victoria and I gather you had a similar impact on young Laura.'

'If Kelly loses her father in violent and distressing circumstances, I'm sure she'll be equally vulnerable. Until then, DS Tyson is blissfully ignorant of my charms.'

'Not so ignorant that she couldn't do her job properly.'

'No thanks to you and your Disciples.'

Sorenson's head dropped. 'I can only apologise for McQuarry's actions. I didn't sanction that. Such violence goes against everything we stand for.'

'Is that a joke?'

'What do you mean? My Disciples are under strict instructions...'

'Five minutes ago, the head of your network was about to put a bullet in my head.'

'That was not my wish.'

'It was your wish that Fulbright ran your network.'

'He'll be dealt with. It won't happen again.'

'Yes, it will. It's inevitable because ordinary mortals can't rationalise the violence the way you can.'

'With my guidance...'

'They've had your guidance. It didn't prevent Mike from getting shot and I would've followed. Don't you see? Killing degrades the perpetrator as well as the victim. The more you kill, the more poison seeps into you, until every cell is infected. McQuarry was unrecognisable as the person Mike knew and, if he hadn't been armed, we'd both be dead.'

For the first time Sorenson was subdued. 'I would never sanction the murder of police officers.'

'Somebody did,' said Brook.

Sorenson glanced at the patio door. 'How did Laura react?'

'As you would have,' said Brook. 'She tried to talk sense into McQuarry and, after we got Mike to the hospital, she was mortified about her role.'

'Her scruples do her credit,' said Sorenson. 'And now?'

'Now she struggles with what she did and lives in fear of the consequences of her betrayal.'

Sorenson's black eyes burned into Brook. 'I hope you put her mind at ease on that.'

'How could I? A member of the network *you* created, tried to execute two police officers, in front of her.'

'Speak to her, reassure her that she has nothing to fear.'

'No.'

'Please, Damen. She's like a daughter to me. I'd do it myself but Laura thinks I'm dead and it's better it stays that way.'

'Then why are you having her followed?'

'Followed?' Brook felt a twinge of pleasure at Sorenson's shock. 'By whom?'

'By whoever gutted the Reaper safe house in Brighton,' said Brook. 'Fulbright's lapdog, DS Ross, if I had to guess.'

Sorenson's eyes narrowed. 'You know about Ross?'

'Of course, I know. Kelly Tyson wasn't in your study the night of your supposed suicide but Ross was. That had to be deliberate.'

'Kelly interviewed me,' said Sorenson. 'She'd have known it wasn't my body. That doesn't mean...'

'Ross falsified the Reaper file with that nonsense about Elphick and Muir,' said Brook.

Sorenson nodded. 'No detail too small.' He nodded. 'I'll have Richard speak to Ross about Laura.'

A noise at the patio door turned their heads.

'What the...' Drexler stood shivering at the door, his hands still bound, his face blue from the cold. He blinked theatrically and approached Sorenson, eyes burning into him. 'No. No. No.'

'Hello, Michael,' said Sorenson. 'Come and get warm.'

Drexler turned to Brook. 'Then who...?'

'An ex-con called Vinny Muir,' said Brook.

'My body double,' said Sorenson. 'By the time the alarm was raised about my suicide, I was on a private jet to Los Angeles.'

Sorenson handed the scalpel to Brook who cut Drexler's bonds. Drexler swooped on his gun, pointing it at Sorenson, his hand shaking. 'You tried to kill us.'

'Put that down, Michael. I get enough drama from Richard. Have a drink.'

After a beat, Drexler lowered the gun and accepted the offered glass. He swallowed the large measure in one gulp, wincing at the heat in his throat.

'You and Damen are my friends,' said Sorenson. 'Richard overstepped the mark and I was unaware of his intentions. If Damen hadn't turned up the music when he did...'

Drexler tucked the pistol into the waistband behind his back. 'So, Fulbright's the one I need to thank for getting shot.'

'I'm so sorry,' said Sorenson. 'My organisation does not execute police officers.'

'Sounds like whoever's in charge is losing their grip,' said Drexler.

Sorenson's head bowed in supplication. 'Rest assured, I will be taking steps.'

'Good because he's out there with a gun,' said Drexler.

'It's not loaded,' said Sorenson, patting his pocket. 'If you see him on the way back to your car, tell him I want a word.'

'We can go?' said Drexler.

'There's nothing to keep you here. Unless one of you would like to stay. I have a position of some responsibility that's about to become vacant.'

'And if we call the FBI?' said Drexler.

'And say what?'

'You're a self-confessed killer who's supposed to be dead,' said Drexler. 'Not to mention, our homicidal friend out there, passing himself off as his dead brother.'

'Go ahead,' said Sorenson. 'Maybe you'll get lucky and speak to an agent who isn't part of my network. In which case, we can all confess our sins and take the consequences. You could spend decades in prison while I only have a few months and may not live to see a cell.'

'Fool me once...' said Brook.

'I'm not immortal, Damen,' said Sorenson. 'My resources have allowed me to slow the advance of my cancer but I will die soon.'

'But the Reaper lives on,' said Brook.

'The Reaper is no longer a man, he's an idea and *will* live on through others.'

'Will these other Reapers shoot police officers too?' said Brook.

'That was a mistake!'

'What about a nurse?' said Brook.

'What are you talking about?'

'Jason Wallis killed his aunt last week then dressed it up as a Reaper attack,' said Drexler.

'She was a nurse,' said Brook. 'She helped people.'

'I don't believe you,' said Sorenson.

'He cut her throat and used her blood to write SAVED on the front window then drugged himself to fake an alibi.'

'That little punk doesn't have the skills,' said Sorenson.

'He does now,' said Brook. 'He's been exposed to your methods so often that he knows exactly what to do. And when he found the Reaper flat in Derby, he had all the equipment he needed.'

'Flat?' said Sorenson.

'Magnet House, near the station.'

'Richard didn't mention...'

'He doesn't know!' said Brook. 'I covered it up to protect Laura. The night I found the flat, Mike followed me there and that's why McQuarry decided to kill us.' Sorenson glanced at Drexler for confirmation.

'It's true,' said Drexler.

'But why would Jason Wallis kill his aunt?' demanded Sorenson.

'Does it matter?' said Brook.

Sorenson stared at the ground then fiercely back at Brook. 'How did an uneducated thug like that find an apartment it took the finest detective I've ever known, two years to find?'

'Jason followed me there. After he killed Denise Ottoman...'

'Who?'

Brook was quick to anger. 'The teacher Jason assaulted! The attack that brought Wallis to your attention. You don't even remember her name.'

Sorenson nodded. 'She was killed?'

'She died of heart failure and it was written off as natural causes,' said Brook. 'But her heart failed when Jason attacked her. I went to the house to investigate and...'

'Jason was watching,' said Sorenson.

Brook nodded. 'After I left the flat, he broke in and found all the tools he needed to kill his aunt and inherit her money.'

'Has he been arrested?'

'I'm the only one who knows and I can't touch him,' said Brook.

'What are you going to do about it?' demanded Sorenson.

'Whatever I can,' said Brook.

'This is at your door, Damen. How many chances have you had to put young Wallis down?'

'I don't work for you,' growled Brook.

'So, he gets away with it,' said Sorenson.

'Not if I have anything to do with it,' said Brook. 'But that doesn't mean I'm going to execute him.'

'Why not?' snarled Sorenson. 'Wallis is a killer, born *and* bred.'

'Then he's your equal,' said Brook.

'You're being ridiculous,' said Sorenson. 'Our motives are worlds apart.'

'But the result is the same. Death and more death. This has all got to end, professor. The Reaper. The Disciples. Tonight. And you can start with Reaper Armageddon.'

Sorenson blanched. 'What?'

'Your grand design,' said Brook. 'I know it exists and I know it's happening on your next birthday.'

Sorenson's good humour returned. 'My final contribution. What do you know about it?'

'Nothing. But I suspect it's a mass extinction event, Reaper killings co-ordinated to happen simultaneously around the world.'

'Very good,' said Sorenson.

'No, it isn't,' said Drexler. 'You have to stop it.'

'I'll do no such thing,' replied Sorenson. 'It's taken years of careful recruitment and planning across the entire planet.'

'I don't care,' said Brook. 'Put an end to it!'

Sorenson smiled. 'Give me one good reason.'

'Because it's wrong,' said Brook.

'Wrong?' Sorenson chuckled. 'Right. Good. Evil. Light. Dark. When will you stop being so naïve? People like you and I must act. We have to change things before it's too late and, thanks to the Reaper, that change is coming.'

'You're insane,' said Drexler.

'And yet I am unmoved by your scorn,' said Sorenson. 'Your sentimentality appals me. To change the world, we have to be ruthless for the greater good. We can't go on like this.'

'Yes, we can,' said Brook. 'And we will. Because life is too complex for your simplistic social engineering. Wiping out problem families and serial offenders does *not* make room for the virtuous to flourish. When you removed the Wallis family, the Inghams sprang up to take their place...'

'I cut out a tumour,' said Sorenson.

'But the patient is still sick,' said Drexler.

'Then I'll cut deeper,' said Sorenson.

'Professor...' began Brook.

'No!' said Sorenson. 'Honest people are depending on the Reaper...'

'Honest people depend on good to defeat evil...'

'And how is that working out?' said Sorenson.

'Sometimes we win,' said Brook. 'Sometimes we lose.'

'Not good enough,' retorted Sorenson.

'It has to be,' said Brook. 'It's all we have. The Reaper offers nothing but violence...'

'The Reaper delivers justice!' declared Sorenson.

'Vengeance isn't justice!' said Brook. 'Society isn't an algorithm. It can't be reduced to absolutes. What I offer isn't perfect but you cannot justify murdering children on the off-chance they might follow in a parent's footsteps. And all this killing infects decent people. McQuarry. Fulbright. Laura. All of them warped by their own pain and anger, twisted by you into a cry for vengeance, for blood. And so, they kill until the killing becomes no more than a meaningless ritual. I know it. Mike knows it. Charlie Rowlands knew it and now Laura knows it.' He jabbed a finger towards Sorenson. 'Why don't you?'

The wind howled outside as Brook got his breath back. After a few seconds, Sorenson's features cracked into a big smile and he brought his hands together in slow-motion applause. 'Wonderful, Damen. Wonderful.' Brook closed his eyes in despair. 'You're right, of course. There needs to be a moral component to my work.'

'Professor...'

'No, Damen, I'm way ahead of you. Your scruples are the final piece of the jigsaw - an asset, not a hindrance. You and Mike have the necessary moral compass that *every* Disciple needs.'

Drexler's eye was drawn to the CCTV monitor at the other end of the room. The main gates were open and the hire car was gone. Tyre tracks on the drive marked the vehicle's passage towards the house. 'Damen,' he said softly.

'You were always the one to take my work forward, Damen,' said Sorenson. 'I knew from the first moment.' He marched to a bureau, opened it and returned with a laptop then proceeded to tap the keys.

'Damen,' said Drexler, with a little more urgency. 'We're about to have company.'

'There!' said Sorenson, flipping the laptop round to Brook. A cursor flashed on a black screen. 'The Armageddon program. Press the correct key and the abort message is sent.'

'Which key?' said Brook.

'I'll press it when you promise to take charge of my work and lead the Disciples into a new era,' said Sorenson. 'What do you say, Damen?'

'You'd trust me to take over after all I've done to thwart you?' said Brook.

'That's the reason I trust you more than anyone,' said Sorenson. 'Give me your word you'll take control and I'll cancel the Armageddon program and deliver the levers of power into your hands.'

'Damen?' said Drexler, a warning in his voice.

'Think what you can achieve,' said Sorenson. Brook blew out his cheeks.

'You're not actually considering it?' said Drexler. Brook glanced at him. 'Tell him no and let's get out of here.'

'And do what?' said Brook. 'Put our feet up while Fulbright wreaks havoc? You've seen the man. He's unhinged.'

'Damen's right,' nodded Sorenson. 'Richard's out of his depth.' He smiled at Brook. 'But with you as its head, the Disciples can bring real order and stability. Just say the word.'

Resigned, Brook nodded at Sorenson.

'I need you to say it,' said Sorenson.

'Damen!' said Drexler. 'You can't do this.'

'Mike, I have to.'

'No, you don't. I can shoot the guy and we can be on our way.'

'That solves nothing.'

'I'm waiting,' said Sorenson.

'Yes,' said Brook. 'I'll take over the network.' A groan emanated from Drexler.

Sorenson exhaled a sigh of pleasure and tapped at a key. 'It's done.'

'Sorry, Mike.'

'Don't apologise,' said Drexler, his gaze fixed beyond them. 'Your reign may be short-lived.'

37

Brook followed Drexler's gaze to where Fulbright stood, his face flushed, eyes gleaming like coals, clutching a rifle aimed at Brook's chest. 'Richard.'

Sorenson's head turned. 'There you are. Come in. We were just talking about the future.'

'I heard,' said Fulbright, through tight lips. 'Anointing your successor?'

'No, Richard,' said Sorenson. 'Recruiting more members for you to work with. Damen will be a valuable partner when I depart.'

'A partner who demands the cancellation of Armageddon?' Fulbright's eyes tunnelled into Sorenson. 'And without so much as a word to me, you go along.'

'Richard...'

'After all the work I did. All the weeks and months I spent developing contacts across Europe and Asia.'

'I'm truly sorry,' said Sorenson. 'But Damen is too valuable a resource and I thought it a price worth paying.'

'And if I don't?' snarled Fulbright.

Sorenson's features hardened. 'I'm still in charge. Now come and have a drink.'

'Are we celebrating?' sneered Fulbright.

'Why not?' replied Sorenson, moving to the whisky bottle. He produced another glass and poured a generous measure, holding it out to Fulbright, who ignored the outstretched arm. Sorenson put the glass down, replenished Drexler's empty glass and raised his own. 'To the future.' He took a sip, eyes locked onto the quietly seething Fulbright.

'The future,' mumbled Brook and Drexler, taking their own sips. Brook glared pointedly at Drexler before taking a small step to his right. Drexler looked away without acknowledgement and took a similar step to his left.

'Where are you going, Brook?' said Fulbright, following him with the rifle.

'Putting my drink down,' said Brook, moving further to his right to the coffee table. 'I'm flying back to Manchester tomorrow so Mike and I are going to call it a night.'

'Is that what you think?' said Fulbright.

'I need to get my affairs in order,' said Brook. 'I can hardly drop everything and become the new head of the Disciples overnight.' Fulbright's expression turned to stone and he gripped the rifle with renewed vigour.

'Damen,' said Sorenson, his expression tight. 'That's not what we agreed.'

'Oh, right,' said Brook. 'Sorry. Mum's the word.' He winked at Fulbright.

'Do you know how long I've been setting up this network?' growled Fulbright.

'I'm sure you did your best, Richard,' said Brook.

'My best?' said Fulbright, breathless.

'Ignore him, Richard,' said Sorenson. 'He's pulling your leg.'

'It's easy to go stale if you don't have a vision,' said Brook, taking another step to the right, mirrored by Drexler's to the left. 'That's where I come in.'

'Damen,' warned Sorenson.

'A break will do you good,' continued Brook. 'When you're refreshed, I'm sure you'll be an asset to the organisation, a natural Number Two.' Fulbright's knuckles whitened.

'Stop it!' snapped Sorenson.

'Another toast,' said Brook, picking up his glass. 'To new beginnings.'

'Why, you...'

'No, Richard,' shouted Sorenson, moving across the line of fire as Fulbright brought the rifle up to his eye.

Fulbright pulled the trigger, hitting Sorenson in the chest. Out of his eyeline, Drexler drew his pistol and fired at Fulbright whose forehead exploded, his body jack knifing backwards and, as the rifle fell to earth, Sorenson and Fulbright fell with it.

Brook caught Sorenson's shoulders, while Drexler leapt to kick the rifle away from Fulbright.

'Professor,' said Brook. Sorenson's eyes were closed, blood filling his mouth, his teeth jamming together in a grimace of pain. 'Professor.'

Sorenson's black eyes opened and shock gave way to recognition. 'Damen,' he whispered, blood bubbling from the corner of his mouth.

'Don't try to speak.'

'I must,' said Sorenson, panting. 'I need to thank you.'

Brook was nonplussed. 'For what?'

'Your friendship. It means everything.' He coughed up blood.

'Take it easy.'

'But I'm dying.'

'I know.'

Sorenson chuckled, coughing up more blood. 'Honest to a fault.'

'Sorry,' said Brook. 'Thank you, too.'

'For what?' croaked Sorenson.

Brook took a second to consider. 'For ruining my life.'

'Pleasure,' said Sorenson, laughing through the pain. A smile creased Brook's mouth in return.

From the speakers, music began to flow over the pair of them and Sorenson's expression turned to joy. Drexler threw the remote onto the sofa.

'Beautiful,' sighed Sorenson, closing his eyes to better appreciate the music. 'Richard?'

'Gone,' said Brook.

'Good,' said Sorenson. 'Clean break. New broom.'

'Some water, Mike,' said Brook, over his shoulder. Drexler disappeared to find a tap.

'All these years, waiting for you...'

'A lifetime,' said Brook, feeling a pressure on his arm. 'Does it hurt?'

'Not a bit,' spluttered Sorenson. 'Hold my hand.'

Brook took Sorenson's long lifeless fingers in his hand. Once, the strength of Sorenson's grip had astonished him but now the professor's hand was cold and limp.

'Pavarotti and my best friend to see me on my way,' said Sorenson, smiling. 'Beat that.'

Brook felt Sorenson stiffen and his black eyes widened. A second later, his body slackened. A single tear rolled down Brook's face. He wasn't sure why. The release of years of tension and self-doubt, certainly, but also a tear for Victor Sorenson. Not a great human being but a man like no other, a man who had chosen Brook to be his friend, bringing terror and wonder in his wake.

Drexler returned with the water as Brook got to his feet.

'He's dead.'

Drexler stared at the body. 'Hard to believe.' The gun was still in his right hand. He eyed Brook. 'Looks like you're *it*, Damen.'

'It?'

'The head of the network.'

Brook stared at the blood on his hands then at Drexler. 'I lied.'

Drexler nodded, pushed the gun back into his waistband. 'And you an officer of the law.'

'Do you still know the locals?'

'Andy Dupree was County Sherriff in Markleeville but I think he retired.'

'What about local FBI?'

'Damen, they're both dead.' Brook stared at Drexler, uncomprehending. 'They were dead before we got here.'

Brook blinked and nodded. 'Right. Sorry. Not thinking straight.'

'You're in shock. Sit down, have another drink. I'll see if I can find a tarp and some rope. There might be some in the boathouse.'

'Are you sure we shouldn't...?'

'Dead man kills second dead man so I shoot the first dead man dead?' said Drexler. 'I'm sure.'

'It was self-defence,' offered Brook.

'Doesn't matter. With our connections to them, we'll be answering questions until next Christmas.'

∽

BROOK AND DREXLER stood at the end of the pier, staring out at what they could see of the darkened lake. Night had blackened the water and snow swirled about their heads, restricting visibility. Drexler had discovered a small launch in the boathouse, now tethered to a post, its outboard motor chugging away.

'You're sure you can handle that thing?' said Brook.

'I'm Californian, Damen. Boats are in my blood.' Brook frowned. 'I got it out of the boathouse, didn't I?'

'Not without hitting things.'

'It's been a while.'

'What if someone sees us out there?'

'Another boat on the water in these conditions?' said Drexler. 'They'd be crazy.'

'That's reassuring.'

'Don't worry. It's a straight shoot to the middle of the lake.'

'It's getting back to the dock that worries me.'

'Damen, you could see the house from space.'

Brook looked over his shoulder. After they'd turned on every working light inside and outside the property, the house shone like a beacon. 'Okay. Let's get this over.'

Drexler bent down to lift one end of the nearest body-shaped tarpaulin on the pier and Brook gripped the other end. Despite the heavy anchor, wrapped and bound inside the tarp, they managed to heave Fulbright onto the boat. Sorenson's tarpaulin was lighter and easier to manoeuvre and a few minutes later the boat was heading out to deeper waters, Brook looking constantly over his shoulder to keep the house's receding lights in view.

After several minutes, Drexler throttled back and the boat slowed which made it more susceptible to being tossed around by the choppy waters. The two men manoeuvred themselves into position and grabbed Fulbright's body, tossing his remains into the lake then solemnly watching the body sink into the depths. Drexler threw in his recently-purchased gun followed by Fulbright's rifle and Brook tossed Sorenson's laptop over the side.

With Sorenson's corpse, the pair were a little more deliberate as they hoisted the tarpaulin to the gunwale.

'Want to say a few words?' said Drexler.

Brook shook his head. 'Sorenson loathed sentimentality.'

They gripped both ends of the tarpaulin and dropped it over the side, watching it sink into the icy depths.

∼

THREE HOURS LATER, Brook and Drexler were ready to leave the lakeside home. They'd cleaned and bleached the bloodstains from furniture and floorboards as best they could, wiped down every surface for blood spatter and fingerprints and done a sweep of the house for any documents connected to Sorenson and Fulbright. They found very little and what they did discover - fake passports, driving licenses, credit cards and other identifying documents - they consigned to the rekindled log fire. They found nothing pertaining to membership or even the existence of Sorenson's Disciple network.

With the house clean, in every sense, Brook and Drexler poured themselves a small glass of Sorenson's favourite malt whisky and shared a few moments of silence. After washing out the glasses and turning off all the house lights, the two men trudged to the car and drove back to their motel, where they both collapsed on their beds and slept the sleep of the dead.

∼

'THAT'S MY FLIGHT,' said Drexler, gathering his bags at the announcement at San Francisco Airport. He held out a hand to Brook who shook it firmly. 'Happy New Year, Damen. Keep in touch.'

'I'll try,' said Brook, honesty trumping even the simplest small talk. Drexler was the bridge to a past he needed to forget and he was certain they'd never meet again. Drexler seemed to understand. He smiled and turned towards the crowd heading for the flight gate. Brook watched until he disappeared from view.

38

December 28th, 2010

Brook left Manchester Airport for the drive south along the M6 towards Stoke then the A50 to Derby. He'd slept on the plane but the time difference left him groggy and he would have loved nothing better than to head straight back to his cottage and fall into bed. Unfortunately, Noble had his house keys so Brook texted flight details before boarding the plane in San Francisco. He received a swift reply.

Come straight to the station. J

Brook brooded about what to expect when he walked into St Mary's Wharf. Leaving Jason Wallis to fend for himself with a compound leg fracture, was a dereliction of duty and could lead to a charge - and that's assuming young Wallis hadn't concocted an even more unflattering version of events. No doubt the murdering little sod had complained long and loud though his grievances might have been tempered by the Reaper artefacts in his rucksack and his unauthorised presence in Brook's home.

On arrival, Brook trudged wearily through the pale winter sunshine and marched up to his office. Noble was working on the computer.

'Welcome back,' said Noble. 'How was America?'

'Fine,' replied Brook.

The Resurrection

'And Mike?'

'Fine,' said Brook.

'Is it worth asking how you are?' said Noble.

'I'm fine,' yawned Brook.

'That wasn't the question.' Brook blinked in confusion. Noble took pity. 'You look shattered.'

'I'm fine.' Noble shook his head. 'You have my keys?'

Noble rummaged in a drawer then tossed Brook his house keys. 'No intruder at your cottage, no commotion and nothing taken as far as I could tell, though a trapdoor up to your roof space was dislodged. I fixed it.' Brook stared. 'Problem?'

'No. It does that sometimes. Wind. Sorry to drag you out there.'

'I'm not. There was a cat trapped in the house. Would've been a nasty homecoming present.'

'A cat?'

'Lying across your top step. I chased it out and locked up, if you can call it that with the state of your security. A child could get in.'

'So, I've been told. Thanks, John.'

'Words are cheap,' said Noble. 'You owe me beers for hauling my carcass out to the boondocks.'

'Are you American?' said Brook.

'Don't you want to know where I found the keys?' enquired Noble. Brook tried to look interested. 'On the kitchen table.'

'Seriously?' Brook shook his head. 'What am I like?'

'Still working on that one. In the plus column, it looks like you were on the money about Jason Wallis.'

Brook's heart missed a beat. 'Wallis? What about him?'

'Don't gloat but he seems to have done a runner.' Brook had a mental image of Jason's snapped leg. 'He hasn't been seen since protective detail tucked him up in his hotel the night before you flew to the States. We're reassessing his aunt's murder.'

'With Greatorix on the case, he probably panicked.'

'Didn't I just ask you not to gloat?' said Noble, frowning.

'Sorry. How's Bob taking it?'

'Like a bear with a sore head. We've issued local and national bulletins but no sightings yet and no ANPR hits on his bike. Got to hand it to him. It's pretty impressive, dropping off the grid like that with so few resources. His friends and KA's are all dead and his last known was crawling with SOCO when he vanished - suggestions gratefully received.'

'Media?'

'In the pipeline.'
'Mobile?'
'Left at his aunt's the night of the murder.'
'Finances?'
'Wallis doesn't have a credit card or even a bank account, so no spending to follow.'

Brook nodded. 'So, his inheritance is just sitting there untouched...'

Noble grinned. 'The irony.'

'Hospitals?' said Brook. 'Transport hubs?' Noble raised an eyebrow. 'Sorry. You did ask. I could speak to Greatorix, offer to help.'

'Now for that I could sell tickets,' said Noble.

∼

BROOK DROVE BACK TO HARTINGTON, replaying the night of Jason's attack in his head. How could Jason be missing with such a debilitating injury? He couldn't have got far without assistance or transport. Had he brought an accomplice with him, someone waiting outside, someone who helped him away, *before* Noble turned up to check the place over a few hours later? It was the only explanation. How else could the cat have got in?

'But who?' mumbled Brook. *And where was Jason?*

After pulling onto his drive, Brook unlocked the front door and dragged his tired body across the kitchen to the spot where he'd last seen the stricken Wallis. There wasn't so much as a bloodstain, if there'd ever been one.

In the office, Brook picked up the phone to check the last number dialled. It was to his energy provider a month ago - Jason hadn't crawled through to the office to use the phone. Struggling to keep his eyes open, Brook gave it up and climbed the stairs to flop, fully-clothed, onto his unmade bed and, after a glance at the trapdoor in the ceiling, fell into a deep sleep.

∼

IT WAS dark when Brook woke but the clock revealed it was only eight in the evening so he swung his feet to the floor and padded downstairs. Sitting at the kitchen table with a mug of black tea, Brook realised, in the search for Jason, he had an advantage over Noble. Wallis must have ridden his Kawasaki to Hartington on the night he'd disappeared and being in no condition to ride away, it could still be in the village.

And, even if it wasn't, Brook knew when and where to start looking on traffic film. On the negative side, he could hardly breeze into St Mary's Wharf and start doing so, without inviting questions.

Brook grabbed his coat to walk around the village but, forty minutes later, the Kawasaki was nowhere to be seen. At the bottom of his lane, he called into the corner shop, just about to close, where he bought milk and a few groceries. While the proprietor bagged his purchases, Brook's eye alighted on a monitor behind the counter. It displayed a view of the shop door and, beyond that, the main road through the village and the junction of the small back lane that wound up to his cottage.

'Are those images stored?' asked Brook, nodding in the monitor's direction.

'For a while.'

'Would you have a copy of the weekend before Christmas?'

'Just about. The discs go back two weeks before we record over them.'

'Could I take a copy for the night of Saturday the 18th and all of Sunday?'

'Now?'

'If it's no trouble.'

The proprietor sighed. 'It's a bit of pain, we're closing in five minutes.'

'You know I'm a police officer, right?' said Brook, looking round for a way to seal the deal. His eye landed on a poster promoting a local raffle in the window. 'And while I'm waiting, why don't I buy ten pounds worth of tickets for the raffle?'

The proprietor's expression brightened, sensing an opportunity. 'They're drawing the damn thing on Friday and I'm lumbered with thirty quid's-worth.'

Brook drew out three tens from his wallet. 'Thirty pounds worth of tickets, please and feel free to put your name on them.'

The satisfied proprietor accepted the notes and disappeared into the backroom, emerging a few minutes later with a disc.

After dumping his bags on the kitchen table, Brook loaded the disc into his computer and spent a few minutes getting familiar with the format, before loading images from the night of Jason's attack.

Jason claimed to have been staking out John Ottoman's house in the dark until the arrival of a patrol car, so Brook arbitrarily set the tape rolling at 8pm and eased back with tea and a cheese sandwich to watch people and vehicles moving past the shop.

At 9.41pm, Brook was roused from his torpor by a motorbike travelling towards the heart of the village and past the turn-off to Brook's cottage. He replayed the footage a couple of times but it was too dark to distinguish details. It was clear, however, that the bike was travelling away from his cottage.

'Parking?'

Sure enough, three minutes after restarting the film, a figure walked past the shop's door in full view of the camera, turned and headed up the hill towards Brook's cottage. He paused the film and gazed at the image of Jason Wallis, rucksack on his back, motorcycle helmet tucked under his arm.

'Helmet?' muttered Brook, realising he hadn't seen one on the night of Jason's attack. He considered this for a few minutes before rewinding the film to review Jason's arrival on the bike.

On second viewing, Brook noticed a car a hundred yards behind the motorbike. He rewound the film to view the footage again but, no matter how many times he watched it, he couldn't identify the model, let alone a plate. The headlights were too dazzling and the camera too basic.

Instead, Brook watched Jason walk past the shop again and let the film roll. Two minutes later, another familiar figure walked past the darkened shop front. Dark clothing, gloves and a woollen hat, pulled over his head, were not enough to mask his identity.

39

Nearing midnight, Brook pulled to the side of the road and locked his car under the one working street lamp, having already driven round the block twice to check there was no patrol car watching the house.

Approaching the neglected, semi-detached property on the Drayfin Estate, Brook was reminded of his first visit, over two years ago, when he and Noble had interviewed Denise and John Ottoman about the brutal slaughter of Jason's family. It seemed like a lifetime ago which, sadly for Ottoman's late wife, it was.

Brook glanced at the For-Sale sign nailed to the gatepost. He took a further moment to run an eye over the Nissan Micra parked on the crumbling drive before striding along the weed-infested path to rap on the front door. Lights burned inside.

John Ottoman opened the door a split-second after Brook's knock, greeting him with a warm, if quizzical, smile.

'Inspector? Nice to see you.'

'Sorry to call so late.'

'Don't apologise, come in.' The beaming ex-teacher pulled the door back and Brook crossed the threshold into a cramped kitchen. Two tea chests held newspaper-wrapped crockery, utensils and glassware.

'You're moving?'

'I am,' said Ottoman. 'Staying with my sister until the house is sold and then...who knows? France? Spain? Too many memories here. Well, you can imagine. Tea?'

'Please,' said Brook. 'You saw me drive up?'

Ottoman stopped searching for teabags to glance at Brook. 'No. Why?'

'The speed with which you opened the door.'

'I was already in the kitchen.'

'Of a house I warned you to avoid.'

'You did,' said Ottoman. 'But if I'm to sell the place, I couldn't stay away forever, despite the threat of Jason Wallis.'

'True. But after my warning, you might have answered my knock with a little more circumspection.'

Ottoman stared back. 'What did you want to talk about?' he said, pouring hot water into two mugs.

'Where were you on the night of December 18th and the early hours of the 19th?'

Ottoman studied Brook. 'You're talking to a teacher, Inspector.'

'What does that mean?'

'Teachers don't ask questions of students to which they don't know the answer. I expect it's the same for a detective.'

'Do you have an answer?'

'The early part of the evening, I was here, sorting out the house and then I followed Jason Wallis on his motorbike to Hartington.'

'Thank you for not lying.'

'How did you know?'

'You were caught on camera,' said Brook.

Ottoman handed Brook a mug of tea. 'Should I pack a bag?'

'For what?'

'A night in the cells.'

'Is that where this ends?' said Brook.

'That's up to you,' replied Ottoman. 'I've no intention of lying to you so, if you're here to arrest me, I'll come quietly.'

'Why did you come back to this house?'

'Because, the night you warned me Jason was planning to kill me, I had an epiphany.'

'And what was that?'

'I decided I'd rather be dead than live in fear a moment longer. That's how Denise lived. Even in daylight, she'd cower in the house, unable to leave. At night, the smallest noise would wake her and she'd sob until dawn while I lay helpless, beside her. In the end, it was her fear that killed her.

'Your warning made me realise I had to come back and face Wallis or end up like Denise. So, I made my plans and returned the following afternoon. If Jason wanted to kill me, I was going to die on my own terms, in my own home. No more creeping around, no more looking over my shoulder. When I returned, I opened the curtains and turned on the lights to wait for him.'

'Lucky I persuaded DS Noble to station a car outside your home.'

'I no longer believe in luck, Inspector.'

'What do you believe in?'

'My power to act.'

'Your power to act?' *Sorenson's phrase.* Brook studied the retired teacher, small and lean, late middle-aged, his grey hair and timid demeanour. 'You baited him.'

'I did. So, thank you for your warning.'

'I was concerned for your safety.'

'Be concerned no more.'

'What happened?'

'I started packing and waited for Wallis to show his face,' said Ottoman. 'When darkness fell and there was still no sign, I realised, even with youth and vigour on his side, he wouldn't come at me in the light. So, I changed my strategy, thinking he might be happier breaking into an empty house, like the night he killed Denise. So, I went out for a drive and left him to break in.'

'Say he *had* broken in, what chance would you have had against a younger, fitter man?'

'Virtually none,' said Ottoman. 'And if that police car hadn't turned up when it did, I'd probably be lying on a mortuary slab and Jason would be behind bars.'

'You were prepared to sacrifice yourself?'

'I was.'

'And how would we know to put Jason behind bars?'

'I'm an IT teacher,' said Ottoman, prompting Brook with an eyebrow.

Brook glanced at a sturdy PC World box, now filled with wrapped plates. 'Webcams.'

'Installed in every room,' said Ottoman. 'I left my sister a letter to be opened in the event of my death, directing the police to my server where a copy of the film would be stored. After Jason killed me, you'd receive everything you needed to put him away for life.'

Brook nodded. 'But the patrol car turned up and Jason fled.'

'I'd just reversed off the drive when I saw it in my rear-view mirror.' Ottoman shook his head. 'All the times I called you lot when Denise was alive, only to be ignored. You can't imagine what a slap in the face that was.'

'I'm sorry,' said Brook.

'It's not your fault. You've done more than I had any right to expect. You listened when I needed you to listen and you set my mind at rest about Denise. I couldn't have asked for more.'

'And Jason?'

'Jason wasn't going to break in with a patrol car outside, so I drove round the block, intending to return to the house.' Ottoman smiled. 'Then fate took a hand. As I turned the corner into the next street, Jason emerged from the garden of a house, right in front of me so I parked and watched him pull on his rucksack and helmet and ride away on his motorbike.'

'And you followed?'

'Yes.'

'All the way to Hartington.'

'I didn't know where he was going and that's the truth, Inspector. I followed him, without any real intent beyond a vague notion of finding out where he lived. But when he picked up the Ashbourne road, I remembered from the papers that you lived in the Peak District, so I just kept going. Forty minutes later, he led me right to your door.'

'On the bike?'

'No. He parked next to some outdoor toilets on the other side of the village and, when he walked back past the Devonshire Arms, I got out and followed him. He turned up the hill, past a corner shop and I lost him for a moment but, halfway up the hill, I saw him in the distance, approaching what I assumed was your door. But, by the time I got to your cottage, he'd disappeared.'

'What did you do?'

Ottoman shrugged. 'There were no lights on and I wasn't certain he was inside or even that you actually lived there so I went back for my car...'

'And parked it across from my house,' said Brook.

'I saw you looking at it when you came out with your suitcase,' said Ottoman.

'I hadn't seen it in the lane before.'

'Did you know it was mine?'

'Not until this evening,' said Brook. 'Where were you?'

'Watching from behind a wall, in the field,' said Ottoman.

'And when I arrived home?'

The Resurrection

'I was in the driver's seat.'

'Any reason you didn't get out and warn me about Jason?'

Ottoman's eyes lowered. 'After I parked up, I reclined the seat so I wouldn't be visible...'

Brook pre-empted Ottoman's hesitation. 'You fell asleep.'

'I was exhausted - all that rushing about. When I eventually woke up, I saw your car on the drive and realised I'd missed you.'

'You could've knocked on my door to warn me.'

'I considered it,' said Ottoman. 'But, having fallen asleep, I couldn't be sure Jason was even in there so I walked back through the village to check his bike. When I saw it was where he'd left it, I realised you were in terrible danger so I hurried back but, when I got there, I decided it was too late to warn you.'

'Too late?'

Ottoman turned away, switched on the kettle and threw two more tea bags into fresh mugs. 'I couldn't risk it.'

'So much for sacrificing yourself.'

'I didn't *want* to die, Inspector, but I was prepared *if* it served a purpose. But if I'd charged in to warn you and you were dead, Wallis would have killed me too and maybe gotten away with it. I couldn't risk that. When I saw you come out with your suitcase, you can't imagine my relief.'

'From behind the wall,' said Brook.

'I'd nipped out to take a leak. You came out to put the case in your car then went next door. I was freezing but I didn't want you coming back out and seeing me, so I stayed where I was. Twenty minutes later, you came out with your neighbour and his cases and drove away.'

'And that's when you went into my house,' said Brook, quietly.

Ottoman pushed the fresh mug of tea at Brook. 'I meant what I said, Inspector. I owe you. If you need me to take the blame for Wallis, I'm your man. I've got my story ready and I can say it all happened after you drove away. You'd be in the clear.'

'Are you serious?'

'If I was prepared to let Jason kill me to get him off the streets, a long spell in prison isn't going to deter me.' Brook didn't answer. 'Of course, there is a second option.'

'And what's that?'

'We drink our tea, agree that the world is a better place without Jason then go our separate ways.'

'What have you done?' said Brook.

'What you couldn't manage.'

'Jason's dead?'

'Gone for good.'

'He had a broken leg,' said Brook.

'I saw. Nasty injury.'

'That wasn't my doing. Help was on the way.'

Ottoman chuckled. 'You left him there to suffer and die. He told me. Good for you. You wanted him gone. He's gone.'

'You killed him?'

'Technically, no,' said Ottoman. 'I just let nature take its course. And I wasn't the one who stuck a needle in his arm...'

'Needle?'

'A hypodermic. It was hanging out of a vein, empty. Some sort of narcotic, I assumed.'

'That was none of my doing,' said Brook. 'He must have injected himself to dull the pain. He was planning to cut my throat and he brought that to pacify me.'

'Then what the hell are you worried about?' protested Ottoman. 'Jason took the easy option, like the coward he is. Was. Don't give him another thought. I only wish I'd had the courage to kill him at the Ingham house. We both let the side down that night.'

'Side?'

'This Reaper who killed Jason's family and then the Ingham scum - he did all the heavy lifting and left Jason for us to finish. We had a job to do and my Denise would be alive today if we'd done it. We failed her. He didn't suffer if that's what you're wondering.' Ottoman narrowed his eyes. 'Or did you want him to?'

'Tell me what happened?'

'After you and your neighbour drove off, I waited a few minutes before going in. Jason was babbling incoherently so I put the hypodermic inside his rucksack and threw it on the passenger seat so there'd be nothing to link him to your cottage. It was still dark so I helped him out to the car and pushed him into the boot. I even went back to wipe up some of his blood to make it look as though he was never there.

'When I got him back here, I left him in the car on the drive and let nature take its course. I worried about noise at first but he was mostly too out of it, drifting in and out of consciousness. Plus, his pulse was very weak. I don't think he had the strength to kick up a fuss. Even so, it took him three days to die.'

The Resurrection

'In the boot of your car?' said Brook, putting his head in his hands. 'What have I done?'

'Something every right-minded person would applaud,' said Ottoman. 'Thanks to us, Jason's in the ground and the world is a safer place.'

'Where's the body?'

Ottoman shook his head. 'You'll have to arrest me to find out.'

'I have to know.'

'Then charge me. I'll take you to the grave and make a full confession. Otherwise, accept the gift of ignorance.'

'What happened to the Kawasaki?'

'The next day, I took the bus out to Hartington with the keys from his rucksack and rode it away. It was cold and dark when the bus rolled into the village - not many around to take notice and even if there was, who's going to remember an inoffensive soul like me.'

'What about Jason's helmet?'

'I wondered about that because I remembered him carrying it to your cottage. After I got off the bus, I went to look for it but the house was locked up, which was a bit disconcerting...'

'My sergeant,' mumbled Brook.

'Good job he didn't search the garden. The helmet was under a bush. I walked back to the Kawasaki, put the helmet on and rode it back to Derby. Quite exhilarating, actually. I might get something similar when this is all over.'

'Where's the bike now?'

'Gone.'

'Gone where?'

'That's the best bit. I've no idea.' Ottoman chuckled. 'I rode it back to the Drayfin and left it on the street with the helmet on the seat and the keys in the ignition.'

'And it was gone within the hour.'

'Try ten minutes,' laughed Ottoman. 'An elegant solution, I think you'll agree.' He drained his tea. 'So, what's it to be, Inspector? Do you want my freedom to compensate for Jason's life? I'll surrender it gladly. Although there is a third option.' He reached into a drawer and drew out a scalpel. 'This was also in Jason's rucksack.'

Brook stared as Ottoman held the blade of the scalpel against his left wrist. 'What are you doing?'

'I think you want to give me a free pass but may not feel I can be trusted to stick to the arrangement. From your perspective, that makes me a loose end. Say the word and I'll tie it up for you.'

'You're not serious?'

'Why? Nobody would be surprised. I've just buried my wife...'

Brook held out a hand. 'Give it to me.' Ottoman handed the scalpel over, handle first, and Brook slipped it into a pocket. 'You're insane.'

'Do you know, I've actually considered that,' said Ottoman. 'I'm definitely not myself, I admit. I feel liberated, like I can do anything. Nothing scares me. Is that what losing your mind feels like? I'm sorry, that sounds rude. I know you've had issues. But, honestly, I'm embracing the change, ready to achieve my goals.'

'Do your goals include killing your enemies?'

Ottoman laughed. 'I no longer have enemies, Inspector, so please don't worry I might start slaughtering anyone who looks at me the wrong way. Jason's death was for the greater good and I couldn't have done it without you. But now I'm done.' Brook's eyes began to close so he rubbed them to try and focus. 'Are you okay?'

'Jet lag,' muttered Brook. Or at least that's what he tried to say. His mouth wasn't as compliant as usual and when the world began to melt and his knee buckled, Ottoman was at his side to support him.

'Easy now,' said Ottoman. 'You're feeling it, I think.'

'What...?'

'Just a little something to help you relax,' said Ottoman. 'Denise left behind a bucketful of sleeping pills.' He guided Brook through into the lounge and eased him into an armchair. 'I'm sorry but I've decided to plump for Option Two and I can't be sure how you'll react so the *new* me has decided to take no chances. Don't worry, Inspector, you'll be fine in the morning.'

Brook tried to get to his feet but failed.

'Relax,' said Ottoman. 'You're in no danger, I promise.' He leaned into Brook's ear. 'I'll send you a postcard.' He held Brook's chin with his hand and gazed down at him. 'Thank you.'

Brook's skeleton turned to jelly and the night closed in around him.

40

Brook's eyes opened at the sound of loud knocking, followed by a door opening. He was lying on a sofa and from the look of the dormant log burner six feet away, that sofa was in his living room.

'Hello!'

A light came on in the kitchen and Brook's eyes settled on a blurred figure, silhouetted against the glare.

'Alright for some.' Noble's voice.

'John.' Brook swung his legs to the floor. 'How long have I been out?'

'If you want me to watch you sleep, you'll have to pay me.'

Brook blinked up at Noble. 'I can't hear the kettle.'

The silhouette disappeared and Brook tottered after him. Reaching the kitchen table, he sank onto a chair.

'Jet lag? Booze? Old age?' enquired Noble, pouring hot water into mugs.

'Yes,' said Brook.

Noble plonked down two mugs of tea. An A4 brown envelope was already on the table. 'Belated Christmas present. Sorry about the wrapping.'

Brook stared at Noble then picked up the envelope and slid out a thin document. It was the photocopy of Victor Sorenson's post mortem examination. 'Where did you get this?'

Noble raised a mocking eyebrow. 'Please don't patronise me. And don't worry - no-one knows I searched Mike's cottage. I didn't apply for a warrant and I haven't logged it into evidence. I thought with your friend safely back in the States, you might want it.'

Brook took a sip of tea and a moment to form a reply. 'Mike knew Sorenson,' he said quietly. 'McQuarry and Drexler interviewed him in the Ghost Road case.'

'Tell me something I don't know,' said Noble.

'He always suspected Sorenson executed the Ashwell family.'

'I wouldn't expect that to be in his book,' said Noble, 'On the other hand, I would expect some mention of an interview.'

'McQuarry filleted the record,' said Brook. 'She was the lead detective on the case and she hung Mike out to dry. The argument that provoked the shootout was partly about that.'

'And partly about the *reason* she tried to hide Sorenson's involvement,' said Noble. 'What do you suppose that was?'

'I have the feeling you're about to tell me.'

'It was McQuarry who fell under Sorenson's influence, not Mike. And, under that influence, she murdered Jacob Ashwell at the Golden Nugget Motel, using Mike's gun.'

Brook stared. 'How do you know that?'

'Until your reaction, I didn't,' said Noble. 'But Mike had a reprimand for losing one of his service weapons when he resigned so I put two and two together. McQuarry carried out the killings at the Ingham house last month, didn't she?' No answer from Brook. 'Quite some influence this Sorenson has.'

'Sorenson's dead,' said Brook.

'So, I've heard,' said Noble. He nodded at the post mortem document. 'Though, like Mike, I had begun to wonder. I still don't know *why* McQuarry was killing people on Sorenson's say-so, two years after his death, but I assume she was the face at the window across from the Ingham house, planning the attack. Presumably Mike was on her trail, trying to stop her, and that's what provoked the gunfight. Did you know?'

'Not until the night of the shooting. You have to believe that, John.'

'If you say it's so, I'll believe it,' said Noble. 'And now?'

'Now what?'

'You can't reveal all to the world because Mike will be vulnerable to exposure. Is that it?'

'Something like that.'

'Which presupposes there are others like McQuarry who are still around to wield this leverage over him.' Noble's gaze tunnelled through Brook. 'And, perhaps other current and former law enforcement officers who might also have been manipulated by Sorenson in the past.' Noble took out his cigarettes and offered one to Brook, who declined with a shake of the head. Noble lit up then picked up the photocopy of Sorenson's post mortem and held a corner against the flame from his lighter.

'With McQuarry and Sorenson dead, the only question left is who killed Jason's aunt,' said Noble.

Brook stared through the blue-brown smoke. 'The Reaper doesn't kill nurses, John.'

'No,' agreed Noble. 'Just vicious slags like Jason Wallis. Odd the way the Reaper keeps fluffing his lines when it comes to him. Almost like Sorenson wants someone else to step up and take Jason out.' Noble looked at Brook. 'Someone over whom he thinks he has leverage, say.'

'Sorenson's dead,' repeated Brook. 'It's over.'

The paper burned to ash. 'That's it, then. Another time for that beer?'

Unsteady, Brook got to his feet and held out his hand for Noble to shake. 'Count on it, John.'

∼

THE NEXT MORNING, Brook drove to the Drayfin Estate. The Ottoman house was locked up, the curtains drawn and the drive empty.

His next call was to Ottoman's sister to confirm that her brother had cleared out all his belongings and set off for pastures new. She didn't know where he'd gone because Ottoman hadn't known either but he'd promised to ring her in a couple of days when he got there.

'Honestly, he's a changed man, Inspector,' said Ottoman's sister, laughing. 'You should see the difference.'

'I have,' said Brook.

'And he says he has you to thank.'

Back in his car, Brook drove to the centre of Derby. He parked at the railway station for the short walk to Magnet House, carrying a roll of bin bags under his arm.

When he opened the Reaper flat's door, he saw at once it had been cleared out. Gone were the boxes of wine, the mountain bike and the flasks of Twilight Sleep. Under the sink the box of forensic suits had been removed, the cartons of scalpels and hypodermics too. Even the freezer had been emptied of all meats and the appliance turned off. The smell of chemicals confirmed the depth of the cleaning.

In the bedroom, the bedside lamp, mattress, computer and the shelf full of classical CDs had gone too.

Brook left the flat and trudged back to his car, dropping the keys down a grate on the way. Before driving home, Brook bought a new year's calendar at the newsagents on the station concourse.

Back at the cottage, he made tea and unwrapped the calendar, flicked through the months of the year and circled a date in November in red pen. From the attic he extracted a framed painting and hung it on the wall in the kitchen. The picture - of a half-eaten meal of bread and cheese next to a pitcher of wine - was painted in the characteristic broad strokes of Vincent Van Gogh. Half the table was brightly painted to represent the dazzling Provencal light of a noonday sun and the other half was in the shadow of an unseen figure, standing nearby.

Brook stood back to admire the painting, a gift from Victor Sorenson. The professor had claimed it was an original and unknown work by the tortured genius. True or not, the picture was magnificent and Brook poured a small measure of Lagavulin and lifted the glass towards it.

'Rest in peace, professor. And this time...' He put the glass of liquid smoke to his lips. '...stay that way.'

41

30th November 2011

DS Frank Ross sat in the chair, going over his mental checklist as he had a thousand times before. When he was satisfied all was ready, he took a final glimpse through the binoculars then stood to do his work. Dressed head to toe in a black one-piece boiler suit, he checked his watch. Three in the morning. It was time.

He opened the door of the flat and was astonished to see a figure standing in his way. 'What the fuck...'

'Hello, Frank.'

'Brook! What the hell are you doing here?'

Brook smiled at Ross. 'Sorenson's dead. So is Fulbright.'

'Thanks for the history lesson...'

'No, I mean *really* dead not just pretend dead. They died last Christmas in California.'

Ross hesitated. 'You're lying.'

'Believe me. I was there. Why do you think there's been no contact for nearly a year? And how do you think I knew you'd be in Vinny Muir's flat, planning to kill his family?'

Ross hesitated, glancing over Brook's shoulder, feeling the scalpel against his thigh.

'Don't worry,' said Brook. 'I'm not here to arrest you.'

'Arrest me for what?' Ross tightened his grip on the blade.

'Kelly says hi, by the way.'

Ross blinked in shock. 'Kelly Tyson?'

'She's waiting for us in the car. It's just me and her.'

'What?'

'We should talk inside.' Brook stepped over the threshold and closed the door behind him.

'Why are you really here, Brook?'

'I'm the new head of the Disciples, Frank, and I've come to stand you down. Reaper Armageddon is dead and we're closing the network. Didn't you get the message?'

Ross hesitated. 'I got it but I didn't believe it.'

'Believe it,' said Brook. 'Now get out of that ridiculous outfit and let's go and have some breakfast. I'm buying.' Ross didn't move, didn't speak. Brook smiled. 'You're in shock. Perhaps a stiff drink might be better. Get changed, Frank. It's over. All that's left is a conversation about the rest of your life.'

The two men stared at each other until Ross moved his hand to the zipper and began to remove his protective suit, overshoes and gloves. He pulled on his jacket and walked towards Brook, the scalpel in his hand. 'I could kill you right now and no-one would know for months.'

'You'd know,' said Brook, opening the door for him. 'And, trust me, Frank, whatever you think of me, that knowledge would ruin your life.'

Ross glared. Eventually, his eyes dropped and the scalpel clattered to the concrete floor. 'Kelly isn't really here, is she? You just said her name to blindside me.'

Smiling, Brook raised an arm to show the way. 'After you, Frank.'

THE END

Printed in Great Britain
by Amazon